A Suitable Affair

Erica Taylor

Amberjack Publishing
New York, New York

Amberjack Publishing
228 Park Avenue S #89611
New York, NY 10003-1502
http://amberjackpublishing.com

Publisher's Cataloging-in-Publication data
Names: Taylor, Erica, author.
Title: A Suitable Affair / by Erica Taylor.
Description: New York, NY : Amberjack Publishing Company, 2016.
Identifiers: ISBN 978-1- 944995-15-7 (pbk.) | 978-1- 944995-19-5 (ebook) | LCCN 2016957552
Subjects: LCSH Murder--Fiction. | Kidnapping--Fiction. | Marriage--Fiction. | England--Social life and customs--Fiction. | Historical fiction. | Love stories. | Regency fiction. | BISAC FICTION / Romance / Historical / Regency
Classification: LCC PS3620.A9432 S85 2016 | DDC 813.6--dc23

Cover Design: Red Couch Creative

Chapter One

❁

September 1813
London, England

I t was not an everyday occurrence that Lady Susanna Macalister was nearly trampled to death in the middle of Hyde Park. The pounding of hooves should have been her first intimation there was something amiss that fine Tuesday afternoon, but her thoughts at the time were scattered, delaying her response to the potential danger. As she turned to see a great, black beast charging straight towards her, Susanna stood helplessly frozen in shock, wondering how the day could have gone so terribly wrong.

Fortunately, her walking companion, Viscount Riverton, managed to keep his wits and push her out of the rider's path, shouting as the great, black horse reared up.

Susanna caught herself against a tree and turned to see her would-be assailant, tilting her head against the afternoon sun to where he was perched atop a very large horse. As the rider pulled sharply on the reins to regain control of his animal, she could see that his very handsome face was highly displeased, his gaze boring into Lord Riverton with something akin to hatred.

She could just barely make out the color of the rider's hair tucked beneath a cap—dark blond, matching the scruff around his mouth, chin, and jaw—but as he narrowed his gaze and focused solely on her, the color of his eyes was inscrutable, which was a shame because Susanna believed everything was in the eyes. She felt warmth rush through her, coloring her cheeks red, more from the heat of anger in the insolent gaze of the rider, than the adrenaline from her near-death rendezvous with the horse's hooves. The beast neighed angrily, clearly unhappy that the slight form of Susanna had curtailed his romp through the park.

"D'artagnan, will you cease?" the rider cried at the horse, pulling him in a circle, attempting to regain control. The horse did not appreciate his master's tone in his command; he reared up again and spun about. Susanna took a few steps backward again, and Lord Riverton darted out of the way.

"Westcott, contain your cattle!" Lord Riverton exclaimed, grasping his jewel topped cane and waving it at the horse, which only angered the beast further. The rider glared again at Lord Riverton before digging his heels into the horse's flanks and taking off in the direction he had been initially headed.

"Goodness!" came a cry from Susanna's sister-in-law, as she hurried towards them. Clara, the Duchess of Bradstone, was close in age to Susanna, though half a head shorter and remarkably pretty. "What was that?"

"That, your grace, was the Earl of Westcott," Lord Riverton replied with indignation as he replaced the beaver hat that had toppled off his head, tucking his dark hair beneath the brim. He pulled out a handkerchief and dabbed at the perspiration on his neck before replacing it in his pocket. Riverton was a solid fellow, taller than Susanna—but only just—with dark brown hair and eyes. He was decidedly attractive yet not alarmingly so. Not someone you would necessarily notice in a crowd.

Susanna watched as he fiddled with the angle of his hat, expecting more of an explanation. "And *who* is the Earl of Westcott?" she asked impatiently, since he seemed more acquainted with the earl than either she or Clara were.

Lord Riverton did not meet her gaze, but answered her query. "Westcott was once almost my brother-in-law, when I was affianced to his sister, Lady Elizabeth, before she was tragically taken from me."

"How terribly sad for Lord Westcott to have to endure such a terrible loss," Susanna said, and Clara discreetly nudged her with her elbow. "And you too, of course, Lord Riverton," Susanna added.

He nodded sadly and looked away. "I am sorry for his appearance, Lady Susanna."

"No bother," Susanna said dismissively. "You cannot control the comings and goings of the earl."

"Quite right," Lord Riverton said, but he still looked crestfallen and quite shaken by the episode. "I beg for your apology, but I must take my leave. Westcott's appearance has quite thrown me into despondency. I was unaware he had returned to town."

Susanna nodded, though she was less traumatized than the viscount, and she was the one who had been throw into a tree and almost trampled by a horse. "Yes, of course."

"You will be able to find your way safely home, yes?" he asked, and took a few steps backwards, his dark eyes glancing around nervously.

Susanna glanced at her sister-in-law, who looked as bewildered as Susanna felt. "Yes, we will manage," Susanna replied with a roll of her eyes.

Riverton shot her a look that was so brief she almost thought she had imagined it. She stared at him for a moment longer, wondering if the anger that had flashed across his face was intended for her or for the man who almost trampled her. Lord Riverton tipped his hat and walked quickly away.

Susanna shook off the feeling of unease creeping up her back.

Having been courted by him for months, Susanna thought she had assessed Lord Riverton's disposition fairly accurately, but she had never seen him agitated or frightened, never anxious, and certainly never hateful. He seemed to be a very calm and even-tempered fellow—steadfast—though almost boring if she was being completely honest. She must have misinterpreted his facial expression.

"Well, what an interesting turn of events," Clara said, raising an eyebrow at the viscount's retreating back.

Susanna couldn't agree more. The day had begun normally enough: her maid, Annette, had laid out a wonderfully pretty, lavender morning dress with a cream, satin sash across the midsection. After dressing, she broke her fast with her sisters in the breakfast room, then did some light reading in the garden. It was a bright day in early September, and Susanna was pleased when Lord Riverton had made a surprise appearance after tea and invited her to go for a walk. She donned her best bonnet and made sure her chaperone was the proper distance behind her as she and her fiancé strolled through the park.

Well, almost fiancé. Susanna had been hoping her suitor's unannounced appearance today would mean there would be a ring on her finger by the end of the afternoon. Apparently she had quite mistaken his intentions. He had merely come to ask for her forgiveness for being unable to attend the house party this coming weekend.

Clara linked her arm through Susanna's, and they turned back toward Bradstone House on the other side of Hyde Park. Riverton had forwardly introduced himself during a mutual friend's house party in July, and while his suit wasn't unwanted, it was surprising. Until then, Susanna had never heard of him. Her brother Andrew, the Duke of Bradstone, had been initially hesitant about him. Lord Riverton was the first to openly approach the stoic family patriarch and ask for permission to court her. Susanna knew her position in society and her family connections opened many doors, but they closed just as many when it came to her marriageable prospects.

Not only was she the daughter and sister of the Dukes of Bradstone, but she had four additional brothers, and not many suitors were willing to take on the lot of them in order to pursue her hand. Some proclaimed they were not intimidated by her pack of brothers, but, in the end, she had not been worth the hassle. The fact that Riverton had been willing to brave the Macalister clan had been enough for Susanna to give the viscount a chance.

It had been over two months since Lord Riverton had begun to court her. She was expecting a declaration any day now, but there was something holding him back, and she wasn't certain how to push him along.

"It is curious that Lord Riverton seemed more shaken by seeing someone from his past than you were by almost getting trampled by a horse," Clara commented, slyly glancing at Susanna for a reaction. Careful not to give her one, Susanna nodded in agreement.

"I've not known him to be so skittish," Susanna replied evenly. "Odd, yes, and peculiar in his choice of friends, but perhaps it was the memory of his lost fiancée that bothered him so?"

Clara shrugged. "Either way. At least this gives us a chance to walk by ourselves without a male looming over our shoulders and interfering with our conversation."

"Was there a topic you wanted to discuss in particular?" Clara glanced at her and nodded. "There was, actually."

Susanna sighed. "You've been dancing around this since last week, Clara. Let us have it out and see how we can fix whatever problem you have created."

"It is not I who created this problem," the duchess rectified. "It is you."

"Me? What could I have possibly done?"

"I know Andrew has approved of this match mainly because you asked him to," Clara began. "I want to make certain you know you do not have to engage with him any longer if you truly do not want to. I fear you are agreeing to Riverton's courtship based solely on a desire for a husband and not due to actual affection for the viscount."

Susanna stopped walking and eyed her sister-in-law. "You think I am merely accepting the first man to ask?"

"Of course not," Clara said. "But I must tell you what a bore Lord Riverton is."

"He is not a bore."

"He is quite peculiar, as you have already mentioned," Clara responded. "And his manners are uncouth."

"He was startled," Susanna said in Riverton's defense.

"He left us in the middle of the park with no footman or means to get safely home," Clara replied. "It was quite ungentlemanly."

"But we are home," Susanna said, indicating the large Park Lane mansion just on the other side of the street.

Clara crossed her arms and sighed. "I do not want to quarrel with you. I simply wish you to be as happy as I. You need not settle simply because the viscount showed you some semblance of attention. You deserve a little romance, Susanna, and I do not think Riverton possesses anything of the sort. Yes, he would provide a good, solid household and position, and a reasonable companion, but you should be *wooed*, Susanna, not simply courted. Courting is boring."

"This is coming from the expert on courtships," Susanna said, rolling her eyes. Her brother's courtship of Clara was not exactly the example by which all courtships were expected to follow.

"My courtship may not have been traditional, but the end result was the same," Clara said defensively.

"I know, Duchess Clara," Susanna replied, using the family's pet name for their new duchess. "I do appreciate your concern, but I think the situation with Riverton simply needs to run its course."

Clara nodded. "I am merely a champion for your happiness, dear."

Susanna smiled genuinely at her. In the few short months she had known Clara—through her very unconventional and dramatic courtship to her brother—the duchess had become more than simply a friend. She really felt as though Clara was truly her sister.

"I am famished," Susanna said. "Let's see what Cookie has set up for luncheon."

Clara laughed and linked her arm through Susanna's as they made their way across the cobblestone street, the events of the park pushed to the back of their minds.

Ian Carlisle, the Earl of Westcott, was not pleased.

He had been late to his meeting, and it was all his brother-in-law's fault.

Almost brother-in-law. And it was not *entirely* Viscount Riverton's fault. Had the viscount's dark-haired walking companion not stepped into his path, Ian would not have been forced to give up his course in order to not trample the poor girl to death. Still, Riverton was present and that gave Ian reason enough to blame his almost brother-in-law.

He glanced around the rose tea room he had fashioned into a makeshift study in his father's London home. It had been Beth's favorite room, and while his first instinct had been to board it up upon her death, he found himself unable to do so. It comforted him to be here, to hold onto a piece of his poor, dead sister.

"Problems, cousin?"

Ian was startled out of his brooding thoughts by Lord Rheneas Warren, the Earl of Bexley.

"Same problem as always, Rheneas," Ian answered and watched his cousin as he strode into the room. The earl winced at his Christian name but did not correct him, though Ian was the only person aside from Bexley's mother whom he permitted to call him Rheneas. They had once been boys together at Ashford Hall in Wiltshire. Ian had not been allowed to attend Eton, on his father's orders, and had envied his cousin's time spent there and the friends he had cultivated. As soon as he could muster enough courage, Ian bought himself a commission and left the country, leaving his sister in the care of his senile mother and father. He would never forgive himself for his moment of rebellion.

"I came over as soon as I heard," Bexley said, taking a seat across from Ian's desk. "Heard what?" Ian asked, looking back down at the missive in his hands.

"That you have officially returned to town," Bexley replied, popping off his hat and gloves and setting them aside. "It's been three years, cousin."

Ian looked up at him shrewdly. "I saw you not six months ago at Easter."

"Yes, but Easter was not spent in town."

"So the startling revelation is that I am in London?" Ian asked, placing the parchment in a file. "Nice to know I can still cause a stir. Besides, I have been here many times in the past three years."

Bexley scoffed. "But no one was paying attention then. Your appearance will turn some heads, though not as many had you waited until the regular season. At least now people will not think you are here to look for a wife."

"Gads no," Ian replied, shaking his head. "Last thing on my mind, I assure you."

"However, the fact that you raced hellbent through Hyde Park, almost trampling Lady Susanna Macalister, is bound to cause some commotion."

"Is that who that was?" Ian asked, the surname ringing a bell. Bexley nodded. "I am friends with her brother, you know."

"The duke, right?"

Bexley nodded again. "He was most displeased to hear you were causing quite a dangerous disturbance in the park."

"Is he the Hyde Park Watch now?"

Bexley chuckled. "No, just very protective of his kin."

"I assume you sent my utmost apologies for offending his grace's sensibilities?"

"He demanded a personal apology for himself and his sister,"

Bexley responded. "The duke is hosting a house party this weekend, and he has issued you an invitation. Or rather, his new duchess has."

"I am honored," Ian replied sarcastically, weary at the thought of having to attend a society function. "I suppose I cannot refuse?" he asked, rubbing his brow.

Bexley shook his head. "No one refuses the Duchess of Bradstone." His cousin stood and retrieved his hat and gloves from the side table. "I will be here at nine sharp Friday morning to collect you."

Ian nodded and Bexley left, leaving Ian alone with his thoughts. As much as he avoided London, he really did not avoid society. Truth be told, he never had a proper season. He left the country just before he was old enough to make his own bows before the King, only doing so when his father forced him while home on a brief leave. Ian was gone again after having only attended a few balls, one musical, and two nights at Almack's Assembly Rooms. He had not returned again until his sister's betrothal three years ago. Since then, the Home Office had kept him busy enough, not allowing him to spend much time in England, much less London.

Ian threw his quill down on the table and sighed, resigning to his fate. His appearance in London this time was only spurred by a summons from his superiors; it was the unfortunate encounter with Lady Susanna that had made him tardy this morning.

He supposed he owed Lady Susanna a sensible explanation and apology. It wasn't very gentlemanly of him to nearly crush a lady of quality with his horse, especially when that lady was the sister of a duke who was a friend of his cousin. Plus, he felt oddly obligated to warn Lady Susanna of his past with Riverton. He knew not of her connection to the viscount, but if she was walking with him in Hyde Park, she should know the sort of character Riverton was. Ian did not think the viscount was fit company for any lady, and he doubted Lady Susanna was aware of that just yet. He could not divulge everything he knew about the viscount, but he would think of something to get Lady Susanna away from Riverton. Ian would be damned if another unsuspecting young lady fell victim to Riverton's whims.

Chapter Two

Three days later, Ian sat in his cousin's carriage, dreading the upcoming weekend. It was exactly the type of lull he had avoided during the past three years. Idleness did not suit him.

When the formal, elegantly penned invitation to the house party had come the day before, he knew he could not refuse. He half expected his cousin to tease him about being invited; it was the sort of prank Bexley would have found amusing. He gritted his teeth as the carriage rolled them closer to Bradstone Park, his head thumping against the glass of the window with every bump in the road. His cousin sat across from him, slumped against the window fast asleep.

Occasionally a bump would jolt him enough to elicit a loud snore but not enough to wake him. The carriage slowed as it rounded a corner, and Ian had his first glimpse of Bradstone Park. As the heir to a Marquessate, Ian was no stranger to grandeur, but even he was a little awed by the massive beauty and opulence of Bradstone Park. Rising high above the freshly manicured lawns, the Tudor structure sat in an unwavering position of solidarity and authority. The stones were a reddish-brown, offset by white-painted window frames. A pair of Tudor wings stretched out towards the drive, and white columns framed the opulent main entrance. Ashford Castle, his father's country seat in Northumberland, was literally a castle, but this structure was just outlandish.

"Rather ostentatious, isn't it?" Bexley asked, and Ian glanced at his cousin. Bexley yawned. "Bradstone agrees. But he cannot do anything about it, as it's his family seat."

"Does he primarily reside in London then?" Ian asked, looking back at the structure, noting the fountain and reflecting pool in the front circle drive.

"No, he uses one of his other estates for his time away from London," Bexley replied.

Ian nodded absently, reminded that he should make a trip to his father's country seat even if it wasn't the residence he chose to utilize. Not that he really utilized any of them.

Ian and Bexley were among the last to arrive, and they were quickly shown to their rooms. A luncheon had been set up on the back lawn for the guests as they arrived. Ian went ahead, leaving Bexley alone with the chamber pot.

As he made his way through the extravagant interiors of Bradstone House, Ian pondered how he should proceed with his warning to Lady Susanna Macalister. He did not know the lady personally, but he knew the type that came from such homes and such families: young women born to lords and ladies, schooled out of the nursery to produce another generation of lords and ladies. As the daughter of a duke, no doubt she would be demure and courteous, probably boring to a fault—most young debutants were. Granted, he did not know much about the Macalister family, only that they were one of the oldest families in England with titles that were just as old, and he had a thin sliver of past doings with the duke. Bradstone was born to the type of aristocratic family to expect such blind submission to the will and needs of the title, much as his own title boasted the same opinions. Yes, he had a fair assumption of what type of "Society Miss" Lady Susanna would be.

He was briefly reminded of the fiery, blue gaze that had been staring up at him in shock days earlier in the park, but he did not have time to ponder the matter further as the subject of his thoughts came barreling around a corner, plowing right into him. She bounced off his broad chest harmlessly, though shaken and surprised to find a solid body in front of her. Ian recognized her immediately—her dark chocolate hair and startlingly bright blue eyes giving her away. Her face was round, her nose slightly narrow. Her irises were ringed with a darker blue halo, echoing the late summer sky outside. Her hair was pulled away from her face and wound at the base of her neck. Her perfect, ivory skin was barely sun-kissed, though he could tell there were a few rebellious freckles she had tried to fade with powder.

"Goodness, I do beg your pardon," Lady Susanna said as he helped her right herself. She brushed an errant wisp of dark hair back from her eyes and looked up to his face. Intelligent eyes stared back at him as recognition flashed through them.

"You are fully pardoned, I assure you," he said smoothly, chuckling under his breath, as if the mere thought of her had summoned the very lovely Lady Susanna to him. "I am prone to not peeking around a corner before I stand in a lovely lady's way."

Her eyes narrowed. "You, sir, should be more careful where you walk and where you ride."

"Is it not proper for one to walk in a hallway?" he asked, looking around curiously. "Or to ride a horse in a park? Perhaps it is you who should be careful to not wander into the path of a rider on horseback. Or a man walking down a hall."

"*You* should ride more carefully and not at such a great speed," she said, pointing her finger at him. "I cannot imagine what was so important that required breakneck speeds through a crowded park."

"I apologize, my lady, for not being more courteous on your designated walking paths," he said, dramatically placing a hand over his heart in mock sorrow. "I assure you my future romps will take place where you are not present."

She glared at him for his mocking tone. "You should be vigilant of your surroundings."

Ian laughed to himself at her choice of words. If she only knew how vigilant he truly was. "And you, my dear, might want to be more cautious when choosing your company," Ian drawled before grinning. "Present company excluded, of course." Her eyes flashed blue fire just as he had expected them to. He was oddly satisfied he had correctly predicted the reaction.

"How dare you have the audacity to tell me with whom I may and may not associate. And I am not your *dear*. You do not have permission to be so forward."

"One must have permission to be forward?" Ian asked. "Isn't that the point of being forward?"

"You are insufferable, my lord."

"I've been told that once or twice," he replied. "But in all seriousness, Lady Susanna, you should stay away from Lord Riverton."

"He is my fiancé."

Ian's eyebrows rose. "Is he now?"

The lovely Lady Susanna flushed a very pretty shade of pink. "Well, not exactly. He is courting me, and I expect a proposal any day now."

"I cannot possibly see what could be so appealing about the man," Ian said, irritated. "He is barely respectable. I am surprised that a lady such as yourself would lower herself to be a mere viscountess." He clicked his tongue and shook his head. "You could do much better."

"I am not interested in his title, and I have plenty of money of my own," Susanna said crossing her arms. "But, I will have you know he will one day be an earl. I cannot imagine you have anything better to offer."

"Ah, but I wasn't offering," Ian said grinning. "But since you brought me into the conversation, I will have you know I am the heir to the Marquess of Ashford. They say that my father will drop dead any day now. Marquess always out-ranks earl."

Lady Susanna's face softened. "Your father is ill? Will it really be any day?"

He eyed her, curious at her change in tone. Was she actually concerned for his father's health, or did the prospect of becoming a marchioness interest her?

"The physician has been saying he will go any day for the past two years," Ian finally replied. "It is his mind that is ill, not his body. He appears the epitome of physical health to me. Either way, I am not waiting with bated breath for the news of his death. I have a life to live in the meantime."

She nodded and looked down at the lavishly carpeted floors. He felt the strange stirrings of curiosity regarding the enigmatic Lady Susanna, a puzzle that needed to be solved, and Ian loved a good puzzle.

"I thank you for your warning, Lord Westcott," she said, lifting her head. Her blue eyes were soft and distant, but not at all meek, and he was surprised to find she knew his name.

Apparently Riverton had shared something of their entwined past. "I will heed your advice, but since it is only advice, which has been presented with no evidence to support the claims, please do not be offended if I choose to ignore your words of wisdom."

"Perhaps if we discussed this at a later date you might be more satisfied?" he asked. He saw something in Lady Susanna that quite surprised him, something he had not anticipated.

Behind her appearances as a sophisticated English lady, she possessed something he had not thought existed in a lady of the *ton*. Lady Susanna had strength.

"I do not think it needs further discussion, my lord," she said, challenging him with a tilt of her head.

She was dismissing him, he realized, and he wanted to laugh at her. She had spunk, he would give her that, but her loyalties were severely misplaced, and he would be damned if he allowed another genteel young lady to fall victim to Riverton's bad character.

"There are things you should know about your soon-to-be fiancé," he added cryptically. "I would be happy to share my knowledge, if you were interested in learning who he really is."

She eyed him, his words turning over in her pretty head, and after a long moment, she nodded. "I do not know when you expect to discuss this with me. It is not proper for me to be seen with you."

"What's wrong with me?" he asked in mock defense.

She glowered at him. "An unmarried, unchaperoned woman in the company of a man she does not know."

"Ah, much like we are now?" he asked, a teasing edge to his voice. "Not to worry, my dear. My cousin is the Earl of Bexley, and he should do the introductions later, which we should make certain to appear genuine. I would hate to upset the duke."

"Are you afraid of my brother?" she asked curiously.

Ian replied without hesitation. "Not in the slightest, but I respect him. I would hate to make an enemy of him. My cousin thinks very highly of him, and Bexley is a stickler for a person's character, so I have no reason to fear the duke."

She nodded pensively and then smiled softly at him. "Yes, it would do us both good if we pretend our 'first meeting' is in truth our first. How wise you are to think of it, my lord."

"And then it would not be improper for us to walk together on the way into town or on some other silly excursion planned for this house party."

"There is a walk into Whitstable planned for tomorrow mid-morning," she admitted. "It would still be inappropriate for me to walk with you directly, so if I happen to fall back due to an injured ankle or knot in my bonnet, you will gallantly offer your assistance. But should there be an audience, you will wait until another opportunity presents itself."

"And you will listen to what I have to say?" he asked, impressed with her demands. She certainly knew who she was and her place in this world. Not a shred of self-doubt in this lady.

"Yes, I will listen to what you have to say," she agreed. "But I will not promise to do as you say. You will leave and never bother me with this again, and you will accept my decisions regarding the matters discussed."

"Fair enough," he nodded. "I think it is time you returned to your party before someone starts to look for you."

"Oh, this is not my party," she replied, shaking her head. "It's the duchess's. And she is most eager to meet you, my lord."

"My friends call me Westcott, you know," he said to her.

"Ah, but we are not friends, are we?" she asked, grinning at him. "Please excuse me, my lord. I was off to fetch a new bonnet, for this one refuses to stay upon my head."

"Until we meet for the first time, again," he said gallantly and bowed. She held his gaze for a moment before stepping around him and headed towards the inside of the manor house.

Ian shook his head, smiling to himself. Lady Susanna was not the simple, mindless chit he had assumed her to be. *Well*, he thought to himself as he shook his head again to clear his thoughts, *serves me right to judge the book by its rather expensively adorned bindings.*

"You needn't have waited for me," Bexley said as he stepped around the corner from a different direction than Susanna had disappeared. Ian did not answer, and his cousin shrugged. "No matter. Come, I will do the introductions. Remember to be gracious and apologetic."

"Yes, Mother," Ian replied sardonically. Bexley shot him a glare but said nothing. He led the way outside, and Ian had his first look at the other members of their house party menagerie.

He glanced around the expansive lawn, vibrant green despite the warm summer. There was a soft breeze coming off the ocean he could see beyond the cliffs at the far edge of the property, and he breathed in the salty, ocean air. Thirty or so people mingled in little sextets scattered across the lawn, chattering between sips of lemonade and bites of chicken. He followed his cousin down the steps to where a tall, dark-haired gentleman stood with a pretty blonde on his arm, another dark-haired lady, and a solemn blond gentleman beside them.

"Bexley, so good to see you've arrived," the dark-haired gentlemen said. Bexley nodded and shook his hand before turning towards Ian.

"Allow me to introduce my cousin, the scoundrel who seems to think Hyde Park the perfect place for a horse race. Ian Carlisle, the Earl of Westcott. Ian, the Duke and Duchess of Bradstone."

"Your graces," Ian said, dipping into a bow.

The duke looked very unhappy as he nodded to Ian, the dark scowl not leaving his face. His eyes narrowed a fraction as he searched Ian's face. Ian knew he looked familiar to him and that he was probably trying to place his face. Ian had had dealings with their graces the previous spring.

The duchess's pretty brown eyes widened as recognition hit her much sooner than it did her husband. She smiled sweetly at him.

"Forgive me, but it seems we met before the day in the park, though you were not introduced to us then. It is a pleasure to finally know your name, Lord Westcott," the duchess said warmly and introduced Lady Norah Macalister, another sister of the duke, and Lady Norah's friend, Lord Niles Hawley. Susanna rejoined their group just then, a fresh bonnet upon her head.

"And this is Lady Susanna Macalister, the young lady you almost trampled to death three mornings ago," the duchess said, smiling at him. He nodded to Susanna, and she nodded in return.

"It is reassuring to see you did not break your neck riding at such a dangerous speed through the park," Susanna said to him pleasantly, but he could hear the rebuke all the same. She had a very warm smile that quite disarmed him, though even with her approachable nature, she radiated sophistication. He smiled, quite unable to help himself.

"I do beg for your forgiveness, Lady Susanna," he said with all honestly. "I was in quite a hurry, and it was very reckless to traverse the park in such a fashion. I assure you it will not happen again. Riding at such speeds through Hyde Park is not safe in the slightest."

"Quite right," the duke replied and his wife gave him a scathing look. Ian was intrigued by how the three Macalister siblings resembled each other: dark brown hair, same straight nose, and blue eyes. He could not imagine growing up as part of such a large family. It had only been Beth and himself and he had been eight years Beth's senior. He and his sister looked nothing alike.

"Lord Bexley tells us you are newly returned to London," Susanna remarked.

"Yes," he replied but did not elaborate. Her expression clearly showed she expected him to continue. "I have been gone for three years and have been everywhere since then. Or so it often seems."

"On the continent?" she asked curiously.

"Some," he admitted. "But England also, just not London."

"I can understand your confusion regarding the etiquette of horsemanship within city limits," Susanna retorted. "I agree there is no proper room to run a horse in the city. In the country, walking paths do not coincide with the horse paths."

"I assure you, Lady Susanna, you will be safe from my horsemanship whilst in town," Ian said. "I learned my lesson. You have no need to fear me."

Susanna blinked at him. "I do not fear you, my lord. I do not even know you."

"That is such a shame," he replied. "I am very likable once you know me."

"I find I am quite set for friends at the moment, my lord," she stated with a dismissive shrug of her shoulder. "Perhaps you can apply again in a few months."

"I will wait with bated breath, holding out until you decide the time is ripe for an acquaintance with me."

"I certainly hope you hold your breath the entire time you wait," Susanna replied sweetly, crossing her arms. "I look forward to watching you suffocate."

"Ah, but you will be watching."

Susanna looked away, blushing. He grinned at her, then all too late realized their exchange had happened in the audience of his own cousin, their graces, Lady Norah, Lord Niles, all watching with curiosity. Ian inwardly cringed.

"Well," the duchess said brightly, looking curiously between Susanna and Bexley. "Susanna, would you be a dear and step inside with me. I wish to see Cook about dinner."

Susanna smiled warmly but very falsely. "Yes, of course." Both Susanna and the duchess dipped into a curtsy before leaving their company.

The duke looked wistfully after his wife before turning back towards Ian and Bexley.

Lord Niles murmured some excuse, and he and Lady Norah left the group to rejoin another on the other end of the lawn.

A footman appeared and the three gentlemen each plucked a glass of cool lemonade from the tray.

"I assume any intentions you have towards my sister are completely honorable," Bradstone said bluntly. Ian would have choked on his lemonade had he not quickly swallowed it down. Bexley laughed.

"I assure you, your grace, I have no intentions towards your sister, or any other female for that matter," Ian replied and Bexley laughed again. "Not that I do not enjoy the company of a woman from time to time, but, uh, I have no thoughts about Lady Susanna in such terms."

Bradstone scowled. "Is she not fit company for someone as yourself? You are what, an earl?"

"Heir to a Marquessate, in fact," Bexley interjected.

"Lady Susanna seems to be a very lovely person, and while I can surmise she would be wonderful company, you will not have to worry about my actions with her. I am not looking for a wife nor any dalliance. I was merely called to London for a meeting and happened to cross the ladies' path, and then I was summoned here.

After this, you shall never see me again."

"Oh, come now, Ian," Bexley said. "You are not that bad of company. You needn't haul yourself back to the wilds of the English countryside, doing whatever it is you do for King and Country and whatnot."

"Yes, but my superiors say otherwise," Ian replied.

Bradstone's brows were pinched together as he studied Ian. "You work for the Home Office?"

Ian nodded. "In a certain capacity." Bradstone nodded but did not comment.

Bexley chattered on, filling the silence as neither Bradstone nor Ian seemed inclined to speak. Bradstone scowled across the lawn, and Ian listened to his cousin rattle on about some actress *de jour* he had taken an interest in. Ian managed to intercept another glass of lemonade from a passing footman and downed the contents. Looking back at the scowling duke, his own idiot cousin, and the expansive green lawns littered with the duchess's guests, Ian wondered what he had gotten himself into.

Susanna had never met a more insufferable man in her entire life. Once they were safely inside the house and away from gossiping party guests, she let her displeasure be known.

"Can you believe his nerve?" Susanna whispered to Clara as she and the duchess walked away from the subject of her ire.

Clara caught Susanna's arm in the hallway. "You do not know who he is, do you?"

Susanna was bewildered. "Westcott? I know exactly who he is!"

Clara shook her head. "He was the one who brought my sister's husband to London last spring, Susanna. He is more than he seems."

"You approve of him?" Susanna asked, a bit taken back at her grace's sudden support of the scoundrel.

"I feel grateful to him," Clara replied honestly. "But my feelings are irrelevant. You do not like him? He seemed perfectly charming to me."

"You did not hear what he said to me when I met him in the hallway moments before," Susanna replied, crossing her arms across her chest. "He called Riverton's character into question without giving any sort of explanation. And he practically questioned my judgment and implied I was a title-seeking fortune hunter!"

"Maybe you should heed his advice," Clara said slowly, her lip pulling to the side as she chewed the inside of her cheek.

Susanna huffed. "There you go again, taking his side!"

"There are no sides to take, Susanna!" the duchess replied, exasperated. "I knew not who he was that day in the park, but I can tell you, Lord Westcott is the man I saw last spring; perhaps what he says has some merit."

Susanna remembered the somewhat exciting events during the spring season earlier in the year. Clara's relationship with Andrew began amidst rather unpleasant events. Clara's brother had wanted her killed to inherit a fortune Clara had not even known she possessed, which made Andrew go a little mad trying to protect her. It had been an interesting season, to say the least, but it all turned out well in the end. Andrew and Clara were made for each other, and Susanna was relieved her brother's sensibilities had returned to him once Clara's destructive brother had been dealt with. But Susanna did remember the story Clara had told her about the man who aided them in the spring, and apparently that man was the Earl of Westcott. But it did not excuse Westcott's intrusion in her life.

Susanna shook her head. "Men like to control things, I think. Thinking they own and possess makes them feel better. When they feel things are out of their control, they turn to rash behavior."

"Perhaps," the duchess replied slowly, a mischievous twinkle returning to her bright brown eyes. "But perhaps some men just need to be tamed."

Susanna rolled her eyes. "I assure you, I have no intention of taming anyone, least of all that ludicrous creature."

Her sister-in-law smiled sweetly at her. "Listen to what West-cott has to tell you with an open mind, Susanna. Do not shut him off because you think he is overstepping."

Susanna shook her head again. She did not need another man in her life telling her what to do. She was happy and comfortable with Riverton. Westcott was nothing but a nuisance.

A nuisance that could make her tingle with a single look.

Chapter Three

———— ❁ ————

*L*ate in the morning on the following day, Susanna was greatly annoyed that she was actually anticipating spending a few unattended moments with Lord Westcott. She walked beside Lady Monica Summers and Miss Gemma Scott, two of her dearest friends, accompanied by her cousin, Lord George Cordell. They were a few paces behind most of the walking party on their way into Whitstable. The air was crisp, almost too chilly for September. The leaves had not yet changed to the vibrant gold and red that herald the oncoming winter, and Susanna was grateful for the last few moments of summer.

She glanced around curiously, looking for Westcott, wondering when and how he would assault her this time. "Assault" may be a rather dramatic way for her to view what would most likely just be a simple conversation, but she could not help but wonder what he could possibly tell her about Riverton that would change her opinion of him. Susanna had always felt there was something amiss with Riverton, and Lord Westcott had piqued her interest. Riverton had seemed too perfect, too stable, and too safe. Lord Westcott had irritated and provoked her, but at the same time he had also stirred something else in her. His laughing, grey-green eyes, swaggering smile, and flirtatious banter challenged her, and that was something Lord Riverton did not do.

She was almost excited to see Westcott again.

Susanna rolled her eyes skyward at her silent admission. This just would not do. The man irritated her; he had almost killed her the first time they met. She knew hardly anything about him. He had no right to elicit such curiosity from her.

She glanced around again, wondering where he had gone, discreetly loosening her bonnet ribbons. Lord Westcott had not spoken directly to her since the luncheon yesterday afternoon, choosing to be on the opposite side of every gathering since then. He sat as far away from her at dinner as he could manage; he was on the opposite side of the room when Lady Monica graced them with a singing performance after dinner. He had not been at breakfast but appeared as their party was setting out for Whitstable soon after. And now, he was nowhere to be found.

"Susie, you look awfully peaked," Monica commented, her dark auburn hair trying to escape her bonnet. She looked at Susanna as she swatted away an errant curl. "What has ruffled your feathers so?"

Susanna straightened her posture and gave herself a mental shake to clear her head. She wasn't sure how to explain what, or rather who, had her on edge.

"Nothing of importance," Susanna replied with a dismissive shrug. "I am merely concerned about the new ribbons the haberdasher should have in. You know how I am fond of ribbons."

Her friends shared a disbelieving look but did not comment.

"Ribbons are an eternal bore, Susanna," Gemma interjected, her pale blonde hair barely visible beneath her wide-brimmed bonnet, and Monica snickered.

Smiling up at their male companion, Monica asked, "What do you think, Lord George?"

Lord George shrugged dismissively and tossed the rock in his palm against a tree. He and Susanna were paternal cousins and they both shared the dark Macalister hair, but that was about all they had in common. Susanna knew he was invited merely for the numbers, but since they were of a similar age, he and Susanna had been tossed together on numerous family outings throughout their lives. He was as strange an adult as he was a child.

Monica gave Susanna a sideways look that Susanna clearly understood to mean, "Why must we put up with your absurd, immature cousin?"

"Georgie, there is a good snuff shop in town, should you wish to deposit us once we are content with our ribbons," Susanna added to draw him into the conversation.

"I think I might like to see the snuff shop," Monica said cheekily. "Come on, Susie, ribbons *are* a bore."

Susanna shook her head. "Snuff gives me a headache. Besides, his grace would be rather put out with me if I went into a gentlemen's shop."

"Hang proper and hang his grace!" Monica said, dramatically waving her fist in the air. "Your brother is bound to loosen the leading strings someday."

Susanna laughed. "He is overbearing and over protective, but a good brother nonetheless."

"And do not say such things, for goodness' sake," Gemma chided. "Clara would be quite put out with you."

"And one mustn't cross the duchess," Georgie replied solemnly, as he kicked a rock with the toe of his shoe, making an uncharacteristically satirical comment. Though for him, it could have been said in complete seriousness.

The three ladies looked at him peculiarly before returning to their usual female chatter. "Did you hear what she did to Lady Laura?" Monica asked, whipping her head around to Gemma's, grinning beneath her wide-brimmed bonnet with her latest bit of gossip. Until recently, Susanna would have jumped in with her friend to share the newest bit of *haute ton* news, but gossip had recently been leaving a disturbing taste in her mouth.

"I did not," Gemma replied without looking at her.

"She cut her!" Monica replied giddily. "In the middle of Hyde Park. Not two days ago."

"She did not!" Gemma looked surprised, turning to Susanna with grin, her eyes bright with excitement.

"I was there," Susanna confirmed, nodding. "Clara does not like Lady Laura and made it quite clear she had better start groveling for her behavior last spring if she expected any invites come next season."

"How splendid of her grace!" Gemma said with a bark of laughter. "I do quite like her."

Susanna nodded. "As do I."

"And what about this new earl of yours?" Monica asked, returning her sparkling green eyes to Susanna. "Who is he?"

"He is not *my* earl," Susanna replied, knowing it was pointless to pretend to not know who Monica was speaking of. "He is the Earl of Westcott and he almost ran me over in the park."

"It sounds romantic," Monica said wistfully.

"It sounds dangerous," George interjected gruffly. "A gentleman does not ride at dangerous speeds through a crowded park."

"And a gentleman can admit when he was wrong," came Westcott's amused voice. Their quartet stopped as he approached on horseback.

Susanna tilted her head back to see his face and as she did so, her bonnet slipped off her head and into a muddy puddle.

She gasped and silently cursed her own mistake as her bonnet sank below the muddy surface. Another bonnet ruined in less than twenty-four hours. Though that had been her intention all along: create a situation where they could have a private conversation. It was tragic the lovely bonnet had to be the victim.

"Oh, good heavens, Susie, honestly," Monica chided her, though the glint in her green eyes hinted she was on to Susanna's scheme.

"Well done," Gemma said over dramatically and it seemed both her friends were in on her ploy. Westcott swung his leg over his massive black horse, the same one who had nearly galloped over her head in Hyde Park.

He nodded to them and gave a quick, tight bow. "Lady Monica, Miss Scott, Lord George."

The ladies curtsied and George nodded absently.

"Lord Westcott," Gemma began, "would you be so kind to offer our clumsy friend some assistance? It seems she is in need of a new bonnet."

Susanna thought about swatting her friends with her reticule and fetching her own bonnet, but she kept her mouth shut, and smiled ruefully at Westcott, who had bent to retrieve the soggy bonnet dripping with mud. He vigorously shook the bonnet, sending water and mud splattering across the ground, though thankfully not on any of the ladies. He glanced at Susanna and for a moment she thought he was going to plop it back on her head and declare it good as new.

"It is clearly ruined, my lord," Susanna declared in warning. He grinned. Apparently she had been fairly accurate in predicting the direction of his thoughts.

"Clearly," he replied, winking. He tied the ribbons around the horse's neck, the bonnet positioned perfectly upon the beast's head. The sight of the massive black horse wearing a soggy, mud-soaked bonnet was rather ridiculous and Susanna laughed at the sight. The horse did not seem to appreciate his master's humor and shook his head, the bonnet falling under his throat.

"Oh, D'artagnon, have a sense of humor, boy!" Westcott said affectionately to the horse and patted his neck. The earl looked at Susanna and smiled. "I would be pleased to offer assistance, my lady, should you require it."

Susanna hesitated. He was giving her the option to refuse his help, to refuse to listen to his information. He was giving her a choice.

"Your help would be greatly appreciated," Susanna replied and turned to her friends and cousin. "Please go on ahead of me. Lord Westcott will convey me back to Bradstone Park so I may retrieve another bonnet and we will meet you in Whitstable."

George nodded absently while Monica and Gemma smiled brightly.

"Come along, Miss Gemma," Monica said brightly, linking her arm through the young woman's and pulling her down the roadway, George lumbering along behind them. "This way we can visit the snuff shop without Susie complaining about the smell."

Susanna sighed, looking again at the ruined bonnet hanging from the horse's neck. "You really are quite absurd," she said to Westcott.

He shrugged. "I do what amuses me," he replied evasively. "Shall we?" He looked ready to regain his seat atop the horse.

"I am not riding that horse with you."

"Why not?" he asked, looking at the horse.

"To start with, this horse almost killed me," she stated, crossing her arms before her. "And second, it would be quite inappropriate for me to do so."

"Ah, yes, the rules of propriety," he said, his voice reverberating with mock reverence.

He set his foot off the stirrup. "Let us all bow down to the all-mighty rules."

"The rules you so mock are what govern our world, my lord," Susanna replied.

"Then were the whispers about you untrue?" he accused. "I've been recently informed how you flaunt the rules and dare anyone to question your actions."

Susanna sighed. "Well, yes, I try to do as I please. But even so, some rules must remain intact. Wearing a dark blue gown to a ball is one thing; gallivanting through the countryside with a man who is not my husband would shatter some of the most important guidelines inflicted upon an unwed lady. Walking alone with you is as much as I am willing to push for now, especially since I am not quite sure what has persuaded me to do so."

"You wish to know what I know," he replied, easily answering the question with the answer she was afraid of.

She eyed him, wondering if he was toying with her, if he really knew something about Riverton that could have any weight on her relationship with the viscount. "I will walk with you; that is all. You may tether your horse and retrieve it upon our return, or he may walk with you."

"I am not leaving him here," Westcott replied determinedly. "This horse crossed France with me, he can walk back to the manor house." He shook the reins off the neck of the horse and tugged, urging the horse to follow them. "Might I say you look quite lovely this morning, Lady Susanna."

She turned to regard him with a haughty look. "Is that to say I do not look equally lovely at other times of the day?"

"That is precisely what it says," he nodded. "But since I've seen you indoors and outdoors, at morning and evening, I consider myself an expert."

"What about trampled in the park in mid-afternoon?" she asked.

"Will you not let me live that one down?" he asked sincerely and looked sideways at her. "One transgression and I am forever written off. I assure you, I am not a bad person."

"I never said you were, Lord Westcott," Susanna replied. "Ian."

"I beg your pardon?"

"Please call me by my given name, Ian," he said. "Well, technically it is Lord Ian Joshua Walden Englebrett Carlisle, but that's a mouthful. Simply Ian will do."

She stared impatiently at him. "We are not at the stage in our relationship where it would be proper for me to call you any part of that."

"But you do admit to us having a relationship then?"

She sighed, exasperated.

He chuckled softly and she was reminded how very handsome he was. His hair was a tawny brown-blond, not quite one or the other. His eyes were a curious grey-green. His nose was straight and thin, his face youthful, though she thought him close to Andrew's age, more than a few years her senior. He had not shaven, and the scruff from the day in the park had grown.

"My sister-in-law says I should listen to what you have to say regarding Riverton," Susanna said. "She seems to think you know what you are talking about."

"Does she now?" Ian asked. "What else did the duchess disclose about me?"

Susanna glanced at him sideways but did not turn her head. "Nothing much. Merely that she recognized you from last spring."

"Indeed," Ian replied. "I was asked to find a man who was proving difficult to obtain and I did my best to oblige."

"That's very vague," Susanna stated.

Ian shrugged. "There isn't any more to the story."

"So what have you to tell me about Lord Riverton?" she asked, eager to get to the point of this little interview.

"Ah yes, the Viscount Riverton," he said, his voice laced with bitterness. It was curious, but Susanna realized Ian—for now that he had told her his Christian name, she could no longer think of him as Westcott—did not care for the viscount. He paused for a moment longer before continuing. "Lord Riverton was engaged to my sister."

"Yes, Riverton said as much the other day in the park," Susanna replied.

"Did he happen to mention how he was too cowardly to pay the ransom request?" Ian asked. "And then demanded her dowry for the breach of contract?"

"No," Susanna admitted. "He failed to mention anything of the sort."

Ian sighed and ran his hand through his hair. "Beth was kidnapped and a ransom was requested. Riverton refused to pay the kidnappers a penny Ranted and raved about the whole thing, as if it was all somehow my fault, then stormed out of the house. I agreed to pay it—anything to get my sister back unharmed. I withdrew the funds from my father's safe, put them into a large traveling bag and waited. No one ever came to collect it."

Susanna was puzzled. "They asked for a ransom but never expected payment?"

He shrugged. "Best I could tell, something went wrong, though on my end or the kidnappers' is unclear. We found her body two days later in Hyde Park." He glanced at her, her face carefully hiding her horror.

"I remember this from the papers," Susanna admitted, frowning. "I do not understand how this should alter my perception of him."

"He refused to pay the ransom for his beloved fiancée," Ian reiterated. "And then demanded her dowry. Does that not say something of his character? Have you ever seen him behave less than a gentleman?"

Susanna opened her mouth to say something in Riverton's defense, but she shut it quickly, remembering how he left herself and Clara in the middle of the park. She looked away from his inquisitive eyes. "He is a peculiar man, I will admit, but perhaps there is another explanation. Did you ever speak to him about it?"

Ian shook his head. "The first time I saw him after Beth's funeral was when he was walking with you in the park."

"Why were you racing so fast across a public park?" she asked, curious, unable to stop herself.

He shrugged nonchalantly. "I was eager to get to a waistcoat fitting."

Susanna did not believe him, but he returned to the reason for their interview before she could press him further.

"Lord Riverton does not possess a desirable character one would seek in a husband," Ian continued. "Had I been home during their courtship, I would have never allowed my father to approve the match. I am certain your brother will come to same conclusion as well. Riverton is after your dowry, Lady Susanna."

"Have you mentioned any of this to Andrew?" she asked, though none of what he was telling her made any sense.

Ian shook his head. "No. As imperative as it was, it seemed more prudent to come to you directly. Had I initially gone to his grace and he forced your hand at crying off, I feared you might take matters into your own hands and elope, or worse, find a way for Riverton to compromise you."

She smiled lightly at how well he had judged her potential reaction; she did not like being told what to do. "I appreciate the courtesy. Andrew can be overprotective at times and I would rather not trouble him with this just yet. Plus, you have only impugned the viscount's character. It is not exactly grounds to break off a perfectly decent courtship."

He stopped walking and scowled darkly at her. "You would saddle yourself to a gentleman who is beyond repugnant, willingly? Have you a death wish?"

Susanna's mouth popped open in surprise. His tone was much harsher than she had expected. His displeasure with Riverton seemed to be much deeper than a financial dispute. How did one make the leap from bad character to death wish?

He shook his head and looked away. "I've frightened you. I am sorry—"

"I am not frightened," she corrected. "Only confused. You have insulted the man's character and his honor, though none of this makes sense to me. A death wish? What sort of question is that? And what right do you have to judge a man's character so harshly?"

Ian stared directly into her eyes and with no hesitation or doubt, he stated, "I have every right to criticize the man I firmly believe is responsible for my sister's death. You may think me impertinent, my dear, but trust my experience in these matters. The truth of his character is all you need concern yourself with and you would be wise to heed my advice and create a hasty distance from that man, as he is not what he seems. I have given as much evidence as I am at liberty to divulge, but believe me, he is not the man for you."

"I do not think you could have concocted a more confusing answer had you tried," she replied, crossing her arms. "Do not be afraid of offending my delicate sensibilities, my lord. I assure you I am capable of comprehending what you seem to unwilling to share."

Ian laughed and she could see the tension leave his body, clearly feeling more at ease when the mood was light.

"I doubt your sensibilities are anything but delicate, Susanna. And I am sorry I cannot give you a more convincing argument, but please take my word as a gentleman that he is very bad sort."

"Why are you suddenly championing my cause?" she asked curiously. "You do not even know me."

"True," he admitted and looked down at his hands, a stormy, haunted look crossing over his face again. "I saw Lord Riverton in times of a great crisis and, in my experience, this is when a person's true character is revealed. In the end, I saw that he was only after my sister's money and cared not for Beth herself. I am certain that had he not been engaged to my sister, she would not have met such an untimely death. I am convinced his presence in her life brought her death upon her, though I have no explanation as to how. I will forever carry the guilt of my absence during their courtship. I was unable to save my sister. I hope, by overstepping my bounds, I can save you."

Susanna stared at Ian and he stared back, his grey-green eyes intense and honest, and she understood his reasoning. The loss of his sister had devastated him, completely and utterly changed him, much as her father's and brother's deaths twelve years earlier had changed her.

Whatever he thought about Riverton, she might as well give it some credence. The little she had ascertained of Ian's character during their barely one-day acquaintance, told her he did not seem like the sort to go off insulting every gentleman's quality.

She nodded and looked away, not wanting to see the pain in his face any longer.

"I will take what you have told me into dutiful consideration," she replied and they started walking again. "I thank you for taking the time to look out for my well-being."

"I am merely a servant at your beck and call, my dear Susanna," he said dramatically, and she fought the urge to lift her eyes towards the heavens. Again, he turned the conversation to much lighter topics, choosing the coverlet of humor instead of facing reality.

She was, however, quite touched at his protective attitude towards of her. He did not know her and yet he had deliberately sought her out to warn her. Susanna had five overbearing brothers who felt it their duty to give their opinions and dictate how her life should unfold. Andrew issued orders, Luke treated her like a child, Bennett was not in England, Nick was too self-absorbed to aid her in any way, and it was usually difficult to get Charlie to look at anything that wasn't under a microscope. But this man, who was of no relation, saw a problem and had taken the initiative to speak to her like a person, rather than go directly to one of her brothers and demand his opinion be heeded. It seemed this unknown gentleman had more blind respect for her than her five brothers combined.

They neared the front door of the Bradstone Park manor house, and he stopped and turned to her.

"I will leave you to fetch your bonnet," he said and untied the ribbons from under D'artagnon's neck. Susanna giggled again, remembering the sight of the horse in her bonnet. Ian glanced at her and grinned. "Will you need an escort back to town?"

Susanna paused for a moment before smiling warmly. "Thank you, my lord. I would appreciate that."

Susanna could feel his eyes on her as she quickly entered the house in search of a new bonnet. Perhaps Clara was right, she pondered as she swept into her room and rang for her maid. Annette was by her side in less than a minute and she took the disgraced bonnet from Susanna's grasp.

The man did radiate something she was not familiar with. He had power and charisma, but there was something else, something that made her tingle when he smiled. He was being truthful with her in sharing his very poor opinion of Lord Riverton. Perhaps his accusations warranted some sort of inquiry. She would ask Riverton directly and gauge his reaction. She would make her decision in a logical and civilized manner, and not on gut feelings and beliefs.

With a fresh bonnet atop her head, Susanna stepped back into the morning sunlight and smiled again at Ian. Ian smiled rakishly back at her and offered his arm, which she accepted. She was beginning to feel the stirrings of friendship building with Lord Westcott. In her experience, men did not over worry or offer genuine advice to young women for whom they did not have legal or familial responsibility. Then again, her experience was rather limited to her brothers and various family members. Most of the males in society smiled and were courteous, but did not pay her any further attention. None sought her out directly, except for Riverton, and now Ian.

Perhaps he did have some sort of tender feelings for her.

Maybe, just maybe, she thought, he could be the one she had been waiting for.

Ian quite enjoyed his stroll into the small village of Whitstable, especially with the lovely brunette on his arm.

Susanna chatted idly about ribbons as they made the twenty-minute walk into town. She smiled warmly when he made sardonic remarks about ribbons and bonnets and other female apparel he truly knew nothing about. He enjoyed himself nonetheless; her enthusiasm and the way her face lit up was truly remarkable. They were discussing ribbons, after all.

"I appreciate you feigning interest in what I have to say," Susanna said coyly.

"On the contrary, I find your enthusiasm for ribbons quite refreshing," he replied. "It has been a while since I've seen such a small thing give someone so much joy."

Susanna grimaced. "I am not excited about mere ribbons. It is the shopping I enjoy."

"Ah, yes, shopping."

She grimaced again and looked away. "I am not going to explain it to you."

"The acquisition of fine things, like a quest or a grand adventure in search of something no one else has or of something better. It's a game, a challenge issued by the other ladies of society. Who will have the newest trends, who will outshine the others; who can spend the most and be the most desirable?"

Susanna's brows knitted together and she frowned. "No, that's not it at all. Well, it is partly that, the challenge of finding something new is rather exciting, but I have no desire to set trends or show up the other girls. They are not my competition."

"Are they not?"

She looked up at him, and there was something in her bright blue eyes that made him uneasy in his assessment. He had already realized she was not as he expected her to be; when would he learn he did not quite have her pegged as well as he thought he did?

"No, my lord," she replied. "I have no desire to step to the exact tune society deems appropriate. I want to marry and have a family, but there are few women of my age who do not. Women do not have as many opportunities as men do, especially unmarried women. It would be nice to run my own home instead of feeling like an intruder in my family's ancestral seat."

"However," Susanna continued, "it is not my ultimate goal in life to find the richest gentleman with the grandest title. Should I marry down, or never at all, I would be content, I think. It is this perspective that does not put me in competition with the other ladies in society. If anything, I am staying out of the competition. I do not giggle in the presence of a duke nor do I drop my handkerchief hoping some lordly fellow will favor me with his attention. I have a mind and if a gentleman chooses to appreciate that, then the better for us both. If not, I do not want to waste my life with a husband who does not appreciate me for the person I am. Married or not, I want to actually do something with my life."

"I did not mean to offend, Lady Susanna," Ian said, thinking over her rant. Would he ever tire of being wrong where she was concerned?

"I take no offense, Lord Westcott," Susanna replied, tilting her head towards him so he could fully see her face beneath her wide-brimmed bonnet. "But I would ask you not to assume to know me, when clearly you do not."

Ian smiled apologetically and patted her hand on his arm, attempting to bring some levity back to the conversation. "Then I aspire to get to know you better, so I will not make such grievous accusations in the future," he replied. "In fact, I—"

Ian whipped his head around at the sound of someone calling his name, and instantaneously his senses kicked into full attention. The bright midday sun suddenly seemed dim, and he could make out each face in the village square, taking every detail to permanent memory: the baker arguing with a cobbler over three loaves of bread, three lads trying to sneak into the pub four doors down, and the bells chiming from the church steeple at the end of the lane.

"Westcott!" he heard his named called again and spotted the owner of the voice: his partner, Mayne. His muscles relaxed slightly as the familiar man came into full view, hurrying towards him from across the square.

"Lady Susanna, please meet Mr. Charles Mayne."

"Mr. Mayne," Susanna said, dipping into a curtsy.

Mayne touched his hat with a curt, "M'lady." His attention was focused on Ian as he handed him a folded paper.

"Yes, what is it?" Ian asked.

"From Leeds," Mayne responded as Ian scanned the quickly scrawled sentences before handing the paper back to his associate.

Ian nodded to him and said, "We leave straight away. Send for my things."

Mayne gave a quick bow and took off across the square.

Excitement washed over Ian as he rolled the new information around in his head, but his excitement was quickly replaced with regret. He looked down at the gentle face of the extraordinary young woman he wished so desperately he could get to know better and he did the worst thing he could have done: he shrugged her off as if he did not care.

"I am terribly sorry, my dear, but I must be going," he said with as much distance in his voice he could manage.

"Back to the park?" she asked, her brow furrowing in confusion. "But we aren't due back for over an hour."

He shrugged again. "Actually, I have to leave the house party altogether."

Her eyes widened a fraction and she took a half-step back, a telling sign of her feelings of rejection. Ian cringed. He did not want to hurt Susanna, and he knew what she must think of him now. Gentlemen rarely pay such careful and courteous attention to random young ladies, and they certainly do not go out of their way to warn them away from another gentlemen when they have no intention of persuing them for themselves. He knew what he was doing when he decided to warn her off, and this was the ultimate conclusion. His work at the Home Office did not allow any normalcy in his life.

"You know the duchess will be quite put out with you," she said, attempting an idle threat. "This will make the numbers uneven. And an unhappy duchess makes for an unhappy duke."

Ian shrugged again because there really was nothing he could say to make this any better.

"Their graces will get over it. I was a last minute invite anyway. No one will miss me." Cold and detached was the best way out now. He was already in much deeper than he wanted to admit.

He sighed and swallowed the pitiful confession he so desperately wanted to make. "I hope you take my warnings seriously."

Her eyes darkened and she stood a little straighter, her shoulders squaring in defense. "Yes, I will take what you have said with as much seriousness as you seem to possess."

"Susanna—"

"Oh I see Lady Monica and Miss Scott," she said dismissively and waved to them across the square. Lady Monica beamed and waved back before pulling Miss Scott along across the square.

"Susie, dear, we must have missed you at the ribbon shop," Monica said, glancing between Ian and Susanna. "Are we to return for luncheon?"

"Not quite yet," Susanna replied and looked coolly at Ian. "But his lordship is eager to return for some important business matter. Estate business or trampling people in the park, no doubt. He is most eager to be off."

Lady Monica blinked once but, to her credit, did not miss a beat in smiling up at him and bidding him farewell.

Ian was eager to leave the house party, even if he was not eager to leave Susanna. How very wrong he had been about her character from the very onset. She was no simpleton, no giggling miss with marriage on the mind. Her confidence was empowering and her matter-of-fact attitude was refreshing. He wished he could have more time to know her better, to siphon out all her secrets, to see what made her heart flutter with excitement. He wished he were a whole man who deserved someone as kind and strong as Lady Susanna.

"Goodbye Susanna," he said softly, taking her gloved hand and placing a chaste kiss along her knuckles.

She bade him a firm, "Goodbye," before turning her back to him and walking quickly up the walk with Monica and Gemma on either side.

He watched them disappear into the crowd, before turning on

his heel and hurrying back to where he had tethered D'Artangnon.

In his line of work, wishing was pointless. He could wish and hope and plead with fate all he liked but the fact of the matter was, he would never see Lady Susanna again.

Chapter Four

———— ✿ ————

It had been two weeks since Ian had last left London, but it felt like a mere few days. It was a dreary day in London, the rain and drizzle out of character for the previous fortnight of warmth and humidity. It seemed the mournful haze of gray would come early this year, leaving all Londoners craving the days of color and light and warmth again.

He strolled into Brook's, catching the eye of the barman, who nodded to him. He found a seat near the warm hearth and waited only a short moment before a decanter of brandy and a single glass were placed on the table beside him. He stretched out his long legs and snapped his paper open, content to simply sit in silence and read the day's news.

The past two weeks had not been so relaxing for him. With the latest string of robberies in Bath nicely wrapped up and the culprits on their way to Newgate, Ian simply wanted a moment to breathe. He craved a moment that did not involve the underbelly of society—of the death, decay, and desperation he saw so often on the faces of his fellow humankind. He had no idea when his next assignment was going to begin, so choosing to do nothing sat very well with him, indeed, even though he could only stand it for a brief hour. The warmth of the fire and the brandy, and the simple luxury of reading the paper in silence would sustain him through his next mission.

His silent reprieve, however, was short lived, as a laughing voice caught his attention. He tried his best not to roll his eyes as he recognized the joyful timbre of his cousin's laugh.

"And he sits there thinking he is just too damned good to spend his time with anyone of importance, much less his own cousin," Bexley said loudly, laughing from a few chairs away. "How he missed me upon entering I have not yet ascertained."

"I hope he comes over here and pummels you," the man beside him replied. "You can be such a prick sometimes."

Ian turned his head to regard his cousin and his cousin's light-haired friend. "What is it I can do for you?" he asked his cousin.

"You could say 'hello,'" Bexley replied.

Ian huffed and tossed his paper down. He gathered his cup and brandy into one hand and moved to the empty chair beside his cousin.

"Watch it, Rheneas, or I will force you to endure my company endlessly," Ian said, pouring himself another drink. The light-haired man snickered. "Through good moods and bad, you will be so sick of me you will be begging me to leave you alone. And I will refuse, citing my endless desire to be close to the oppressive cousin who adores me so. Does that suit you well enough?"

"Oh, Connolly, will you cease?" Bexley asked, slapping his friend on the back, as his laughter had caused him to choke on his drink.

"Emmett Connolly, Viscount Barrington," the man said as he recovered his wits and extended his hand. Ian shook it.

"Connolly, if you please."

"Ian Carlisle, Earl of Westcott," he replied.

"We are off to the theater this evening," Connolly said. "One last look at the soprano performing before I must be off into the depths of Wales."

Ian's face twisted in revulsion. "Whatever for?"

Connolly took a swig of his brandy. "I have been summoned by the Duke of Newport. Apparently he is a distant relation."

"Well, I wish you luck, I think," Ian said tipping his glass towards Connolly.

Connolly nodded. "Hence the soprano."

"Here, here!" Bexley cheered, clinking glasses with Ian and Connolly.

Ian's first instinct was to decline. But the feeling of the night—the camaraderie he felt with these two men and the brandy racing through his veins—made him change his mind. He had not had a night out on the town in quite a while and felt he was due some frivolity. Having a bit of fun tonight sounded like just the thing he needed to pull himself out of the gloomy mood that had overtaken him over the past two weeks.

He followed the two men out of the club, not even considering what would happen if he encountered the *reason* for his gloomy mood.

In Susanna's opinion, Covent Garden was one of the highlights of London. She loved the theater. The drama and the romance, and even the tragedy was such a welcome contrast to her usual, boring existence. Routs, house parties, musicals, balls, picnics, and social calls; even this past season had been boring, with the slight exception of Andrew and his new duchess throwing a little entertainment and excitement into her life. But now it had settled back into its tedious mind-numbing routine. The Little Season had provided little distraction; even if her courtship with Lord Riverton was a welcome change, it did not transform her life in any drastic way.

Sometimes she wished for the epic romance her sister-in-law

thought she deserved, someone to make her knees weak and her nerves flutter. She was afraid she would settle for stable and safe. Susanna knew she wasn't getting any younger, and—though still far from old—her number of years past her debut would soon put her on the shelf. What options did she have?

She watched the performance, the sounds of music washing over her in a comforting way. Even as a child, she had forced her siblings to put on plays and productions with her, though none would admit to it now. Mother had enjoyed watching them perform, laughing as they forgot their lines or ran into each other on their make-shift stages. Father never attended and had never allowed Sam to attend or participate.

Susanna frowned as she remembered her eldest brother, the brother who had been her father's heir before they both tragically died. It was sad, really, how boring his existence must have been. Not allowed to attend Eton or Oxford, simply stuck indoors with tutors all day long. Though all children were devastated and shocked by their passings, Andrew had been most affected. He was forced to take up Father and Sam's positions and step into the role of the Duke of Bradstone. He had done his best, mostly shutting himself off from the world and throwing up the façade of the Stone Duke, but Susanna knew better. There was a soft, gentle side to her stoic elder brother and his love for Clara clearly demonstrated that to the world.

Susanna watched Andrew and Clara in the row before her as they glanced at each other, their eyes melting into each other's, sharing small private smiles, clearly very much in love.

She sighed again, wishing Riverton would look at her like that and that she would want to look at him with the same intensity. What did it feel like to be loved so passionately? She couldn't imagine an all-consuming love, but it was the blunt absence of it that made it all the more devastating. She glanced at Lord Riverton seated next to her, his dark hair curling behind his ears. She had asked him about Ian's claims, and he admitted to everything.

Remembering the look of anguish on the viscount's face made her look away from him now. He would declare himself any day and she was terrified at what she would say. If she said yes, she was sentencing herself to a life without enduring adoration. If she said no, she could be dismissing a chance for a perfectly content life. She did not long for greatness, but happiness did not seem like too much to ask for.

Susanna wasn't certain what she had expected from her brief encounter with Ian. He had been quite charming, and his face had been so painfully honest, that for one, brief moment she had seen something real in him, something true and sincere. He was the master of hiding behind a comedic façade, and it was a relief to see there was someone of some substance beneath. He had come into her life in a whirlwind of sarcasm and teasing looks, and had left just as quickly, though she couldn't fathom what had pulled him away so suddenly. She swore she saw him while shopping with Monica on a last minute quick trip to Bath, but Monica claimed she was lovesick and seeing things.

Riverton, on the other hand, had no jokes or humor. Over the past two weeks, she had come to realize he was, in fact, rather dull, and that was her biggest problem with him. He was a perfectly suitable, stable, and comfortable match, everything a lady of quality should hope for in a marriage. She would acquire a title, a sizable income, and a home to run as her own. She would host society events, head charity organizations, and become a great matron of society. She would deliver him an heir and a spare and, hopefully, a dark-haired little lady too. They would live in the country most of the year, coming to London for the season. She would be content and comfortable. And *bored*.

Riverton was not exciting. He was not dramatic. He was plain and dull and very, very safe. His eyes were never intense; his smiles did not make her weak in the knees. Their relationship would be that of companionship, a content happiness. There would be no darkness, no uncertainty. There would be no sparks, no fire; there would be no all-encompassing, burning, passionate love.

It wasn't as if she had many other options. Her brief daydreams of what could have been with Ian were just that—dreams. They would never come true.

Days after he disappeared, she had mourned as if she were losing some great love.

Truth was, she did not even know him. She was foolish to let her thoughts and dreams run away with her. She knew better than to count her eggs before there was even a rooster in the hen house.

Aside from marriage to Riverton, the only other immediate option was not marrying at all. Susanna wasn't sure what was worse, a loveless marriage or no marriage at all.

They rose from their seats and clapped politely as the curtain fell on the stage. The theater audience made their way to the corridors for the traditional intermission promenade and Susanna cringed, not feeling in the mood to smile and be social.

Lord Riverton offered his arm as they left the Bradstone box, and she accepted. They walked along the hallways, smiling and nodding at acquaintances. Riverton stopped to talk with a friend from Oxford, and Susanna stood demurely at his side, bored beyond belief. She looked helplessly around the room for someone she recognized, for something to relieve her from her doldrums, anything to yank her out of this boring nightmare she found herself in.

Was this to be her life? A life without love? Without passion? Six months ago, she would not have thought twice about it—the type of man and marriage Riverton had to offer were just the type she had always expected. Her parents had had a great romance, but since both were gone when she was so young, she really did not remember anything of it. Her sister Sarah's marriage had been of equal affection, but not a love match. It was Andrew and Clara that made her realize such a thing was possible. She had barely had any time to process such a possibility when Riverton had begun his courtship. And now she was stuck.

"Please excuse me," Susanna said to Riverton. "I believe I see an acquaintance." He nodded to her, barely acknowledging her words and turned back to his Oxford chum.

Susanna left quickly, swallowing her lie. She craved some sort of distraction from the oppressive possibility of becoming Lady Riverton.

It was a good match, she told herself, albeit not a perfect one. It was a safe, reliable solution to spending a lifetime at Bradstone House. But it made her sad to think this might be all she would be allowed in life. Would Riverton let her continue her charity work? What about the work she wished to do to help reform the prisons? And goodness, what would she do about Lady Day?

A firm hand caught her arm and she was pulled behind a curtain into a side alcove.

Another hand came across her mouth and she went to scream.

"Shhhh, Susanna, it is only me," Ian said gently. 'Her eyes grew round at the sight of him, and she could not help but stare wide-eyed, every fiber of her body springing to life. The man who had haunted her dreams for a fortnight was flesh before her, and her memory had not done his handsomeness justice. His face was more tanned, unfashionably so, but his eyes were clear and lit with fire.

"What are you doing here?" she asked as he lowered his hand. His eyes narrowed into a hard glare.

"I should ask you the same thing," he replied in a hard hushed tone. "Or rather, why are you here with *him*?"

"I asked Riverton about your accusations, and he confessed to everything," she replied.

"Did he?" he said, taken back. "What exactly did he confess?"

"He admitted to not paying the ransom, and that he had never forgiven himself for his oversight. He claimed to have been devastated at the loss of Lady Beth and not thinking correctly when he asked for her dowry. He said he mourned her even though they were not properly married. He said he felt they were married in his heart."

"He is playing you, Susanna," he replied, shaking his head.

"I have not given you permission to use my given name," she snapped at him. "And you do not have the right to speak to me so. You told me your suspicions about Riverton and I have done what I saw fit."

"Do you still intend to marry Riverton if he offers?" he asked.

"I—" she stopped, unable to give an answer she did not know herself.

"Ah ha," he said, a satisfied smile coming across his face. "Not so sure of your viscount anymore, are you?"

"I have no doubts about Riverton," she said harshly. "He has even told me he will refuse my dowry, that we should give the money to a charity that needs it."

Ian scoffed. "He is lying."

"How do I know you are not lying?" she accused. "How do I know that in your grief-stricken state you did not invent his whole thing in your head to seek revenge on the man you blamed for your sister's death?"

The last thing she expected him to do was kiss her. She let out a surprised gasp as he roughly pressed his lips to hers and for a brief moment, she forgot to breathe. But when she did, she breathed in the scent of him—a fresh, earthy smell combined with a hint of peppermint and a spiciness lingering on his breath. Her eyes fluttered closed and she relaxed, wrapping her arms around his neck and pressing herself into him, molding her body to his. His arms wound around her back, lifting her closer. He nibbled on her lip, letting himself inside and pummeled her mouth with his tongue. It was not the kiss of a gentle suitor, and it shook her senses wide-awake. It was a passionate kiss, meant to punish. She wound her fingers into his hair, wrapping his locks into her hands and closed her fists. He groaned.

"Lady Susanna?" a sweet voice called, and Susanna pulled away from Ian, breathless. His eyes were dark with desire and he smelled of brandy. He released her, and they stood staring at each other for a long moment before she heard Clara calling her name again, this time closer to their curtained alcove.

Ian reached up and wiped the moisture of his kiss from her mouth and nodded, deeming her presentable. She did not speak as she quickly stepped out of the curtain to face her sister-in-law standing alone in the empty corridor. It appeared intermission was over.

The duchess eyed her suspiciously, glancing at the curtain she had just stepped away from.

"Lord Riverton mentioned you went to find an acquaintance," Clara said. "I suggested perhaps you returned to your acquaintance's box at the end of intermission, but I would check the refreshing rooms for you just in case."

"Yes, um, an acquaintance," Susanna managed to say. Her lips felt raw from Ian's kiss and she knew she looked a little more rumpled than appropriate. "I did not know my friend was in attendance tonight."

"Are you certain your acquaintance is reliable?" Clara asked her, a knowing look in her eye.

"I certainly hope so," Susanna admitted.

"I hope your acquaintance understands that while he may have Andrew's bark to deal with it, is my bite that should be feared," Clara threatened in a very sweet tone.

Susanna nodded, certain Ian was hearing everything she was saying. He was only a foot behind her, hidden by the curtain, but she could still feel him all over her.

"Might I recommend you return to Bradstone House, claiming a dastardly headache?" Clara suggested. "You look awfully flushed, as if you might be coming down with a fever. I will make excuses for you and not speak a word of this to Andrew. I am your friend, Susanna, but my limits of impropriety can only be stretched so far. Please do not put me in a situation where I must lie to Andrew for you. I assure you, I could not do it."

"Yes, I understand," Susanna nodded. "I am feeling rather . . .

warm. Perhaps it is best if I return home."

Clara nodded. "Please take the Bradstone carriage. Garnet can convey you home and return for the rest of us. I would offer to accompany you, but I must stay and make your excuses. Beverell will be sufficient enough as an escort."

Susanna nodded again, squeezing Clara's hand as she stepped past the duchess and quickly made her exit. The Bradstone carriage was before her in moments. Beverell, their brawny footman, helped her into the carriage and the footman shut the door with a soft click before hopping onto the back of the carriage. The carriage rocked into motion as the driver, Garnet, transported her home. She wrapped the warm blanket around her for their ten-minute journey back to Bradstone House.

What a disgraceful mistake that could have been. She applauded Clara's quick thinking and was thankful she made her exit before anyone saw her alone with Ian in the corridor, or discovered them behind the curtain. She sighed, leaning back against the plush cushions of the Bradstone coach. Her head rolled to the side and she took in the night skyline, a bright full moon giving the evening an eerie glow in the incoming fog.

Fog. That was what Ian did to her; he clouded her mind, robbing her of rational thought. He made her crazy, and she was not prone to madness. The memory of his honesty and his teasing smiles had plagued her for a fortnight, and yet, when she first saw him, she had been elated. Despite the near scandal she had just escaped, she could not regret it. No one had ever kissed her like that.

She glanced at the interior of the coach, staring dejectedly at the expensive seat cushions.

If she married Riverton she would never be kissed like that again.

Ian waited for Susanna to leave before stepping around the

curtain where he knew the duchess was still standing. Her arms were crossed across her chest and she glared up at him.

"I expect you to call tomorrow," she stated, and he felt he was being sternly set down. "I can condone flirting and being a bit too forward, but do not expect a dalliance with Lady Susanna. No more secret alcove moments and no more secluded walks through the woods."

Ian opened his mouth to ask how she expected to stop him from doing as he pleased with Lady Susanna, but she cut him off, holding her hand up toward him, acting as a physical barrier to the charm they both knew he possessed.

"I may not have any control over you or Susanna," she said, "but I do have the duke's ear. If he were to hear of this little tryst, he would not be pleased. You know he would demand you do the honorable thing and marry Susanna. Are you prepared for that?"

He grimaced at her question. Marriage was not an option for him.

"I thought as much," she replied softy, though he wasn't certain what conclusion she had taken from his silence. "If you desire to see Susanna again you will do so in a proper fashion."

"Her almost fiancé and I do not get on," he informed her.

She shrugged, her arm falling to her side, all barriers removed. "You do not seem like the type to let someone like Viscount Riverton stand in your way. Do you foresee him being a problem?"

He shook his head slowly.

"Besides, he is leaving town tomorrow, for three weeks," she continued. "Something about business at a Northumberland estate. He is set to leave tomorrow morning. Tomorrow afternoon, when you call to take Susanna on a curricle ride through Hyde Park, you will be quite free of his prying eyes. You do own a curricle?"

"Yes, your grace," he replied, smiling at her.

"Good. I'd hate to be denied the use of my own curricle because I would have to lend it to you."

"You will not be accompanying us?" he asked.

She shook her head. "No, I believe Susanna's maid will be sufficient chaperonage. Do you think she should need someone more?"

"No, your grace."

"Good. Now that that is settled, I suggest you return to your box or your home, whichever you see fit."

"Quite right," he agreed and stepped around her. "I say, your grace, might I ask how long you have been married to his grace?"

"Just over three months."

"You have been a duchess for three months?" he asked and she nodded. "I thought you had been a duchess for years. You could give some of the old dragons of society a run for their rubies." He smiled brightly at her.

She beamed at him before shooing him away, shaking her head.

Chapter Five

The lilac sitting room was one of Susanna's favorite rooms in the house, and not only because it was mostly decorated in shades of purple, which happened to be her favorite color. It was the room her mother had let her assist in decorating, almost two decades past, and she still remembered sitting with her mother, poring over fabric sample books, comparing paint samples and furniture designs. When she was in this room, she felt her mother there with her. Even as a grown woman, she missed her mother each day, and sitting in this room made her feel a bit closer. It was the one thing they had done together, just the two of them.

"This was much less complicated when I did not have to chaperone both of you," Clara said, sitting down in a chair opposite Susanna. Most of the settees and sofas were in shades of white and silver, the walls were lilac with damask print curtains draped artfully over the windows. The dark hardwood flooring added a contrast, as did the dark wood of the tables and writing desk in the corner.

"It seems silly that *you* must chaperone both Norah and I,"

Susanna commented. "I mean, chaperones are usually old and crusty an—"

"And married," Clara interjected. "Since your sister, Sarah, has gone off to the country with her sister-in-law, the chaperone duties have fallen to me entirely. What is silly is that you and Norah cannot each receive callers in the same room."

Susanna glanced through the lilac drawing room door, across the hall to the apricot drawing room where Norah was holding court. Normally her older sister Sarah, Lady Radcliff, sat with her younger sister Norah during her days at home, and Clara sat with Susanna, since they shared the same friends. But Sarah, like much of society, had high-tailed it out of the city a few months ago when the heat set in.

Susanna sighed. She and Norah were on separate ends of the metaphorical social balance.

Both at the top of the social heap, yet Norah was far more conservative than the very liberal Susanna. The sisters got along with each other, but their views on society were quite different. Where Norah opted to do exactly what society expected of her, Susanna and her friends chose to test the waters, daring the *haute ton* to disgrace them.

"You know why Norah and I cannot receive callers together," Susanna began but Clara waved her off.

"Yes, yes, I understand. It is just exhausting having to go back and forth between the two rooms. You know I cannot stand her friends."

Susanna nodded and smiled. "Though, it is rather wonderful to see them falling at your feet when they wanted nothing to do with you mere months ago. Norah has such silly friends."

Clara pursed her lips. "That is what makes it worse."

"Just wait until the regular season begins," Susanna said, laughing. "You will be much in demand. You will not have time to chaperone Norah and I as you will be entertaining yourself. Then Sarah will take up her chaperone duties again."

"Yes, well perhaps you could just make it easy on all of us and marry some nice gentleman, and then you can conduct your own social calls in your own house," Clara said with hopeful optimism. Susanna looked away from Clara's cheerful face, not wanting the duchess to see how much the topic bothered her.

"Yes, well," Susanna replied, looking down at her green-print day dress. It was a lovely fabric she had found just at the end of the season, a soft, olive-green with burgundy and cream flowers scattered throughout the print. Annette had paired it with a cream, satin sash.

"Oh bother, Susanna, you know you are welcome here as long as you desire," Clara said, shaking her head. "Andrew and I truly enjoy having you here."

Susanna looked up at her friend, and something clicked into place in her mind; an inkling that had been dancing around for months finally became a full-fledged realization. This was no longer Susanna's home. As sincerely as her sweet sister-in-law might have intended the offer, Clara's words were further proof of Susanna's position as guest in their home. This was the home of the Duke and Duchess of Bradstone, and Susanna was neither. Andrew and Clara would soon start their own Macalister family, and really, how long could Susanna dawdle as a doting aunt?

Susanna fought back the tears that threatened to take over because she was afraid once she began crying she would never stop. What on earth was she to do with herself?

Clara smiled apologetically and glanced at the timepiece on the mantle. Giggling caught both their attention and Clara leaned forward to see who was in the hall.

"Norah and Lord Niles?" Susanna asked.

"And Lady Laura," Clara added with a sigh.

Susanna ruffled her nose in disgust. "I cannot believe Norah forgave her after her atrocious outburst last spring. Your cut was superb, by the way."

"Yes, well, that is why I am hiding in here. But now that Lord

Niles has arrived, it seems I must return." The duchess looked at her pleadingly. "You could join me for moral support."

Susanna laughed. "Silly Duchess, do you need me there to fend off the evil, blonde gossipmongers? Shall I slay them in your honor? I am happy to play your knight, your grace."

"Oh, hush," Clara scolded, rolling her eyes, but Susanna knew her sister-in-law enjoyed her teasing. The duchess stood, shaking out the skirts of her gold-and-cream-striped, silk, day dress. The colors complemented her complexion perfectly. She sighed before straightening her back, lifting her chin, and sweeping determinedly and very duchess-like out of the room.

Susanna sat back in her chair and closed her eyes. As with each time she had closed her eyes since the night before, she was thrown back into the moment Ian had kissed her. His kiss haunted her, teased her for its lack of completion. Goodness—what had she been thinking? If Clara had not come looking for her, who knew what would have happened?

"Might I return when you are awake, Lady Susanna?" a male voice asked and she snapped her eyes open, jumping up from the chair. As if pulled straight from her dreams, there stood Ian in the doorway. He looked smart in buff breeches, a navy jacket, and white waistcoat, his cravat simply tied into an uncomplicated knot. He was effortlessly elegant and sublimely masculine and she could not fight the smile that broke across her face.

He smiled brightly at her in return and bowed before pulling a bouquet of fresh daisies from behind his back.

"For you, my dear," he said, his eyes teasing.

She sent him a scathing look but accepted the flowers all the same. Daisies, after all, were her favorite flower, though he could not have known that.

"These are lovely, my lord," she said. "Thank you."

"Will you not call me Ian?" he asked and she shook her head.

"And you may not call me Susanna," she replied. He sighed and shrugged but did not look too bothered by this current stalemate. She stepped to the bell pull and rang for a maid.

"How are you this afternoon?" he asked.

"Splendid," she replied. "Though I am quite surprised to see you here."

"I am quite surprised to see myself here as well," he replied honestly, glancing around at the room like he had never seen a drawing room before. "I snuck in behind that Niles fellow, and, before your butler noticed me, I found my way here. I have arrived in a most splendidly sprung curricle and it would be a great honor to me if you would join me in a ride around Hyde Park."

Susanna blinked stupidly at him while she processed what he had just suggested.

"You want to drive with me, just the two of us, through the park during the fashionable hour where everyone will see?"

He nodded. "Yes. Well, not completely alone, that would be most improper, you know. Rules and propriety and all that. Shame on you for suggesting something so scandalous, Susanna."

Susanna fought the urge to roll her eyes.

"If your maid is available," Ian continued, "she is welcome to attend you. And while it may be the fashionable hour, there is a definite chill in the air this afternoon, so not as many people will be in the park. Plus, it is only September and not May, so the most notorious busybodies will not be present. But yes, I wish to be seen with you."

"Why?" Susanna couldn't help herself.

He shrugged. "I like you. You are much more interesting than any other lady I know. Men too, in fact. And I am free this afternoon and thought you might need to see me again."

"I do not ever *need* to see you, my lord," she replied.

"Yes, but you *want* to."

Susanna tried to keep her face stern, but his charming smile and teasing eyes forced a smile from her and she let out a small chuckle.

"I might have wanted to see you," she admitted.

"See, that was not so difficult to confess, was it?" he asked.

"Actually, it was," she replied, tilting her chin up. "I will have you know, you are not as charming as you think you are."

"Yes I am," he replied, and she laughed again. They were interrupted by the arrival of a maid and Susanna handed over the daisies with instruction they be put into water.

"If you fetch your cloak and your maid, we might be on our way," Ian instructed as the maid left. "I even have a firebox heating a blanket for you, should you require it."

"I think my cloak should do just fine," she replied. She excused herself and stepped around him, careful not to touch him as she passed, though she could feel the heat radiating off him nonetheless. She saw Clara in the hallway, haughty airs and one blonde eyebrow raised in question.

"Westcott is taking me for a curricle ride through the park," she quickly explained. "I will bring Annette; all will be proper. He is just a friend, Clara, please do not make this into more than it needs to be."

"It is your happiness that I care about," Clara said softly. "You are a great friend to me and I am attempting to return the favor."

Susanna stepped around her, pausing to buss her cheek. "Thank you!"

There was a definite chill in the air as she stepped outside Bradstone House, her arm tightly tucked into Ian's. His curricle was parked in front of the house along the brick drive, the two bays accompanying the curricle matched perfectly together. The top folding hood stood up, covering them in a half cocoon, a blanket was folded on the seat and waves of heat wafted up from the warming box beneath the seat. He lifted her into the high-pitched curricle, and she scooted across the bench as he launched himself into the seat. Susanna glanced behind her where her maid, Annette, was wrapped in a cloak and perched on the back step.

"Please do not drive too fast," Susanna said to Ian as he took the reins from the groom. "I would hate for Annette to fall off the back perch."

He turned in the seat to regard her. "Why is it you are end-lessly concerned with the speed at which I drive?"

She leveled a scathing look at him and he nodded.

"Oh yes, *that*," he said and flicked the reins. "It seems I am never to live down that one moment. And I assure you, Susanna, it was but one moment."

"Do not—"

"But you need not fear for your maid, my dear," he continued. "I will drive so slowly you will not even know we are moving."

She scowled at him but remained silent. It seemed he was going to call her whatever he wanted and there was nothing she could do about it.

"If you insist on using my Christian name, please do not do so when someone might overhear. It would be unseemly for a virtually unknown man to use my given name."

"Why do you insist that we do not know each other?" he asked, maneuvering the matched horses through the traffic. "Even more so, you seem determined not to know me."

"I have no aversion to you, my lord," she replied. "Just your impropriety."

"You might find my forwardness alluring once you knew my character better," he suggested. "Ask me something and I swear to answer it honestly."

"Anything?' she asked.

He nodded.

"What about seriously?" she asked. "I know you are capable of honesty, but seriousness is something that might be intriguing to see."

"Bah," he complained, turning into the park. "Being serious is boring. You will find you would enjoy life much more if you were not so serious all the time."

"Another diverted answer. You are quite good at them."

"Yes, I will answer you as honestly and seriously as I can

manage," he replied. "That is the best I can do, I am afraid. In return, all I require is that you allow me the same privilege."

She mulled this over for a moment before nodding. She could not deny the fact that she was overtly curious about this man.

He grinned. "Fabulous, we are agreed then," he said and turned the curricle onto the well-worn path around the park. There were a few other carriages out, but since they were a bit early for the sociable hour, they were in the minority for their age group.

"How old are you?" she asked, glancing at him out of the corner of her eye.

"Almost nine and twenty," he replied.

Hmm, she would have thought he were further along into his thirties.

"How old are you?" he asked in return.

She swallowed an exasperated sigh at his improper question but answered him. "Two and twenty. Have you any siblings other than Lady Beth?"

He shook his head. "My parents were well past their child bearing years when I came along and Beth was quite the surprise eight years later. You Macalisters . . . How many of you are there?"

"Ten," she replied, "though only nine living. My eldest brother and father died when I was ten. Andrew is, of course, the next oldest son, but Sarah is older than he. Ben and Luke come after Andrew, then myself, then Norah and her twin Nick, and Charlie and Mara are at the end of the line."

"There certainly are a gaggle of you," he replied. "I've only just met the duke, and I've worked with Lord Luke before."

"In what capacity did you work with Luke?" she asked curiously, as her brother Luke was seldom in town.

He sent her a sideways glance before shrugging. "On the continent. We played a hand of whist, if I am not mistaken." There seemed to be more to the story but Susanna moved on.

"I assume you attended Eton and Oxford?"

"Neither, actually," he replied. "I was tutored at home before

I reached my majority. Then I ran off and joined the Royal Army."

"You went off to war when you were your father's heir?" she asked curiously.

"I was rebelling," he explained, shrugging. "Father had me sequestered in the country my entire life. I was not allowed to attend Eton or Oxford, and one afternoon I snapped. After one particularly nasty argument over spending some time abroad for a celebratory nineteenth birthday tour, I jumped on my horse to ride off my frustrations, and before I knew it I was riding into London to the Home Office to purchase a commission. I was out of the country in a week."

"They allowed you to purchase your own commission?"

Ian smiled sheepishly. "I may have forged letters from my father instructing the purchase of a commission for his only son. Luckily for me, one had become available the week prior and there was no delay."

"That must not have gone over well with your father," she commented.

"Not at all," he agreed. "I received multiple letters summoning me home, but I refused. Eventually the letters tapered off. Beth continued to write me and keep me apprised of what was going on at home, but I was much happier where I was. Besides, I wasn't actually fighting in the war. I can count on one hand how many times I actually saw battle."

Susanna was confused. "If you did not fight in the war, then what did you do?"

He opened his mouth to respond, but snapped it shut, his brow furrowing and he thought for a moment before continuing. "I was in the army, I had a rank and pay and all the privileges. One of my superiors noticed my knack for solving puzzles, and I have an excellent memory. He recommended me for another sect of the army. I was more involved in the background side of things"

"You were a spy?"

He laughed loudly and slapped his knee. "Good lord, no, not at all. Could you see me as a spy?"

She honestly couldn't and she told him so.

"That's rich," he laughed again, shaking his head. "No, I was plucked from the battlefield and worked with the Home Office.

"Were you a diplomat?" she asked, wondering what other positions one could hold within the Home Office.

Ian shook his head. "It was an experimental position to begin with, but now there are six of us. Nothing too exciting, I assure you. Mostly paperwork." He shrugged again and Susanna was starting to see a pattern. He probably did not even know he was doing it, though it must be his way of maneuvering away from anything too serious or truly personal.

"You were schooled at home, I assume?" Ian asked.

Susanna shook her head, noting how he turned the focus of conversation back on her. "Actually, no. When I turned thirteen, Andrew sent me to Miss Katherine's Finishing School for Young Ladies. Norah and I both were sent there and recently my youngest sister Mara has begun as well. It was quite an extensive education."

"What is taught there?"

"The usual things: watercolors, how to manage a household, literature, arithmetic, and French," she replied. "But the subject entitled, 'Practical Matters' was my favorite. It was a different topic every two months. Sometimes it was current events, then history of England, then military history and traditions. I particularly enjoyed the sessions on social classes and charity work. Some of the topics were more liberal, like social reform and foreign affairs."

"Sounds like quite an interesting education," Ian commented. "Not the normal topics you would find at a ladies' finishing school."

Susanna beamed, nodding. "That was the purpose. Miss Katherine was very exclusive in who she accepted. She felt she had a duty to her girls to make them more than society mammas, but women who could use their positions to help and change our society at large."

"She taught her girls to think for themselves, rather than

follow blindly."

"Precisely."

"Then I suppose your reactions of last night are not as surprising," he added.

"How so?"

"You did not collapse into a fit of vapors when I kissed you," he answered and glanced at her. "And you did not run off to your brother demanding I pay for my crimes."

Susanna shifted uncomfortably in her seat. "I would never have done that."

"Because you would not want to be saddled to me or because you do not want your brother dictating your life?"

Susanna chewed over her answer, wondering how their light-hearted conversation had taken such a turn for the serious. They were rounding the last curve of the carriage path in the park and there were more carriages out now than before.

"I did not want you to get into trouble," she replied softly and looked down at her hands. "You have tried to help me, and it did not seem a very polite way to return such a kindness."

"You do me a great favor by assuming my intentions are completely honorable," he said. "You, my dear, are quite lovely. And you must know I was quite foxed last night."

She chuckled softly. "Later I realized that. You tasted like brandy."

He raised his eyebrows and looked down at her, mirth racing through his green eyes. "You tasted like strawberries."

She laughed and shook her head. "It's a good thing it is simply the Little Season. Were it next spring, there would be five times as many people and you would not be able to speak to me so."

He grinned at her and she knew that he would still say such things even if they were surrounded by five hundred of the strictest sticklers. He seemed to do as he pleased and she couldn't help but admire him for it.

They made another loop around the park, smiling and nodding

at a few people they each knew. Susanna did not miss the inquisitive glances she was receiving and hoped her outing with Ian would not cause too much of a scene, though she was afraid it would.

"No more questions?" he asked.

She shrugged gracefully. "I do not know. Let us not spoil all the fun in one afternoon."

"Quite right," he nodded. "Very logical of you. From here on out, we shall limit our daily interview to five questions each to avoid running out of things to talk about."

Susanna regarded him, tilting her head to the side just so. "What will we do when we run out of things to talk about?"

"When we no longer have anything to say to each other, then we shall part ways, never to speak again," he replied. "Because, really, what would two people who have run out of things to say have to say to each other?"

She laughed and shook her head at his absurdity, but smiled despite herself. He grinned brightly in return.

He made another loop around the park before returning her to Bradstone House. He leapt from the curricle before turning to help her down, his wide hands wrapping gently around her slender waist. He lifted her down from the curricle, setting her down a fraction too close to be considered proper. The heat from his gloved hands burned through her day dress and she looked up into his handsome face with a warning, expecting to see some sort of teasing smile. What she saw was fire and some sort of raw emotion she did not recognize.

"I apologize, Lady Susanna," he said and took a step away.

"Thank you for your assistance, Lord Westcott," she said and took a step backwards. The heel of her shoe caught on an uneven cobblestone and she felt herself falling backwards. Ian's warm hands caught her again, hauling her upright and pulling her into his torso. Her hands pressed against his solid chest. She could feel heat from his body radiate down the length of her. Staring at his cravat, she embraced the shock and fire that raced through her before taking a steadying breath and looking up into his amused face.

"It seems I step away from you to prevent causing a scene and you take it upon yourself to fall, so I must do just that," he said, a sultry timbre in his voice. His words teased and his face was laced with a smirk, but there was a primal longing swirling about in the depths of his grey-green eyes. "Really, Susanna, be prepared to make an honest man out of me."

"Oh, stop," she said, laughing, swatting him with her hand and removing herself from his embrace. "You know I fell in earnest, so do not get rakish with me."

He laughed and shook his head. "I doubt anyone would ever peg me as a rake."

"No, you are too indecent to be a rake," she agreed nodding. "You are something different altogether."

"I will leave you to your evening, then," he said and hauled himself up onto the perch of his curricle. She heard the door open behind her and caught the red and white of the Bradstone livery out of the corner of her eye.

"Thank you for a lovely afternoon, Lord Westcott," she replied and took a step towards the house, reluctant to go inside. She wanted to know more about him, she wanted to watch him shrug and evade her questions. It only made her more curious about what he had to hide. She wanted to see the fire in his eyes when he looked at her, she wanted to feel the warmth his teasing grin sent down to her toes.

"Until our paths cross again, my dear," he said softly, not breaking her eye contact.

"For goodness' sake, Susanna, stop dawdling on the stoop," came Norah's voice as she stepped from the house.

Susanna whipped her head around as her sister was followed by Lady Laura and Lord Niles. She turned back towards Ian to make introductions or spout some sort of explanation, but he was already rounding the front gate, perched smartly upon his curricle.

"Who on earth was that?" Lady Laura asked and Susanna hurried up the front steps, pausing as she passed Norah and her friends.

Susanna looked directly at the young blonde before turning her head and marching inside the house, cutting her directly.

"You know your cuts mean nothing on your own doorstep?" Lady Laura called after her.

Susanna spun around. "Your welcome in this house is very thin and very conditional. It would behoove you to at least appear to respect that."

Lady Laura glared. "It is charming to see you making threats as if you were the Duchess of Bradstone. But wait—Lady Susanna—you have no husband and you have no title and you have no home of your own. So forgive me that I do not see anything before me worth respecting." Susanna slammed the heavy door shut, the sounds echoing through the front hall.

"How dare she," Susanna muttered to herself before spinning around, determined to make it to her room before she broke something, only to have her steps halted when she saw who was standing behind her.

"Andrew," Susanna said, her voice calm, not giving away the extent of her rage.

"Susanna," he replied, nodding. "I trust you had an enjoyable afternoon?"

She wasn't certain to which aspect of her afternoon her brother was referring to so she simply smiled. "Splendid. Please excuse me, I must dress for dinner."

"I share your frustrations with Lady Laura," her brother said as her slipper hit the first step. "She is uncouth and should not be welcome here. However, she is a friend of Norah's for some reason, and it would be rude of me to deny her entrance. But there is one point where she and I are in agreement."

Susanna slowly turned to regard her brother, waiting for him to continue. "You are not the Duchess of Bradstone," he stated.

"Yes," Susanna said slowly. "I am aware of that."

Andrew shook his head and looked down at the envelopes in his hands. "I have noticed there has been a shift of balance in this house since Clara became my wife. Prior to my marriage, you and Sarah seemed to take up portions of duchess duties, Sarah more so than you. It is not a coincidence Sarah has taken her sister-in-law up on her offer for a summer in the country and has yet to return. While I am certain there is no animosity towards Clara in any regard, I am not blind. Everyone is adjusting to the new arrangements."

"Andrew, I've never known you to mince words," Susanna said. "Just spit out whatever it is you want to say."

"You should marry and have a home of your own," he replied. "You will always be welcome here for as long as you need, but you should want to move on in your life. The duties as duchess that you and Sarah took on are no longer required of you. You and Norah both are of marrying age and it is time you married and got on with your lives—found your own happiness. You do not need to tend to the Bradstone name any longer."

Susanna stiffened at his words, knowing he was right and that while he spoke from a place of sincerity, as usual his execution was a bit cold.

He ran his hand through his hair and looked directly at her. "You think me uncaring, but I care too much, Susanna. Your happiness is of the highest importance to me."

She nodded in acknowledgement. She knew he loved each of them. He just had a strange way of showing it.

"I shall see you for dinner then." He bowed stiffly then turned and quit the entrance hall, disappearing into the depths of the house. She sighed as she ascended the stairs, knowing one way or another, her days in the house were numbered.

Ian sat alone in his rose-colored study, flipping through the papers on his desk, looking for something he knew he was missing. One small detail to connect everything together. It had to be here, it had to all be linked.

He should have been working on the assignment he had received this morning: movements of stolen items turning up in other parts of the country, watch fobs and earrings missing from London but found in Cardiff and Portsmouth. So far, the only link was a merchant ship owned by a wealthy London merchant.

What he was thinking about was his sister's murder and the dozens of other similar deaths he had come across in the past three years. Affianced girls kidnapped, ransoms paid, then days later their bodies found, and the fiancé in the wind. What was troubling was not the occurrences across the country, but that aside from the similarities in the methodology, there were no other connections, save one.

A small knock came from the drawing room door and he sighed, calling for the knocker to enter.

"Ah, Mayne," Ian said as he glanced up at his associate. "Just the report I was waiting for."

"Westcott," Mayne nodded as he sat down in the chair opposite Ian's desk.

Ian did not offer tea or brandy, knowing the man would not accept. Mayne was a peculiarly paranoid chap who refused to drink anything but his own stores for fear of being poisoned.

Mayne opened up a large file of papers wrapped in leather and handed Ian a few sheets.

Ian accepted them, scanning the words, and smiling at what he saw.

"So nice to see the magistrate saw it our way in the end," Ian said, flipping through the other papers, new reports on the stolen goods. "When will the ship come into port? What is it called again? The—"

"*Anna Marianne*," Mayne replied shaking his head. "Ridiculous name for a ship. Reports put her in at the end of next week."

"Make certain we are notified when she passes Gravesend," Ian said. The lookouts along the southern end of the Thames would help with a more accurate arrival time.

"Yes, my lord," Mayne replied.

"Where is—"

"He was last seen outside Oxfordshire," Mayne replied.

"Which is not exactly on the way to Northhamptonshire," Ian replied, setting a new page down. "How many do you have?"

"Three," Mayne replied. "Traveling as a father and son on their way north with their driver.

"Any word from—"

"No, but the dispatches have just gone out," Mayne replied. "It might take them a while to hold any meaning."

Ian nodded, leaning back in his chair. He linked his hands behind his head and sighed.

"Something amiss, my lord?" Mayne asked. They were partners, equals in their place of employment, but Mayne refused to drop the formalities when it came to Ian's rank and title.

"Mayne, this whole investigation is completely secret, only three other men outside of this room know the entirety of its details, and those are the three currently pursuing him."

"Yes, my lord."

"So theoretically, if there was another girl who was being targeted, do not we have some sort of obligation to warn her away from the blackguard?"

Mayne scratched his head. "Not if we wanted to nab the bloke, my lord. If we tip off his mark, we tip him off and he could be gone for another year, like he did in '11. All we have right now is circumstantial, nothing we can actually arrest him on. We need to catch him literally in the act, blood on his hands, as they say."

Ian grimaced. "What if we fail again? What if this one time we are certain we know his target and we still cannot apprehend him and she dies, just like the others? Her death is our fault, is it not?"

"It will be him doing the killing, my lord," Mayne replied. "To save the poor girl we have to arrest and detain him before he can harm her."

"But to do that we have to use her as bait," Ian replied, irritated. "We cannot arrest without proof of wrongdoing and we cannot get proof until he does something wrong."

"Rock and a hard place, my lord," Mayne replied.

Ian shook his head. "I still do not like it."

Mayne narrowed his eyes at Ian. "Are we truly speaking theoretically?"

Ian shrugged. "Perhaps."

"One girl's safety is not necessarily more important than justice for all the girls before her," Mayne reminded him. "Let us not forget what started this entire investigation. It is your vengeance that has gotten us this far."

Ian nodded. "Rock and a hard place indeed."

"Is there anything further?" Mayne asked.

Ian shook his head. "Not that I can think of."

"Good day, Westcott," Mayne said and stood.

"Good day." Ian watched absently as his associate quickly left the rose study. No one commented on his choice for office any longer. Everyone knew why he was here, why he was so determined. He would not fail Beth a second time.

A knock came from the door and his butler stepped inside.

"My lord, the doctor is here for his lordship and her ladyship's examination."

"I will be along in a moment," Ian replied and the butler left. Ian rubbed his hands over his face, pressing his palms deeply into his eyes before standing up. He couldn't tell Susanna about his concerns without jeopardizing the entire mission, but he was desperate to have her safe. If only he could get Riverton interested in some other girl, then Susanna would be free of him.

As he stood, a piece of information fell into place.

"If I cannot arrest until I have proof, then I must obtain proof,"

Ian said to himself, and shuffled through the papers Mayne had handed him earlier.

Oxfordshire was not on the way to Northhamptonshire. Out of town for three weeks, on the heels of another hasty trip out of town.

"There is already another girl," Ian said to his empty study. He quickly hurried into the hall, calling for someone to fetch Mayne before his associate disappeared into the underbelly of London.

Chapter Six

❀

Susanna took another glance at herself in the reflecting glass in the front hall before declaring herself presentable. Not perfect, she had not had enough sleep to achieve that. A demonic, sandy-haired cat with big, grey-green eyes and a teasing smile had chased her through her dreams all night long.

"Have you finished primping?" Norah asked as she came down the stairs. Susanna looked up at her younger sister and smiled. Despite her choice in friends, Norah was still her sister and she did love her.

"Have you finished your latest love note to Lord Niles?"

Norah grimaced. "Oh please. If I am writing love notes, you are composing sonnets with 'hair spun from gold' as one of the beginning lines."

"Westcott's hair is not spun from gold," Susanna said, adjusting the hem of her gloves. "And furthermore—"

The mischievous glint in Norah's turquoise eyes made Susanna stop and she fought the urge to groan. Something about that man had her quite befuddled, she could barely think straight where he was concerned.

"Where is Duchess Clara?" Susanna asked, choosing to ignore her previous comment. Norah gave a very unladylike shrug. "Last I saw her was at breakfast."

"Here I am," Clara called down as she descended the stairs.

Norah and Susanna exchanged a look after looking at the duchess. Her face was red and puffy and her brow looked a bit clammy. Her hand was gripping the top rail tightly, knuckles white.

"Clara, dear, are you all right?" Susanna asked.

Clara nodded and straightened her back. "Something did not agree with me at breakfast, I am afraid. My eggs must have been touching the kippers; you know how they upset my constitution. But no matter, I will weather through. We have planned this shopping trip for weeks. I know you two are eager to see the new bolts Madame Deveroux has just received. Pay me no mind, my dears. My sensitive stomach will not make us tardy any longer."

"Yes, but Clara, if you are truly not feeling well, we understand," Susanna began.

"We do?" Norah asked, looking at her sister.

Susanna sent a discreet elbow into her sister's side as Clara swallowed deeply, closing her eyes with a few deep breaths.

Norah swallowed as well and Susanna felt an impending doom. If Clara threw up her breakfast in the front hall, she knew Norah was soon to follow. Norah's stomach was even more sensitive than Clara's.

"Yes, Clara, if you are not feeling well—" Susanna began again.

A loud knock came from the front door and Susanna and Norah turned as the butler opened the large wooden door.

"Hello, Howards," Ian said as he strode pleasantly into the front hall. "I am here to see his—"

He smiled when his eyes fell onto hers, surprised to see her in the front hall. Susanna's eyes widened appreciatively as she took him in, standing handsomely in the foyer. Dressed smartly in buff breaches, gray vest, and dark green jacket, he looked every inch the devilish earl. He'd even shaved off the scruff of hair from his face, revealing a strongly shaped chin and the lightest of dimples. Would she never tire of looking at him?

"I've come to . . ." Ian began, but trailed off, spying the ill duchess. "I say, your grace, are you feeling well?" He took a few steps towards the duchess and stopped as she shook her head, her hand covering her mouth.

"I am fine, I assure you," she said, swallowing again. He handed her his handkerchief and she dabbed at her forehead.

She really does not look well at all, Susanna mused.

"Has his grace left for the day?" Ian asked, glancing at the butler.

"No, my lord," Howards said and, understanding the reason for Ian's question, he hurried into the depths of the house to fetch the duke.

"We are going shopping," Clara said determinedly, handing Ian his handkerchief back.

He shook his head.

"It is yours to keep, your grace," he replied.

She nodded and swallowed again, holding the handkerchief to her mouth.

Andrew came into the front hall just then, took one glance at Clara and was beside her in an instant.

"Clara, why do you not stay in bed when you are unwell?" he asked.

"We are shopping, Andrew," she repeated. "Susanna and Norah have been looking forward to this for over a month. I will not let the kippers keep me from joining them."

"No more kippers at breakfast," Andrew replied. "If they make you this sick, I do not want them in the house."

She nodded, closing her eyes and swallowing again, trying to breathe deeply. Andrew glanced at Susanna and Norah then to Ian. Ian stepped forward and handed Andrew a folded parchment, ignoring the looks of three curious ladies.

Andrew quickly ready through the contents of the note before tucking it inside his jacket pocket. "Westcott will escort them on their shopping," Andrew announced, meeting Ian's eyes. "Yes, of course, your grace," Ian replied. "I would be happy to accompany them."

"Really, that is not necessary," Susanna said. "I am certain his lordship has better things to do than attend to our shopping."

"He does not," Andrew replied and at the same time Ian said, "I do not."

"It is settled," Andrew said. He bent and scooped Clara, who was turning a peculiar shade of yellow, into his arms and carried her up the stairs, calling for the doctor as he went.

Howards nodded to one of the footmen in the front hall who left quickly out the front door.

"An indisposed duchess?" Ian asked, raising an eyebrow.

"Clara and fish do not get along," Susanna explained.

"It truly was miraculous that you came along just as we needed an escort, Lord Westcott," Norah said sweetly. "How kind of you to offer your assistance."

Ian glanced from Susanna to Norah and smiled. "I am delighted to attend to your shopping excursion, Lady Norah. Shall we?"

Norah smiled her dazzling smile at him and Susanna wanted to roll her eyes. She sent Ian an apologetic look and he shrugged, following the two ladies out the door and into the Bradstone carriage.

"Lord Westcott, I understand you haven't been in London for very long," Norah said as the carriage rocked into motion. Susanna cringed at her sister's tone, the way she was practically purring Westcott's name.

"That is partly correct, Lady Norah," Ian replied. "I have a residence in London but I am out of town more than I am in it."

"This must explain why we haven't seen you out in society before," Norah said.

"Yes, it does," Ian replied.

Susanna recognized the avoided answer and felt an iota of triumph. At least she wasn't the only one he dodged questions with.

"All that traveling must leave you eager for home," Norah commented. "I have been invited on a Grand Tour. Tell me, have you any advice to avoid homesickness?"

"Who invited you on a Grand Tour?" Susanna asked, looking at her sister.

"Lady Laura, if you must know, nosybody," Norah replied before smiling at Ian. "The Earl of Swanley and his family are dear friends of mine. They are leaving for a tour of England in a few weeks. Lady Laura asked me just yesterday if I wanted to join her."

"A tour of England is hardly a Grand Tour," Susanna said. "Besides, why would you want to even be near her after what she has done to Clara?"

"I choose my friends, you choose yours," Norah replied, shrugging. "And it seems you've made a wonderful choice in his lordship here."

"Is Lady Laura the young lady who accompanied you yesterday, Lady Norah?" Ian asked.

Smiling, Norah replied, "Yes, that was her. And our good friend Lord Niles. You met him briefly at the house party."

Ian nodded. "Well I am certain you will have a splendid time on your tour, Lady Norah. Good friends are hard to come by, especially friends you are willing to put up with for weeks at a time. You should be commended for your generosity to put up with your friend's ugly character. Fact is, it says something of your character that you are able to manage someone so trying."

Susanna beamed at him. Norah opened her mouth to say something but the carriage lurched to a halt and Ian bounded out before either lady could say something.

Norah glared at her. "If he makes this day miserable, I am blaming you."

Susanna laughed. "Lord Westcott is perfectly amiable if you

drop your flirty airs. You are no match for him."

"Perhaps," Norah said, a glint of challenge in her eye. Susanna sighed and followed her sister out of the carriage.

Bond Street was virtually empty, as it was still early, but Ian did not mind.

"Where to?" Ian asked, looking up and down the street. It was early yet, so the crush of ladies shopping for bonnets and baubles did not clutter the lane. A few gentlemen strolled the streets, three carriages rolled up the street, one hackney passing by going the other direction, and two street hawkers stood across from each other on the street corner, one boasting candied apples, the other hothouse flowers. Ian nodded, taking note of each detail and accepting it as normal street activity for Bond Street.

"Here," Susanna said, motioning to the storefront before them. He glanced at the establishment before them: a dark, wood front with a large display window where a solo mannequin stood exhibiting a lovely blue satin ball gown. Beside her, a small pedestal table with a hand-painted sign read, "Closed."

"Sorry to disappoint, love, but it appears to be closed," Ian said, pointing to the sign.

At Ian's choice of pet names, Norah looked sharply at Susanna who shook her head before turning and leveling Ian with a scathing look. He met her gaze and shrugged. He was not going to apologize for his slip, though a slip it had been. He was much too comfortable with Susanna, and, even in the presence of her silly sister, he was letting his guard down.

"Madame Deveroux is never closed for us," Norah replied as she pushed the door open.

"Well, technically she is closed today," Susanna explained to Ian as they followed Norah inside. "The last Friday of the month she closes for inventory and takes in new shipments of fabric bolts. She has merchant brothers in Paris, Venice, and Bombay who send her the finest linens. She always has the newest trends in fabrics."

Ian leaned closer to whisper conspiringly, "Does not this play into the bit about the fashion game and competition with the other girls?"

Susanna shook her head. "For Norah, yes. She thrives on the competition and being the Belle of the season. For me it is about the purchases, about giving back to the merchants. Our patronage helps keep them in business. Madame Deveroux is a widow who has provided for her children with the profits from this shop and her extension in Bath. She has a son at Oxford studying to be a doctor, and her daughter just married a wealthy merchant. We are an interlocked puzzle of systems, the aristocracy, the merchant class, and the lower classes. Madame Deveroux is seen as the highest quality and trend of fashion, she has amazing fabrics and colors available."

Ian puzzled this over in his head for a moment before nodding.

"I do enjoy the actual act of shopping," Susanna said. "I find it relaxing. I do love wearing pretty things, and I am lucky to have a wealthy brother who pays for it all. But I recognize that without us, as in the ladies of the *haute ton*, Madame Deveroux would not have been able to provide for her children as she has. And without Madame Deveroux's spectacular selection, we would not have such beautiful things to wear. Our patronage helps her stay on top."

Ian looked at her oddly and nodded again. It was surprising how astutely aware she was of her place in life.

Norah was on the other side of the shop, though Ian wasn't certain she was out of earshot. He doubted she shared her sister's views.

"It seems my initial presumption of your character was quite incorrect," Ian said, trying to look uninterested, though he truly was fascinated by everything she had to say. "You continually surprise me."

Susanna smiled. "You thought me society-obsessed with marriage on the mind, angling to get a better title than the next girl, using all my feminine wiles to whatever extreme I felt necessary to achieve my goal."

Ian shrugged. "Something along those lines, yes."

Susanna laughed, shaking her head. "Well, then I am certainly glad my ruse is working. If people think me in line with the other silly ninnies, with the likes of Norah and Lady Laura, then no one will notice what I am actually doing."

Ian opened his mouth to ask what she meant, but he was cut off by the arrival of the shop's proprietor.

"Ah, my favorite ladies have come to pick at my fabrics again!" a woman said boisterously in a thick French accent as she came in from the back room. Her eyes locked onto Ian. "And who might this charming chap be?"

"Madame Deveroux, may I introduce the Earl of Westcott," Susanna said, smiling brightly. "He graciously offered to escort us today when her grace was indisposed."

"You know we are quite excited to see your new fabrics," Norah added.

"Yes, you two are the sweetest of the bunch," Madame Deveroux replied affectionately. "Come along, let us see what we have today." Both Susanna and Norah stepped into the back of the shop, bussing Madame on the cheek as they passed.

"Madame Deveroux," Ian said, making his bow as he passed, smiling charmingly at her and following the ladies into the back room.

Whatever he had been expecting from the tiny front shop was completely different than what he saw. The entirety of the two floors had been gutted into one enormously large room.

Floor to ceiling shelves lined each wall, with stacks and stacks of bolts of fabrics neatly arranged into some method of organization known only to Madame Deveroux.

He was careful to keep his expressions in control despite his shock and interest in the contents of the room. Who knew such a thing existed?

Susanna looked at him curiously and smiled when she caught his eye.

"Fascinating, the inner workings of the female life," he commented absently. She rolled her eyes.

For the next hour—and Ian knew the time exactly because he was discreetly watching the timepiece on the far wall—Madame Deveroux pulled out bolt after bolt of fabric, each one delighting the girls more. It was interesting to watch the dynamics of the sisters. Susanna favored bolder colors, bright pinks and blues and purples, while Norah, who Ian discerned had finished her second season, was still confined to the debutant whites. She smiled appreciatively at the light pinks and faint blues. Ian started to understand their relationship more.

"Norah, you really should think about that dark turquoise," Susanna said to her sister. "It would go perfectly with your eyes."

Norah looked wistfully at the color before shaking her head. "No, it will just not suit. I truly love this peach. The embroidered flowers and eyelets are darling."

Susanna had already chosen a deep blue, a rich cream with gold and pink embroidery, and a dark green with vine-like print.

"But for Christmas no one will think twice about such a dark color," Susanna replied. "In the winter especially. Besides, we will be with family."

"What if I choose to extend my tour with Lady Laura?"

Susanna waved her comment off. "You would never miss a family Christmas." Norah shrugged, but Ian was certain she did not disagree.

"I truly like this red," Susanna said, fingering the silk fabric. "These white and gold flowers are divine. I will take this one too."

"Susanna, where ever will you wear it?" Norah asked.

"The Macalister Birthday Ball next season," Susanna replied and Norah stared at her agape. Susanna laughed. "Just teasing you, Norah, do not look so offended. I was thinking the Masquerade Ball Newcastle puts on each All Hallows Eve. An Elizabethan gown with off-the-shoulder sleeves and long, white gloves. Saber, Thomas, and Walters Milliners have a selection of masks arriving from Vienna and I am certain I could find one to match perfectly."

Norah eyed her warily, and looked again at the dark fabric that was neither blue nor green but some magical combination of the two.

"If this is a masked ball, no one will know who you are, Lady Norah," Ian interjected. "At least until the unmasking."

"Oh there is no unmasking," Susanna said. "It is more than a masked ball, it's a masquerade—over the top costumes and circus performers and palm readers. It is quite an extravagant affair."

"It's *the* event of the Little Season," Norah added still looking at the dark fabric.

"Come on, Norah, just buy it," Susanna pleaded. "Step outside your debutante world for just one moment. You will quite enjoy the freedom, I assure you."

Norah shook her head. "No, I will not buy it. I already have my masquerade costume planned with Lady Laura, and I refuse to wear such a daring color at Christmas. Regardless of my company, it would be quite improper. I will take these four, Madame Deveroux." She indicated the four, light pastel fabrics she had set aside. Susanna added to her order a few yards of a deep brown that shimmered into gold.

She caught Ian's inquisitive look as she passed by him.

"For Clara," she explained. "It will go perfect with her coloring and it might help cheer her up since she missed this."

The fabrics were cut and wrapped and handed over to Ian for carrying and safekeeping as they made their way back to the carriage.

"Newcastle hosts a Little Season ball?" Ian inquired once they were comfortably seated in the carriage. He rapped on the roof and the carriage rocked into motion.

Susanna nodded eagerly. "It is all the rage. Everyone comes back into town for the ball weekend and then leaves again. London is filled to the brim for the one evening. And everyone's costumes are spectacular. Riverton has promised to be back in time to escort me. We really must get you an invitation, Westcott, it is quite a crush."

"Why would you assume I had not already received one?" he asked, his tone a little too harsh. Her continued association with Riverton was beginning to annoy him, though he knew there was nothing he could do about it.

"I only thought that since you are not in London often—"

"That I do not know the Duke of Newcastle?" Ian asked. "I am an earl, Susanna, not some lowly, second-rate merchant boy."

Susanna narrowed at him. "You needn't be so offended, *Lord Westcott*." She emphasized his title, reminding him to watch his speech. "I merely expressed an interest in seeing you there. Of course you are an earl, and of course you would know the Duke of Newcastle."

Ian gave himself a mental shake, pulling himself back under control. In fact, he did not know the Duke of Newcastle, he barely knew anyone outside of work, but he had been invited to the masquerade nonetheless.

"You two bicker like Andrew and Clara do," Norah said absently, not looking away from the window. "And it is even more annoying because the two of you are not married."

Ian grinned, pleased at the fact he had been able to annoy Lady Norah. He found he enjoyed having someone to tease. He had never really teased Beth.

He glanced at Susanna and she was grinning as well.

"Westcott is much better company than you are most of the time," Susanna replied.

Norah turned to regard her sister and some unspoken challenge passed between the two. Norah turned her striking green-blue eyes toward Ian and smiled sweetly.

"You really should come to the masquerade, Lord Westcott," she said, her voice almost purring. "Susanna is quite right, it is a crush. Everyone will be there."

Ian eyed her apprehensively. "I will see if I can manage a costume in time," he replied, not sure what the young lady was playing at. There was something more to her words than he could immediately ascertain.

"You will be sure to save me a dance if you do," Lady Norah continued. "You look like you would be a superb partner for the evening."

Ian understood. The young Lady Norah thought she could out-flirt him. Susanna had practically challenged her with her look, apparently feeling Ian would be the winner.

Not wanting to let his lovely lady down, he replied, "Of course, Lady Norah. I think I would find the experience quite pleasurable. One dance it is, though you might be inclined to ask for more and I might just find myself willing to oblige you."

Norah's smile did not falter, but her eyes widened a fraction. "I am curious to see what a well-traveled man of the world could teach a demure lady such as myself. It seems I could be in for quite an evening."

Ian responded, "There are all sorts of dances I could teach you, both on and off your feet. Tell me, Lady Norah, which ones would you prefer?"

Lady Norah's mouth popped open and she quickly looked away, a deep blush rising up her neck to her face.

Susanna laughed and he grinned, winking at her despite himself. Norah sat with her arms crossed for the last few minutes of their trip to Bradstone House. She bolted out of the carriage the moment it stopped, not waiting for one of the attending footmen to open the carriage door.

"What's gotten into her?" Ian asked innocently.

Susanna swatted him with her reticule. "You were rather wicked to her," Susanna replied.

"You knew exactly the sort of things that come out of my mouth," Ian replied in mock defense. "You understood what would happen when you silently challenged her."

"Well, you are a scoundrel for playing along," Susanna chided. "She is not as accustomed to your talent for shocking people as I. She is barely out of the schoolroom."

Ian shrugged. "I still say it is your fault."

"It will not be my fault when she tattles to Andrew about your deplorable behavior," she replied. "And it will not be my fault when he forbids me from seeing you again."

"It was good for her," Ian replied and bounded out of the carriage, holding his hand out to assist her. She accepted and stepped gracefully from the carriage. "Besides," he continued, tucking her arm into the crook of his arm. "You would find a way to see me if you so desired."

"Would I?" she asked.

"Oh, yes. I am quite certain you would fight your way through hell and high water for what you wanted, especially if someone told you not to."

She nodded. "I do hate being told 'no.'" They stepped into the house and Susanna peeled off her gloves and handed them and her bonnet over to her awaiting maid. She glanced at Ian. "You have forgiven me for whatever I said to upset you?"

Ian shrugged and was delighted when she set her lips into a firm line at his averted answer.

"Whatever did I say to bother you so?" she inquired.

Ian sighed. "Riverton. You are choosing to trust him over me."

Susanna crossed her arms. "I barely know you."

"You barely know *him*," Ian replied.

"Right now, he is offering something you are not," Susanna replied. "And until that is different, I will not change my mind."

Ian looked away from her, shaking his head. "I have nothing to offer you, Susanna."

He could feel her eyes on him. She made little flinching movements, as if she wanted to wrap her arms around him, but she was stopping herself. The movements cut into him, like a knife twisting into his gut.

"Oh, Ian, that's not what I meant," she said softly and he closed his eyes at the sound of his name on her voice—the first time she had ever used his Christian name. She was so beautiful, her dark hair tucked into a knot at the top of her neck, her lovely face contorted with genuine concern. Whatever she wanted from him, he was in no position to offer, and the thought had started to bother him. Why couldn't he have a life with her? Had not he sacrificed enough?

He shook his head, replacing his top hat upon his head, halting his thoughts before they ventured into dark and dangerous territory. He knew why he could not have happiness, why he did not deserve a life with a lady such as of Susanna. He had a duty and he would not be selfish again.

"Enjoy the rest of your afternoon, Lady Susanna," he said. Ignoring the worry in her bright blue eyes, he quickly left the house.

He hurried down the front steps and onto his horse the Bradstone groom had waiting for him, digging his heels into D'artagnon's flanks, wanting nothing more than a stiff drink and to forget the longing in Lady Susanna's voice and more so, the longing in his own heart.

Chapter Seven

Saturday morning, Susanna woke from another evening of tormented sleep. Instead of a charming, orange tabby torturing her in her sleep, it was a small, innocent kitten with big grey-green eyes, stranded on an island in the middle of a large lake. It sat mewing and mewing for someone to rescue it and Susanna frantically searched for a boat and oars, only to find there were none.

Her maid, Annette, tended to her morning tonic, a hot water and lemon juice mixture, Susanna's secret to being wide awake on early mornings such as the one she found herself in.

"Which morning dress do you prefer?" Annette asked. Susanna smiled at her maid, sent to her from France by her brother Bennett. French maids were all the rage and Susanna reveled in the fact she had an actual French lady's maid and not an English one parading as French.

"The striped blue for this morning," Susanna replied. "I do not anticipate any outings today, but best press the dark cyan in case Lady Monica demands my presence somewhere."

"And for this evening?" Annette asked, pulling Susanna's selections from her side wardrobe.

Susanna took a sip of her tonic, mentally going through her list of evening gowns. "The orchid," she replied. "Not the dark one, the medium with the long sleeves and the lace along the bust line."

"Very good, my lady," Annette said and curtsied before stepping into the antechamber Susanna used for her evening and ball gowns. She shared it through a connecting door with Norah. Her room was simply appointed, mostly because she had no need for the acquisition of clutter, unlike her sister Norah. The walls were white and gold vertical stripes, with a few paintings in ornate golden frames. Her bed boasted an oversized padded headboard trimmed in a light wood, with matching side tables on each side of the bed. A small sitting area sat before the fireplace, two sofas upholstered in beiges and creams facing each other with a curved, light wood table in between. There were a few dark purple pillows on the sofas matched by a lush, purple rug underneath the sitting pieces before the fireplace, and heavy, dark purple drapes hung before the windows, reaching from ceiling to floor. She had a dressing table adjacent to the fireplace, which had excellent lighting during the day, a dark purple, cushioned, backless chair tucked underneath.

Susanna took another sip of her tonic, her senses finally starting to wake up from their slumber. She looked curiously at the two floral arrangements on her dressing table. One was an overlarge arrangement of random hothouse flowers—the same one that arrived every morning from Riverton. The second was slightly shorter, though the vase was filled with white daises.

"Annette?" Susanna called.

Annette poked her head out of the antechamber and followed Susanna's gaze to the flowers.

"Yes, my lady, those came for you this morning."

"Yes, but who are the daisies from?" Susanna asked.

Annette went to the flowers and plucked the card off the

arrangement, handing it to her before curtsying and reentering the antechamber.

Susanna flipped the envelope flap back and pulled the little card out. Scribbled in a hasty scrawl was written,

> These flowers are all I have to offer for now,
> and for that I am truly sorry.
> —Ian.

Susanna smiled, remembering he had brought her daisies the day he came to call. She swung her legs over the bed, wrapping her dressing gown around her as she stepped towards the dressing table. She picked up the vase of daisies and moved them to the table beside her bed, just behind the small clock Norah had given her for her birthday three years earlier.

She returned to the dressing table, slipped the card into her top drawer, and moved the larger arrangement from Riverton to the middle of the dressing table. It was a lovely arrangement, Susanna thought, even if it was lacking in personality, much like its sender.

Annette stepped back into the main room again, the medium orchid dress slung over her arm.

"I think I will have a bath this morning, Annette," Susanna said.

Annette nodded. "Of course, my lady. I will have one sent up immediately."

"Thank you," Susanna replied and stepped over to her second wardrobe where all her day dresses were housed. Annette left, but returned moments later with two large, plush towels.

"Annette, take this one, will you please?" Susanna pulled out an olive green dress and offered it to her maid. "And the midnight blue evening gown as well, the one I wore to the Macalister Birthday Ball this year. I have no need for them as I bought similar fabrics yesterday at Madame Deveroux's. The green color will be lovely with your coloring. Hold it up, please."

Annette smiled and blushed, but accepted the green day dress from her mistress. She held it up in front of her and Susanna smiled brightly.

"Yes, that is just it. Pulls out the pink in your cheeks, and the cream in the stripes truly complements your soft complexion and fair hair. The blue one is yours as well, though if you choose not to keep it you are welcome to do with it as you wish. But the green one is lovely on you."

Annette blushed again and curtsied. "Thank you, Lady Susanna."

"You are quite welcome," Susanna replied. She moved to the side table and poured herself another cup of lemon tonic. She watched Annette move about the room, finding stockings and stays and slippers to accompany her morning dress. Soon there was a claw-foot tub sitting before the large fireplace, steam from the warm water wafting up towards the ceiling. Annette set two glass bottles of soap into the table beside the tub before turning towards Susanna to offer her assistance.

"I can manage, Annette, but thank you," Susanna said.

Annette curtsied and left the room, collecting her two new gowns as she went. "Annette?" Susanna called as the maid opened the door.

"Was there something else, my lady?"

"Which arrangement do you prefer?" Susanna asked, gesturing to the two different arrangements of blooms.

Annette's blue eyes twinkled. "The daisies are a new addition to your morning deliveries," the maid began, smiling pleasantly. "And they do fit rather nicely into the room." She curtsied again before leaving Susanna alone in the room with just her flowers.

She soaked in her bath water until the water had lost most of its heat, thinking of the gentleman who wanted her but whom she did not want, and the gentleman she wanted but who seemed not to want her in return.

Ian blinked painfully into the bright sunlight streaming into the drawing room. The room was sideways and it took him a long moment to realize it was because he was sitting upright with his head on the table. He lifted his head slowly, a paper sticking to his cheek and pain rushing into his brain, stinging his senses.

"You had quite the rousing evening last night," Bexley drawled, and Ian blinked again, pulling the paper off his face. He tried to make his eyes focus on the room, but everything had started to spin. He leaned back in his chair, pressing his palms into his eyes, rubbing away the vertigo.

"I cannot recall if I did anything spectacularly entertaining," Ian said, opening his eyes again.

"You did not," his cousin replied. He was standing along the side of the room, stirring something in a glass. "You drank your way through Brook's before needing my assistance home, where you drank through another entire decanter of brandy, mumbling away at these papers all night. You finally passed out around six this morning. Here, drink this."

Ian eyed the offered beverage suspiciously, but accepted it.

"Best not to smell it," Bexley warned. "Just gulp it down and you'll feel better in an hour or so."

"What on earth is it?"

"Uncle Rudolph's Overindulgence Cure," Bexley replied.

"Oh yes, good old Uncle Rudolph," Ian muttered and downed the contents of the glass.

Salty and sweet and horribly acidic, it burned his mouth and throat. He accepted the glass of milk his cousin was handing him and drank it down as well.

"That was disgusting," Ian replied. "What was in it?"

"I cannot give you the official recipe or Uncle Rudolph would cut me out of his will and since he is richer than Midas, I am not about to jeopardize that. But it's a combination of juice from a pickle, molasses, and the dried, macerated rind from an orange."

Ian leaned back in his chair again, willing the spinning to stop. "Why are you here, Rheneas?"

"I slept here, actually," Bexley replied. "After our dear friend Bradstone bowed out on our evening frivolity—"

"His wife was sick yesterday," Ian said in his defense.

"Yes, I am well aware," Bexley said. "He took off before the drinking got too out of control and some hours later, you and I adjourned here to where you drank and I slept—rather restlessly—since you refused to fall asleep yourself. I've returned to make sure you are presentable for dinner this evening."

"Dinner?" Ian asked. "What time is it?"

"Four in the afternoon."

"Four?" Ian exclaimed and then immediately regretted it as the sound of his own voice made his head pound. "And what dinner are you talking about?"

"My mother's," Bexley replied. "Your dearest aunt requests you join us in a family dinner. As Mother likes to remind me almost every time you are mentioned in conversation, she is your mother's baby sister and it is her job to take care of you, like your mother took care of her."

"My mother is not dead, you know," Ian replied.

"She is also not in any condition to make certain you are properly fed."

Ian knew his cousin was right in regard to meals. The cook he employed did not cook for him.

"And then you and I will attend an art review."

"I am not attending anything with art," Ian groaned, folding his arms on the table and resting his head on his arms.

"Oh, yes, you are," Bexley replied, chuckling. "There is a young widow I have been quite taken with and her great uncle is hosting a showing of his acclaimed snuff boxes," Bexley explained. "I wish to make an appearance."

"Snuff boxes are considered art?"

"Semantics," his cousin replied. "She has the most wonderfully plump lips that just imagining them on—"

"That's quite enough, Rheneas," Ian cut him off, not wanting to think about lips anywhere. The only lips he wanted were Susanna's and those lips expected something from him, something he was unable to give.

"You will understand when we meet her," Bexley replied. "But first you need a bath and some proper evening attire. You do own something presentable, correct?"

"Yes."

"Well, then, we have dinner at five-thirty and the art showing at seven, so we had best get you moving."

Just over an hour later, Ian was feeling much better, though whether it was due to the bath or his Uncle Rudolph's remedy, he wasn't sure. He sat in his own carriage with his cousin, trying to piece together the previous night. It had been barely lunchtime when he had started drinking at Brook's. He rarely drank to excess, and knowing that Susanna could push him to those extremes bothered him.

"Did you say I was drinking with the Duke of Bradstone last night?" Ian asked, remembering something of his cousin's tale.

"Yes, though not for long."

"Did I say anything particularly embarrassing?" Ian asked, wondering if he should make his apologies the next morning.

"Not really," Bexley replied. "Though you might have mentioned how, and I quote, 'Susanna is the finest among all diamonds and his grace is a dolt for allowing Riverton to court her.' End quote."

Ian cringed. "I actually called her Susanna? No 'Lady' in there at all?" His cousin shook his head, chuckling. "You also called his grace a dolt."

"I will be barred entrance to Bradstone House."

"No, Andrew was really not bothered by your comments,"

Bexley said. "He actually agreed with you. It was lucky he left after two drinks, there is no telling what you might have said to him if he stayed. Which reminds me, there was something you kept saying over and over as you went through your papers into the wee hours. You said you needed to break the chains, the links had to be weak somewhere and the money was somewhere. Well, I flipped through those papers you had, and the flowers he sends every morning were not mentioned."

"What flowers?" he asked. "Wait, you looked through my papers? Those are official, you know."

Bexley shrugged. "Riverton sends Susanna a bouquet of flowers every morning," Bexley replied. "Andrew has mentioned it on several occasions. The same arrangement each morning arrives by courier, but there is no mention of them in his financial reports."

"So he must be using a different account," Ian said, thinking quickly. "He has an account we do not know about. But this florist is paid somehow." He stopped and looked curiously at his cousin. "How did you know I was investigating Riverton?"

"Please," Bexley chided. "My quota for 'acquaintances who might be a spy' might be fuller than most—"

"I am not a spy," Ian interjected, rubbing the bridge of his nose.

"And I may be just a mere peer of the realm, but I can be just as observant as the rest of you," Bexley continued. "You hate the man, Ian. Clearly you think he is not what he seems. And his name is all over the papers on your desk. Official or not, we are family. I am here to help."

Ian looked gratefully at his cousin and nodded. "Could you get me the name of the florist?"

Bexley shook his head. "I asked Andrew about it this morning and he said it is not one of the well-known ones, certainly not one from Mayfair."

Ian nodded as the carriage rounded a corner and he saw Bexley's London home, Warren House. He twisted in his seat and spotted Bradstone House out the other window, further down the lane. He smiled as a few more pieces of the puzzle fell into place.

Later the same evening, Susanna stood in a very charmingly decorated music room, even though cherubs and clouds were not her taste in décor. Not that she had a particular interest in snuff boxes—the 'art' on display around the room. She was here at the request of her two friends, as she was in the Garden Club with their host's wife, the Countess of Fanthome, and was able to procure them all an invite, although somehow again she had been shackled to her cousin, Lord George. He seemed to have a knack for popping up in her company lately.

"Really, Susie, pace yourself," Gemma chided under her breath as Susanna plucked a third glass of champagne from a passing footman, taking a long sip. She giggled again and batted her lashes at George. She knew she had no effect on him, regardless of their relationship as cousins. Lord George looked at her with vague recognition and rolled his eyes, which was the most amount of sass she had ever seen from him. His presence in their troupe was bothersome, though he was not the reason for her third glass of champagne. No, the reason for her more than normal drinking and excessive giggling was on the opposite side of the room, chatting up a pair of very well-endowed ladies with too much rouge on their lips.

She had watched wide-eyed as Ian had entered with his cousin, his eyes darting around the room, taking in the guests. His gaze had passed right over her and he had floated along effortlessly beside his cousin. He had not looked her way the entire evening, choosing to flirt shamelessly with the merry widows. It was refreshing to see how he behaved when not in her company.

"I say, Lord George, you are looking quite charming tonight," Susanna said, blinking up at the man by her side. "Do not you agree, Lady Monica?"

"Georgie always looks dashing," Monica replied, winking at

George. "He was born that way, I am sure."

"I am certain I was," George replied flatly and looked away from Monica.

"I have been so terribly bored lately," Susanna whined, aware she sounded like a complaining teenager. Her complaint effectively changed the awkward silence created by her awkward cousin.

"How could you be bored with that Adonis playing you court?" Monica asked, looking pointedly at Ian. Susanna turned and looked at him again and this time he turned his head and stared back. She held his gaze for a moment before turning away and looking back at her two friends.

"He is not playing me court," Susanna said.

"No, of course he is not," Gemma said. "Though he is coming this way."

"Excuse me," Susanna said and hurried past her friends in a panic, not even stopping to check behind her. She escaped to the refreshing room before Ian could speak to her—could trap her with his laughing, grey-green eyes. She sat on one of the plush chairs and counted to one hundred before downing the last of her third glass of champagne and standing up. She truly believed a person's soul could be seen through their eyes, and the beauty of Ian's soul quite caught her off guard, especially because it was veiled behind humor and absurdity.

"Get ahold of yourself, Susanna," she said to her reflection. Her reflection looked back unconvincingly, before she stood straighter, empowered by the alcohol.

She cautiously stepped out of the refreshing room, glancing left and right.

"Did you think you'd made your escape?" Ian asked, and she spun around to see him standing directly behind her.

"I was not attempting to escape anything," Susanna answered, straightening her back and tilting her nose a little higher than necessary.

Ian chuckled. "I am quite surprised to see you here, my dear.

Had I known you would attend tonight I would have asked to escort you."

"Had you seen me earlier you might have not flirted so long with that widowed hussy," Susanna replied, much more vehemently than she intended.

"Jealous, are we?" he asked, taking a step towards her, to which she took a step backwards. "Careful, Susanna, green is not your color."

"Ha!" Susanna laughed. "What, pray tell, would I have to be jealous of?"

"The 'hussy,' as you call her, happens to be a very friendly woman who is the good friend of a widow my cousin is in pursuit of. I was merely here as a secondary chap, waiting in the wings to help out and occupy as necessary. She is of no interest to me."

Susanna swallowed, taking another step backwards. "You are free to do as you wish. I care not. I am merely your unworldly, invisible friend."

"You are hardly invisible, Susanna," Ian replied, taking another step. "And I saw you earlier, laughing with your darling cronies. You seemed quite smitten with the tall, dark-haired fellow. Fact, I think you make a rather nice couple."

Susanna took another step backwards. "Who is jealous now?" she asked.

"Do you think of me when you flirt with him?" he asked. "Because all I can think about is you."

"George isn't even aware people are in the same room, much less flirting with him," she replied, avoiding his question though her body was burning for him with each word he spoke. "Besides, the fellow I looked smitten with is in fact my cousin. I am not smitten, I am friendly."

"Ah, so you are not smitten with me?" he asked, taking another step.

"Nope," she lied, smiling brightly. "Merely friendly." She took a step back and her foot hit a wall. He had backed her into a literal corner, wall to her left and large curtain to her right. Ian took another step and she was blocked from the view of the hallway. What was with this man and curtained alcoves?

"You know we are much more than friends," he whispered into her ear, his hot breath sending tingles down her spine.

"No, we are nothing," she whispered in return.

"Nothing?"

"Nothing."

"Keep telling yourself that," he whispered, a teasing glint in his eyes before he captured her mouth with his. His kiss pummeled her mouth, gently then forcefully, over and over and she was more than willing to comply. She matched him as best she could, but she was barely in control of her actions, her mind clouded with the smell of him and the effects of the champagne.

Susanna pressed herself into him, arching as he wound his arms around her back, moving down to caress her bottom.

"Susanna we have to stop," he breathed heavily as he tore himself away from her lips.

"Why is it you can kiss me when you are foxed, but I cannot kiss you when I am foxed?" she asked, watching the passion and torment raging war in his uniquely-colored eyes. "Your eyes are the color of a tempest, by the way."

He laughed and kissed her again before setting her away from him, wiping his kiss off her lips with his thumb. "I am much better at handling myself while severely impaired."

"I only had three glasses of champagne, Westcott," Susanna said, slipping her hand into his evening jacket, and running her fingertips over his chest. "I am not severely impaired." He closed his eyes, enjoying the sensation.

"Apparently you are," he said, pulling her hand down. "Three glasses of champagne and you are drunk. Duly noted."

"I am not drunk," Susanna said. "I am merely . . . free."

She gazed at him, thinking of his kisses, of his kindness and his jokes. He leaned down and kissed her again, long and drugging, enough to fill her senses.

"You are much too tempting for your own good, Susanna," he whispered huskily against her lips.

"Then let me tempt you, Westcott," she replied.

"Why will you not call me Ian?" he asked, softly, capturing her face in his hand, rubbing the pad of his thumb over her soft skin of her cheek. "You did so the other day."

"When you are Westcott, you are detached from me, I have no claim on you," she explained thickly, looking at him through her dark lashes. "When you are Ian, you are mine. And because you will not let me have you, it is too painful to call you Ian. Even though that is who you are to me."

With a feral sounding growl he captured her mouth with his, pushing her back into the wall, completely hiding her from view. Her hands wound around him, lacing her fingers through his hair, pulling him closer, pulling him to her. His mouth was hot, and his roaming hands left a path of fire as he trailed them down her breasts and to her waist, cupping her bottom and pulling her against the hard bulge in his trousers.

Moving on wanton need, she slowly lifted up and down on her toes, rubbing her body against his, the spot at the apex of her thighs burning as she pulsed against his erection. Susanna was lost, the heat of his mouth on hers, and his body so close, it drove her mad, stirring a desire deep within her she had not known could exist. She was no longer in control of her actions, her hands, body, and mouth moving on primal instinct as she returned his kisses, feeling freedom from the propriety that held her in check so often. True, she pushed the limits of what was acceptable, but she was fairly certain that wantonly kissing an earl who was not her husband was not socially acceptable. If someone found them . . .

Ian sensed her hesitation and pulled away, looking into her eyes, conflicting emotions rushing through his gaze, his breathing coming in thick pants, matching Susanna breath for breath.

"There you are," he said, his voice laced with humor. "For a second there I wondered where my darling lady went. Do not get me wrong, I quite enjoy Susanna the Minx, but she could do some damage if left to her own devices."

Susanna shook her head, trying to hide her smile, but the absurd man had a way of pulling one out of her, even in the most uncomfortable situations.

"Have you regained your head?" he asked, cradling her head in his hands, his thumb pads passing softly over her cheeks.

She nodded, feeling in control of her senses, and mostly in control of her actions. "I do think I should leave, though."

"Shall I fetch your carriage?" he asked and she nodded again.

"Am I presentable?" she asked, patting down her dark curls that were pulled off her neck. "Passably," he teased. "You could passably pass the most passable inspection."

Susanna chuckled again and he stepped away from her. The hallway was still mercifully empty, though the sounds of the guests could be heard down the corridor. They made their way swiftly towards the front of the house.

Susanna groaned. "Everyone will notice we are both absent."

Ian shrugged. "I will return alone and make your excuses."

"Clara will know this has happened," Susanna said.

"Well, then, huzzah for Clara," Ian replied sarcastically, waving to the footman waiting near the front door. "No one will know unless we tell them, which seem like slim odds to me." He instructed the footman to bring around the Bradstone carriage.

Susanna stopped and regarded him. "I have a question to ask, and, per our agreement, you must answer honestly."

"Now?" he asked, glancing around.

She nodded. "It's as good a time as any."

He sighed. "Very well, ask away."

"Are you a gambling man, my lord?"

"Are you a gambling lady?" he asked and she looked pointedly at him. He sighed, resigning to answer with as much seriousness and honesty as he could manage. "When the occasion warrants a bet, I have been known to place one."

"Which means you are willing to take a chance?" she asked.

"A calculated chance is hardly a risk," he replied.

"But it is within your capability to put faith in something and hope for the best?" she asked.

"Yes, but not blindly."

She nodded. "Fair enough."

"Why do you ask?"

She shrugged as the Bradstone carriage rounded the corner. "Good evening, Lord Westcott."

"Come now, Susanna, you cannot possibly ask me such a thing and not explain why you are inquiring," Ian replied, grabbing her hand as she stepped towards the carriage.

"I inquired for no reason other than my own morbid curiosity," she replied. "And perhaps because I am still a tad drink. I mean drunk. I am still a tad drunk."

"You know if you tell me how drunk you are, I will feel compelled to kiss you into sobriety," he said tugging on her arm. She did not budge.

"I am no longer that intoxicated," she replied. "Just enough to appreciate the complex man you are, Westcott."

"Ian."

She raised her eyebrows and ducked inside the carriage. It was off within seconds and she was gone, rolling away into the darkness of the night.

Chapter Eight

Susanna looked again at the arrangement of daisies sitting on her dressing table. It was three days since she had last seen Ian, but his arrangements of daisies had come both the morning after the snuff box showing, yesterday, and also today. Each was different than the one before it, each one accompanied by a card with something sweetly honest written inside. The cards were all neatly tucked into her desk drawer—she did not need Norah or Clara swooping in and snatching the cards from her fingers. Somehow she did not want to share this with anyone.

Whatever she and Ian had, regardless of its longevity, was theirs and theirs alone.

Which brought her to the second arrangement, the large hothouse florals Riverton sent every morning with only his calling card attached. No sweet nothings, no stirrings of passion or heat from his kisses. In fact, Riverton had never kissed her. She wasn't even certain of his first name—Robert perhaps? Or Zachary?

"What has you in such a bother lately?" Norah asked, coming through the antechamber that connected their rooms.

"Nothing of importance," Susanna said, sipping her morning tonic. Norah was already dressed in a lovely, soft blue morning dress and plopped herself very ungracefully onto the end of Susanna's bed, handing over her morning correspondence.

"Sarah has written," Norah noted.

Susanna accepted the mail and tore into Sarah's letter, though there was nothing new for her sister to write. The same old routines and daily activities as usual.

"Are you not ever bored?" Susanna asked her sister absently, folding up her letter.

"With what?" Norah asked, looking at her cuticles.

"With all this?" Susanna said, waving her hand around the room. "With the calls and the balls and, well, everything. It is so tedious and tiresome."

Norah thought for a moment before shrugging one shoulder. "I suspect I could get bored, eventually. You have been at this longer than I, Susanna."

"Yes, thank you for reminding me," Susanna replied irritably. "Have you come to bring my mail and make snide remarks or did you come with a purpose?"

Norah sighed. "I understand what you mean by boredom, Susanna. You know I do not mean to irritate, not usually, at least. I've spent the past three days with Lady Laura, sometimes I forget to turn the snide-ness off."

Susanna nodded. "Yes, it must be exhausting to have to pretend to be a snot."

"You have no idea," Norah said, leaning against the wooden post of Susanna's four-poster bed with a sigh. "Laura is quite trying and while sometimes I can tune her out and answer automatically, lately I've been finding myself actually responding in ways that are quite worrisome."

"You could just not be friends with her," Susanna suggested. "You know she is the one who—"

"Yes, I am well aware," Norah answered quickly, cutting her

off. "And it is not very friendly of me to berate her for her past indiscretions."

"I'd hardly call it an 'indiscretion,'" Susanna replied, pursing her lips.

Norah shrugged. "I know what I am doing, Susanna."

"I trust that you do," Susanna replied. "Her presence is just worrisome. And she is annoying."

Norah laughed. "She is that for certain. But I am in too deep now. Were I to show my cards too soon, she would completely turn the entire *ton* against me."

"You care too much," Susanna scolded. "You will be much more comfortable if you allow yourself to be who you are. You are not such a society-obsessed miss as you appear to be."

"Oh, but I am," Norah said with a laugh. "I have my reasons, and it will all play out in time. Besides, you've done a fine job of not caring for the both of us. It must be difficult to be courted by two equally handsome gentlemen."

"Lord Westcott is not courting me," Susanna replied.

"You've seen him almost every day for a week," Norah replied. "He sends you flowers, he fetches your lemonade, and he cares enough to send you home when you are indisposed, instead of merely looking the other way. And he makes those gooey eyes at you like Andrew makes at Clara."

"He does not."

"And you make them back," Norah accused. "You smile too much when he is near."

Susanna fought the smile that came over her face, turning her head so her sister would not see.

"See, you are smiling now!" Norah said, laughing. "It is quite refreshing to see you finally fall in love with someone."

"I am not in love with Westcott," Susanna protested.

Norah quirked an eyebrow. "Truly?"

Susanna shook her head and repeated her statement, wanting to see if she could actually say it again with a straight face. She managed, barely, but Norah simply shrugged and looked away with a knowing glint in her blue-green eyes.

"It seems I shall be the only one not in love in this house," Norah continued. "Once you marry and leave, it will be me and the love birds. I do adore Clara, but sometimes their love is rather . . . nauseating."

Susanna laughed. "Then you should find some gentlemen to love and marry and get out of here. It might be good for us both to be away from this house."

Norah nodded. "Let us say that if neither one of us is married by the end of next season than we shall take a tour together."

"There is a war on the continent, remember?" Susanna reminded her. "And your stomach could not handle a ship. It can barely handle a carriage."

"Then we make multiple stops on our way to Ireland," Norah replied. "Or we write to Bennett and demand he take us away somewhere exotic. He will magically make the seas calm for our passage."

Susanna laughed, smiling at her sister.

"Oh, Norah darling, Lady Laura does not deserve you as a friend," Susanna said. "You are much too wonderful for the likes of her."

"Oh, I know," Norah replied. "She is rather vicious."

"Whyever do you remain her friend if she makes you so miserable?"

Norah shrugged. "I have my reasons. Trust me, Susanna, my reasons are sound."

"I trust you know what you are doing," Susanna answered. "As long as you are not becoming Lady Laura, and you keep your head with her."

"She is trying, but I promise I will not turn into her brunette twin," Norah replied. "I already have a twin. Another would simply be a bother."

Susanna laughed again and Annette entered with her pressed

gowns for the day.

"I will leave you to dress, then," Norah said, standing. "We are attending the reading today at Hammer and Sons. Best to not be late."

Susanna sighed and downed the last of her now cold tonic. She gave herself a mental shake. She truly was looking forward to the reading; Miss Calla Jennings was one of her favorite authors and it was a treat to be invited.

Susanna nodded to Annette, approving of the soft marigold day dress she had laid out. This was her life. She was resigned to the endless parade of outings and routs and social calls and balls. Such was a life of a lady of the *ton,* and Susanna did not mind the mindlessness of it all. She just could not help feel that there could be more.

Ian stood outside Hammer and Sons Booksellers, absently listening to the reading of some dreadful woman's author inside. He leaned leisurely against the shop wall, scanning the street for Mayne's messenger. He glanced again inside the shop window, scanning the small gathering of women, looking past them to the shop's proprietor, Mr. Hammer, senior. The man flicked his eyes towards the back room, shifting uncomfortably from foot to foot.

Ian smiled to himself, straightening as he heard light footsteps approaching.

"You be Mayne's gent?" the grimy boy asked, his blond hair dirtied into a darker color than was probably natural, bright brown eyes peering up at him through a mire-covered face. His clothes looked as though they had been pulled from the trash heap three years prior and not washed since. His two front teeth were missing, his adult teeth beginning to pop through his gums. He couldn't have been older than seven, Ian surmised uneasily.

Ian harrumphed. "You lot keep getting younger, do not you? What happened to the other boy, the one he usually sends?"

The boy shrugged. "Lady Day snatched him up."

"Lady Day?" Ian asked, though this was not the first time he had heard of the illusive lady.

The boy nodded. "Gone for three days now, the lucky bugger. Anywhere is better than the dump I am livin' in now."

"Hmmm." Ian paused and glanced back at the shop owner. He was still in place. Looking back at the messenger boy he asked, "What have you to report then?"

"Mr. Mayne says there is another entrance in the back of the shop and he is watching it personally."

"Very good," Ian replied and tipped the lad a coin. Ian glanced again inside the shop once more, not putting too much thought into Lady Day. So far she was mostly a myth, something the older boys told the younger ones to give them hope. Who or what Lady Day actually was was not important now. What was important was the shady shopkeeper and the dealings he had with the captain of the *Anna Marianne* and the reported stolen possessions turning up all over the coast.

It was a clever idea, Ian had to admit. Too risky getting caught selling stolen items in London, better to send them to other cities and hawk them where no one would recognize them. Until a gentleman whose sister's rubies had gone missing in London saw them in a jewelry shop in Cardiff; messages were then dispatched to the different port cities along the coast of England and Wales and soon missing pieces were turning up all over the coast. A watch fob in Portsmouth, pearls in Southampton, signet ring in Plymouth. It was Susanna who had given him the idea, actually, when she mentioned that Madame Deveroux contracted with suppliers all over the world. All it took was organizing the found items into trade routes the *Anna Marianne* used and learning the identity of the captain's largest patron.

He glanced again as the soft applause ended and the women in the shop all rose and began to file out of the bookshop. He tugged his cap down a little farther, ducking inside as the last of the ladies came out. He scanned the shop and, save for two whispering ladies on the other side of the shelves, the shop was empty. He had two associates outside the front door, Mayne was watching the back so Mr. Hammer could not make an easy escape. The shop owner had already disappeared into the back of the store, but a younger man, who must have been one of the sons in Hammer and Sons, stood at the counter, looking at him curiously.

"Have you something to pick up, sir?" the younger Mr. Hammer asked.

"Actually I have a need to speak with the owner of this fine establishment," Ian said, lowering his voice. "It is of a private manner."

The man nodded and stepped into the book room.

"Well, if my eyes have not deceived me, I do believe the Earl of Westcott has graced us with his presence," a sweet feminine voice purred and Ian inwardly cringed.

"Lady Susanna," he said, turning around slowly, schooling his features to that of detached amusement. Of course she had to be here. "And the lovely Lady Norah too."

Susanna smiled. "We have just heard the most invigorating story by a favorite author of ours," she said.

Ian was cursing himself for his oversight. He should have looked at the two girls behind the shelving more closely, and he certainly should have made sure Susanna was not in attendance. How did he not see her or her sister? He had peered into the shop no less than four times in the last ten minutes. How had he not noticed her?

"Miss Jennings is a favorite author of yours?" he asked her.

"She is better than Ms. Radcliff and her gothics," she replied, showing him the inside cover of her book. "See? She even inscribed our books for us. She is quite the dear."

"Who knew the grisly gothic was your cup of tea, Lady Susanna?" he drawled, looking for a way to get her out of the shop.

"She writes the most deliciously supernatural death scenes,"

Susanna replied.

Ian scoffed. "There is nothing delicious about death, Susanna."

Her eyes narrowed a fraction before shrugging. "Come along, Norah, we really mustn't be late. Luncheon will be served soon and I am quite peckish. Good day to you, my lord." He nodded in response to their light curtsies, and they left the store, skirts swaying as they went.

Ian let out a very ungentlemanly swear word and rubbed the back of his neck. That had been a near miss. He could not have questioned Mr. Hammer properly had she remained in the store.

Ian whipped his head around, looking at the curtain separating the front from the back of the shop. Mr. Hammer Senior should have been out by now.

Ian pulled the curtain back, ducking into the back room, which looked the same as the front room only with more books. It appeared deserted.

He swore again, pulling his pistol out of his side holster. He prowled the main pathway through the shelves of books, checking each aisle as he passed until he reached the back door. Pushing it open, he blinked into the morning sun and spotted Mayne waiting a few feet away.

"Where is he?" Ian asked.

"Not come this way, Westcott," Mayne replied. Ian swore for the third time in as many minutes. Mayne's eyebrows raised. Ian was not a man who was prone to swearing.

"Must have missed something because I came in through the front," Ian said, yanking the back door open again. Mayne grunted in his agreement and followed him inside.

A thorough examination of the back room revealed a trap door along one of the bookshelves that lead to the cellar where they found an unconscious Mr. Hammer Senior, bleeding from a head wound.

Mayne wrapped a strip of cloth around his wound, torn from the man's shirt. The cellar was damp and cramped with a desk along one wall, which was littered with papers and maps and a decrepit looking lantern. Along the far wall there was a hole in the brickwork, as if someone had pried the bricks away to shove something past it.

Ian bent down, looking into the hole. "I hear water and there is a foul stench. This must connect to the sewer."

"That'll take him straight to the docks, if he knows the way," Mayne commented, pointing towards the tunnel with a stubby finger. "Shall we flip for who gets to follow the blackguard?"

"Nah," Ian replied. "He ran, therefore he is likely done something wrong. His next move will be to get out of the city, either by boat, horse, or on foot. The first seems most likely, especially with the *Anna Marianne* due in soon. Let's patrol the docks, send his description along to the routes out of town. Someone will see him."

"Did you get a good enough look at the younger Mr. Hammer while you were dawdling in the shop?" Mayne asked.

Ian nodded, ignoring his associate's jibe. "Enough to do a sketch."

"Surprised he spotted you as trouble the way you are dressed, m'lord."

Ian thought for a moment, wondering the same thing and then he realized what must have given him away. His attire was suitable for his role as a lower class gent, simple brown trousers with a faded white shirt, loosely tied cravat and brown tweed coat which was fraying at the seams. Combined with his cap no one would take him for an aristocrat. Except, of course, for the lovely Lady Susanna.

Ian groaned. Susanna and her sister had seen him in this getup. No wonder she had looked at him peculiarly and made a hasty exit. And she had inadvertently given him away, allowing their perpetrator to escape. Plus, the culprit had seen Susanna and Norah in the shop—he could very well know them by name.

"Right, well now we know which Mr. Hammer to look for," Ian replied, mentally adding "shake Susanna senseless" to his list of things to do. It was his own fault, but really, why did the girl have to turn up at every wrong opportunity?

"Collect everything," Ian said, turning to climb the cellar stairs. "Invoices, ledgers, manifests, anything and everything. I want it all sent to my home office."

Mayne nodded. "Yes m'lord. Where be you off to?"

Ian grimaced. "To make certain no harm comes to our pretty little bait."

She was not normally prone to napping, but since her nights were often disturbed with grey-green eyed tabby cats and their ridiculous schemes, she had taken to having a quick nap before dinner. The afternoon of the book reading was no exception and as she dozed lightly on the chaise in her bedroom, she did not hear her sister-in-law knocking lightly on her door.

"Susanna," Clara said softly, gently shaking her shoulder. Susanna opened her eyes, blinked away her sleepy daze, and focused on the duchess's face.

"You fell asleep again, Susanna," Clara said. "What has you so exhausted?"

Susanna leaned against the back of the chaise, stretching her spine. "I have not been sleeping properly."

Clara nodded. "You have a gentlemen caller."

Susanna blinked dumbly. "Currently?"

Clara laughed. "Yes, he is downstairs."

"Is it—"

"It is Westcott," Clara replied. "And he seems to be in a rather serious mood. Shall I send him away?"

"No, I will meet with him," she replied, glancing at the clock on her mantle. "Does he know it is well past the socially acceptable hours to call?"

"He did not seem like he was here to make a social call," Clara replied cautiously and stood as Susanna did. "He was rather . . .

professional."

"Oh." Well now her curiosity was definitely piqued. A serious and professional Ian? This she had to see.

She checked her appearance in her dressing table mirror and attempted to smooth out the wrinkles her dress had acquired whilst she was asleep.

"You look marvelous, dear," Clara said. "He will not mind a few wrinkles."

Susanna followed her grace out of her room, down the stairs to the first floor, and into the blue drawing room reserved for the gentlemen callers when they called upon the gentlemen of the house. Susanna rarely set foot in there.

"Good afternoon, Lord Westcott," Susanna said, and dipped into a curtsy. He nodded, but did not smile, did not make some sarcastic remark. His expression was solemn, serious even. It quite unnerved her.

"Shall I ring for tea?" Clara asked, reaching for the bell pull.

"No, thank you, your grace," he replied, his voice much more commanding without its traces of humor. "And I would ask that Lady Susanna and I be allowed to conduct this interview in private."

A single blonde eyebrow rose above Clara's curious eyes and she regarded him.

"That is most improper, my lord," Susanna replied, glancing at her sister-in-law for support.

"You have fifteen minutes, Lord Westcott," Clara replied. "The door shall remain partially open."

"Agreed."

Clara swept from the room, patting Susanna on the arm as she passed. Susanna looked back at the earl, not sure what to think.

"Goodness, Westcott, has someone died?" she asked, thinking who it could be. "

No, nothing of the sort," he replied. "Please have a seat."

"I think I would prefer to stand, thank you," she replied, crossing her arms. "What is this about?"

"I would appreciate your cooperation by sitting down."

The way he said the word "down" made her want to sit down immediately. Everything in her told her not to do as he demanded, yet everything about him was telling her to do exactly as he said.

With an incredulous look in her eyes, she walked demurely to the sofa and gracefully sat on the edge of the cushion.

"Thank you," he replied. "I know this is most irregular, but I must ask you about what you saw at the booksellers today."

"What I saw?" she repeated. "What I saw was you in a short temper dressed as a ruffian. Much as you are now, actually. Why are you dressed in such a deplorable state, Westcott?"

"I will ask the questions, if you please."

Susanna laughed. "What is this, an interrogation? Am I under suspicion of something?" His silence stunned her and she felt her smile fade from her face. "Goodness, Westcott, what is going on?"

He did not look away from her as he asked, "How familiar are you with the younger Mr. Hammer of Hammer and Sons bookseller?"

"I am not familiar with him at all," she replied. "If you are implying that I—"

"Susanna, just answer my questions," he replied sternly, but his grey-green eyes were pleading.

She swallowed. "I would recognize the younger Mr. Hammer on sight, I suppose," she said slowly. "I am not certain of his first name. We do not go to Hammer and Sons normally, but occasionally they have something the other booksellers do not."

"Has he helped you before?" he asked, jotting something down in a small notebook.

Susanna watched him curiously. "Yes, I believe he was in the store last week when we went for another book reading. Clara was with us then, and she bought a book on roses."

"How often does this author have readings at that store?" he asked.

"Just last week and this week, to coincide with her new novel being published," she replied. "But there are others often, we just do not attend those."

He jotted something more. "Your information is on record at the store?"

Susanna nodded. "I would assume so."

"Have you ever taken deliveries from that establishment?"

"No," Susanna replied, wondering what was going on. He did not seem ready to divulge any of that information yet, so she kept her tongue.

"In the times you have been there for a reading, have you found something missing afterwards?"

"Missing?" she asked. "Like what?"

"Earring. Ring, items from your reticule."

Susanna thought for a moment and shook her head. "No."

"How do the readings normally go about?" he asked. "Is there time for milling about? I noticed everyone exited the shop quickly this afternoon; is that normal?"

"When we arrive, we take our seats. I suspect we would hand our cloaks over to Mr. Hammer should we have one. We sit in a few rows and listen to the reading, which is probably half an hour at most. There are about twenty of us that went last week and today."

"Twenty-four actually," he replied.

"Last week, after the reading, we all headed to our carriages to meet for tea at Gunter's."

"And you and your sister chose not to attend today?"

Susanna shook her head. "Norah wanted to find something Lady Laura had told her about, but we did not see it on the shelving. We had stepped out to ask Mr. Hammer about it when we saw you."

"Did you tell anyone you saw me?" he asked.

She blinked at him. "No, of course not."

"What about Lady Norah?" he asked. "Is she likely to gossip

about such a thing?"

"Possibly," Susanna replied, and he wrote something more. "But I will speak with her. She is truly not as silly as she seems. If I ask her not to say anything, she will not."

He regarded her before nodding and writing something else.

"Have you more questions, interrogator?" she asked. He glanced at her, giving her a warning glare.

"I have other questions, but about a different subject," he replied and stepped around the sofa to sit before her. "I wish to ask you about Riverton."

"Goodness, not that again, Westcott," Susanna replied with a massive sigh, much like steam escaping from a vent. "I've told you that topic is closed."

"I do not wish to persuade you to call it off," he replied. "Well, I still do—make no mistake—but that is not what I want to ask you about."

She eyed him peculiarly but nodded, curious again at this new side of him. "Riverton sends you flowers each morning, correct?"

"How could you possibly know that?" she asked.

"Just the answers, please."

She sighed.

"Fine. Yes, he sends me flowers, the same arrangement every morning."

"Is there a florist card?"

"No, just his calling card."

"Do you see who delivers them?"

"No, they are normally in my room by the time I awake," she replied. "You'd best ask Howards, or my maid Annette who receives them."

He jotted the two names down. "What do you know of his friends?" he asked.

"Only that he has two good friends, but they are peculiar sorts," she replied. "Not the sort of people you would think a viscount befriends, but he swears to their character."

"Have you met them?"

"Once," she replied. "At a fair near the docks last month."

"If you saw a sketch, could you recognize them?" he asked.

"Possibly," she replied.

"And their names?"

"The names I am not as clear on," she replied, and thought for a long moment. "The tall one was a Mr. Slate, a banker's son, I believe. The other was a rounder fellow with rather unfortunate eyebrows. "Mr. Gabble, Gobble, Bobble, something to that effect. He did not address them by their first names."

"Why do you feel these are peculiar friends for a viscount?" he asked, looking up from his notebook.

"For starters, Riverton is rather handsome and, in my experience, wealthy, titled, attractive people run with people of equal stature," she began, feeling oddly satisfied at the way his mouth tightened at her appreciation of Riverton's appearance.

"Generally one can be overlooked with an abundance of two; for instance, an heiress would be forgiven for her lack of title if her beauty and dowry compensate. A wealthy lord would be forgiven if he had an unpleasant face. But these friends of Riverton were not attractive. They were not titled; they were not even merchants. They were commoners, and low-class commoners at that. You normally do not see a handsome, wealthy, titled man associating with such people. I do not particularly care who he is friends with, meaning I do not have an issue with the classes mixing; it is just not typical. It was also the only time I have seen them. He consorts with his Oxford chums at routs and balls and the like, but he was much more familiar and comfortable with these men."

"What did they talk about?"

Susanna blushed and looked down. "Me, in fact."

"Did he mention who your relations were?"

Susanna thought for a moment and slowly nodded. "Yes, he did."

"Has there ever been anything unusual about him, anything

out of the ordinary?" Ian asked.

"If you are trying to discourage his suit, I am tired of repeating myself—"

"I am not discouraging anything, Susanna," he clipped. "I just need the information.'"

Susanna sighed. "No, there has never been anything . . ." She trailed off, remembering the times she had seen such hatred on his face, so fleeting that she was still half convinced she had imagined it.

"You have noticed something?"

Susanna frowned. "On occasion, there seems to be an underlying level of anger or hatred that peeks through when he does not think anyone will notice. Sometimes he is perfectly amiable, and others a complete bore, but there have been a few instances when his face has been so full of rage that it completely catches me off guard, as if he is a completely different person. But it is so quick that I almost think I am seeing things."

Remembering his face on those occasions sent a shiver down her spine, and she pushed away the uneasiness of the memories.

Ian gave her arm a light, comforting squeeze and a reassuring smile.

"I am sure I am just being silly, and it is simply my imagination running wild," Susanna said with a shrug.

Ian did not comment, he merely wrote something more in his notebook before tucking his pencil lead into a page and snapping it shut, stuffing it into the breast pocket of his frayed coat. He looked at her expectantly. "Will you stand, please?"

"I beg your pardon?" she asked, knitting her brows together.

"Propriety requires me to sit until you stand, and I cannot leave unless I am standing, and I very much need to leave now."

"Oh," she said and jumped to her feet. "What on earth was that all about?"

He donned his cap, looking quite out of place for the very elegant and formal sitting room. The contrast was striking. He stepped around the table between them, bending to whisper in her ear, "I will tell you later. Leave your window open when you go to sleep." He kissed her cheek, and she closed her eyes at the brief contact. He was gone before she could register he was leaving her standing alone in the sitting room.

"Is he gone already?" she heard Clara ask, and Susanna nodded. "What on earth was that about?" Clara asked, echoing Susanna's exact words from moments earlier.

"I have no idea," Susanna replied. "I am awake, am I not? This was not all some sort of dream?"

Clara chuckled. "I assure you, you are as real as I am. Truly, Lord Westcott was here. What did he speak of?"

"He quizzed me about the readings at Hammer and Sons and then about Riverton's friends," Susanna replied, and then remembered she had promised to speak to Norah for him. "Excuse me, Clara dear, but I must speak with Norah."

She hurried past the duchess and was up the stairs in moments, knocking on Norah's door. Norah pulled it open and appeared in the middle of dressing.

"We must speak," Susanna said and pushed her way inside. Norah's face showed her concern, and she nodded, closing the door with a soft click.

Chapter Nine

———— ❀ ————

It was nearing one o'clock in the morning, and Susanna could not sleep. Not because of fitful dreams, but because of a live and in-person earl who tormented her thoughts.

Leave her window open? He would explain later? If she had not been confused before, she certainly was now.

The *tick, tick, tick* of the clock on her bedside table was driving her mad, and she rolled over, pulling her pillow over her head. She had left the window open as instructed, and it was making her room cold. The cool evening breeze wafted gracefully over her coverlet before drifting off into the late September night. The sky was dark—the only light for those out at night was from the street lamps the lamplighter had lit hours earlier. Susanna sighed and sat up, glaring at the offending window.

"Do you always toss and turn this much?" came Ian's voice in the darkness.

Susanna jumped. "What are you doing here?" she asked in a harsh whisper. A match was lit and his face was illuminated by the single flame. He was grinning at her. He lit the candelabra on her bedside table and sat of the edge of her bed.

Susanna closed her eyes. "I cannot believe this is happening," she muttered, and he laughed quietly in the darkness. She snapped her eyes open, glaring at him. "You know this is not a good idea," she said quietly. "If someone were to find you in here—"

"No one will find me in here," he reassured her.

"Norah's room is just through the connecting door in the side closet," she replied, pointing at the antechamber.

"And she is fast asleep, and a rather sound sleeper I might add."

Susanna huffed. "Will you please tell me the meaning of this? What happened earlier? Why did you ask me all those questions? And why are you here?"

"Why are any of us here, my dear?"

She huffed again and he smiled. He scooted himself forward on the bed, pulling her into his lap and kissed her. She was still for a brief moment before her body gave in and returned his kisses. He did not deepen them, though Susanna belatedly realized this was their first kiss when neither one was intoxicated.

He pulled away from her, resting his head on hers and sighed.

"I wish I could stay here, wrapped in the darkness and your kisses for an eternity," he muttered thickly. "You have bewitched me, you damn irritating woman, and I find I cannot stay away."

"You know you can stay," she said softly, pushing his sandy hair from his face. "You do not have to let me go."

He set her off of him and looked away. "No, Susanna, I cannot. I was not lying when I told you I have nothing to offer you."

"Is that why you were dressed so shabbily this morning?" she asked, leaning against the headboard of her four poster bed. "Because you are want for funds? I have a substantial dowry, you know."

He chucked quietly in the darkness. "Goodness, no, Susanna. I did not mean to imply I have nothing monetarily to offer you. I meant . . . damnation, never mind. Do not worry about my financial state, I assure you I am quite well off. Now, onto this morning—"

"You are dodging questions again," she chided him.

"It is what I do, Susanna," he replied, a tad irritably.

"What is that supposed to mean?" she asked.

He sighed. "I told you I worked for the Home Office while I was in the army. What I failed to mention is that I am technically still in the army, working for the Home Office as a sort of investigator within the government, between Bow Street and the Royal Court, the military and the various covert agencies. I conduct investigations."

"You have a profession?" she asked, surprised.

He took her surprise for repugnance. "I've got to do something with my time while I wait for my father to wither away into nothingness."

"I am not condemning it, Westcott," she replied. "I was merely surprised you did not mention it before."

"I could not," he replied. "The establishment I work for is a separate organization which reports directly to the Home Secretary. We work within each of the different aspects of military and law enforcement, the Army, the Marines, the Navy, Bow Street Runners, and the Watch, investigating everyone and everything equally."

"What sort of things do you investigate?" she asked, curiously.

He sighed and scratched the side of his chin where a layer of stubble had begun to appear. "In France, there was a sergeant who was over-ordering supplies and selling them off, telling his men that England was not sending anything. We were able to track him down through shipments and apprehend him. There was also a series of violent home invasions throughout the same area, and we investigated and determined the regiment behind it. I've dealt with highway robberies, art theft, and fratricide to gain a title. All sorts of things."

"So you were working on a case this morning," she said, and

suddenly everything made sense. The clothing, his short attitude followed by his interrogation. "Blimey, Norah and I walked right into the middle of it."

"Right on the nose, my dear."

"I am terribly sorry, Ian," she said hurriedly. "If we had known . . . Heavens! Did we give you away? I called you by your title."

"I am afraid you might have, my dear," he replied. "But no worries, the gentleman is currently being held by the Bow Street Runners."

"You caught him?"

Ian nodded with a cocky grin. "Of course we did, darling. That is what I do. Your tip-off did not help matters, nor did the man's ignorance about how the shipping business works. He was merely sending stolen goods out on merchant ships. He never knew he couldn't just hop on any ship he desired."

"Is it wise to boast about catching a stupid criminal?" she asked, tilting her head to the side. "Does not that say something about your investigative skills?"

"Not at all," he replied. "Though it only took us four days to crack a case and catch the culprit. Bow Street has been after these gents for weeks."

That explained his absence over the past few days, she realized. "So you are handed the cases others are not able to solve?"

"Usually," he replied. "My skills are used by numerous sources. I aided your brother and his friend last spring when a rather unsavory, former footman needed to be found. Turns out I have extremely keen observation skills and am quite adept at solving riddles and puzzles. Keeps my mind off of, well, everything else."

"Why the questions about Riverton?" she asked.

"If you are asking me that, then you already know the answer," he replied.

"You are investigating him for something," she replied slowly, thinking it through. "You suspect him of something."

"In a manner of speaking," Ian answered. "Though the extent to which I cannot tell you, not just yet."

"I am practically engaged to the man, Westcott," she said.

"And as you recall, I've advised you against that on multiple occasions," he replied.

"But if you haven't arrested him yet, then you cannot prove he has done anything wrong," she continued.

"And that is the rub of it, my dear," he said.

"Am I in danger?" Susanna asked. "Will he hurt me?"

Ian shook his head. "I want to tell you all the sordid details, Susanna, but I cannot. I am deeply sorry, but just know that I am desperate to have you away from him."

"So I should break it off?"

"There is the other side of the coin," he replied. "Even if I did not tell you exactly what he was suspected of, were you to call it off we might not be able to catch him in any sort of wrongdoing. I do not want you to marry him, but I am afraid I must ask you not to cry off. You are unfortunately perfect just where you are."

"You are going to use me as bait?" she asked.

"Again, you are asking questions you know the answers to."

"And again you are dodging the answers," she replied. "Which I notice you only do when you do not want to answer truthfully. So I am to be bait for some suspected criminal whose crimes I do not know the extent of."

"If you please."

"Well, at least you said 'please'," she replied and sighed. "I am sleepy, Westcott. This is all making my head quite ache. Are you planning on staying until morning, or are you going to slip out as silently as you came in?"

"Is that an invitation?" he asked, quirking an eyebrow.

"You are insufferable."

He chuckled and puffed out the candles before pulling himself to the other side of the bed, parallel to her, and rolled her so she was half laying on him, her head resting on his chest.

"Sleep, Lady Susanna," he said softly and kissed her hair.

"This is most improper," she replied, closing her eyes.

"All the more reason to do it," he whispered in the darkness. Susanna did not really want to fall asleep on him, but she was suddenly overcome with exhaustion. Perhaps it was her emotional turmoil throughout the day, or learning what she had from Ian. But within moments, she was sound asleep.

The next morning, she awoke as the bright morning sunlight lit her face when Annette pulled the heavy curtains open, welcoming the start of a new day.

Susanna sat upright in bed and looked wildly around her. Realizing Ian was no longer there, she breathed a deep sigh of relief and fell back against her pillows.

"Are you well, miss?" Annette asked, pulling the other set of curtains open.

"Yes, perfectly," Susanna replied. "I was just confused." She glanced at the window, and it was closed shut, the latch firmly in place. She sat up, looking to the candelabra, and each of the candles were new and unburned as they had been the night before.

Had it just been a dream?

What an absurd thing to dream about, she thought, looking around the room for something to prove he had been there. *Absurd, but absolutely wonderful.* She turned and swung her legs over the side of the bed, and she saw it. A small grey box, wrapped in a white satin ribbon, sitting beside the vase of daisies from Ian delivered the morning before. Susanna glanced at Annette, who was busy in the antechamber, before she hopped up and snatched the box before scrambling back into bed.

Checking for her maid again—still busy with stockings and stays—Susanna pulled the ribbon from the box and snapped the lid back.

A white card fell from the box and it read:

Should you need assistance, please utilise this pin

to your advantage. Be warned, it can be quite
sharp. I hope you slept well.

Yours,
Ian.

Inside the box was a delicate-looking hairpin with three long
pointed prongs, the middle a tad longer than the other two. At the
base, woven into the gold of the finger prongs, were diamonds nestled in a pattern to look like flowers.

Daisies, Susanna realized. Ian had sent her daisies to use for
protection.

"You are sure you are well, my lady?" Annette asked, startling
her out of her thoughts. Annette continued, looking at Susanna
with concern. "Her grace is sick again this morning. You aren't
coming down with what is ailing her, are you?"

"No, Annette, I am well," Susanna reassured her maid. She had
a pretty good idea about what was ailing the new duchess and was
certain she was not plagued by the same affliction. "Just trying to
pull myself from a wonderful dream is all. My mind does not seem
to want to let it go."

"Very good, miss," Annette replied and smiled. She set the
breakfast tray on the table beside the bed before dipping into a
quick curtsey and exiting the room. Setting the hairpin in its box,
she used her maid's momentary absence to place it safely in her
dressing table drawer with Ian's other cards, securely away from
the prying eyes of her sisters. She did not know what to make of
any of this just yet: Ian sleeping soundly beside her all night—it
was the most sleep she'd had all week—his veiled revelations about
Riverton and knowledge that Ian himself was investigating him for
something, and his reassurances she was not in danger. Then awak-
ing to a diamond encrusted hairpin, which looked an awful lot like
a dagger—what sort of gift was that?

It was beautiful and generous, and it warmed her heart that Ian had bought her something, but she did not want her growing affection for Ian to overshadow the inkling that he was not telling her something important.

She sat back on her bed, pulling her thick down comforter around her to trample out the morning cold and the thread of doubt in Riverton that was slowly weaving itself into something more substantial. The prickling sensation at the base of her neck crept back, the image of his face that day in the park, so full of hate, flashed through her mind. Knowing more of Ian's work with the Crown than she had before, a thick layer of worry had begun to settle in, and while she had faith he was capable of taking care of himself, she could not shake the feeling that there was something more to all of this.

A fire had already been started in the hearth across the room, but it did little to provide warmth just yet. The day looked to be another miserable and dreary one. As she sipped her steaming mug of hot lemon water, she hoped Ian, wherever he was, was warm on such a morning.

Ian flicked the collar of his thick wool coat up around his neck, rubbing his hands together to warm them. The holes in the tattered, knit gloves did not exactly provide much warmth, and the fog rolling in from the river did little to keep him dry.

He had escaped the warmth of Susanna's bed scarcely an hour before dawn, with the intention of seeking the warmth of his own, only to find Mayne waiting at his doorstep with another case to investigate. A Mr. Bose was suspected of harboring French spies on English soil. Another set of investigators had gotten the case this far, but they were almost certain Mr. Bose would recognize them, and, therefore, needed Ian and Mayne to finish it out. A simple tail and Mr. Bose would lead them right to the safe house. Unpretentious and uneventful, albeit cold.

He hoped he had not scared Susanna with his talk of investigating Riverton, though if she would only heed his warning and take him seriously, he might not need to resort to scare tactics to keep her safe. The hairpin had been a marvelous find, and it fit perfectly with what he had been saying all along. If she refused to listen to him, then at least she would be armed.

He wondered if she would see it for what it truly was, though knowing Susanna as he had come to, she would understand its alternative uses.

He watched the subject of his surveillance with detached interest, making note of his movements and mannerisms as he moved through the rookery, stopping to speak with anyone who would listen. Mr. Bose claimed to be looking for someone, explaining someone's appearance over and over, attempting to generate sympathy for the lost relative, though Ian suspected it was a ruse. This case held little interest for him and he was vaguely annoyed he had been handed the tedious task of finishing someone else's work when he could have been warm in his bed, though he preferred sleeping beside the lovely Susanna.

For the first time in as long as Ian could remember, he had slept soundly. Normally he tossed and turned, his nights afflicted with fitful sleep. Much to his surprise, he had fallen asleep with Susanna snuggled beside him and awoke in much the same position. Had he known sleeping with a warm body pressed up against him would be so comforting, he might have sought the solution earlier. As it stood, he was already contemplating ways in which he could return night after night and steal away the sleeping hours beside her.

I could just marry her and be done with it, Ian mused. Though the thought of bringing her home to Westcott House was not a peaceful one. The Marquess and Marchioness were still in residence, and with the wailing that went on nightly, it was a wonder his neighbors had not made a fuss about their sleep being interrupted. No, Susanna did not belong at Westcott House any more than he did. There was no happiness left there.

Mr. Bose was just turning a corner, and Ian quickened his pace to catch up. As he rounded the corner, the man in question turned towards him, and Ian quickly ducked into the nearest doorway, slumping down against the side of the door frame, disappearing from sight for the briefest of moments before Mr. Bose found him.

Mr. Bose stared down at him, and Ian pretended to doze drunkenly.

The man poked him with the toe of his boot, nudging him. Ian slept on. Bending down, Mr. Bose pulled a knife from his pocket and pressed it into Ian's rib. A little thrust and the knife would go through Ian's heavy wool coat and pierce his flesh.

"Who are you, you bounder?" the man demanded. "Why are you following me?"

Ian slept on.

"I know you are faking it," the man added, shoving his shoulder to rouse him. "I've seen you following me for the past four blocks, and yesterday another gent was on my coattails all day. Did she send you?"

Ian slept on, perfectly willing to have the subject of the investigation reveal all his evildoings. It would make arresting him much easier.

"Christ, she probably did," he grumbled. He had not yet removed the knife from Ian's side. "Damn a meddling woman! Whatever she said I did, it is an outright lie!" Mr. Bose shoved him again.

Ian startled awake, feinting drunkenness, his head wobbling from side to side.

"What d'ya want?" he demanded with a slurred Cockney in his voice. "Lemme 'lone!"

"You cannot fool me, you rat," Mr. Bose claimed. "Why are you following me?"

Ian squinted his eyes and peered at him in confusion. "I am na followin' ya, I am sleepin', can ya see?"

Mr. Bose dragged him to his feet. Ian stood on falsely drunken legs, curious to what Mr. Bose would do next.

"I've got this knife ready to plunge into your side, ya hear?" Mr. Bose asked. "You'll do as I say."

Ian nodded and slumped as Mr. Bose forced him along, apparently not buying his drunken act. His mind raced at the different ways this could play out, filtering through the different scenarios. He caught Mayne from the corner of his eye, walking towards them to intervene, but Ian waved him off with the slightest of movements of his free arm. Mayne walked past. Ian decided to continue with his drunken ruse, hoping Mr. Bose would just take him to the safe house and waltz him through the front door.

To Ian's minor irritation, that's exactly what Mr. Bose did. Criminals were nothing if not stupid. Susanna was right: there wasn't much enjoyment in outsmarting an idiot.

Ian was roughly tossed into a hackney, and he slumped in the corner, snoring loudly as they traveled through the city for perhaps ten minutes. He paid careful attention to the directions the hack turned and the sounds from outside the carriage. Before long, they came to a stop and he was yanked from the carriage and thrown to the ground. The street was quieter and the pavement cleaner. Not the Rookery.

Mr. Bose pulled him to his feet, and practically dragged him past a wrought iron gate and into a nicely appointed house with neat flowers in the beds.

"Mr. Bose!" a woman's voice exclaimed as the man dropped Ian in a drunken heap on the floor. "What is the meaning of this? Who is this man?"

Ian gave her a merry wave before slumping onto the ground again. Intoxicated was always the best ruse and the easiest to pull off, though he would have been a little more convincing had he smelled like a draught house. He would have to make sure his performance was convincing. Not knowing what he had just walked into, he hoped Mayne had been able to keep up with them or Ian would have to manufacture his own means of escape.

"He is been followin' me, Mrs. Windham," Mr. Bose replied.

"And your solution was to bring him here?" Mrs. Windham asked.

"I couldn't let him follow me!"

Mrs. Windham eyed Ian doubtfully. "He is so deep in his cups, he cannot even stand."

"That's just an act," Mr. Bose said, and nudged Ian with his boot.

"What is your name?" Mrs. Windham asked Ian.

Ian gave another wave with a hearty, "I am the bonny Prince Charlie!"

"He is drunk, Mr. Bose," Mrs. Windham concluded. "I do not think he could have followed you if he tried."

"He was, I swear to it! He—" but Mr. Bose was cut off by a knocking on the door. He exchanged a look with the woman before grabbing Ian by the arm, yanking him to his feet and pulling him behind the door, the knife again at his ribs. Mr. Bose gave a curt nod to Mrs. Windham in permission before she opened the door.

"Good morning, Madame," came Mayne's voice from the door. "Might you have seen a little, black dog around these parts? Little bugger slipped his leash."

Ian moved quicker than Mr. Bose was expecting, completely catching him off guard as he disarmed the man, knocking him in the jaw with a forceful jab of the elbow. Mr. Bose slumped to the floor.

"Quite sorry about your dog, sir," Mrs. Windham was saying and Ian yanked the door open. Startled, she spun around and gasped, Mayne's hands came over her mouth before she could scream, and he stepped into the house. Ian shut the door.

"Nicely done," Mayne said, offering Ian a swatch of cloth to bind Mr. Bose. Ian nodded and bent to the man, wrapping his hands securely behind his back.

"Thanks for keeping up with the carriage," Ian said. "The driver took so many turns I wasn't certain I could keep them all clear in my head."

"I was a bit dodgy at the end, and I did not see which house he had taken you in to," Mayne admitted.

"How did you find the right house then?"

"This was the third door I knocked on looking for my little, black dog," Mayne replied, and Ian chuckled.

Fifteen minutes later, there were five more women, three maids, and two footmen secured in one of the sitting rooms, with two other men who worked with Ian and Mayne combing the house for information. It seemed this was the home for the girls who worked in a high-end brothel. The girls slept and lived here and went to work in the brothel in the Rookery, where they managed to acquire secrets and information from their customers— customers who were members of parliament and held positions within the government. The girls then reported the information back to Mr. Bose and Mrs. Windham, and they passed it along to Mrs. Windham's brother, who took it to a man at the docks who then sailed with the information to France.

Ian wrapped up his notes before handing them over to the case's original investigators, Mr. Reginald Harvey and Lord Eric Pastel. Reggie, as he preferred to be called, was a dark-haired fellow from northern England, the son of a baker if Ian remembered correctly. Lord Eric was a fair-haired chap with dark brown eyes and was a third or fourth son from a prominent family.

Reggie smirked at Ian, nodding his thanks. "Heard your intoxicated act wasn't convincing."

Ian shrugged. "It was passable. Best I could do on the spot."

"Thanks for your help with this one, Westcott," Lord Eric said gratefully. "No matter what we did, we could not trail him here."

"He spotted you days ago," Ian replied. "He spotted me, too. Seems he thought it was wiser to bring the person directly to the house as not to risk them following you there."

"He probably meant to kill you once you were here," Mayne

added.

"Probably," Ian admitted. "Luckily he wasn't the brightest of criminals."

"Luckily for us and you, I suppose," Reggie replied. They chatted about some inane details of the case, then moved from the house as those suspected of espionage were loaded into a jailer carriage headed for Newgate. Thinking he deserved a hot bath, a meal, and perhaps a nap, Ian was stopped by Lord Eric before he could mount his horse.

"My father heard you were in town," Lord Eric began with a grimace, and Ian shot his eyes skyward in a silent prayer for patience. That damnable trample through the park had done unknown damage in announcing his presence in the city.

"It seems it's become a rousing bit of information," Ian replied.

Lord Eric nodded. "Indeed. But the damage has been done, and Father is insisting you attend the ball tomorrow."

"The ball?" Ian dared to ask.

Lord Eric nodded solemnly. "Normally not my scene, but Father hosts one each Little Season and apparently it's quite a crush. He is insisting you attend."

"How does he even know you know me?"

"He does not," Lord Eric replied. "He announced it to the room at large, and I suspect an invitation will be at your house soon. I merely wanted to give you warning. It's a highly formal affair. Come for fifteen minutes, shake the earl's hand, let him reminisce about his Eton days with your father, and you can be off."

Ian sighed, knowing he should do the lad a favor and attend his father's ball, even though it would be a miserable evening with falsely genuine inquiries about the state of his father.

"Fine," Ian agreed. "But you owe me a bottle of brandy, something good and old."

"Done," Lord Eric said with a laugh.

With a nod, Ian was off, wondering what other consequences his treacherous ride through Hyde Park would bring to light.

Chapter Ten

———— ❀ ————

It had been two whole days since Susanna had last seen Ian, and she was not sure what to make of his absence. She was rather put out with the man. He showed up sporadically over the past week and just when she started to get used to him, he disappeared. Worst of all, he pulled a feat like sleeping in her bed and gifting her with a dagger hairpin and then did not call on her for two days.

"You look wonderful, Susanna," Clara declared, smiling sweetly at her. Clara was as radiant as ever in a lavender gown with long strands of pearls around her neck. Susanna had chosen a darker shade of turquoise blue, perfectly matching the peacock plume in her hair.

"This plume will not stay in place," Susanna said, fiddling with the feather tucked into the back of her curls.

"Then take the thing off," Andrew said impatiently, his brow hard with irritation.

Clara turned and raised an eyebrow at him. He gave her a long, exasperated stare before huffing and flipping open the evening paper.

"Will Lord Westcott be there?" Clara asked, looking back at Susanna.

"I have no idea," she replied, fiddling with the feather again. "I am not his keeper. He does not disclose his schedule with me."

"I was merely asking if you had heard from him," Clara replied. "After his, ah, interesting call the other day."

"No, I haven't," Susanna admitted, giving her an apologetic glance. She needn't take her ire toward Ian out on the duchess.

Clara patted her arm but did not offer any words of comfort, not that Susanna wanted to hear any. Again she had allowed herself to be duped by the earl, tricked into thinking he cared, that there was more between them than some arbitrary need to protect her from an invisible foe.

She sighed, giving herself one last rueful glance in the mirror. The feather was fine, but for some reason she was a jumble of nerves. It was true what she told Clara; she was not aware of his social calendar, but did he even have a social calendar? Would he attend a ball? He had made it clear he was not in town for the Little Season, and yet he was making his presence known.

The clock on the table ticked down the seconds until their departure, but it brought Susanna no comfort. Unfortunately, she had done nothing for the past two days but think about Ian and wonder what it would be like when she saw him. How could things be as they were after sleeping so closely in her bed? Had anything changed? She felt as though things were different between them, but she had no explanation as to what or why. But after two days of silence, she could only take that to demonstrate he was not afflicted the same as she was.

"I find it curious that Westcott is courting you without my permission," Andrew stated gruffly and took a sip of his brandy.

"Westcott is not courting me," Susanna replied, turning towards her brother. "We are simply friends."

"Friends who spend more time together than courting couples," Andrew replied.

"I am allowed male friends," Susanna countered, stepping around the sofa and claiming a seat beside the hearth. "Besides, I haven't seen him in two days. Surely if he was courting me he would have shown his face since Tuesday."

"People will talk, Susanna," Andrew continued.

"Since when did you care about idle gossip?" she asked, looking back at her brother in surprise, her gaze without humor.

He lowered his paper and looked sternly at her. "I care not about the gossip, but I do care about you."

"I am sure Lord Westcott is just being . . . kind," Clara interjected and glanced at her husband. "If he were to court Susanna he would come to you first, of course." She sent a pointed look at Susanna, but she did not understand the reason for the look. Ian was *not* courting her! The idea was ludicrous.

Or was it?

Susanna shook her head, not allowing herself to complete the thought. "He has no interest in me, I assure you. We are simply friends."

Andrew grumbled something under his breath that Susanna did not hear, but his wife gasped and smacked his arm.

"Where is Norah?" Susanna wondered aloud.

"I am here," Norah said from the doorway. She smiled tersely at them, stuffing something into her reticule.

Susanna eyed her sister curiously, but Norah did not meet her gaze. "What has taken you so long?"

"Change in gown choice is all," Norah explained quickly, smiling a bit too brightly at them. Her eyes were clear and bright, as if she had been crying, though her coloring seemed fine. Susanna pursed her lips. Something was amiss with her younger sister, but she chose to drop it, for now.

Her family proved an adequate distraction as they journeyed to the Mathgram Manor, and she did not think about the Earl of Westcott until after she and her siblings had been announced and settled into the ballroom. Soon Gemma and Monica were by her side and all felt right in the world . . . almost. The ballroom was filled to the brim; the Mathgram Ball was the crush of the Little Season, though had it been held during the regular season it would not have stood out from any of the other balls. The room was adorned in golds and blues, with high curtains draped over curved top windows set in little alcoves. Lords and ladies shifted through the tightly packed room. At a crush such as this, there wasn't much personal space allowed.

Susanna was distracted by Monica's tale of her footman chasing an errant parasol through the park, laughing lightly at the image. A single glass of champagne was settling warmly into her system, and for the briefest of moments, Susanna forgot to wonder about Ian or worry over Riverton or contemplate about what she was to do with her life. Her peace was short-lived.

"The Earl of Westcott and the Earl of Bexley," the footman said, announcing Ian and his cousin to the ball. Most of the heads in the ballroom turned to watch the cousins, who looked nothing alike, walk leisurely into the room. Ian's presence was not the usual, and it seemed everyone was curious about who he was and why he was here. The Little Season was a strange place to suddenly pop up in society without a purpose. As Ian and Bexley made their way through the crowd, a wave of whispers swept through the room, everyone eager for any information pertaining to the two lords.

"You would think he were a piece of horseflesh up for auction with the twitters he is causing," Susanna said to herself.

"What was that, dear?" Clara asked, and Susanna looked at the duchess.

"Oh, nothing," Susanna said, waving her hand in front of her. "I was merely thinking out loud."

Clara raised an eyebrow but did not comment further.

"He is much more handsome than I remember," Monica added, and Susanna smiled at her friend.

"Yes, and he is still as absurd," Susanna commented, turning away from the cousins as they disappeared into the crowd. "He says the most shocking things."

Monica snickered, shaking her head. "Only you would find that a fault, Susanna."

"Is it so wrong to want to speak to someone with a level head and a steady character?" Susanna asked.

"No, not at all," Lady Monica replied. "But we both know that would bore you after the first ten minutes. Are you ever bored with his lordship?"

Susanna did not answer, knowing her friend was right. She would never be bored with Ian. "It does not matter what I think of his lordship," Susanna said. "Currently, I only have one potential offer on the table. It is best to focus on what I can accomplish rather than chasing after wild dreams."

Monica gave her a sympathetic look and patted her arm. "Dreams can come true, Susie. Just look at my mother. Born to a butcher's son, made her treads on the stage where her Savior Prince came and swept her out of the theater and into the halls of a well-born lady. I am their dream come true."

What Monica left out was the part where her father's family ostracized her father for marrying an actress, forcibly removing her and her mother from their home, her mother turning back to the stage, raising Monica behind the curtains of the theater. Five years ago, upon her father's death, an aunt found Monica and dumped her at Lady Katherine's with a lump sum of funds and the instructions to never contact their family.

Susanna sighed and nodded. "I will try to be more hopeful and open to a happy ending," she lied, smiling sweetly at her friend.

Her point was adequate, but the story of Monica's parents wasn't the most inspiring example of a happy ending. People rarely got what they wanted in the end. That was the problem, she realized; maybe she wanted too much.

Gemma launched into a story to fill the moment of silence, and Susanna forced herself not to think of the future at this exact moment. She was at a ball, she was dressed in a gorgeous gown, she was well fed, had a warm bed, and was well-loved. She had no right to ask for more.

"Mrs. Barfield, how lovely to see you again," Clara said to the woman standing before her. Mrs. Barfield smiled and curtsied, her three daughters behind her doing the same: Marianne, Rosemary, and Annabelle—three auburn-haired sisters who were notorious title hunters. The oldest sister had actually married herself a title, thus promoting Marianne to Miss Barfield, and the next sister trying to gain a title. The youngest, Miss Annabelle, had debuted the season before last with Norah. The three smiled sweetly at Susanna, and she refrained from rolling her eyes. The sisters were manageable as individuals; all at once, plus their mother, was a recipe for a migraine.

"Good evening, your graces," Mrs. Barfield said. "Please excuse my forwardness, but I was told you were an acquaintance with the Earl of Westcott?"

Clara smiled at Mrs. Barfield. "I am acquainted with the earl, though that is the extent of my knowledge of him. I have only formally met him once."

"He was at your house party, was he not, your grace?" Mrs. Barfield asked Clara.

"For only one night of the four," Clara replied. "He had to leave early to attend to unexpected business."

Mrs. Barfield frowned, which wasn't an unusual expression for her. "Left at the beginning of a party? Leaving your numbers uneven? How dreadful for you, your grace."

Clara flipped open her fan and fanned her face. "One of the young ladies fell ill incidentally, which was quite upsetting, I assure you. But it worked out in the end, for our numbers stayed even."

"Are his manners up to par?" Mrs. Barfield forwardly asked and Susanna fought the giggle threatening to escape.

"He was the perfect gentleman," Clara replied.

"Who is his family?"

"I suspect his father was once the Earl of Westcott," Clara replied.

Mrs. Barfield sucked in a sharp breath at Clara's snarky reply. Susanna had dealt with the Barfields much longer than Clara and stepped in to help keep the Barfield drama to a minimum.

"His father is the Marquess of Ashford, I believe," Susanna replied. "He is a cousin to the Earl of Bexley, as you may have heard when he was announced a few moments ago. Though I cannot imagine we know any more about him than anyone else. Like her grace told you, we barely know him."

This did not seem to dissuade Mrs. Barfield, and she looked directly at Susanna. "He is courting you, is he not?"

Susanna impressed herself with her composure. Why did everyone think Ian was courting her? "He is not. He is merely a family acquaintance."

Mrs. Barfield narrowed her eyes at Susanna, but Susanna did not back down. She met the woman's stare straight on, a pleasant, unemotional look firmly on her face.

"I do not know what you think you are playing at, missy, but you do not have the right to string along two eligible lords at the same time."

A few people surrounding them gasped, and she saw Andrew open his mouth to rebuke the woman, but Susanna cut him off.

"I assure you I am not dallying with the earl," Susanna replied. "And from what I know of his character, he is not the type to dally with an unsuspecting lady of quality. I have no claim on him. However, he does seem to be very selective with his acquaintances, and since he is rarely in town, it is difficult to gain an introduction. I am sure if you'd like an introduction, her grace would be happy to assist. I know you would be most grateful for such an invitation, especially if his lordship were to take a liking to one of your daughters. Though should he not, you would not want to embarrass her grace, or yourself, by lingering too long where you are not wanted."

Mrs. Barfield glanced quickly at her daughters before her face contorted into a tight smile. "If her grace would be so kind," she said, looking at the duchess.

"I will see what I can do," Clara sweetly. The duchess was truly too nice for her own good.

"Good," Susanna said, smiling brightly albeit falsely at the Barfields. "Now that is settled, is there any other way we can be of assistance?"

"No, my lady," Mrs. Barfield replied, curtsying to their graces and nodding at Susanna. The three daughters did the same, shooting apologetic glances at Susanna before following their mother into the crowd.

It was then, after they had gone, that Susanna realized her heart was pounding in her ears. The buzz around them returned to normal, and Susanna looked at her brother and his duchess. "Who knew the Little Season could be so exciting?" Susanna asked with a tight shrug. Clara grinned at her; Andrew looked irritated.

"Yes, who knew?" a voice asked from behind her and Susanna spun around to see Ian standing tall before her. The sounds of the room around her disappeared as Susanna took in a formally dressed Ian, something she had not seen before. Evening attire was nice, day wear was comforting, even his worn and tattered look made her think unmentionable thoughts, but goodness, the boy cleaned up nicely. Gone was the ruffian from his investigations at the booksellers and the silly casualness of their afternoon turn about the park. He stood tall, head tilted up just a bit, every inch the aristocrat he was, as much as he was wont to deny it. His finely fit, black coat curved deliciously around his arms and back, and black breeches that formed his shape to perfection were neatly tucked into black boots. His face was freshly shaven, grey-green eyes bright, and his sandy hair had been parted and slicked to one side. He was a morsel to behold.

He smiled and kissed her gloved knuckles, and she couldn't help the dreamy smile that crept onto her face.

"So nice to see your disapproval directed at someone else for a change," he added, winking.

"My what?" Susanna asked absently before recovering her wits. He had quite befuddled her. "Oh, yes, well, I suspect my disapproval for you will return momentarily."

"Probably," Ian replied. Glancing down he spotted her dance card dangling from her wrist. He nicked her card. "How long have you been out of your debutante whites?"

"Four seasons," Susanna replied cautiously.

"Good, then you can dance more than two dances with me," he said, penning his name onto her dance card. She snatched it away from him.

"You would not dare," she said, horrified. "That is not proper, my lord." More than two dances? Was he mad? Apparently people already had their suspicions about her relationship with Ian, and more than two dances would solidify their assumptions and secure Susanna's downfall. His brow furrowed together.

"Is that not proper?" he asked and shrugged. "It is not as if I am courting you."

She glared at him. "Have you no respect for my reputation? Two dances is at the edge of scandal; more than two dances and you might as well announce our engagement with the amount of attention you've been paying me, for that is what everyone thinks."

"Truly?" he asked. "Have I been paying you too much attention?"

Susanna glared at him. He knew he had.

Ian rolled his eyes. He took Norah's card from her and wrote his name on two slots before handing it back to her. Turning to Clara, he smiled charmingly and the duchess, who had been watching their exchange, handed over her card as well. Andrew opened his mouth to protest but snapped it shut when his wife elbowed him in the ribs. Ian wrote his name on two of Clara's lines also before handing it back to her and did the same with Monica's and Gemma's dance cards.

"There, two dance sets with each of you," Ian announced

proudly. "No one will think we are courting if I dance with your friends, your sister, and the duchess just as often."

Reluctantly, she handed her card back to him, and he wrote his name on the final line, the last before dinner.

"There," he said, letting go of the card so it swung lightly on her wrist. "Problem solved."

Susanna let out an exasperated sigh. "If only it were that easy. In fact—" She stopped as she caught sight of the Barfields heading straight for them, apparently returning now that Westcott had joined them. Susanna groaned.

Ian glanced in the direction Susanna was looking and he looked back at her, smiling.

"Returning for more of your barbed tongue, love?" Susanna glared at him, and he winked at her.

"It is your fault, Susanna," Clara said to her through her teeth, turning to smile at Mrs. Barfield as they approached.

"Your grace," Mrs. Barfield said, dipping into a curtsey.

"Mrs. Barfield, allow me to introduce you to the Earl of Westcott," Clara said demurely, though Susanna could tell that she was irritated.

Mrs. Barfield smiled too sweetly as she introduced her girls, each smiling and blinking rapidly. Ian smiled back, bowing as he was introduced to each girl, shooting a reproachful look Susanna's way.

"My three younger girls are unattached presently, as my oldest Petunia made a wonderful match with Viscount Samburg this past summer," Mrs. Barfield was saying. "My Annabelle plays a wonderful clarinet, and Rosemary is quite skilled with watercolors."

The music changed from softly wafting in the background of the ball to more enforced tones, and couples began gathering on the dance floor.

Mrs. Barfield's eyes widened in hunger at the change in music. "My Marianne is a most accomplished dancer, my lord. Were you in need of a dance partner for the first set—"

"I appreciate your kindness, Mrs. Barfield, but I am afraid I am already taken," Ian replied. Grasping Susanna by the hand, he pulled her from the safety of the crowd, away from the fuming Barfield matron, and onto the dance floor.

Oh my, Susanna thought as he turned towards her. The first dance had to be a waltz, of course. She had never danced with Ian. His hands had been on her body, but this was different. Before, it had been behind curtains, in private, something just between them. Here, everyone saw, everyone was witness to his hand on her hip, his warm glove clasped tightly in hers. Even though it was completely acceptable, it felt illicit—forbidden—turning with him around the room, her arm on his shoulder, feeling the strength of him beneath her.

"What on earth are you thinking about?" he asked, his eyes narrowed mischievously.

She grinned. "We've never danced before. I am quite surprised you know how."

"I have many talents you have yet to see," he replied and winked.

"Yes, well keep those to yourself, please," she said. "You've already caused quite a stir tonight."

"I doubt anyone has taken notice of me when I am dancing with such a charming beauty," he replied. "You look lovely tonight, love."

Susanna blushed and looked away. "Yes, thank you. Though you really should not call me such things where others can hear. Everyone already thinks you are courting me."

He shrugged. "I care not what people think. I did not realize you were the type to weigh yourself down with other people's opinions."

Susanna pursed her lips. "A lady's reputation is all she has to offer a husband, aside from a dowry."

"It helps then that your dowry is substantial."

"Perhaps," she allowed. "I permit myself leniency where the

rules of society are concerned. However, there are hard limits even I cannot step beyond without social ruin. Dallying with an earl who will turn me out will damage my reputation beyond repair."

"What is your point?"

"That we have already created enough speculation, Ian," Susanna said softly. "Please, do not ruin me."

"Whatever you want from me, you know I cannot—"

"I am not asking for a declaration of anything, my lord," she replied interrupting him. "I am merely asking you to be respectful in your dealings with me, especially in public. You do pay me an awful lot attention for a gentleman who is not courting."

"And what if I was courting you?" he asked. "Would that permit me to spend time with you? Would you allow me to call you whatever I want?"

Susanna eyed him peculiarly. Their conversation had taken a turn in a direction Susanna had not anticipated. What did he mean by that?

"You can call me whatever you please when we are alone. I've realized I cannot stop you from doing so," she replied. "I am simply reminding you that since we are not courting, you need to watch how your actions towards me in public will be perceived. Since you do not seem keen on the position, I would hate if my association with you ruined my chances with another potential suitor."

"What makes you think I am not keen on the position?" he asked.

"Your blatant statement that you have nothing to offer me," she replied. "I know you are fond of me, though beyond that I do not understand your hesitancy."

"It is not you I hesitate against," Ian said slowly. "But I do admit you are quite the enjoyable distraction."

"If that's what you need from me, fine," she said softly. "Just do not leave me in tatters when you eventually leave me. I enjoy your company, Westcott. You have made the Little Season more enjoyable than normal."

His lips quirked into a smile, and she understood the random seriousness of their conversation was over.

"You lofting me onto the Barfield sisters was not exactly playing fair, Susanna," he said. "Each Barfield sister I dance with tonight will require a favor from you."

"A favor?" she asked, intrigued. "What might these favors entail?"

"Whatever I desire," he replied.

"Well, I might be inclined to accept, if you agree to keep it within those limits society deems hard lines."

"Come now, you aren't willing to walk on the side of impropriety?"

She shook her head.

"Susanna, you are wearing dark turquoise," he pointed out. "Not exactly a color of a women looking for a husband."

"I am not looking for a husband," she replied. "Well, I am always on the lookout for a husband, should the opportunity present itself, but I am not actively pursuing the men in this room as potential suitors. I am well beyond the debutante whites, and bold colors are all the rage right now, for those with enough confidence to wear them."

"You do wear it well," he commented, glancing down at her.

"Contain yourself, please," she chided as the music came to an end.

"Until later in private?" he asked, hopeful.

"You are incorrigible, my lord."

"You love it," he replied softly in her ear.

She rolled her eyes, praying to the heavens for the patience to deal with this man.

The rest of the evening passed in uneventful splendor. Ian danced with Norah, Monica, Gemma, Clara and all three Barfield sisters. As he returned with each sister, he discreetly held up an additional finger for her to see and count her favors owed. It really wasn't her fault he had been foisted upon the Barfield sisters.

If Mrs. Barfield had not irked her, she might have kept her nose out of it, but the idea of one of the Barfield sisters impressing Ian enough to catch his eye was preposterous.

Although he was smiling awfully genuinely at Miss Annabelle as they came off the dance floor. He laughed at Miss Rosemary's awful duck impression, and he seemed sincerely impressed as Miss Barfield regaled him with some tale about her horse.

"You are staring, Susanna," Andrew said to her as he danced with her around the room.

She glared at her brother. She appreciated their dancing arrangement, but she did not need his comments.

"I am not staring," she argued. "I am observing the other couples in the room. Did you notice Lady Sadett's new shoes? Splendid color with such delicate lace work. I must remember to ask the countess where she found them. I simply must have a pair."

"Buy the shoes if you must, but I know you better than that," Andrew replied.

"I am not staring," she insisted.

"He is a charming chap," Andrew commented, nodding towards Ian. "Much better company than that Riverton fellow. Why hasn't he been around in a while?"

"Out of town on estate business or something," Susanna replied.

"Will he ever ask for your hand?" her brother asked.

"I am sure he will as soon as he returns."

"Shame," Andrew said. "I should not want him as a brother-in-law."

Susanna looked up at her brother, into bright blue eyes so much like her own. "And whyever not?"

Andrew gave a half shrug. "The man always came across as a bit odd, you know? As if he is play-acting his role as the Viscount Riverton. He has never seemed truly genuine."

Susanna pursed her lips. Her brother had just actually pinned her uncertainties with the viscount perfectly, not that she was going to tell him she agreed. "If you dislike him so, why have you consented to his courtship?"

"Because you seemed to be in favor of it," he replied, as if this should have been obvious. "If it makes you happy, I am often willing to oblige."

Susanna thought about this for a moment, realizing he was correct. He never denied her anything.

"I think your duchess has brought out the softer side of you," she commented.

"Nonsense," he replied. "I have no softer side." Although in his eyes she saw something she had not seen in her brother in a very long time. Humor and mischief—it had to be Clara's doing. She came into their lives and completely turned her brother on his head, causing such uproar in his neat and orderly and decisively dull life that he had no option but to take notice. Much like Ian had done to her. The thought of him leaving made her sad. He drove her crazy; he was impulsive and inappropriate, but he brought out a side of her she rather liked.

"Since you are not staring again, I should mention the dance has ended," Andrew said.

Susanna blinked and realized they were standing in the middle of the dance floor, the other dancing couples having moved off.

"Yes, of course," she replied, giving herself a mental shake. "I was merely catching my breath."

Andrew let out a rather unduke-like noise—half chortle and half snort—and a few heads turned to look at him peculiarly.

Susanna smiled softly at her brother. "I am glad you married Clara. She is good for you."

He nodded. "You have no idea."

They returned to their party, where Clara stood chatting with Monica. Andrew moved to stand beside his wife, glancing down at her with an expression that made Susanna's heart melt. Discreetly, Susanna glanced across the room where Ian was depositing Miss Barfield with her Mamma, and she felt her heart ache with longing.

This would not do.

"It is so nice to have such an energetic ball during the Little Season," Susanna said, looking away from Ian. "Helps liven up the *ennui*."

Monica nodded in agreement. "Such a wonderful crush."

"Luckily, we have no shortage of events the coming weeks," Clara added. "Makes the time in town go much faster."

"Come now, your grace, you would not want to leave the splendor just yet?" Monica teased. "I daresay you've started to become comfortable in your new title."

"Comfortable as a duchess, yes," Clara agreed. "Though I will never truly be as comfortable in the city as I am in the country."

"Agreed," Susanna said, nodding. "As much as I enjoy town, it will be nice to return to the open fields of the country."

"Where one can walk without being trampled?" Ian asked from behind her, and she turned to look up into his handsome face.

"I was going to drop it, but since you brought it up, yes, my lord. It will be most relaxing to walk without the fear of being trampled to death by an angry piece of horse flesh."

"D'artagnon was not angry," Ian argued. "He was simply frustrated you stepped in his path."

Susanna was chagrined. "I stepped into his way?" Why did this man have the ability to wind her up so? "I will have you know riding at anything faster than a leisurely pace is illegal in the park. You of all people should know the law."

His eyes hardened for a moment before letting out a bark of laughter. "What, did you research the Hyde Park laws?"

A tight smile crept across Susanna's lips as she fought to control her amusement. "As a matter of fact, I did."

Ian shook his head. "Whatever will I do with you?"

Susanna opened her mouth to reply, but a threesome of ladies cut her off.

"Oh, Lady Susanna, we are most looking forward to your event on Friday!" Lady Orthernshire exclaimed and Susanna turned to welcome her with a smile.

"Your event?" Ian inquired.

Susanna gave him a warning look before returning her attention to the three ladies: Lady Pippa Lee, the Countess of Orthernshire; Lady Samantha Spencer, the Countess of Leister; and Lady Athena Hamilton, Viscountess Holland. Three girls she had debuted with, three who were already established in marriages.

"May I introduce the Earl of Westcott?" Susanna said as Ian bowed and the ladies curtsied.

"A pleasure to meet you, my lord," Lady Orthernshire said brightly. "Will we see you at the Lady Day Benefit?"

Ian's eyebrows peaked up. "The Lady Day Benefit?"

Lady Leister nodded. "It's a benefit brunch to assist the Lady Day Foundation."

"Forgive me, but I have no clue to what you speak of," Ian said apologetically.

"The Lady Day Foundation helps orphans in the city," Lady Holland answered.

Ian nodded. "And there is a brunch to help aid with donations?"

"The brunch is simply because we adore brunch," Susanna replied. "The silent auction is what helps the charity."

"And why is this your event?" Ian asked, looking down at her.

Susanna hesitated to give the answer, though she wasn't sure why. She was almost embarrassed for Ian to know of the depth of her involvement.

"Because Lady Susanna is on the board of trustees, of course," Lady Leister supplied for her.

"I only oversee the event planning," Susanna said quickly. "Merely an honorary position."

"It's a splendid event," Lady Orthernshire added. "You would truly enjoy it, my lord."

"Indeed I would," Ian said absently, looking at Susanna peculiarly.

"You are welcome to attend, Lord Westcott," Susanna replied, regaining her composure. "Everyone is welcome, you do not need an invitation."

"Would you like me to attend?"

Susanna blinked rapidly at him, cringing at the way the three married ladies were eating up his every word, watching as he brazenly flirted with her right in front of them.

Susanna looked away and shrugged. "Should you wish to join, we would love to have your support. There is an hour of boxing with Gentleman Jackson up for auction this year. Perhaps that might be something you are interested in?" She looked up at him again in mock inquiry.

"I have a great many interests, Lady Susanna," Ian said simply. "Perhaps something might catch my eye."

Susanna looked away from him, it was just too much. Why would he not stay the proper course, especially when they were in public? Why must he flaunt their would-be relationship in front of these girls? These three ladies from decent families who had married directly after their first season? Three lords who had danced with Susanna at her coming out ball, three lords who had shown a glimmer of interest before they realized they would have to go through the Stone Duke of Bradstone in order to court his grace's sister. Three lords, three among many, who had decided not to pursue her and found brides in other ladies presented that year. Not that she wanted their husbands. Susanna merely wanted what they had already attained and what seemed to elude her at every turn. She may not be on the hunt for a husband, but a happy marriage, family, and household of her own was always something she would desire.

Ian was dangling her above the precipice of social ruin, blatantly, and he did not care. He may not approve of the rules, but Susanna had to live by them. The room was suddenly very hot; her stays felt much too tight.

She forced a smile onto her face and looked at the three titled ladies. "We appreciate your patronage and I look forward to seeing you tomorrow. If you would excuse me, I am in need of some refreshments."

There was more curtsying and bowing before Susanna made her escape, ignoring Clara's concerned look or Andrew's halting arm on his wife's elbow. She made her way through the crowd, craving the fresh air of the outdoors, hoping no one would see her tears or hear her gasping breath.

Ian was not prepared for a weeping Susanna.

The outer balcony was thankfully free of guests, but he was stopped in his tracks by the sight of his strong Susanna reduced to tears. Knowing he was somehow responsible made his heart sink like lead to the bottom of the sea.

He took a few steps towards her, lightly placing his gloved hands on her shoulders and pulling her towards him, her back to his chest.

"Please, Ian, just let me be," she pleaded softly.

He shook his head and softly answered, "Never."

She spun around, glaring at him, wiping tears from her eyes. "See, that—that is what I cannot understand. You pursue, then you withdraw. I cannot make any sense of you. You risk my reputation with your joking and flirting and yet stake no claim. Why cannot you just respect that I need you to make up your mind?"

"I have the utmost respect for you, Susanna," he replied truthfully. "I do not like that I have caused you this pain."

She pulled a handkerchief from her reticule and dabbed her eyes before stuffing it back inside.

"If you do not want to cause me pain, then please leave me alone," she begged.

"You know I cannot do that," he answered.

"Why?"

"You know why."

She shook her head and looked down. "I do not." There was a long pause before she looked back up at him. "You say you want to be friends, then let us be friends. You say you want to protect me and yet use me as bait and I agreed. But I cannot have you acting as you are in front of other people. We discussed this scarcely two hours ago, and then you do it again, in front of those ladies of all the people in the ballroom."

"What is wrong with those ladies?" he asked.

She pursed her lips. "I debuted with those ladies four years ago, and they made very advantageous matches during their debut season, matches that could have been mine had my brother not been a duke whose mere expression would frighten the suitors away. The only two men who felt I was worth involvement with the Stone Duke have been Riverton and you. Compared to those three women, I am a failure. You may call it a competition, and while I am not actively competing, I still have to play the game. And I am losing miserably."

Ian couldn't take it anymore. He hated seeing the hurt and loss in her eyes, realizing that her list of suitors was ridiculously short. And as much as she preached about not needing a husband, she truly wanted a husband and a family of her own. He took a step towards her, wrapping a hand behind her head and pulling her towards him, he kissed her. He took a long sip of her delectable kiss before she pushed him away.

"This is what I am talking about!" she exclaimed. "You cannot kiss me in full view of a crowded ballroom! Have you no sense?"

He shook his head, her kiss having a drugging effect on him. "I seem to lose all common sense when you are around, Susanna."

She smirked. "I doubt you ever had common sense."

He shrugged. "It is one of my more endearing qualities."

"Yes, it is," she said softly. "However, you cannot lose reason when we are surrounded by a ballroom full of people. Or while at the theater or Hyde Park or a dinner party. I enjoy the time I spend with you, but we cannot abandon all propriety and be as we want."

"Why the damned hell not?" he asked.

"Because that is not the world we live in."

"It's not the world I live in," he said, frustration creeping into his words. "I understand rules and propriety and proper and scandals, Susanna. But do not you see the absurdity of all those constraints?"

"I do," she said determinedly. "I hate having to live like this. Were I to have my way, I would wear trousers and ride through the park as fast as I wanted. I would put everything I have into Lady Day and not care about what the *ton* thought. I would wear red gowns and I would dance every dance with you.

However, that is not my place in the world. As a well-bred lady, I have expectations and responsibilities to my family and it would be very selfish of me to do as I please and bring them down with me. My reputation is connected to Clara's reputation and Norah's and Mara's—who has yet to even debut! Why would I wish to cause her undue turmoil? I care too much for them to hurt them that way. So I push what rules I can, bend them where I know they are lenient. I wear bright turquoise to a ball instead of the scandalous red, and I dance a little too closely with an earl who is not my betrothed. However, society has a breaking point and I refuse to break what cannot be mended. I cannot imagine your family would appreciate the way you have been carrying on."

"Oh, do not get started on me, love," Ian said, shaking his head. "My life is fine the way it is."

"Is it?" she asked. "You live a life on the road, at the disposal of an invisible dictator who determines where you go, what cases to work. All fine and dandy, except how is your father's estate? As his regent, do you spend the necessary time on estate business? Have you bothered to learn the politics and positions of bills you must one day vote to pass? You do as you want and act as you want, but truly, who are you, Ian? Have you taken responsibility for the title you will one day inherit, one that you are supposed to be executing in everything but name? Because all I see from you is silliness and idle boredom suppressed by solving every little puzzle that comes your way!"

Ian shook his head at her, anger coursing through him. "You know nothing of who I am!" he snapped at her.

"How could I?" she cried. "You hardly share anything of your personal life, everything I get from you is half-veiled comments and flirting. I know nothing of you because you know not who you are!"

He shook his head angrily at her and turned to walk away. He spun on his heels and stomped the few steps back to her, getting close to her face as he said, "You know nothing of my life, Susanna. You are just a silly, little girl who play acts at being an independent thinker when truly you are the worst of society's sheep."

She blinked at him, her face void of expression. "I may be a silly, little girl to you, Ian, but at least I know my place in this world and do not throw away what I have been given."

He glared hard at her, unable to say anything, no apology, no jokes, no clever retort. He regretted his words the instant they escaped his mouth, for he truly did not think that of her.

He respected her for her brazen outlook on society and her daring wit. She was loyal and bold, and he could not ask for a better friend. But it was impossible to form those words. He was so angry—with her, with himself, with his life—that the only thing he could do was turn and disappear into the darkness.

Chapter Eleven

———— ❁ ————

Susanna ignored Clara and Norah's inquiries, her mood turning foul. That damn man was the reason, but she just couldn't bring herself to share with her sisters. Not only was she angry with Ian for his lack of decorum, she was worried about him. He had never lashed out at her, never had she seen him so upset. Damn that man for causing her concern to overtake her anger!

They returned to Bradstone House just before midnight. Susanna shut herself in her rooms—ignoring her family—simply wanting to be alone. Appreciative as she was for their concern, so many family members in residence could be suffocating.

Annette came in to help her undress, yawning in the candlelight. Susanna felt a twinge of guilt for forcing her maid to be up as late as she.

"This came while you were out, my lady," Annette said, setting a cream envelope down on the dressing table. Susanna looked at the envelope curiously, and quickly tore it open.

As she read, her heart sank, which was not exactly a healthy response to the news that her potential fiancé had returned and would call upon her tomorrow.

It was harebrained and ridiculous, but she was terrified of Riverton's return, terrified of what he would ask her and what she would say. She barely had half the truth from Ian about the viscount; how was she to make the right decision if he would not tell her all the facts?

Having Riverton back in town would also limit her time with Ian. She did not want the last time she spoke to him to be an argument. The hurt on his face, the pain in his eyes—how was she to fix that with Riverton in town?

"Annette, I can manage from here," she announced, rather sharply to her maid. Her harsh tone was unnecessary, but Susanna just desperately wanted to be alone. Annette blinked at her in surprise. Susanna managed a soft, apologetic smile. "You are tired, I am sure. Please retire for the evening. And tomorrow I wish to have a good-lie in so please do not disturb me until well past noon. I hope you are able to get a good night's sleep."

Annette bobbed a curtsey but did not seem willing to argue the point with her mistress and she quickly quit the room.

Susanna peeled her corset, shift, and stockings off, tossing them to the chair. She found a nightgown Annette had pulled from her drawers and she shrugged it on over her hair, still done up from the ball. The pins came out and her chocolate hair came tumbling down, but she had not the energy to weave it into a plait.

She was exhausted. Riverton and Ian, they both were so trying. Riverton seemed interested, but not eager, where Ian was much too eager with less serious interest.

The look on his face plagued her, his eyes so full of pain, his tone so different than when he was charming and teasing. To mask all that pain behind a veneer of charm and sarcasm, he had to be mentally drained. She hoped he would still attend the Lady Day Brunch; she needed to know he was all right. She needed him to understand that somewhere along the way she had become much more deeply imbedded in their relationship than she intended.

He claimed he had nothing to offer her, but she wasn't certain that was the case. There was something more he wasn't telling her, of that much there was no question, but his investigations with the Crown and into Riverton was only a way to block out the pain of something much deeper. She had seen a glimpse of the broken man tonight, and it shook her to her core. How could a man so capable of good not see the good in himself?

Something told her that Ian needed her in his life. And she was pretty sure she needed him.

Later that evening, Ian found himself half-drunk and standing in his sister's bedroom. He glanced around at the yellow and gold striped wallpaper, the four poster bed, the trinkets on the dressing table. Nothing had been touched since his sister had died. He had not been able to set foot inside the room until now. The heavy drapes were pulled closed, protecting the contents from a cruel world. He pulled one drape open and sighed, exhausted after his spat with Susanna and frustrated that she was more correct about him than he was willing to admit. White sheets covered the chairs like formless ghosts haunting the room of a girl long passed. He pulled one drape off the chair, slowly, the dust puffing up in the candle light, and sat down. The soft autumn moon drifted in, illuminating the dull polish on the hard wooden floors, another reminder that perhaps he wasn't doing as well managing his father's estate as he had led himself to believe.

He sat, the bottle of brandy from Lord Eric clutched tightly in his hand, careful not to disturb the peace of the room. When had he last seen the properties belonging to the Marquessate? When had he last traveled to Northumberland, to his family's country seat and the root of his centuries-old title? He conversed with his steward monthly about important business with the estate, but really, how much did he know about his father's holdings? Did he even know how to be Ashford when it came his time?

He ran away from his home, family, and responsibilities when he was nineteen years old.

He should have been at Oxford, he chose the wilds of France, a part of the war but not truly participating. He plowed his way through investigations, keeping occupied through his early twenties so he couldn't be reminded of what he had walked away from at home. He expected to return eventually. He presumed Beth would have been safe in his absence. She had been eleven when he left and had been eighteen and engaged when she had died. Looking around the room, the music box on the night stand, the brush and mirror on the dressing table, a porcelain parakeet figurine on a table with a vase—these were from a person he did not know. For whom did he mourn all these years? A grown sister he knew only from letters, or a kid sister he had walked away from?

Lady Susanna, as maddening as she was, was right. He was not handling his responsibilities. He was not doing his duty to his father's title. The Marquess was in no state to run the estate, much less sign his own name. It fell upon Ian to correct the evils he had committed when he had walked away all those years ago. Finding his way back felt impossible.

A crash from down the hall set him on edge, and the cries of a mad woman reminded him of where he was, as if he could somehow forget. It seemed the Marchioness was awake for her nightly tantrum. His father would soon follow. Ian would not go to them, as the things they reminded him of were not something he could handle at the moment. The nurses and staff he employed here excelled; besides, his parents' dementia was severe, and they did not even know who he was.

He stood, setting the decanter of brandy on the side table, hoping he remembered to retrieve it in the morning. Taking another longing look across the empty room, he sighed and shook his head. What a mess he was.

Chapter Twelve

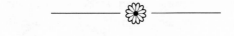

Ignoring the dull throb in his head and putting his pride aside, Ian attended the Lady Day Benefit Brunch the second morning following the Mathgram Ball. He really had behaved rather badly to Lady Susanna and at the very least he owed her an apology before she cut off all ties with him.

The day was bright and warm, the last bits of summer giving one last appearance before fall turned into winter. The morning was cheerful and held a tone of optimism, but as it was a charity event, the purpose was to keep everyone in good spirits so they would open their pocketbooks. At least the weather was willing to play its part.

Ian surveyed the grounds of Coleford Park. He was impressed with the number of people willing to make the drive to Surrey. Whether it be the charity they were in support of or the lady at the helm, he wasn't sure, but Susanna had set up quite an event.

The house sat beside a long, man-made pond. The green lawn was expansive, wrapping around the pool and the sides of the house. The room at the back sat further out than the rest of the house, a wall of mirrored glass reflecting the pool back at the party guests. Along the side of the house were four pavilions set up with tables of items arranged in U shapes within each tent.

Poles were posted along the edges of the party, pennants and long banners fluttered in the breeze, footmen wove in and out of the *haute ton*, delivering a lemony champagne drink.

Everyone seemed to have adopted a more casual air than the formality one saw at the ball. Pastels and whites adorned the ladies with parasols and wicker bonnets, shading the sun from their faces. Men chose mostly buff breeches and coats in earth tones.

In the middle of it all was Lady Susanna, radiant in her element. Ian watched her as she chatted brightly about the charity she seemed to support with all her heart. It had surprised him that she had an association with the enigmatic Lady Day and the charity that snatched troubled, young boys from the streets and whisked them away to a magical land. None of the lads who had been taken by Lady Day had ever returned, and no one heard from them ever again. Ian had made a few inquiries about the Lady Day Foundation and some of the information had intrigued him.

Susanna's involvement in the charity seemed to go deeper than she had previously let on. He wanted to know more about Lady Day and what it meant to Susanna, but after his behavior the other night, he wasn't sure if she would reveal any more of herself. What was worse is he knew he did not deserve her confidence.

Susanna tried not to fiddle with the scrap of paper in her palm, the note she had written for Ian seemingly burning a hole through her glove. Her heart felt like it was going to leap out of her chest. He looked well, but Susanna was dying to actually speak to him. Try as she might, she was worried about him. She cared about him, she admitted it to herself, and once Susanna cared about something, she was hell-bent on making sure it was put to rights.

She had seen him watching her from across the lawn for a

good twenty minutes before he downed his goblet of lemon champagne and made his way towards her. The sight of him sent a tingle of electricity down to her toes, even with Riverton at her arm to dampen any feelings of excitement.

"Lord Westcott," Susanna said and curtsied. "I believe you know my dear friend, Lord Riverton?" Ian nodded curtly to Riverton, barely paying him any attention.

"Good to see you looking well, Westcott," Riverton said politely.

Ian glanced at him and nodded again. "You as well," he responded.

"Are you enjoying your morning, my lord?" Susanna asked.

"Quite," he replied, glancing at Riverton again. Riverton had turned to chat with the couple behind him. "I, ah . . ." Ian cleared his throat, looking down at his toes before meeting her gaze. So much raced through his eyes, Susanna could see, and she desperately wanted to be alone with him.

"Have you seen the silent auction, my lord?" she asked him. "Make sure you take a peek and see if there is something you find worth bidding on." She held her hand aloft indicating he should take it. A peculiar expression flashed through his eyes, almost as if he were trying to decipher a possible double meaning in her words.

He took her hand and she let go of the folded note, sliding it into his hand as he brushed a chaste kiss over her gloved knuckles.

Her eyes flashed a warning that only he could see and he nodded in understanding. "I will peruse the auction tables, my lady," he agreed. "Anything I can do to help the orphans."

She smiled sweetly at him, partly for show, but partly because she truly had grown fond of him over the past couple weeks. He nodded again to her and Riverton before stepping aside and disappearing into the crowd.

"He is not very agreeable company," Riverton stated once Ian was gone.

Susanna quirked her head to the side and asked, "Why would

you think that?"

"Because I know him much better than you do," Riverton replied, a dark look crossing over his face. It was gone when he turned his eyes to her. "Trust me, he is not a man for polite company."

Susanna smiled demurely, Riverton taking it as an agreement and turning the subject on to a new shipping venture. Susanna counted silently in her head, ticking away the seconds until she could safely slip away. She got to two hundred and politely excused herself from the company of her would-be fiancé, claiming a need to check on the refreshments.

"I am the hostess, after all," she explained. Riverton looked less than interested and nodded, before turning back to the gentleman to engage in more shipping lore.

Susanna knew he would be occupied for a good half-hour before he would start to wonder where she was. She hurried as best she could through the crowd, across the lawn, up the stairs and into the back doors of Coleford Park.

Ian fiddled with the note in his gloved fingers, running through what he had to say to the lovely Lady Susanna.

> *Please meet me in the back library in five minutes.*

It was pretty straightforward as far as directions went, though her motives had Ian stumped.

He spotted her outside, smiling and making her way through the crowd, politely talking to people as she maneuvered closer to the edge of the lawn. She wanted to see him, alone it seemed, and Ian could not fathom why. Their last encounter had been atrocious, and while he knew he must apologize, he wasn't sure if she would be willing to accept.

She came into the room, eyes taking a moment to adjust to the dimness of the room, a striking contrast to the brightness of the day outside.

"I was surprised you would seek me out," he said to her. She squinted her eyes as she spotted him across the room. She fumbled with her bonnet ribbons, winding her way through the various pieces of furniture arranged in the room.

"I was worried about you," she said softly.

Ian was taken aback. "You were worried about me?"

She nodded and stopped a few feet from him, pulling her bonnet gingerly from her head. She set it aside and smoothed her gloved hands over her hair, attempting to tame down the mess her bonnet had made.

"You look lovely, Susanna," he said quietly. "Do not worry about the appearance of your hair for me. Now why would you possibly be worried about me?"

"The other night," she explained, as if it should be obvious. "The night of the Mathgram Ball. You were so angry with me, I had to make sure you were all right."

He watched as a myriad of emotions crossed her face, though he wasn't sure he could understand her reasoning, or rather he wasn't sure he could believe it. He had yelled in her face and still she came to him, still she found him worthy of her care.

Damn it, Ian thought to himself, closing the distance between them and wrapping his arms around her slim frame. *I think I might love this woman.* He breathed in her scent, and her warmth, resting his head against hers, tucking her into him. She held him and took a deep steadying breath.

"I do not particularly enjoy fighting with you," she said into his chest.

"I am sorry for my outburst," he began. "I truly did not mean what I said to you. I felt horrible once it escaped my lips. I was not angry with you; I do not want you to be frightened of me."

"I appreciate your apology, Ian, though you are not the first man to yell at me," she admitted. "It was less frightening and more concerning. I had to see with my own eyes that you were well. You were so upset with me—whatever I said to distress you, I am deeply sorry."

He leaned down and kissed her, arousal suddenly coursing through him. He backed her against the sofa, his mouth demanding hers in a passionate torment. A soft moan vibrated deep in her throat and his pulse quickened. The distant sounds of the event outside filtered into his clouded mind and reason poked at his desire.

"Susanna, we cannot do this here," he said, pulling away from her.

"Yes, we can," she said leaning forward to kiss under his chin, where his pulse was thudding out of control.

"After all your speeches about propriety and witnesses . . ."

"No one knows this room is here, most people would go along to the side entrance where the auction tables are," she said, nipping at the skin along his neck cravat. "And in case you did not notice, the windows are treated with a mirrored effect on the outside, so anyone looking in can only see a reflection of the expansive lawn. So we are effectively alone."

"Even though we can see all those people out there?"

She nodded. "No one can see us."

He grabbed her wrists and looked her in the face. "Have you had any champagne?"

She laughed and shook her head. "No, why?"

He eyed her curiously. "Susanna the Minx is the same as my proper, sober miss?"

She leaned up to him and kissed him long, winding her hands out of his grasp, wrapping her arms around his neck, and pulling him closer to him. "Cannot Sober Susanna be Seductive Susanna?" she asked.

"Oh, God, yes. The things I want to do to you . . ." He groaned as he pulled away. He turned his head and looked away, struggling to catch his breath.

She placed a hand on each side of his face and pulled his face back to hers.

"Ian, do you think you are the only one affected by . . . whatever we have here?" she asked softly. "Do you think me immune to how you make me feel?"

He shook his head, not sure how to explain what he was feeling. "You, Susanna, are so good, so much better than I. You were right to scold me for tempting your social ruin for my own pleasures. I was irresponsible and rash. This . . . whatever it is, cannot go on."

She smirked at him. "You do not get to make those decisions for me, Ian."

"But you said—"

"I said do not act so brazenly in public," she cut him off. "Have I complained about how we behave when we are alone?"

"Well, not exactly," Ian realized.

She nodded. "I do not want you to ruin me in front of two hundred people at a ball, which has not changed. But Ian, I like you. I enjoy being around you. I do not want to lose you."

He sighed and leaned into her warmth. She wrapped her arms around his head, cradling him as he wound his arms around her.

"I do not want to lose you, either," he muttered after a few long moments of him just sitting wrapped in her embrace, content and warm in her comfort. He felt raw, exposed.

Something about this woman made him drop all pretense and she saw more in him than he had ever shared with anyone.

"Then stop trying to break apart our friendship," she said softly.

He straightened, looking into her bright blue eyes and her loving face. "I cannot give you what you want from me, Susanna."

She simply looked at him, her gaze taking in every inch of his face. After a long moment, she said, "You say you cannot offer me what I want, but how can you be certain of what I want? What if—for now—all I want is your friendship, and your companionship? What if all I want is you without promises of obligation?"

He shook his head. "That's basically the opposite of what a lovely, young woman of marriageable age should want, Susanna."

She shrugged. "You'd be surprised to learn how progressive a marriageable-aged young woman I can be."

He chuckled. "What about Riverton?"

She shrugged again. "You said you wanted me as bait for something, which I assume is still current?"

He nodded, though it pained him to admit he needed her to continue her relationship with the viscount, even if it was just for show.

"Then I shall continue on as before," she concluded. "Though I have no intention of marrying him, even if your investigations turn up nothing."

"Please do not hold out for me, darling," he said softly, brushing a wisp of hair from her face. "You cannot put your life on hold me for me."

She shook her head. "Ian Carlisle, you absurd man, without you my life cannot go forward. I am simply waiting for you to catch up."

There was no doubt; he was definitely in love with this woman.

Staring into her blue eyes, he could see the life he should have. A caring wife at his side, raising children in the country, fishing and horseback riding. Bringing up another Lord Westcott, doing it right this time, without all the mental baggage his father had dumped upon him. He could see himself sitting in Parliament, managing his family estates and living a life out of the shadows and schemes of the criminals of the world. Living life with the good and the wonderful away from the misery and the depravity.

It almost brought him to tears. For the first time since he ran away from home and joined the Army, he wanted more. He wanted more than his nomad existence, he wanted more than dipping into the immoral and illegalities, no more to bear witness to what the scum of humanity could do to one another.

"My darling, Susanna," he said softly, trying to maintain his even tone, lest she see how broken he truly was—how her declaration had shaken him. "I do not deserve you."

She nodded. "Yes, you do, Ian."

He sighed and looked down. "There is a chapter in my life I must close before I can fathom any sort of normalcy, and I cannot know how long that will take. It could be weeks, it could be years. But it must be concluded."

"Am I to understand apprehending Riverton in some crime will aid in concluding this chapter?" she asked, and he nodded slowly. "Well, you have my assistance should you require it, and you have my support."

"Do I have your patience?" he asked her.

"Without question," she replied. He sighed again shaking his head.

"I do not want to pull you into this," he said softly. "You deserve much better than me."

"Let me decide what I do and do not deserve," she chided. She leaned up to kiss him again, her soft kiss deepening into something more as he leaned into her. Raw with emotion, he pressed himself into her, pinning her against the sofa once more.

"Last chance to rejoin the party," he warned, grazing kisses along her jaw.

"Oh, I have no intention of returning just yet," she replied breathlessly.

"Good," he murmured, capturing her mouth again. "I believe I am in need of payment."

Perhaps it was the intoxicating effect of his kiss, but Susanna wasn't sure she had heard him correctly. She blinked at him, eyes heavy and lazy. He was such a handsome man.

"Payment?" she murmured. "For what?"

"Three favors, to be exact," he replied, pulling her around the sofa and sitting her down.

He sat beside her and captured her mouth with his. The intensity quickly escalated and she matched him as best as she could, drawing on everything she had learned from him. She loved this man—Lord help her—and she wanted to show him how deep her feelings went.

He held up three fingers. "For Miss Barfield, Miss Rosemary, and Miss Annabelle. You owe me, remember?"

Susanna nodded, biting her lip, remembering his words from the other night. "Dare I ask how you expect to be repaid?"

He grinned at her, his eyes dancing with arousal, and he leaned over to kiss her, long and intoxicating. Ian tugged on the top hem of her gown, loosened from his nimble fingers, and her breast spilled out into his hand. His mouth descended onto her nipple, taking her fully into his mouth, his warm hand massaging as he suckled her.

Her breath caught in her throat and she let out a breathless moan. Sensation and fire seemed to race from where he ravished her, down her spine, pooling with rising intensity at her most private spot.

Ian released her breast and kissed his way back to her mouth, over the curve of her breast, along her collarbone, up the sensitive skin of her neck. She tilted her head back, giving him access to the delicate flesh under her jaw before he recaptured her mouth, pummeling her with his tongue. He pulled away, leaving her to catch her breath, her lips wet and raw.

"First," he whispered, cupping her breast, his thumb lazily rubbing past her nipple. "I am going to touch you, stroke you in a way that will make you cry out." He kissed her again, running his hand down her gown, tugging the hem up until it collected in her lap. Slowly, palming her pale thighs as he went, his hand deliberately crept up to the apex between her legs, leaving strings of fire in its wake. Just as he had promised, he cupped her soft mound, slipping one finger inside of her, and she gasped.

"Oh, Ian," she said breathlessly, her eyes popping open in shock and dismay. Was such a thing even done? Apparently it was. He stroked her gently, back and forth, first one finger, then two, her breath catching with each intrusion.

"Secondly," he whispered, his teeth on the lobe of her ear. "I am going to kiss you, Susanna, and it is going to shock you. But you must trust me, love."

She nodded numbly. "Is there is a third? I am not sure I can handle much more, Ian. I feel like I am about to burst into flames."

His breath was hot on her neck as his teeth nipped the sensitive flesh. He sank off the sofa and onto his knees, pushing her knees apart.

"Ian, this seems most improper," Susanna whispered, pulling her nails through his hair, but allowing him access.

"It is, in fact, most improper, love," he said. "But you quite like it."

"I really do," she replied, her voice a harsh whisper, her blue eyes locked onto his, green swirling with grey in a passionate storm. She could feel the cool air between her thighs, knowing she was completely exposed to him, but dared not look away from his gaze. The moment she did she would lose all nerve; she would be too embarrassed. But the way he looked at her, like an animal hungry for its dinner, it did things inside her, made her feel beautiful and wanton and daring. She leaned back slightly, her knees falling further apart. His eyes glowed in appreciation.

"Thirdly, Susanna, you must keep your eyes open and watch for any intruders," he said.

"You want me to watch *what*?" she asked, brows pulling together.

"Watch your party outside," he said hotly. "They cannot see us, but you can see them. I want you to watch everyone, knowing that you are steps away from them, engaged in something so scandalous, so illicit, and right under their noses. I want you to see everyone else, while I have you exposed to them and they do not even know it."

She was shocked to say the least, but seeing everyone outside somehow made what they were doing more forbidden, and yet, more exciting that they were doing it with everyone in full view.

"What are you going to do?" she asked.

"I am going to kiss you," he replied. Looking at him, she wondered what he meant until he looked pointedly at the apex of her thighs and she felt a blush rush down from her face and puddle in the spot he was looking at.

"Do it," she whispered. "Before I lose my nerve."

Ian chuckled, ducking his head under the hem of her dress.

The contact with his tongue was like nothing she had ever felt before. Susanna rolled her head back against the cushion, a moan escaping her lips. Her eyes flitted shut, but she snapped them back open, remembering the people outside. Any minute someone could get a wild idea and walk up to the glass windows and peek inside. The windows were mirrored, but not completely opaque; goodness, what would they think if they saw her and Ian engaged in this?

Susanna no longer cared. About any of it. It all seemed so silly and insignificant compared with what Ian was doing to her, what he was making her feel. Every fiber in her tingled in anticipation, in pleasure. Each stroke of his tongue brought her deeper and deeper under, she could feel her pulse racing—feel the heat and the burn threaten to engulf her. He devoured her, her thighs and knees draped over his shoulders, his hands hot against her hips, pulling her closer to him. Her toes curled with desire as he savored her, and she dutifully kept her eyes open the whole time, watching the guests of her charity event as they mingled and laughed, no inclination that something so scandalous was happening just on the other side of the glass.

What would she do if they could see her? Part of her was terrified of someone coming in and noticing them, but another part of her, deep down in the pools of pleasure Ian was arousing, wanted them all to see her. She wanted them all to see what she truly was, know her for all her dark and sinful glory and dare the *ton* to not accept her. She almost wanted to be discovered in such a compromising position so she could throw their rules of propriety in their faces.

Waves of pleasure washed over her, the dam breaking inside, and she let out a sultry moan, her eyes rolling shut, every muscle in her body clenching and pulsing with radiating sensations of heaven. She embraced it, letting each wave wash over her as it pulled her farther and farther from herself.

Ian removed himself from her skirts, righting her clothing to its original place. He sat beside her on the sofa, grinning at her from ear-to-ear, quite proud of himself, it seemed.

"Oh, goodness, Ian, why must you make such a wanton woman of me?" she asked, closing her eyes as she floated back down to earth.

"Darling, I merely bring out the parts you are so careful to hide from everyone," he said softly, kissing her gently, her lips raw from their passionate kisses. "Much like you do to me."

She smiled at him lazily, resting her forehead against his as she steadied her breath. "I have to return to the party. I've been gone for too long."

"Not as long as you would think," he replied, checking his pocket watch. "Half an hour, perhaps. I went as quickly as I could manage, you know, in respect to your delicate sensibilities."

Susanna laughed. "Oh, thanks for the charity!"

He stood and pulled her to her feet, her legs feeling weak, but she was able to walk more nimbly than she had thought she would be able to. How was she supposed to go back to the party after all this had happened? How was she to look at anyone in the eye, knowing she had just done something so deliciously scandalous right under their noses? She suspected that was part of the reason Ian made her watch the party, so she never forgot exactly where she was, the act burned into her memory.

"Speaking of charity," he said as she found her bonnet. She

untied the ribbons and pulled it onto her head. Turning towards him, he assisted her with her ribbons. "I was surprised to find your name on the originating foundation papers of the Lady Day Foundation, yet no mention of anyone named Lady Day."

Susanna shrugged. "I told you I was on the board of trustees."

"Yes, but you are the only name on the foundation documents and no one seems to know who Lady Day is."

Susanna shrugged. "The foundation is breaking no law by having my name on the originating documents."

"I never said you were," he replied. "Just that it was curious."

"Not everything is a riddle for you to solve," Susanna chided. "Do not go looking for a problem where there is none."

"Very well," he said, but she doubted he had any intentions of dropping it.

She made her way through the maze of furniture. "I do not know why you were poking about in my charity's foundation documents, but could you please not mention what you discovered to anyone, particularly my brother?"

"He does not know your full involvement in the charity?"

Susanna shook her head. "Andrew is a bit over protective and has been known to overreact easily to non-issues. He knows I am on the board, he just does not know my involvement in its founding."

"I assure you I will not say a word to anyone," Ian told her. "Though it is quite admirable for you to take on such a heavy role alone."

"Not such a silly, little girl, am I?" she teased and moved around a table.

He grabbed her hand as she stepped away, squeezing it. "You were never a silly girl, Susanna," he apologized sincerely. "I am sorry I ever said that."

She squeezed his hand before stepping closer and rose onto her toes and kissed him. She could still taste herself on his lips and it was oddly arousing.

"Your apology is accepted," she said as she pulled away. "So please stop apologizing. Now I am going to exit first; you should wait a bit or go through the house to the side entrance where the auction tables are set up. I can give you directions through the house."

He chuckled. "I can manage, thank you."

"And, um, you should wipe your face off," she said, blushing. "You taste like me."

He winked at her. "You taste wonderful, Susanna."

She rolled her eyes; she truly did love the scandalous things he said to her. She squeezed his hand again and winked before stepping outside into the bright early afternoon sun.

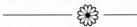

Ian took a deep, calming breath. Their interlude in the library had not gone at all how he expected it. For the better, he supposed, but still it did not ease his worry for her. It did ignite something inside him, and, for the first time in an extremely long time, he felt he had something to protect—something to fight for. And their interlude on the sofa had almost turned into full-fledged deflowering; had he not heard the laughter from outside to pull him back to his senses, it is clear what would have occurred. The moment she came, the noise she had made, had almost caused him to throw all caution to the wind and he would have entered her then. That sound that escaped her would haunt him forever. He longed to cause her to make that sound again.

Even now, he was hard with arousal and incompletion, but there wasn't much he could do about it. She was right about him dangling her virtue over the edge of a cliff, but he seemed to lose all sense when she was around. She pulled something out of him, some part of him he had forgotten existed, and, damnit, he loved her all the more for it.

He waited a few moments before slipping out the door, taking care to wipe down his face before he left, following close to the perimeter of the house towards where the items for auction were set up along tables. Protected from the sunlight and late summer heat, the tables brimming with donated auction items were underneath wide, white tent tops. He made his way through the items— an afternoon of boxing with Gentleman Jackson, a week at a house in Bath, a basket of perfume from France, and more, each with its own card and handwritten lines for each person's donation.

A watercolor in a thin, black frame caught his eye, the colors washed across the canvas in a marriage of skill and imagination. It was a small painting, about the length of Ian's forearm.

The wash of browns and blues, of a young boy standing alone, his clothes ragged and worn. His expression was sad, haunted, lost. He reminded Ian of someone, something, but he was not quite sure what.

"She truly is talented," the Duchess of Bradstone said, coming to stand beside him. He glanced at her; he had not noticed her in the tent, which was odd, as he was usually much more observant. The duchess nodded towards the painting.

"It is unlike anything I've ever seen before," he said quietly. "You know the artist?"

She nodded. "You do, too."

"Susanna painted this?" Ian asked, looking back at the painting with more appreciation. "I had no idea she could paint like this."

"Do not tell her I told you," the duchess replied. "She does not like anyone knowing she has such a talent."

"Whyever not?"

The duchess shrugged. "I am not certain of her reasoning. Some things people choose to keep to themselves." She eyed him curiously before continuing. "I take it you and Susanna know what you are doing?"

He blinked at her and glanced around, though no one was in ear shot. "I saw you come back out of the back library," she admitted.

"Your grace, you have the eyes of a hawk," he said, though it wasn't exactly a compliment.

"I have the eyes and experience of someone who has had to deal with her fair share of scandal and scrutiny," she replied shrewdly. "I notice more than most people because I am overly aware of what people around me are saying and doing. Call it a skill I acquired during my days as a social outcast."

He glanced at her again and realized he did not know enough about her past to judge her so harshly. "I understand your concern for your sister-in-law, I simply ask that you trust Susanna's judgment."

"One's judgment is severely impaired when one is in love," Clara replied.

Ian did not bother to correct the duchess, much to his chagrin. It terrified him to be in love with Susanna, for the exact reason her grace had just stated. His fear for her safety would overtake his rationality. Her proximity to Riverton was troubling, but it was a necessary risk.

Convicting Riverton and solving his sister's murder would give him the closure he needed to move on with his life.

"I ask you to trust me to do what is best for Susanna and her ultimate happiness," he amended. "I would never hurt her."

The duchess nodded. "Not intentionally, but Susanna has a tendency to care too much. She finds a wounded animal and she nurses past survival. She wants those she loves to thrive. She gives so much of herself to others that sometimes she does not realize she needs the same from someone else."

"Do you think I do not realize this?" Ian asked, fully turning towards the duchess. "She will not allow me to walk away from her. I've tried to tell her I am not good for her."

"You also cannot tell Susanna what to do," Clara replied. "It's a Macalister trait, I am afraid. They're all pig-headed and stubborn to a fault. But they are good and they see the good, Susanna the most of them all. Each of them has a need to rescue those around them. If she has chosen you, then there is nothing you can do about it. If she thinks you are worthy, she will nurse you back to health until you are better than you ever were."

"You sound like you are speaking from experience," he observed.

She shrugged. "Susanna has been a dear friend these past few months. She has done more for me in five months than my own family did for me my entire life. Whatever wounds you have from your past, Susanna will make you whole again. You just have to be willing to accept her love."

He turned away from the duchess and looked back at the painting. The young boy, lost and tattered. He realized why it looked familiar; it reminded him of himself.

Ian nodded. "I may not know what I am doing in regards to Lady Susanna," he admitted, looking at the duchess. "But I assure you I intend to get there. In the meantime, Susanna has enough faith and patience for both of us, and I hope that will be enough."

"If there is one thing I have learned from my involvement with this family, they have the ability to love very deeply," the duchess replied. "And if they want something strongly enough, there isn't anything that will prevent that from happening."

He nodded again. Slipping the pen from the slip, he wrote his name on the auction card and an absurd amount of money on the bid line. He was in love with Susanna, that much he knew, and it terrified him. Now he simply had to have enough faith and belief in her that she would be on the other side waiting for him when he was ready to open his life to her.

Trust in Susanna. Seemed easy enough.

Chapter Thirteen

It wasn't often all five of Ian's counterparts were in England at the same time, and it seemed their superiors wanted to take advantage of the rare occasion.

Ian answered the summons to a private residence on Whitehall Place. It was raining when he arrived, a stark contrast to the bright sunshine during the Lady Day Benefit Brunch the morning before. Ian sat in his carriage, glancing up at the house as his driver stepped down and opened the carriage door. Whitehall Place was a row of town homes—white stone fronts and black gates—each one identical to the one beside it.

"Westcott," called a man approaching the house. Ian squinted through the drizzle to see Mayne. He tipped his hat before they both hurried inside the residence.

Ian and Mayne were shown to a first floor study where they were relieved of their hats and overcoats. Reggie and Lord Eric stood along the window watching the street below.

"Anything interesting?" Ian asked, peeking out the window to the street below. There seemed nothing outwardly interesting, simply the street along the back of the house with an entrance to the back courtyard. "What street is that?"

"Nothing of interest, simply watching the rain as it comes down," Reggie replied with a shrug. "That's Great Scotland Yard." He turned with a glance at Ian before moving away from the window. Lord Eric gave Ian a shrug and followed Reggie to a settee.

Ian glanced again at the rain-soaked street, decided it held no interest to him and turned away from the window.

Moments later, two more men were ushered into the room, Mr. Simon White and Lord Oliver Gordon, the newly inherited Earl of Haslett. Ian was familiar with each of these men, though he did not work closely with any of them except for Mayne.

Over a decade prior, on the advice of the then Major General Arthur Wellesley, the Home Secretary at the time, Lord Pelham, had made a case to King George, who agreed to the need of some form of accountability within the ranks of the military. A small, experimental task force was formed consisting of two men who were charged with investigating corruption, disturbances, and crime within the branches of His Majesty's military.

Weeks after Ian had run off to join the Army, and after only three incidents in which he actually discharged his weapon, Ian had been plucked from the battlefield and assigned to this experimental task force. Ian and Mayne were the original founding members of their small troupe, and Ian wasn't even sure they had an official name or title, even after over a decade of work. Occasionally he heard them referred to as Investigating Officers, but it wasn't something he used to describe their jobs within the Home Office. As the years and wars went on, four more men were added, and their jurisdiction widened. They investigated everything from crimes within the military, political corruption, patricide, serial homicide, larceny, and kidnapping. They operated in teams of two, at home and abroad, handling the problems that were too challenging for local magistrate to sort out on their own. Over a decade later, their little experiment seemed a successful one, though Ian was not sure what the nature of their future was.

Lord Sidmouth, the current Home Secretary, entered with a man Ian did not recognize. He was average height with golden blond hair and bright, intelligent eyes. The presence of the Home Secretary was an interesting development as well. Ian did not have time to ponder it further, as a footman entered, followed by his grace, the Duke of Leeds, their reporting superior. Ian stood, along with the other seven men in the room as the duke came into the office.

"Thank you, gentlemen," his grace said, taking a seat behind the large oak desk, a stack of papers in his hands. Ian and the other seven men took their seats on nearby couches, settees, and arm chairs, all conveniently arranged to face the desk.

"This is Mr. Robert Peel," the Duke of Leeds said, gesturing to the newcomer seated beside the Home Secretary. "Lord Sidmouth will explain more about his presence after we have our reviews. White, why do not you begin?"

And so began the process of going through each of their cases, detail by detail, each offering up ideas and opinions, questions and elucidations. It was a room full of clever, intelligent men who all thrived on one thing: the challenge of a good mystery. It was a meeting that normally took place once a month or so, when two teams were near each other for conference. It was a way to share information, get a fresh pair of eyes on a troubling case, and share knowledge and intelligence of the criminal underworld.

A scribe sat in the corner and transcribed their entire conversation. The notations were later copied, sent to this address—his grace's mother's primary residence—with a second copy sent to the Home Office. The Duke of Leeds was their reporting superior, though the phrase was used loosely. As the brother-in-law to their creator, Lord Pelham, Leeds had been engaged as a personal favor to the former Home Secretary to lead up their task force. Leeds had proven a worthy wrangler and stayed the course, even after

Lord Pelham ended his term.

Ian listened to his counterparts run through their information—Mayne took extensive notes but Ian committed most of it to memory. Usually this lengthy interview was the highlight of his month, the sharing of information, misplaced pieces of the puzzle all in one place to form a whole picture. But something was missing this month, something had changed. He did not have to wonder what it was, though he wasn't sure if his blue-eyed minx was the agent for this change, or just the instigator. Somehow all this seemed rather uninteresting.

Mayne launched into an explanation of their caseload and recently closed cases, and Ian added details along the way, mostly allowing his associate to do the talking. The inclusion of the Home Secretary, who was the man they ultimately reported to, was curious, as was the enigmatic Mr. Robert Peel.

It took an hour for the three sets of investigators to lay out all their information, but at last Mayne wrapped up his and Ian's work, snapping the massive leather-bound folder with a click of the spine.

Leeds took off his spectacles and rubbed at the bridge of his nose. "As you can see, we are joined by the Home Secretary, Lord Sidmouth. I will let him explain his presence here."

Lord Sidmouth stood, which was odd, but Ian ignored it.

"Gentlemen. This will be brief, as I know we have already been here long enough. I am joined this evening by Mr. Robert Peel, the chief secretary in Dublin," the Home Secretary explained. "He has some interesting ideas regarding the need for a specialist police force. Mr. Peel, the floor is yours."

"Gentleman," Mr. Peel said, standing up. "We are nearing a time when the need for an organized police force is paramount. You have spoken for over an hour on numerous cases involving the general public, and the public does not know you are doing this service for them. Think what could be accomplished with an organized, ethical police force, essentially citizens in uniform where the police stand as an effective figure of authority. Accountability is key, and the police are the public and the public are the police. The work this task force has done in the past decade is extraordinary."

"The people do not want a police force," Mr. White commented when Mr. Peel paused. "The Bow Street Runners seem sufficient enough."

"If they were sufficient, we would not be here," Ian interjected. The idea of an ethical police force was a thought provoking idea—could it be done?

Mr. Peel was nodding. "We are working on passing an act in Ireland that will set up Irish constables, and I believe this is something we can accomplish in England as well. This task force is part of the groundwork for a larger benefit to come. My presence here today is to ask for your assistance when that day comes."

"What sort of assistance?" Lord Haslett asked, folding his arms across his chest. "Consulting, mostly," Mr. Peel replied. "In Ireland, we are essentially starting from scratch, though the Prefecture of Police of Paris has the best organized police force and is an excellent model to work from. But in England, any form of organization resembling French government is quite unpopular."

"I quite agree," Lord Eric added. "During a time of war, people are less likely to focus on problems in the home state. This is an intriguing idea and I'd be happy to help in any way I can. Though I haven't been doing this as long as Westcott and Mayne have." All the eyes turned to Ian and his partner.

"Yes, I agree the idea is fascinating and I hope it will someday come to pass in London," Ian replied. "The work we do as six could easily be done by many more, if properly taught."

"Thank you for your time tonight, gentlemen," Mr. Peel said. "It was my desire to give you sufficient notice should the organization you work for be altered in the coming years."

Years. Mr. Peel had uttered such a simple and unsuspecting word, but it startled Ian. Did he want to continue doing this for *years*? He had already given ten years to this service, for Crown and

Country and whoever else. But years? Plural?

This was the problem with staying in one place for too long, Ian decided, realizing there was good reason he had never remained stationary. One became comfortable, complacent, relying on certain things and comforts. These additions made him see where the other aspects of his life were lacking. He enjoyed the work, but events of the past two weeks had made him realize something—it was about time he stopped playing at life and grew up.

It was bright and sunny on Sunday afternoon but there was little warmth in the air. Since Sunday was an apt day for rest, the ladies of Macalister House were taking full advantage of such a crisp day. The music room had perfect light for Susanna's watercolors and she was set up there while her two relations joined her in silence.

Norah sat with her nose in a book, eating an apple, her legs draped comfortably, but in a very unladylike way, over the side of the chair. Clara was also engrossed in a book, comfortable on the lounger settee, her legs tucked up under her.

This was how Ian found them—comfortable, no airs, and completely unaware he had been standing in the room for five minutes.

Well, almost unaware. Susanna, of course, had spotted him the moment he walked into the room unannounced. Howards, the butler, had taken a liking to him and sent him up on his own, and although he made no noise upon entering, Susanna's eyes snapped to his the moment he stepped into the room.

"Isn't my interpretation of the afternoon garden divine?" Susanna asked, winking at Ian. "Mmm-hmm," Clara agreed and turned the page.

Susanna giggled. She dipped her brush into the blue and added the highlight to the watercolored hem of Norah's gown. He was certain Norah was unaware that Susanna's watercolor interpretation of the afternoon garden included Norah's ankles propped up on a chair.

Ian paused a moment to take in the sight of Susanna painting in the sunlight. She was beautiful. The beams of light caught her soft yellow morning dress, her hair was pulled to the side in a loose chignon. He glanced at the other two women, realizing it was the most comfortable, relaxed, and unceremonious he had ever seen them. The duchess even had her hair down around her shoulders. Suddenly he felt like he was intruding on something he should not see.

Susanna seemed to sense his panic and grabbed his hand.

"Stay for a few moments," she said. "You came here for a reason, did you not?"

"Mmmm-hmmm," Clara murmured and turned another page.

"Clara dear, will you look at this?" Susanna said, trying to get her sister-in-law's attention.

"In a moment," the duchess replied.

"Lord Westcott is here," Susanna said bluntly.

"Of course," Norah said absently, flipping a page.

"Lovely," Clara agreed.

Susanna looked up at Ian and shrugged. "They have no idea you are even here."

"Perhaps it should stay that way," he replied. The deep timbre of his voice, something different than what the duchess and Norah had expected to hear, pulled them both out of their books long enough to realize his presence.

"Oh!" the duchess gasped. "Goodness, Westcott, how long have you been there?"

"Susanna!" Norah exclaimed, dropping her apple on the floor.

"I tried to tell you he was here," Susanna said, looking back at her painting and frowning. "Well, you moved, so now it is ruined."

"What is ruined?" Clara asked, sitting up in the chair.

"Are you painting me again?" Norah demanded, jumping up from the couch to see her painting.

"Not you, just your feet," Susanna replied cheekily, waving her paintbrush at her sister dismissively.

"Susanna!" Norah cried, snatching the canvas off the easel.

"It really is quite good," Ian offered. Norah glared at him.

"Of course it is good, that's the problem," she snapped.

"Oh, Norah, there is no reason to be rude," Clara scolded.

"You would be if she painted your feet and ankles!" Norah said, flipping the painting around. The paint wasn't completely dry just yet and the movement had started to smear the colors.

Clara sighed. "Susanna, could you have painted something else?"

"I could have," Susanna agreed with a shrug, as if she had not considered it. "But you have such lovely feet, Norah. Perhaps we will save it for your future husband." She glanced wickedly up at Ian. He chuckled at the absurdity of the argument, and the fact that he knew Susanna had painted her sister's feet just to annoy her.

"Oh, no, this is going out with the rubbish," Norah said, stomping away barefooted.

"Some ruffian will find it while going through the rubbish," Ian suggested. "Then some strange man could have your painted feet hanging on the inside of his deplorable dwelling."

Norah turned and glared at him. "Then I will burn it."

Susanna giggled at her sister's dramatics.

"Lord Westcott, what can we help you with?" the duchess asked him after Norah had quit the room.

"Ah, might I have a moment alone with Lady Susanna?" he asked pleadingly. "Literally, just a brief moment."

Clara paused and shot a sideways glance at her book before nodding. She rose from the lounger and abandoned the room, her book tucked under her arm.

Susanna spun around to look at him. "Out with it."

"It is nothing bad, Susanna," he said cautiously. "At least I hope not. I've come to warn you about an impending invitation."

He paused and she looked at him expectedly. "Go on."

Ian swallowed and ran his hand through his hair. "Based on our conversation the other night, it was implied you wanted to get to know me better, to know more of my life. Well, my aunt is hosting a small dinner party and I suggested she invite their graces and yourself."

Susanna's eyebrows pulled together and she thought for a moment. "Your aunt is inviting us to a dinner party?"

He nodded. "She is my mother's baby sister and Lord Bexley's mother. It will be loud and busy, there are so many of them and I do not go over very often because sometimes they are all just too much to handle. But they are family, and well . . . they dine as a family so the younger cousins will be there as well, so I apologize in advance for their behavior. Please, if you do not want to subject yourself to that, I completely understand. She will not be offended if you decline."

Susanna stood and kissed his cheek sweetly. "I would be honored to attend."

"Really?" he asked, and a wave of relief rushed through him. "There really are a lot of them."

Susanna laughed. "Ian, I am one of ten siblings. I am accustomed to large families."

He grinned at her. "Yes, I suppose you are correct."

"Thank you for including me in the invitation," she said, leaning up to place a soft kiss on his lips. The contact was mesmerizing. "I will relay the forewarning to Clara."

"Good idea," he murmured, leaning into her for a deeper kiss, one she was eager to return. His arm wound around her and she molded into him, her body fitting perfectly in his embrace. It wasn't a hungry kiss, but a passionate one, both admitting something to the other.

"*Ahem!*"

Ian took a hasty step away from Susanna. Clara was standing in the doorway, looking slightly amused.

"Uh, your grace, we, uh," Ian stammered, a stupid grin spreading across his face. Susanna chuckled, her face turning pink.

Clara stood, a knowing smirk on her face. "Susanna, you have a gentleman caller."

Susanna glanced at Ian. "Um, yes, I can see that, Clara."

Clara stared at her pointedly. "No, you have *another* caller, downstairs. He arrived as I was sitting on the bottom steps reading my book. I offered to see if you were presentable."

Susanna's face fell. "Riverton is downstairs?"

"Not downstairs anymore," came Riverton's voice from the hall. Susanna looked at Ian in a panic and Ian dropped to his knees, effectively hidden behind the couch, yet hiding nonetheless.

Well, this should be interesting, Ian thought.

Susanna stepped quickly around the couch, reaching the middle of the room by the time Riverton entered the room.

"Lord Riverton," Susanna managed with little squeak in her voice and dipped into a small curtsy. "It is lovely to see you."

"You look lovely," Riverton said, bowing and kissing her bare knuckles. "Though you are a bit flushed. Are you well?"

Susanna nodded a bit too vigorously. "I was just painting. In the sunlight. Too much sunlight, perhaps." She glanced at the window and realized Ian's reflection was clear in the pane of glass. "Uh, let us move further into the shade of the room," she said brightly, linking her arm in the viscount's and practically pulled him to the darker corner of the room.

Clara looked alarmed but did her best to hide it. She glanced at the window and promptly hurried over to close the curtains.

"Oh yes, my lord, too much sunlight adds an unbecoming flush to a young lady's cheeks," the duchess announced. "Sun-kissed is better left as an expression than a facial feature."

Susanna nodded exuberantly and sat on the couch closest to the door, practically pulling Riverton down with her. "Now, to what do we owe the pleasure of this visit?"

Riverton glanced between Susanna and her sister-in-law. "I wished to take you on a ride through the park," he replied slowly. "But if you are too worn from your time in the sun—"

"Noooo, not at all!" Susanna exclaimed, jumping up. "A ride through the park sounds lovely! Allow me to fetch my bonnet and cloak and I will meet you in the foyer?"

Riverton stood slowly after her and nodded apprehensively. "Is everything alright?"

Susanna could see their behavior was completely amiss, and that she had best cover her tracks quickly. "Simply the sun," she replied. "And your surprise visit, of course. I did not expect to see you today and your appearance has me quite . . . elated."

A strange bark came from the other side of the room and both Susanna and Riverton turned to look at the duchess, who was quickly coughing loudly.

"I do beg your pardon, something just was not agreeing with me," Clara coughed. "Perhaps I shall have a lie down while you are out."

Susanna smiled as genuinely as she could, trying to muster enough control to make it out of the house and through an hour in the park with Riverton.

"I will just fetch my things," she said stepping towards the door. "You will wait for me in the foyer?"

Riverton glanced at Clara again before nodding. "Yes, of course."

Slowly and deliberately, Susanna stepped towards the door, Riverton followed her, still looking at her as though she had sprouted a second head. She hurried up the stairs and into her rooms, grabbing the first bonnet and cloak she saw, and was back down the stairs in seconds.

The first floor landing was empty, sans an open door and an alarmed looking duchess. "Is he gone?" Susanna asked in a harsh whisper.

"Which one?" Clara asked pointedly.

"Quite right," Susanna said, pulling her cloak around her.

"Riverton has gone downstairs," Clara replied. "I will stay to make sure you are gone before Westcott is permitted to leave."

Susanna nodded. "Thank you, Clara dear, and I am very sorry about this." She kissed her sister-in-law on the cheek before hurrying down the stairs.

She smiled brightly at Riverton, accepting his arm as soon as she reached the bottom stair.

"Shall we be off?" she asked him. "I am eager for some fresh air."

Riverton led her outside and into his high-pitched phaeton, not quite as flashy as Ian's but still suitable. Her maid followed onto the back perch as Riverton helped Susanna up onto the top seat. She gave a worried glance up to the music room, though there was no one in the window to see it, thanks goodness. The entire affair had been a close call—she shuddered to think what would have happened had Riverton learned of Westcott's presence in the room.

She smiled falsely at him, wrapping her cloak around her and hoping she could make it through the trip around the park, and that Ian would be gone by the time she returned.

Ian had been crouched down for so long his knees had begun to throb.

He could hear the voices in the hallway, Susanna's sweet endearing tone trying to hurry her would-be fiancé out of the door so he could leave the house safely. He wasn't sure what was worse, having to let Susanna leave with that oaf or sit here and listen to her flirt her way out of the situation.

"I say, Clara, why are you standing in the doorway?" came Andrew's voice.

"Andrew, shush, not yet!" the duchess replied in a thick whisper.

"Why are we whispering?" he asked in a whisper.

The heavy door echoed as it closed in the front hall, and a few moments later the sounds of horse hooves were heard departing the front driveway and down the street.

"Clara, what on earth—"

"My lord, please come out now," Clara called, interrupting her husband. Reluctantly, Ian stood up, his knees protesting violently.

"Westcott, what are you doing behind the couch?" Bradstone asked, alarmed. "Clara, what is going on?"

"It is just too complicated," Clara replied shaking her head.

"And just as absurd," Ian finished.

The duke was not pleased. Stomping into the room, he practically shouted, "I demand to know what you are doing hiding in my home!"

"Oh Andrew, calm down," Clara said, placing her hand on his arm. "He was here to see Susanna, we were all in the room, do not worry, or for the most part we were." She frowned but continued. "Anyway, Riverton stopped by unexpectedly and I came to tell Susanna he was here—"

"I thought you were in the room with them," the duke asked.

"Yes, mostly," Clara replied and continued as though he had not interrupted. "And instead of waiting in the foyer downstairs like a proper gentleman, Riverton marched up the stairs and the poor earl had no other choice than to duck behind the couch."

The duke looked between his wife and Ian and Ian couldn't tell if he was annoyed or just did not care anymore.

Andrew shook his head. "My life used to be less complicated," he muttered and left the room.

"I suggest you leave as well," Clara said to Ian and he could not agree more.

"I came to tell Susanna to expect an invitation from my aunt for a dinner party," Ian explained quickly as he stepped towards the door. "For yourself, his grace, and Susanna. Long story, but my aunt would be pleased if you would accept."

"Yes, of course," she said, walking him down the stairs.

"And thank you, your grace, for your assistance," Ian said reaching the front door. He tipped his hat to the butler before hurrying out the door and into the afternoon chill, breathing away the anxiety from the near miss.

Susanna glanced behind her nervously, hoping Ian was able to make a clean getaway.

The man really needed to stop popping up everywhere. She allowed herself a glance at Riverton. He seemed a decent enough fellow, if a bit odd. At times he was good-natured, at others, he was on edge and skittish. Had she still been seriously considering him as a husband, his unstable nature might have been something she could overlook, but knowing Ian suspected him of some wrongdoing, she wondered if his personality flaws were truly an indication of something darker, even sinister. She wished Ian would just confide his suspicions. Though, if they turned out to be false and Susanna had ruined a perfectly agreeable gentleman because of Ian's ridiculousness, she would be furious.

The entire business was beginning to hurt her head. She wanted Ian; that much she knew. She wanted the convoluted man to be happy, but even more, she wanted to be happy with a man she could love. And even if he refused to see it, Ian was entirely lovable. She just hoped he did not make her wait for too long. She promised patience, but if Ian's suspicions of Riverton turned out to be false, and his investigations dragged on, her patience would truly be tested. Had she set her cap for a man who would not come up to snuff? Was she truly sabotaging an acceptable match, misplacing her trust in a man she hardly knew?

Though, she truly did not know that much about Riverton, either.

She stole another glance at him, noting that his dark, curly hair needed a trim as the curls had begun to grace the tops of his ears. He was pleasant enough to look at, though he did not inspire the same wanton thoughts that Ian could elicit with a mere wicked grin. Where she thought Riverton classically tall, dark, and handsome before, she now found his appearance rather lacking. His eyes, a dark brown she had once thought warm, now seemed rather dull and humorless.

What did she know about Riverton? She judged his age to be around thirty, though she truly could not know for certain. He said he had not attended Harrow, Eton, or any of the smaller boy's schools most frequented by aristocrats, so he had not attended school with any of her brothers. No one knew him until Oxford.

"My lord, I hope you do not find this too forward, but do you mind if I ask you a few questions?" she asked, deciding to do a little investigating herself.

He looked at her sideways before returning his gaze to the road. "What sort of questions?" he asked cautiously.

"Oh, nothing too embarrassing, I assure you," she laughed, smiling brightly at him, trying to put him at ease. "There are a few things I find myself wondering when we are apart, truly, silly, girlish queries. I simply wish to know more about you. If you would permit me?" She smiled sweetly at him, innocently blinking her long lashes at him.

He shifted uncomfortably, but nodded. "What would you like to know?"

"Well, to begin with, what is your given name?" she asked. She realized she truly did not know it.

He paused for a breath too long, hesitating to answer before replying, "My given name is Hanson Heubert Avenly. But I choose to be Riverton, therefore I am always Riverton."

She nodded, mentally noting the inflections in his tone and his choice of words. Most peers used their titles as their names, she knew, and men rarely used their Christian names, often even within their own families. It made it all the more scandalous when Ian had practically begged her to call him by his given name. But the way Riverton said he *chose* to be Riverton implied he had another option.

"My middle names are Charlotte and Judith," Susanna replied, hoping to sound as though it was a normal conversation. "Susanna Charlotte Judith Macalister; I am named after a great grandmother and an aunt, I believe."

"Hanson is Lady Riverton's maiden name," he replied. "My mother, that is. It's a common practice for a mother to give her son her maiden name as his first Christian name."

"My father's sister named her eldest son Macalister," Susanna added. "My cousin is now the Earl of Craven. How old are you?" she asked.

He did not hesitate this time. "Five and twenty."

Susanna blinked her surprise, but he did not see it. He was preoccupied with maneuvering the curricle through the traffic in the street, frowning at the owner of an overturned cart, yelling at another man dealing with a broken carriage wheel.

Three years earlier, when he had been engaged to Ian's sister, Riverton had been twenty-two, which was young for a lord to take a wife, at least in her experience. He had only been two years Lady Beth's senior. It wasn't the difference in ages that made her feel uneasy, though.

Three years ago he had chosen a debutant fresh from the schoolroom as his bride—a young, unsuspecting, innocent girl with few at home to protect her. Now he had chosen her with her gaggle of brothers to come to her aid. It was almost as if his prior bride-to-be had been too easy a conquest and he had been looking for a bit of a challenge.

She looked at him again and he was watching her. She smiled.

"Any other questions?" he asked.

She sighed wistfully. "Oh, so many. What was it like growing up with just your sisters? Was it peaceful? And your grandfather is the earl, correct? How old were you when your father passed? Where is your family seat? Where you mischievous as a child? Were you quiet?"

He looked at her in what could be perceived as alarm, which was a curious reaction. "Why would you think such things?" he asked.

Susanna shrugged nonchalantly. "No reason, really, just wanting to know more of you," she repeated. "I told you it was silly."

He looked forward again, his lips pursed. "I do not recall my behavior as a child," he said finally.

"You mentioned before you traveled abroad? Did you ride bulls in Spain, or fight maharajahs in India?"

"I did not fight maharajahs in India or ride bulls in Spain, but I visited the continent, France and Russia mostly."

"Even with the heavy fighting due to the war?" she asked.

He shrugged. "The past couple of years I have toured England extensively."

"Since Lady Beth's passing?"

He shifted uncomfortably. "Yes. It was very upsetting." His tone was even, bored almost.

Susanna blinked at him, expecting more declarations of love and admiration for his former fiancée. That was it? His lack of emotion was startling, especially since the first time Lady Beth had been mentioned, Riverton practically shook from agitation and fled her presence. When she had asked him about Ian's accusations of him, he had been almost in tears. Now he sat cold and collected.

He glanced sideways at her. "I hope the earl has not given you too much trouble over that. I understand he holds me accountable."

Susanna feinted confusion. "The earl?"

Riverton shifted again. "Westcott."

"Oh," she said and waved off the comment. "He has been no bother. I've completely put it from my mind."

"Good," he replied. "I would hate for him to taint your impression of me."

"I am not such a simpleton that I would allow someone else to form an opinion for me," she answered. "I assure you, my opinion of you is all my own."

He nodded at her. "Good. I would like to extend you an invitation of sorts. Lady Riverton—ah—Mother has come into town with the girls and would like to meet you. We wish to host you for a dinner party, with their graces of course."

Susanna wanted to laugh. Dinner parties seemed to be the theme of the day.

"It sounds like a lovely idea," she replied. Clara would get a laugh out of this predicament she found herself in, Susanna thought ruefully. How was she to explain that she was basically being courted by two men, one if unofficially, and yet she did not intend to wed the official suitor because the unofficial suitor deemed it hazardous?

Ian really owed her an explanation.

"They are all interested in meeting you," he continued, unaware of her inner turmoil. "Will the evening after tomorrow work into your schedule?"

She nodded, mentally filling in her social calendar. She had wanted some sort of amusement for the Little Season. She certainly got what she wished for.

Chapter Fourteen

The invitation from Ian's aunt came just as he had warned. Clara accepted with a flourish of her quill pen as soon as the invitation came. She and Susanna were both waiting in the foyer for the invitation, but that only quickened the haste of the reply, not the intent to attend.

Clara gave Susanna a wordless but pointed look as if to say, "Your foot is in it now," before treading the steps up the stairs.

The next evening Susanna stood in the front hall of Bexley House, the Earl of Bexley's mother smiling brightly at her. The Countess of Bexley's head was full of frizzy red hair—barely tamed by her coiffure—a round face, wide brown eyes, and a sweet, motherly voice. Her sincere smile made Susanna feel at ease immediately.

"What a treat for my son to invite some of his friends along for our family dinner," Lady Bexley was saying to them as they made their curtsies and bows.

"It was lovely to receive the invitation, Lady Bexley," Clara replied.

"Well, I should have done it ages ago, your grace," Lady Bexley said to her. "We had his grace around often enough as a lad, so this get together is extremely overdue."

Susanna glanced at her brother who bent to buss Lady Bexley on the cheek, as he did to their own relations. She had not realized her brother had much of a relationship with his friends' families.

"And this is the darling who has caught my nephew's eye," Lady Bexley said turning towards Susanna. Susanna smiled demurely and curtsied.

"It is a pleasure to meet you, Lady Bexley," Susanna said. "And I assure you his lordship and I are simply friends."

For now, a little voice inside her whispered conspiringly, but she trampled it down to where it was a manageable hum. Her feelings for Ian would not suffice here, though it was odd to be with his family and not have him present.

Lady Bexley chattered on about something but Susanna half-paid attention as she discreetly surveyed the room. There was a massing of about a half dozen people, all with bright red hair, much like Lady Bexley's. It truly was a family dinner and Susanna felt as though she was imposing, especially since her most important link to the family was not here. Bexley's older sister, Lady Manning, and her husband Viscount Manning were polite and amiable as she made her way around the room with Andrew and Clara. Lady Mirah Warren was a year younger than Susanna and she eyed Susanna peculiarly as they said hello to each other.

"Have you come to have a go at my brother?" Lady Mirah asked and Andrew coughed into his champagne. Clara turned her head against her husband's bicep and feigned interest in something on the other side of the room to hide her laughter.

Susanna smiled ruefully at the lady. "Not tonight," she answered sweetly.

Lord Rhett Warren, Bexley's younger brother, was entertaining two Warren cousins, Miss Sorrel Warren and Mr. Levant Warren, with some story involving a horse chase. The whole lot of them had bright, flaming red hair. The only people without red hair were Clara, Andrew, and Susanna.

Susanna glanced around, wishing for Ian's sandy locks to disrupt the sea of ginger. It was a Warren trait complete with ancient folklore to go along with their ancient title. If Susanna remembered correctly, it went back to William the Conqueror and the Battle of Hastings. A warlock swore to mark the Warren clan with the distinction of a traitor for turning against Harold II. The Warren ancestor took the side of and fought with William the Conqueror, which won him the earldom.

Ian was the exception to the Warren rule, though Susanna realized he wasn't truly a Warren as they were maternal relations. Still, the sweet, homely face of the countess bespoke more innkeeper's wife than lady of quality. The Warrens were a loud, rambunctious lot, and their teetering lack of elegance was part of their charm. They were good *ton* and a good family, and society just accepted them because the other option was to snub one of the oldest families in England. A title could take one a long way in this town, especially a title bestowed by William the Conqueror.

She felt Ian before she saw him. Turning her head, she spotted his reflection, standing in the doorway behind her. Their eyes connected in the reflecting glass and he smiled brightly at her. She turned quickly and let out a breath of relief. He was here and he was gorgeous and still grinning at her like a fool. Maybe he was a fool, maybe she was too, but his arrival only aided the triumphant voice inside her, puffed up with pride that this man could possibly be hers.

"Why on earth are you grinning like that?" Andrew asked loudly and Susanna broke her eye contact with the earl, looking away. She could feel a blush race up her face.

Clara nudged her husband with her elbow, shaking her head in dismay. Andrew could be so obtuse. How he was able to snare Clara, one of the most observant people Susanna had ever met, she would never comprehend.

"Ian, how wonderful you decided to join us this evening!" Lady Bexley practically shouted at him from across the room. Ian glanced again at Susanna, almost apologetically before crossing the room to his aunt. She watched him with his relation, his gentleness with her, and the soft smile he gave her. It was refreshing to see him caring and genuine with someone and not always the ridiculous joker.

Then Lady Bexley laughed loudly and smacked him on the arm with her fan and he shrugged, grinning wickedly at her.

Susanna sighed and gave a slight shake to her head. He would never change, and she quite liked that about him.

"Dinner is served," a footman announced from the doorway. The dozen or so people in the room began moving toward the doorway through to the dining room. Susanna took a long moment to dig in her reticule for something, hanging towards the back of the group.

"Do not dawdle, Susanna," Andrew's gruff voice said.

"Yes, I am coming," she said, taking a few steps after them. She had hoped to see Ian alone for a moment or two, but he did not seem to be in the drawing room any longer. She snapped her reticule closed and followed after the duke and duchess, making up the rear of the dinner party.

Suddenly an arm snaked out from behind a curtain and snatched hers, pulling her unceremoniously behind the curtain and into the arms of a solid earl. Ian's mouth descended on hers before she could think, but she did not need to think because she wanted him and she wanted this and everything with him felt ridiculously wrong, but entirely right.

It was a quick kiss, but it left them both breathless as they stared into each other's eyes. "Hello," he said softly.

"Hello," she replied. Her eyes flickered to the doorway where their presence was sure to be missed as there were only twelve people dining *en famile* tonight. Ian winked at her and unhooked the back of her earring before mouthing, "Go."

She smiled back at him and stepped out from behind the curtain, clutching her earlobe. "Lady Susanna, is this the bauble you were looking for?" Ian's deep voice asked as she stepped into the dining room.

"Oh, my goodness!" Susanna answered, with feigned gratitude. They were both standing in the dining room now, the entire dining party's eyes on them as she accepted the earring. "Thank you, my lord."

"Ever your servant, my lady," he said nodding to her. But she could see the many inappropriate comments floating in his mind, reflected in his eyes.

No telling what else could fall off you in the drawing room.

If it falls again, I would be happy to oblige you as you search on bended knee.

I could kiss them off next time, darling.

Fortunately, he kept his thoughts to himself, which was a nice change, Susanna realized, as she took her seat beside Clara. He sat across the table from her, beside Bexley, who sat at the head of the table. It seemed, in the right situation, he was able to keep his wits and not rattle off every asinine thought that came into his head.

Dinner progressed in the way most family dinners do when there are three sets of siblings present. Luckily, there were no peas thrown through the air, but Mr. Warren managed to splatter potatoes onto Miss Warren's chest, and when Miss Warren went to smack her brother for his impertinence, she knocked over her glass of champagne, which was thankfully clear but still liquid. As it soaked into the silk table linen, Lady Bexley barked at both of them to quit their antics. Meanwhile, Lord Bexley was ruefully teasing his younger sister Lady Mirah for her silly performance as she had attempted to catch some poor lord's eye at a prior event. Lady Manning was talking over her brother, giving her sister courting advice while at the same time heavily insinuating that Bexley should think about taking a wife himself. Lord Rhett was making gagging sounds every time someone mentioned marriage, which seemed childish for a man fresh out of Oxford. Ian tried to engage Lord Manning in conversation, which was impossible over Lady Bexley's chastising of the Mr. and Miss Warren, Lady Manning explaining the virtues of marriage, and Lord Rhett retching every time she said "marriage." Clara tucked in to her meal and seemed to tune the noise out, though she picked up her glass as a basket of rolls was tipped over and a bread roll came bowling down the table, so she wasn't as unaware as she wanted them to believe.

It was chaos. Susanna watched the antics and teasing and general love this family poured out with every word. It might have seemed like spite and ugliness to an outsider, but Susanna recognized it for what it was—genuine love and affection. No one was overly mean or rude, just interested in each other's lives. She caught her brother watching the scene at the table, her feelings reflected upon his face and knew he must be thinking the same thing she was.

This reminded them of home, of the time when they were all together, not scattered about the globe, when Mother and Father were alive and Sam had been the heir and everything was right in the world.

She caught Andrew's eye and smiled affectionately at him. He returned the expression and winked at her. She looked pointedly down at her potatoes and purposefully twiddled her fork between her fingers, making causal gestures which could possibly resemble a fork made catapult hurling a clump of potatoes.

Andrew took her meaning perfectly and he let out a bark of laughter, which the entire table ignored because no one could really hear him over the ruckus of the dinner table.

Ian caught her eye and shrugged apologetically. She shook her head slightly and grinned at him. The Warren family certainly had a knack for forgetting they were an aristocratic family, and this was undoubtedly different than the other dinner parties as of late. Susanna loved it.

Ian was mortified.

He knew what the Warren family was like, having grown up with them, but for someone else to see them in their own element was horrifying. The Warrens put on a good show in public, though they were still known as an outspoken, rambunctious lot. But here, they were almost on their worst behavior. What must the duke and his lovely duchess and the even lovelier Lady Susanna think of them? Susanna, despite her forward thinking, was still an elegant lady of quality. He couldn't even look up from his plate, not wanting to see her horrified face as she witnessed the scene before them.

The duke's laughter made him snap his head up and he watched as Susanna and her brother grinned at each other, their eyes sharing a secret he wished he could know. He did not often see the duke and his sisters get along, but it was quite touching to see their faces soften as they looked at each other.

Susanna looked at him and he shrugged, begging her with his gaze to not judge him too harshly for his relations. They were a loud bunch, but they took care of him, as best as he would let them. They were the last connection he had to his mother, and he cherished them for it.

Susanna shook her head and grinned brightly at him, and slowly he returned her smile.

Things were quieter once the gentlemen, all six of them, had separated from the ladies and entered the study for cigars and port. It was Bexley's house, technically, though he did not actually reside here, choosing to take a townhouse closer to the Mall. However, he did use the study for business pertaining to the earldom, so it was well stocked with brandy and port.

Ian did not often think of his cousin as an earl, though he had been one for about as long as he could remember. Bexley's father had died long before he had gone off to Eton, passing the title to his juvenile son. Seeing Bexley comfortable in his study, leaning against his heavy mahogany desk was a little jarring. His cousin—his jackanapes, prank-pulling cousin who would rather chase opera singers than find a respectable wife—was actually a respectable member of society. He sat in the House of Lords, and tended to his investments and estates. Ian felt a pang of something, guilt perhaps, as he looked at his cousin and saw for the first time a peer of the realm. Ian had yet to inherit his father's title, though he should have been acting as his regent for some time. Same duties, no title of Marquess, but still a part of him.

He pursed his lips. He did not like where this train of thought was taking him, and he heard Susanna's voice in his head. *Have you taken responsibility for the title you will one day inherit, one that you are supposed to be enacting in everything but name?*

Leave it to Susanna to see right through his charade and straight to the heart of him. "My wife seems to think you have a tender for my sister," the duke said, startling Ian out of his thoughts. Bradstone's appearance was a welcome distraction, though his question was not a light one.

"I beg your pardon?" Ian said. He glanced at Bradstone, expecting anger, but instead he saw amusement on his face.

"Do not pretend you do not know to what I refer," the duke said. "I am not as blind as my wife thinks I am. I know a love-sick man when I see one."

"I am hardly love-sick, your grace," Ian replied, sipping his port. He felt a strange obligation to be honest as possible with Susanna's brother. "Infatuated, certainly, though I am afraid to expect anything deeper on her behalf. I have the upmost respect for her and I consider your sister a friend."

"You told me once you had no intentions towards my sister," Bradstone reminded him. "Has your position changed?"

Ian paused for a moment. "It may have," he admitted.

"Were you not Bexley's cousin, I might consider you a threat to her," Bradstone told him.

"Were you not Bexley's friend, I might consider you a threat to me," Ian replied.

Bradstone regarded him with intelligent eyes, searching his face for any trace of peril. "He is a rather absurd chap, isn't he?" Bradstone asked, his face breaking out in a grin.

Ian laughed, mostly in relief that the duke had not taken offense. "He is indeed. Try growing up with the man."

Bradstone snorted. "Try growing up with Susanna."

"She is a challenging sprite, isn't she? I hold her in the highest esteem, your grace. She has nothing to fear from me."

Bradstone nodded. "Should anything progress past honorable, I will expect you to do what is right."

Ian nodded, though he gave no more commitment past that. He knew what Susanna wanted, and he knew what he wanted. Somehow he would have to figure out how to make everyone happy.

Bradstone eyed him, but said no more on the subject.

"I apologize, your grace," Ian began. "Dinner around here can be quite out of hand. I tried to warn Susanna."

"Think nothing of it," Bradstone replied, taking a sip of his wine. "Dinner was . . . refreshing."

Ian swallowed his port and it went down his throat in a painful lump. Refreshing?

Seeing his confusion, Bradstone gave a rare elaboration. "My sister and I have been without our family in its entirety for some time," he began and took another sip of his wine. "We are but two of nine surviving siblings, so family dinners such as this are not a foreign concept for us. The noise and loving banter are not things we are privileged to experience often anymore."

Ian understood. This is what the Macalister family dinners used to be like, before their family was marked by tragedy. Much like his was.

"I am thankful you and yours were not offended, your grace," Ian said, looking sadly into his port. The night had turned out so much differently than he had intended.

"We were not offended, I assure you, Westcott," Bradstone said, turning towards him, an odd twinkle in his eye, much as he had seen in Susanna's. "Susanna wanted to join in."

Ian laughed. "I have no doubt she did."

"She would not have, though," her brother admitted. "She likes to balk against the constraints society places on her, but really she acknowledges their rules and goes along with the flock because she truly sees she has no other choice. Her obligation to family is great and she is too kind-hearted to ever do us deliberate harm."

Ian nodded. "She told me as much at the Mathgram Ball. I assure you, your grace, I am no danger to Lady Susanna."

"She could very well be a danger to you," he replied. "My wife and sisters think they have the wool pulled over my eyes, but little happens in my household without my permission, whether they know they have it or not."

Ian was silent as he pondered the duke's words, thinking about all the moments he and Susanna had shared. He hoped there were a few that his grace was not privy to.

"I doubt they would agree, your grace," Ian said.

Bradstone nodded. "Probably not." He took another sip of his wine before changing the topic. "Tell me about your work with the Home Office."

It felt rather like an interview, but Ian wanted Susanna's brother to know him, wanted his approval. So he told him what he could about how he had left home, joined the Royal Army, how he had come to investigate crimes within the departments of England's defense—his work within country, his recent case load—Bradstone listened intently, asking intelligent questions along the way, but mostly allowing Ian to talk. He wasn't trying to impress the duke, though he hoped that he was.

"This explains how you know Halcourt," Bradstone said sometime later and Ian nodded. "Clara says you are the man who aided us last spring."

"Yes, that was I. Your wife has a good eye. I am usually not as easily recognized. I looked quite . . . different."

Bradstone rose an eyebrow as if to say, "You think so?"

The clock chimed the end of the hour and they all rose to return to the ladies in the drawing room.

"Thank you for indulging my curiosity," Bradstone said to Ian as they made their way through the hall.

"My pleasure, your grace," Ian said.

Bradstone smiled at him warmly. "I suspect I will see more of you in the future. Please, call me Andrew."

Susanna was relieved when Ian was back at her side. Not that his relations were not pleasant, because truly she quite enjoyed their time together. She simply wanted to see him. She had not had a moment to talk to him—had barely seen him in days. She rather missed his company.

Ian laughed at something Bexley said, some anecdote from their days as boys at Warren Hall in Sussex, and Susanna was warmed to see Ian so relaxed. He was often laughing, usually at her, but here, in his cousin's drawing room, he seemed to drop some of the airs of absurdity he often wore about in society.

Bexley was summoned to the other side of the room by his mother; he reluctantly responded to her beck and call. Clara caught Susanna's eye conspiratorially and winked.

"I say, Andrew dear, I would like to speak with Lady Manning about her darling brooch. Perhaps you could accompany me and see what a splendid shape it is?"

"Why would I need to see her brooch?" he asked.

"In case you feel compelled to buy me one," Clara replied.

Andrew gave Ian an exasperated look, which Susanna did not quite understand, before clapping him on the back with a firm, "Ian," to which Ian replied with a nod, "Andrew."

Susanna looked at Ian appraisingly as Clara practically pulled her husband across the room. "First name basis with the duke, are we?" she inquired.

Ian shrugged. "I think he likes me."

"You are quite likable," Susanna replied. "And after meeting your family, I can understand why."

"They're a difficult lot," Ian rebutted. "I tried to warn you."

"I love it," Susanna replied.

"I had hoped you would understand and know me better if you met them," Ian explained. "I am not in town often, but my aunt insists on sufficiently feeding me when I am."

"Your aunt is your mother's sister?" she asked, remembering her earlier query.

He nodded. "Half-sister, technically, and separated by a good twenty years. Grandmother had my mother and was widowed early in her marriage. Her second marriage was much later and my aunt was a surprise, from what I understand. As I was a late addition to my parents' life, she and her sister ended up bearing children within months of each other, despite their age difference."

"Fascinating," Susanna replied. "You look nothing like your aunt."

"Or the rest of them, yes, I know," Ian said chuckling. "They tease me incessantly about it."

She made up her mind before she could over think it, something she had been mulling over for the past couple days. "I have a strange request, and you are welcome to decline if it does not sound agreeable."

Ian scoffed. "Prim and proper Susanna, what could there be to disapprove of?"

"Will you call upon me on Wednesday morning?" she asked.

"I would do anything for you," he replied, his tone a hint of mockery though she knew he was quite serious. That knowledge sent a warmth down to her toes.

"There is something I would like to show you, something that might help you understand me better."

"What is it you wish me to see?" he asked.

Susanna looked up at him, hoping with all hope that she could trust him. She could feel herself falling—step by step she was closer to the precipice and it terrified her. He was such an enigma, so much sarcasm masking immeasurable pain, and yet he was so gentle with his aunt, such a good sport with his cousins' antics. His life was a nomad's; he shirked everything she took for gospel. How could this man possibly be who she fell in love with? Why did it have to be him?

"It's not a what, but a where," she corrected. "I wish to take you somewhere." She could tell she had piqued his interest and his eyes narrowed as he studied her face. Deciding he was game for her trial, he nodded, his eyes bright with excitement.

"Wherever you wish, I am yours for the taking," he replied, smirking. Yes, it had to be this man.

"Come to Bradstone House the morning after tomorrow around eight, with a carriage preferably without a crest. And dress in your shabby attire—where we are going isn't suitable for finery."

"Well, now I am certainly intrigued," he replied. "But your wish is my command, my dear."

"And please do not mention it to anyone," she added. "Not his grace, not Clara—no one." He rubbed his hands together, clearly captivated. "A top secret mission for the Crown? Lives on the line? Thousands of pounds at stake? Count me in!"

She laughed and shook her head. "No, nothing as grand as that. I just wish for you to know me a little better. You've given me a glimpse into your world, I want you to see mine."

He studied her but nodded. "Wednesday morning it is."

She grinned. "Tomorrow, however, you must make yourself scarce. I am to attend a dinner party with Riverton."

Ian dramatically rolled his eyes. "You had to go and ruin it with mention of that bounder."

"You are the one who wanted me as bait," she reminded him, though she still did not know why. "Just so you know, we will be at his mother's town home for a family dinner."

"You are not serious," he said, though not in jest. "He has invited you to meet his family?"

She nodded, taking note of his investigative tone. The switch was instantaneous. "His family is in town?" he asked. "When did they arrive?"

"Just this weekend, apparently," she replied. "Riverton invited me just yesterday, when we were on our ride through the park. He says his mother is quite interested in meeting me since she has been away from society for some years, since his father's death, I understand."

He was looking at her, but he really wasn't seeing her. His eyes were unfocused as she spoke and she could see him running through information in his mind.

"This . . . is . . . brilliant," he said slowly, his face breaking out into a wide grin. Not the teasing one she had come to cherish, but more maniacal and conniving, his eyes alight with excitement. "Susanna, you little minx, you are a genius! I could kiss you, darling, you have no idea what amazing news this is!" He bounced away excitedly before hurrying back, kissing her knuckles, and winking, then he was gone from the room.

"What happened to the earl?" Clara asked as Susanna approached her after Ian had practically skipped from the room.

Susanna gave a very unladylike shrug. "Dammed if I know," she said under her breath, low enough for only Clara to hear. "I mentioned the dinner party at Riverton's and he was excited about it."

Clara pursed her lips. "You do not think he would show up or anything?"

"No, I do not think so," Susanna replied, thinking over his reaction. "He was pleased to hear Lady Riverton had returned to town, as if her appearance was an indication of something."

"Your choices in men are impeccable," the duchess added.

Susanna nodded, trying to push Ian's odd behavior out of her mind and focus the remainder of the dinner party, which even without Ian by her side, was quite an enjoyable evening.

Chapter Fifteen

Ian called the next day, just hours before the dinner party with Riverton.

Susanna suspected he would, so she had not been surprised when Howards announced him into the lilac drawing room. One look to Clara and her grace scooped up her correspondence and quit the room. Susanna watched the traitorous duchess leave, wondering when her sister-in-law had become such an adamant champion of the earl.

She watched Ian as he paced across the room, his hands behind his back and she realized this wasn't going to be a flirtatious meeting. He was here for work.

"Conversations are best started when one party begins to speak," she said conversationally. He sent her a sardonic look, but continued to pace. Susana sighed, recognizing that she just needed to wait him out. She went back to her needlework.

A good five minutes later, he finally spoke. "I am here on official business."

"That is quite obvious," she retorted, setting her needlework aside. "How can I be of service to the Crown?"

"I wish to ask you more about Riverton," he explained and took a seat in a chair opposite her.

"I assumed as much," she replied. "Please, ask away."

He was very professional and Susanna found it amusing how his demeanor completely changed when he was working. He was a completely different person.

"This ride through the park you took the other day," he began, and was it her imagination or did his face almost darken with displeasure? "What did you discuss?"

Susanna sighed and ran through the conversation as best as she could remember. Ian took notes as she spoke, though she wasn't sure what he could glean from their brief and very vague exchange. He had given her few specifics and mostly answered in broad terms. Other than the few personal details, his answers had been rather detached.

"I need you to pay attention tonight," he explained, putting his notebook away and leaning towards her. "Lady Riverton hasn't been seen in town for at least a decade, and I've never seen any of the sisters. It is extremely curious she would come up herself to meet you and suddenly bring everyone along."

"Would not she want to meet her son's intended?" Susanna asked.

"That is exactly my point," Ian replied. "If his mother is meeting you, that means he intends to actually marry you, or at least wants to make a very good show of the whole thing."

"What else would he want to do but marry me?" she asked, her brows pulling together. "If he wanted to just ruin and leave me he would have done it already; do not you think?"

Ian nodded and continued. "Agreed, this is the longest courtship he has entered into, so something has changed, Susanna." He paused for a long moment before adding, "Beth did not even meet his family."

"You think he is more likely to marry me because he wants me to meet his mother?" Susanna asked. "He was actually engaged to your sister, he has yet to propose to me."

"Actually, the delay of the proposal is another indication that something has changed, that his intentions are actually to marry you."

"That makes no sense." So many questions swamed around in Susanna's head but she couldn't formulate any of them. The whole thing was so confusing and there was a massive chunk of information Ian was withholding. She opened her mouth to ask what was going on, but he cut her off, continuing in his instructions.

"You must be aware of every little detail, every change in tone, posture, veiled threat, anything and everything," he explained. "Take mental note of every conversation, who was there, when they last saw one another, their behavior towards each other, towards Riverton. This meeting is a gift and you are our only inside man, Susanna—woman, whatever. I wish I could do this for you and take your place. I do not relish putting you in this position."

She was still so very confused. "You wish me to spy on Riverton and his family? Whatever for?"

Ian sighed, and she saw a little of his professional façade crumble. "There are things we suspect Riverton to be guilty of, crimes I cannot share with you yet. Accept that what I say is true—he is dangerous and his interest in you puts you unknowingly in danger. However, this dinner party with his family is completely out of character; therefore, something in his operation has changed. It is often that when they are scared or spooked they make mistakes."

"Who?"

"Criminals," Ian replied. "It is in the mistakes that we find the weakness to bring the entire machine down."

"So I am to be bait, again? Still?" She had lost track.

He nodded. "I think you've been promoted to infiltrator, but yes, you are in the perfect position to help us remove a dangerous man from society."

"Alleged dangerous man," Susanna corrected. "If you had any

concrete proof, we would not be here."

He stood and joined her on the couch. "Yes, alleged," he conceded, his green eyes stormy. "But I know he is guilty."

Susanna leaned forward and wove her hands into his. "If he is so dangerous, why have you allowed me to continue this farce?"

He smiled softly at her, tucking a stray wisp of hair behind her ear. "You are never so far away that I cannot swoop in to save you, darling. Have you not noticed how I have dogged your every step these past weeks?"

Susanna shrugged. "I thought you merely liked me."

"I adore you, Susanna," he corrected. "He is dangerous, but only in the right context. You have never been in any true danger."

"Oh, Ian, this entire thing is ridiculous!" she exclaimed, shaking her head. "I cannot spy."

"How is it any different than gossiping about the happenings of a ball the morning after the event?" he asked. "Or when you quizzed Riverton the other day in the carriage. You did that one on your own, my dear. This is something you already do, though you do not realize it. Plus, their graces will be with you. Your little duchess has quite the observant eye. And his grace sees more than he lets on."

"Are you going to question them after the fact?"

"Unfortunately, I may have to," he answered. "I will call this evening and it is going to be late. Please forewarn their graces of this."

She rolled her eyes. "Couldn't it wait until tomorrow?"

He shook his head. "Best to get it out while it is fresh in your mind."

She sighed again and realized he was probably right. He had more experience questioning witnesses than she did, though she wasn't thrilled at being used as a witness. However, if it hastened to free Ian from whatever shackled him to his past, she was apt to oblige.

Susanna leaned back into the cushions of the sofa and sighed.

"Yes, you are right, about all of it, I suppose. I will do whatever I can to aid you in this pursuit, Ian. I want you free of whatever demons are haunting you—driving you to pursue this course. You have my patience, Ian, though soon I will need some explanations."

"You will get them in time," he said standing up before her. Apparently he was no longer standing on ceremony with her, which she rather appreciated. She stood as well and watched as he pulled his gloves onto his long fingers. He grinned his boyish smile at her, winking. "Do not fret, Susanna. Just relax and put on the show of the enchanted fiancée-to-be, the lady of quality who yearns for nothing but a husband and position."

"Should be easy," she replied.

"For a master such as you."

"You could say it was a role I was born to play," she added, almost sardonically.

He pinched her chin between his gloved fingers and lightly kissed her lips. The contact was blissful.

"If only that dolt could understand you are so much more than he deserves," he whispered against her mouth. "If only the *ton* could see you for who you truly are."

"And who is that?" she asked.

He kissed her again, longer this time, breathing her in. "You, my dear, are far better than all of them."

She laughed lightly. "I doubt if everyone truly knew me if they would approve of who I am. I even worry you will stop coming around once you see the real me."

He gave her a peculiar look and shook his head. "There is nothing you could reveal about yourself I would not find wonderful."

"I protest too much," she replied.

"Perhaps," he whispered and gave her a final quick kiss. "Your hair, I think, could benefit from the adornment of a hairpin you recently acquired."

Susanna nodded in understanding. "I think I remember to

what you refer."

"Do not forget," he insisted. "And I want details, Susanna. It is essential."

"I will strive to deliver an adequate report."

"I have means to punish if I find your story lacking," he teased.

"Punishment sounds enticing," she practically purred.

He shook his head. "Stop that or neither one of us will get any work done. You are much too tempting."

She laughed and kissed his cheek. "Go work, do investigative things. Rein in killers and thieves and whatever it is you do away from me."

He teetered on his feet, almost as though he was debating whether or not to leave. The idea of spending a few more uninterrupted moments alone with him was tempting, she had to admit.

"Ian, seriously, go," she said, and playfully pushed him towards the door.

"Ouch, yes, of course I am leaving," he said in mock indignation. "You simply had to ask me to leave, Susanna, no need for violence." He pecked her cheek again before quitting the room. She heard his cheerful farewell to Howards in the front hall before the heavy front door closed behind him.

Four hours later Susanna was closed up in the grand ducal carriage on her way to Lord Riverton's London townhouse in St. James's Square. She had chosen to wear one of her new gowns, a soft mint green with a dainty ruffle along the top and bottom hem. Her hair was woven into a beautiful coiffure, a weave of braid strands creating a nest along the right side of the base of her head, her daisy hairpin tucked into the arrangement.

Her brother and his new wife sat across from her in the carriage and she cringed at what she was about to ask them to do. How could she adequately explain such an inexplicable situation, one she barely comprehended? And why would they possibly go along with it?

Susanna squared her shoulders and looked directly at her brother. She must convince them.

"This may be difficult to understand, but the two of you must pay extra attention to the events of the evening," Susanna said quickly, hoping to catch them off guard with her request, and with little time to argue.

Andrew had been looking out the window, but he snapped his head around to regard her. "Whatever are you talking about?"

"Please Andrew," Susanna said, her voice pleading. "Ian—Lord Westcott—has asked this of us. He will call later after we have returned and we must report back the events of the evening in as much detail as possible."

"Why would it be any of his business?" Andrew asked.

Susanna pursed her lips. "Ian works for the Home Office. He has reason to believe Riverton is guilty of something, though he has not divulged the viscount's supposed crimes. But it is vitally important that he is able to conclude this work. It's a matter of my happiness as well as Ian's."

Her brother's features softened, changing from hard and stern to caring all within a breath.

"Susanna, you know we want happiness for you," Andrew said gently. "If Ian and this strange request is the key to it, then we are willing to accommodate."

Clara nodded in agreement.

Susanna looked at her family in surprise. How could they be so comfortable with this? Clara willingly left her alone with Ian, after she had previously walked in on them kissing. Her brother was calling Ian by his Christian name and had apparently asked Ian to do the same.

Clara smiled softly at Susanna as she wound her fingers into Andrew's and rested her head on his shoulder, her eyes fluttering closed.

They knew, Susanna realized and almost laughed out loud.

They knew she was in love with Ian and they were giving their approval. Somehow they understood this hare-brained request was important to her happiness. Of course they wanted happiness for her, when they were in the midst of wedded bliss. One look at the ducal couple and it was obvious that they were insane for each other. That's how Ian made her feel—insane. She loved the damned man and she was determined to make certain he was as mad as she was.

"I love you both," she said softly to her brother and sister-in-law. "You know that, do not you?"

Clara nodded, her eyes still closed. Andrew looked at her curiously but did not spoil her declaration with a comment and looked back out the window.

The remainder of their journey to St. James's Place, which was ridiculously slow for a trip of less than two miles, was spent in silence. The traffic on Piccadilly made them fashionably fifteen minutes late, but it gave Susanna a chance to gain her composure. Something during this dinner could be the key to Ian's investigation, and the key to him concluding whatever period of his life he felt he could not bring her into. She was determined to share her life with him, and the sooner he got to a place where he was willing to do the same, the better.

They arrived at the address and were quickly ushered inside, for it had begun to drizzle.

Fall, it seemed, had decided to make an appearance and squash summer's last attempts at warmth.

The carriage through the London nighttime to the bright lights of the townhouse was all a blur, and before Susanna knew it, she was standing in the doorway of the drawing room, blinking away the bright candlelight.

It was a simply adorned room, and the furniture did not quite match the wall hangings, but it was cozy and had a crackling fire. Riverton stood by the mantle, his handsome face unmarked by emotion. She smiled sweetly at him and curtsied as they were announced into the room. There were only four other people in the room besides Riverton: an older woman who must be his mother, and three dark-haired young ladies.

"Mother, please meet Lady Susanna Macalister, her brother, the Duke of Bradstone, and his new bride," Riverton said, his hand out to indicate each one of them, as if there was truly a doubt who each of them were. The older woman smiled tightly at her and nodded, her eyes flickering to Riverton for the briefest of moments.

The way he said, "Mother," sent chills down Susanna's spine. "It's a pleasure to meet you, Lady Riverton," Susanna said smiling brightly, hoping to trample out some of the dread she felt seeping into the room.

"Hello," Lady Riverton said simply. Her demeanor was cool but not off-putting. It was if she wasn't certain how to behave.

"My sisters, Misses Harriet, Hortence, and Heather," Riverton continued.

Each stood and curtsied and promptly returned to their seats along the settee. They were older than Susanna had originally assumed, the oldest—Miss Harriet, she guessed—looked closer to her own age. The youngest— Miss Heather?—looked to be nearing the time for her debut.

"So wonderful to meet you all," Clara said.

"Was the rain a bother?" Riverton asked, as a footman came into the room carrying a tray of lemonade. Champagne is what she really wanted, she thought, as she accepted the flute from the viscount. Or maybe a stiff finger of brandy.

"Not at all," she replied and took a sip of the lukewarm liquid. "It was a rather peaceful drive, though we were delayed by the traffic on Piccadilly. Really, on a Tuesday evening, where would they all be going?"

"Almack's?" asked the middle sister—Miss Hortence? Susanna hoped she had guessed correctly which name belonged to whom. Riverton truly did an abysmal job at introductions.

"Sadly no," Susanna answered. "Almack's is only during the

regular season and on Wednesdays, I am afraid. Miss Hortence, is it not?"

The brunette nodded. "Yes, my lady. So silly of me, of course, I remember such a treat would not be in session during the Little Season."

"We haven't been to town for a true season yet," the youngest added. Miss Hortence sent a quick jab to her younger sister's ribs. "I mean, I haven't made my bows yet, so it would not be proper for me to be at Almack's."

It was a smooth cover, but a cover nonetheless.

"Almack's truly isn't all that exciting," Susanna replied. "And not very enjoyable."

"Then why do you go?" Miss Hortence asked.

"Because we must," Susanna replied and took a sip of her lemonade. The three sisters looked confused and the oldest opened her mouth to say something, but shut it just as quickly.

"Riverton, they must come up next season," Susanna said. "I would be happy to act as sponsor. Oh Clara, think what fun that would be!" She looked at her sister-in-law for help. Clara was on point with her quick reply.

"Oh, yes, truly," the duchess agreed, nodding excitedly. "Darling, we could hold a ball in their honor. It would be such a smash."

Andrew did not miss a beat either, answering in his most bored voice, "Yes, if we must."

"What say you, Riverton?" Susanna asked, winking at him. "A London season for your darling sisters?"

Riverton's face was stoic and rather cold. He glared at the girls disapprovingly and, again, a brief moment of anger flashed across his face. It was so quick, but Susanna was certain of what she had seen this time. It was gone before anyone else noticed, and Riverton nodded and repeated his grace's statement. "Yes, if we must."

Susanna had expected a squeal of excitement from the three ladies, but instead she was met with nods and a polite, "Thank you, my lady." So strange. They were clearly terrified of their brother, something Susanna had trouble fathoming. Her brothers were always annoying but never mean or abusive. She glanced at Clara, remembering the stories last spring she had heard of Clara's brother, the late Earl of Morton. Clara's brother had been a despicable brute, but she could not imagine Clara cowering in fear as these ladies did.

Riverton engaged Andrew in conversation and Susanna took the opportunity to speak with the Viscountess of Riverton.

"It truly is nice to meet some of Riverton's family," Susanna said, sitting lightly beside the viscountess. "He rarely speaks of himself, so this invitation was quite an unexpected but delightful surprise."

"My pleasure," she said simply.

It seemed that like Susanna would have to drag information out of the woman.

"He is such a remarkable man, your son," Susanna said. "Tell me a story about Riverton as a boy. Was he mischievous?"

The woman seemed to soften and her eyes glistened. "My Hanson was quite remarkable. Mischievous, yes, but loyal and warm. He could always coax a smile from me, even in my darkest of moods."

Susanna smiled and nodded, encouraging her to go on. She did not. She simply looked at her hands.

"Your husband's passing must have been quite difficult for your family," Susanna said, trying to feel out the reason for her sadness. "I myself lost my father and brother when I was young. I am terribly sorry for your loss, madam."

"It was many years ago," the woman said, straightening her back and looking Susanna square in the eyes. "But I still feel their loss as if it was yesterday."

"Their?" Susanna asked, tilting her head to the side.

Lady Riverton swallowed, her smile faltering. She glanced quickly at Riverton. "Yes, my husband and, ah . . . a local man both died that day. And my Hanson was forever changed after that."

Susanna nodded and patted the woman's hand. "I understand how grief and tragic sudden loss can change a person."

Lady Riverton nodded, looking pointedly into Susanna's eyes. "My Hanson was gone. Riverton took his place from then on."

Something was definitely off. There was fear in the woman's eyes, reflected in those of her daughters. Susanna opened her mouth to inquire further, but was stopped by the appearance of the butler announcing dinner.

Lady Riverton smiled at Susanna, glancing hesitantly at her son. "It was a pleasure chatting with you, Lady Susanna."

Susanna nodded and stood, accepting Riverton's arm as she crossed the sitting room.

They led the small procession through to the dining room. Riverton was seated at the head of the table, Andrew on his left, Susanna on his right. Clara was seated beside her husband, Miss Heather beside her. To Susanna's right were Misses Harriet and Hortence, and Lady Riverton at the end of the table. The table extended further as it was built to seat at least twenty, though it was much too large for the small dining room. Again, it looked like it had been nonchalantly arranged in the space. The long curtains did not match the carpeting, which did not coordinate with the paintings hung on the wall. The frames were mismatched, some gold, some black.

"Riverton, this room is charming," Susanna commented as the footmen made their way around the table, dishing up food along everyone's left. "Wherever did you find such a wonderful array of paintings?"

He glanced at her. "The art came with the house, Lady Susanna. It is all merely rented for the time Mother and the girls are in town."

"Oh, of course," Susanna replied. "So unfortunate, I should like to have that one." She pointed at a landscape of what might have been a lily pond. Really, she did not care for the painting, and she just needed an excuse to ask about the randomness of the room.

"What is so wonderful about that landscape?" Miss Heather asked. "It seems to me an unremarkable talent."

Susanna nodded to her approvingly, but had to continue her feigned interest in the piece. "Ah, but you see the mixture of paints along the edge of the water?" she asked. "It's a masterful technique. Rembrandt originated the technique to create a realistic rendering of wind moving along the landscape."

"Ah, I see now," Miss Heather said, tilting her head at the painting.

"I did not know you were a lover of the arts," Riverton commented, lifting his hand to halt the footman pouring his wine.

"I am sure there are a great many things you do not know about me," she replied cheekily. The more time she spent with Riverton, the more she realized Ian was right about him. As it was, she was completely telling tales about bogus painting techniques and any properly educated Englishman—or woman—would have known her lines to be false.

"I look forward to hearing more of your interests," Riverton said in what Susanna could only surmise was a weak attempt to flirt with her.

"What are your interests, my lord?" Clara asked, giving Susanna a reprieve for her telling nonsense.

"Horsemanship, theater, fishing," he replied automatically, as if reading off a prewritten list. "The usual gentlemanly pursuits."

"Yes, but what do you like to *do*," Clara asked, putting emphasis on the last word. "For instance, when you have a day to yourself, free from obligations, what would you choose to do for that day?"

He looked at her disbelieving. "I assure you I never have such a day."

"I'd spend the entire day reading," Clara replied. "Or in the garden with the roses."

"I would paint," Susanna added. "And read. And sleep."

"I would walk and walk for hours," Miss Harriet commented. "And pick a meadow's worth of wildflowers."

"I would sneak down to the kitchens and bake bread with Cook," Miss Hortence said.

"I would gather up all the leaves that have fallen to the ground, run and jump into the pile so that all the leaves fly up in the air!" Miss Heather said excitedly and everyone laughed, except Riverton. He did not even crack a smile. "What about you, your grace?" Miss Heather looked at Andrew expectedly.

"Miss Heather, I doubt—" Riverton began, but Andrew ignored him and cut him off. "Miss Heather, I would spend the day by the lake skipping rocks. I would probably ride a great deal. Truly a day to spend outdoors doing anything would be a gift compared to tiresome hours in Parliament and committee meetings."

Miss Heather nodded. "Yes, that does sounds rather dull."

The table laughed again, lighter this time, before everyone tucked into their meals.

The dinner progressed in that way, a random bout of conversation about something inane. Riverton would throw around his cold stares and his sisters would quit their questioning or silly conversations and return quietly to their dinner.

It was extremely peculiar. What harm was there in conversing during dinner? Susanna wondered. What was wrong with idle silliness? It was as if he wanted his family to put on a show of respectability for Susanna and their graces, when truly, the Macalisters couldn't care less.

It was a stark contrast from the previous evening spent with Ian's family.

Clara begged a headache after dinner, and they thanked Riverton and his family for their hospitality. Susanna got nothing more from Lady Riverton, but the Averly sisters made sure to remind them of their promise of a ball the next season.

"We will see about this ball," Riverton said, offering Susanna his arm as she finished up with her cloak.

"Yes, of course," she replied, not wanting to seem argumentative. A good wife would accept her husband's decision on things, right? Though she had no intention of actually doing so with her husband, she had to appear as if she were planning on becoming his good and dutiful wife. Hopefully Ian could glean some data from her recollection and she could be done with the whole charade.

"Thank you for joining us for dinner," Riverton said stoically. "It is such a treat to have Mother and the girls in from Lincolnshire."

Really? Susanna wanted to ask, since it did not seem that way at all. "Yes, it was lovely, wasn't it?" Susanna agreed.

"Might I ask to escort you to the theater tomorrow evening?" Riverton asked as they exited the townhouse. Based on his tone, he could have been asking what she thought about paving stones.

"That would be wonderful," she replied. He handed her into the carriage and gave a quick bow.

"Until tomorrow, then," he said before turning on his heel and returning to the house. The three Macalisters sat in silence for a long moment as the carriage rocked into motion.

"That was interesting," Andrew said, breaking the silence.

"It was extremely odd . . . and concerning," Clara replied.

"I am glad I am not the only one feeling this way," Susanna added. "And I am grateful for you two being there with me. Something is terribly wrong and I hope Ian can get to the bottom of this."

"He had better," Andrew muttered.

Ian was waiting for them in Andrew's study when they returned to Bradstone House.

Clara and Susanna sat unceremoniously on the leather couch, Andrew stepped to the side bar and poured himself a stiff drink.

"Well?" Ian asked, looking at them expectedly.

"I hereby withdraw my consent for Susanna to marry that man," Andrew announced. Looking around at his relations, he pointed out the window with the hand holding the glass. "That other man, Riverton." He took a long pull from his glass, nearly downing all its contents. "Ian, you are fine, she can marry you all she wants."

"I wholeheartedly agree," Clara stated.

"As do I," Ian replied. "About the Riverton part. The 'me' part is still sort of . . . complicated."

"Well, make it uncomplicated, and fast," Andrew said, taking the last swig of the brandy. "Because there is something unearthly wrong in that family."

Ian nodded and slipped open his notebook. "Best start from the top."

Chapter Sixteen

*J*an had only bid farewell to Susanna a mere four hours before, but he arrived dutifully at eight the next morning, complete with covered carriage, one that did not bear the eagle and knight of his family crest. He had no idea why that would be a requirement, but he did as instructed.

Susanna stepped from the house before he could knock, surveyed the carriage, and nodded in approval. She was radiant even in a simple day dress that looked more like something a country relation would wear and not the daughter of a duke.

"Where are we headed?" he asked as he handed her into the carriage. Looking around for her maid he asked, "And where is Annette?"

"I do not require her chaperonage this morning," Susanna replied and he hauled himself into the carriage, taking the seat opposite her.

"Will not it be noticed if she is at Bradstone House and you are not?"

She shook her head. "I gave her the morning off. She is to visit her dear friend, who is a maid in Devonshire's employ."

She did not say anything for a long moment, looking longingly out the window as the rows of houses passed them by. He watched her, breathing in her beauty, simple and unassuming in such plain garb, but it was impossible to stamp out or mask her elegance.

"While I do enjoy the cloak and dagger and secrecy of it all, you need to give me an address so my man knows where to go."

"We are going to the Lady Day Home for Boys, outside Wimbledon," she replied. Ian gave the direction to his driver and turned back to her. "You actually go to the orphanage?" he asked.

"Of course," she replied. "The Lady Day Home for Boys is a special project of mine."

"I'd heard of this elusive Lady Day before your brunch was mentioned," he admitted. "She is somewhat of a myth and fantasy amongst the penniless lads in the city. I will admit I've lost a few of my good errand boys to this Lady of yours."

"They are better once off the street and tucked up away safe from the likes of you and your ilk," she replied, rather more venomously than he expected. She had much more invested in this than just her patronage, he realized, noting how she jumped to their defense.

"What connection does this charity have to you?" he asked.

"I told you, I am one of the founding members."

"Yes, you wrote the charter and all that, but why you? Why this charity?"

She shrugged. "It could have been any number of organizations, I suppose. This one just seemed . . . right."

"So you do know who this Lady Day is, if that is even her true name?" he asked.

She hesitated, not looking at him. "I might know who she is."

Ian sat back in his seat, against the uncomfortable cushions of the simple coach. He ran through the known information regarding the Lady Day Home for Boys. The paper work and legalities were all in order, and while there were many names associated with the charity, Susanna's seemed to be a constant thread throughout, more often mentioned than any others.

She did not speak for another half an hour, content to watch the houses turn into open space as they made their way out of London proper. Ian was content to watch her, and he could tell she was wrestling with something, looking for the words to say what she needed to. Their destination was curious, and yet confusing at the same time. He knew she was on the verge of revealing a large portion of herself to him and it had him on pins and needles to see what she would say. Her worrying over his reaction was written on her face, as her brows pulled together. What could she possibly have to show him? He assumed her an innocent, was she not? Did she have a son at the orphanage? That did not make sense though, as he doubted Bradstone would have agreed to that, if he even knew about such a thing happening to her. But no, Ian was certain she was a virgin.

"It helps if you start from the beginning," Ian offered, eager for her to get the words out. "Whatever it is, it cannot be as bad as I am imagining."

"You say you want to know me," she said slowly, not looking away from the window. "What if you do not approve of what you find?"

"Susanna, you could sprout another head and I would still be enchanted by you," he replied.

"What if what I've done could be construed as illegal?" she asked. "Would you be required to arrest me?"

"Have you killed someone?" he asked.

"No, nothing like that."

"Then I should have no reason to arrest you," he concluded. "Please, Susanna, just explain. I swear I will not pass unwonted judgement."

She nodded and took a steadying breath. "Five years ago, the year before my debut, I was walking along Bond Street," Susanna began, sighing as she began her story. "I was shopping and I went out alone, though I had a footman with me. A young boy ran by and snatched my reticule. Where any other lady of the town would have shouted for help, instead I took off in pursuit.

"Luckily, no one saw me. I followed him through the alleyways and into a darker part of the town than I had ever been to. I finally caught up with him; he had not expected me to follow him so long. We were stopped outside a bakery. The lad was so frightened, he apologized and handed me back my purse. It was then I met Mrs. Jensen and her husband. She apologized to me for his behavior and she told me the story about how she and her husband tried to find the boys work and fed them when they could, but they couldn't save them all."

"I was very moved by her story and the struggles of the young boys of the city. Mrs. Jensen said they tried to look after ten boys, but they lacked space and funding. I offered her the money I had with me, but she would only accept a few pounds. I came back the following week and the week after that, and after three months of returning each week, I broached the subject of finding a more permanent solution for the Jensen's, the boys, and the mission they were trying to see to fruition."

"So you started the Lady Day Home for Boys," Ian answered the question that had dodged him for weeks. A realization suddenly hit him like a brick. "You are Lady Day."

Susanna sighed and nodded. "Yes, in a way."

Ian let out a low whistle. "The largest charity for orphans is run by a young lady of quality." His sweet and socially acceptable Lady Susanna was the illusive Lady Day, savior of the ruffian youth of the London underbelly. The risks she had taken, the laws she had bent to her will, not to mention the probable enemies she had made by snatching up the messenger class of young boys used by criminals.

He shook his head and chuckled.

"Please do not laugh at me, Ian," she said.

"No, I would not dare," he replied, looking up at her. "It's the situation I find funny. Does your brother know what you have done? Does anyone?"

She shook her head slowly and looked at her hands. "I've never disclosed this to anyone in my life, until you. Mr. and Mrs. Jensen know, of course, but everything is wrapped in legal jargon, no one has dug deep enough to find the source of the Lady Day Foundation. I sit on the board with three other women, I am a part of the founding charter, but as far as the *ton* is concerned, I am just a titled lady playing at charity."

He shook his head again. "Are you angry?" she asked.

"Angry?" he asked, scratching at the scruff along his chin. "Far from it, Susanna. I am in awe. This news is shocking, to be sure. Terrifying and potentially dangerous, but I am impressed that you did this and kept it a secret for the past four years. How did you write the charter without a lawyer?"

Susanna shrugged. "I asked Andrew's solicitor a few hypothetical questions and the rest I studied."

"You studied law?"

"Well, not as a profession, obviously. But I read through a couple of volumes in Andrew's library and went from there. It wasn't difficult once one understands the legal jargon."

"You were eighteen and you studied law just so you could form a charity charter without getting caught?" he asked and she nodded. "Too bad we cannot get you to run for prime minister; think of what you could accomplish with a country in your hands."

Susanna beamed at him. "Actually, a career in politics has always been my dream. Or a solicitor. Too bad women aren't allowed. They really should be."

Ian nodded. "They should at least make an exception for you."

"So you are not . . . appalled?" she asked hesitantly. "This isn't too much?"

He shook his head. "Susanna, this is incredible. I am quite eager to see it now."

"I had hoped this trip would help you understand me better," she said. "You seem to think me a society obsessed brat, and I am far from it."

Did this help him understand her? Immensely. What he thought about her a month ago was so incredibly wrong that it was amusing how he could have been so far off the mark. She was self-less and generous. She was good, and she was *his*. He did not care what he had to do, she would be his in the end.

The house was a large manor, not grand or opulent, but perfect for a boys' home. The red brick structure stood two stories high with a high shingled roof and black attic windows. Tall woods flanked the house to the east, expansive lawns and a large pond to the west. They had passed through a black iron gate supported by a red brick wall that stretched far along the road in each direction, curving into the lawns and the woods enclosing the perimeter of the property.

"We're here," Susanna said eagerly, smiling at him. "Are you ready?"

He nodded, enjoying the excitement and pride on her face. She truly was a remarkable woman.

She introduced him to Mr. and Mrs. Jensen. She toured him through the rooms, and she talked endlessly about the property, the house, how many rooms it boasted, the repairs they had made to the house and the grounds; it all seemed to pour out of her after five years of having to keep it to herself.

"How is all this funded?" Ian asked.

"Donations mostly," she answered. "The house is in Mr. Jensen's name, as I am not allowed to own property without a husband—" she shot him a rueful glance, as if the law was his fault, and continued. "I employ the Jensens, the two teachers, and the cook. The remainder of the work is done by the boys. They tend to the work outdoors, the gardening, exterior maintenance, upkeep of the drive and lawns. They learn maths, reading, and basic skills to help them become contributing members of society."

"Land management, household service, business management?" he asked.

Susanna nodded. "We want them to be able to make an honest living. We also have a no tolerance for anything disparaging. We pulled them from the filth of the city, and we can put them right back in it should they not wish to be here."

"Have you had to enact that threat?" he asked.

"Once," she replied. "And he got as far as the city limits before he begged to be allowed to return, which we permitted."

"Is it the same group of boys you have had since the beginning?" he asked. It couldn't have been; he knew of three boys who had been taken off to Lady Day in the past year.

"Some of the original boys are still here. Many have found employment and have left. We have a nice relationship with a few mills in the area, in addition to the blacksmith and cobbler in Wimbledon. Two of our former students are employed at Bradstone Park, though Andrew does not know of my connection to them."

"How many are here now?"

Susanna thought for a moment. "Twenty, I believe. No, twenty-one."

"How many do you have room for?"

"Forty at the moment," she replied. "The boys sleep four to a room. For many of these boys, it's the first bed they ever had, much less a space they could make their own. Once I have my dowry, I intend to hire more staff to allow us to double the residents. And I wanted to build a stable so the boys could learn to ride."

"Hold on, you plan to put your entire dowry towards this?" he asked.

She nodded. "Riverton said I could have its entirety, though he did not know I would spend it on this."

"How did you buy the house?"

"One of the things we learned at Miss Katherine's Finishing School for Young Ladies was investments," she explained. "When I was thirteen, my brother Luke agreed to make some for me under his name. Five years later, my investments had paid off, and he sold my stock for me. I used the money from the sale to purchase the home, in Mr. Jensen's name."

Ian's head was spinning. Investing, stocks, buying homes, running an orphanage. Who was this little minx of his? He felt pride welling inside, and admiration, something he was not accustomed to feeling for another person. How extraordinary she had turned out to be!

"Would you like to meet the boys?" she asked hesitantly. He nodded and she grinned.

"They are good boys," she said to him as they climbed the stairs, led by Mrs. Jensen. "But they are a little distrusting of men. So be warned, they might not take to you easily."

They entered through a set of double French doors at the end of the corridor into what seemed to be a study room. Tables were lined in three rows, with adjoining benches, filled with lads of all ages writing with chalk on individual blackboards.

When Susanna entered the room, they all turned and their eyes lit up when they saw her.

There was a rushing of feet and Susanna was encircled with hugs and flowers picked from the flower beds, a chorus of "It's Lady Day!"

"I love Lady Day!" and "I did not know today was Lady Day!" excitedly pulsing through the room.

Susanna smiled at them all, glancing at Ian. "Lady Day isn't a title, you see, it's a day," she explained. "When I would visit the bakery, the lads would call the day Lady Day, the day the lady visited. When we opened this place it seemed the only thing to call it, and most people assumed Lady Day was a person. It's not just one person, it is many who make this whole thing a reality, and make my trips here possible. I love coming for Lady Day. It's the highlight of my tedious time outside this place."

"Why did you bring him around?" one asked, looking untrustingly at Ian.

"This is a very good friend of mine," Susanna explained, stroking the boy's hair. "You must be polite to him."

The boys did not tear their eyes away from Susanna. "Well, I do not like him." It was a popular opinion among the boys, it seemed.

"As you should not," Ian replied, nodding in affirmation. "You do not know me; how can you like me? First, we must be properly introduced. My name is Ian Carlisle, what is yours?" Ian stuck his hand out for the boy to shake. The boy hesitated, glancing at Ian's outstretched hand.

With an encouraging nod from Susanna, the boy clasped Ian's hand and shook. "I am called Roger Thane," the boy replied.

"Nice to meet you, Roger," Ian replied. "You can learn a lot about a person immediately upon meeting them simply from their handshake. You've a strong handshake, lad. I can tell you are confident and stout. If your hand was cold or clammy, I would know you were a weak character or a passive person, nervous even. The blood would run out of your hand and into your arm and leg muscles, keeping you ready to run in a dangerous situation. A good handshake should last only a few seconds, your hand vertical to the ground, squeezing the same amount the other person provides. Do not squeeze too hard; you will come off as too aggressive or disagreeable. Not enough pressure and you'll be seen as inferior or unsure of yourself. Men do not want to hire other men they cannot trust, and a handshake is the first impression and first opportunity you give someone to trust you. Do you understand?"

Roger nodded.

"Good," Ian replied. "Let's all give handshakes a try then?" The boys all jumped into two lines and were quickly practicing handshakes on each other. Some took it very seriously, some made a game out of it, but after a few moments, Ian could see they were absorbing some of what he said. The true leaders in the group had firm but equal handshakes. The weaker boys, more socially awkward, had limps hands while shaking, but after a few tries, they mounted enough courage to shake Ian's hand with confidence. They were soon called down for their afternoon chores, almost all shaking Ian's hand with a, "Nice to meet you, Mr. Carlisle," before hurrying out of the room, eager for some time in the fresh country air. One boy shot Ian a distrustful glare before scurrying after the others.

Susanna's blue eyes twinkled at him as the last boy left the room.

"It's nice to meet you, Mr. Carlisle," Susanna said saucily, extending her bare hand. Ian shook it, realized he had never shaken her hand, always bending over her hand in a bow or kissing her knuckles. Her hand was soft beneath his and he pulled her towards him. Her arm wrapped around his back, his hand lacing through her hair, cradling her head as he leaned down to capture her lips in a kiss.

Kissing Susanna was something he would never tire of, and his new goal was to do it as often as the opportunity arose. He loved the little sighs she made, the way she daringly nipped his bottom lip with her teeth. Susanna the Minx was insatiable and he loved it.

He pulled away and looked at her, taking in her deep blue eyes, her fair complexion marked with a few unruly freckles, hinting at her inner rebel. Her eyes were soft and her face was warm and caring. Try as he might, there was no avoiding falling under her spell. "Hello," he said.

She smiled brightly at him, though her voice was hesitant. "You are pleased with all of this? Truly?"

"I am in awe of all of this, darling, and of you," he replied sincerely, kissing the tip of her nose. He could feel the tension rolling off her, her relief in his acceptance.

"Does this help you understand me a little better?"

He nodded. "Immensely," he replied. "Though I already knew you to be generous and unselfish. I just had no idea those values extended to everyone you ever met, not just rogue earls who you attempt to tame."

She laughed. "I am glad you like it," she said, leaning up and pressing her lips on his.

Ian leaned into her, pressing her into the closed door, the only barrier between them and the rest of Lady Day. How could this conundrum of a woman have chosen him? He was barely in one place long enough to gather any attention and when he did, it was easily rebuffed. She had caught him in her web and as he attempted to learn her secrets, he had fallen hopelessly in love with her, which, for a man of his profession, was not a benefit. He did not need a weakness, he did not need a distraction, and yet Susanna amused and entertained him at every turn. He found himself wondering about her when he was away from her, he wanted to share every moment of his days with her—every little thing he found amusing just to see if she would also.

"Ian, please someone will see," she breathed heavily, her hands on his chest.

"Yes, but I am not certain they would care," he said, trailing kisses down the soft skin below her earlobe to her collarbone.

"Ian," she said with little protest, her voice breathless. "Please."

He wasn't sure what she was asking for, but he wanted to bury himself in her attentions.

Her hand wound its way into his sandy locks and it sent shivers down to his toes. This maddening woman had completely unhinged his world.

"Ian, please," she said again and he pulled away to look at her. So much emotion running through her eyes, reflecting that of his own but he couldn't make himself say the words. He wanted to profess everything, say every sweet thing that the poets had concocted over time, but all that came out was, "You look thoroughly ravished."

She smirked at him, laying a hand on his cheek and he tilted his head slightly into her embrace. "Oh, my Ian, whatever will I do with you?"

You could marry me, he thought. But he couldn't say it to her yet, he would not do her the dishonor of offering something he wasn't even certain he could afford to offer. Not until Riverton was in Newgate. He would not bring Susanna into this darkness, and he would not fail Beth a third time.

She leaned up and placed a last quick kiss on his lips before scooting around him, out the door and disappearing down the stairs.

Chapter Seventeen

The next evening, Ian sat in his rose study, dealing with the worst part of his profession: paperwork. With more details coming to light in the aftermath of the Riverton dinner party, he knew there was a connection, something linking everything together. But as usual, one piece was missing, one important chunk of the maze that was the key to convicting Riverton.

A knock startled him out of his paperwork and he looked up to see Mayne standing in his doorway.

"Good evening," Ian said, setting his quill pen down.

His partner took a seat in the leather chair opposite Ian's desk, nodding to him. He did not say anything right away, just looked at the cream folded parchment he was twiddling between his fingers.

"What is it, Mayne?" Ian asked, sensing something was wrong.

"There's been another kidnapping," he stated and Ian swore, not needing any further explanation. Leaning forward, he reached his arm across the desk for Mayne to hand him the paper. Reading through the summons was Ian's worst nightmare coming true, again. It was the same *modus operandi* as the others—newly engaged girl kidnapped and held for ransom, fiancé not to be found.

"We should leave immediately," Maybe said, rising from his seat.

Ian nodded absently, but a weight came crashing down upon him. *Susanna.* "Give me an hour, please," Ian asked, standing as well.

Mayne nodded, probably understanding more than Ian wanted him to. "We will depart from Whitehall Place," Mayne replied.

"Agreed."

Mayne was gone, and Ian was out of the house in mere minutes, calling for a hackney as he tugged on his hat and gloves. He rattled off Susanna's address on Park Lane before ducking into the hired carriage. His mind was formulating a plan, and he hoped it would work out as he intended. It did not take long to travel to Bradstone House and Ian flipped the driver a coin, asking him to wait for his return.

He knocked on the heavy wooden door and was ushered inside by Howards the butler, another servant heading into the house to fetch Susanna.

He did not have to wait long. Childlike laughter echoed through the halls and Ian whipped around as a petite, blond child hurried into the drawing room in search of a place to hide.

"Oh!" she cried, surprised to see him, her eyes growing wide.

"Hello," he said, wondering who the child could be. She looked an awfully lot like the duchess, but that did not exactly make any sense.

"Susanna!" the little girl called, her voice tinged with worry. "Come quickly, please!"

"Mary Claire, you are not supposed to tell me where you are!" Susanna's voice called from the hall.

"Susanna!" the little girl called again, more alarm in her voice. Susanna burst into the room, a picture of casual elegance.

"What is wrong?" she asked and then saw Ian, her face lighting up. "Ian, what are you doing here?"

"Who is that man?" the little girl asked.

"That, my darling, is a very good friend of mine," Susanna said, stooping to the young girl's level.

"My name is Ian," he said, kneeling beside her and offered his hand. She tentatively shook it.

"My name is Mary," she replied. "You are very tall. But not as tall as my new Papa." Susanna chuckled. "Yes, Ian is quite tall."

He was bewildered, but was thankfully saved by the maid who had been in search of Susanna.

"My lady, oh, I see you've already discovered you have a caller," the maid said, curtsying.

Susanna straightened. "Would you take Mary-Claire down to the kitchens and see if you cannot nick something from Cook? Tell her I sent you," Susanna said, winking at the maid. "I will be along in a moment."

The maid nodded and took the little girl by the hand. "It was nice to meet you, Mr. Ian," the little girl said.

"It was nice to meet you, too," Ian replied. She smiled and waved her little hand at him before being lead out the room.

"Please, let us sit," Susanna said as soon as she was out of the room and sat on the settee. "I've been chasing that little darling all over the house for over an hour. My feet are tired."

Ian sat down opposite her and waited for her explanation.

"That is Miss Meredith Clara Baker-Macalister. She is the orphaned daughter of Clara's twin sister and the man you apprehended and brought to London last spring. Their graces are now her guardians and brought her up to London to finalize her guardianship papers."

"I suspect there is quite a story behind all of that," he said.

She nodded. "Andrew and Clara's relationship began in quite a dramatic fashion."

"I've surmised as much," he answered. "Now is not the time, however, I have come on different news."

"Oh?" she said, sitting up straighter. "Has there been any progress with your investigation?"

"In a manner of speaking," he replied. "I am being sent on assignment out of town." She nodded slowly and he could see her processing this information. "I do not know how long I could be away. Could be a day or two, could be as long as a fortnight."

"And what about Riverton?" she asked, her brows pulling together. "What am I to do about him?"

He sighed. "About the same as you have been, I am afraid. Until I can understand what this new development entails, there really isn't much to be done about him."

"I thought you said he was a danger to me?"

He sighed again and shook his head. "Look, darling, I do not like this any more than you do. But if the pattern holds, you should be in a period of grace for a fortnight at least. But to be safe, do not allow yourself to be alone with him. Always have a chaperone, a male chaperone if you can manage it. And if he proposes, send word immediately."

"I do not understand—if there is still a danger here, why are you being pulled away?"

He hesitated. "There is a girl in confirmed danger and unfortunately that takes precedence over my presumed state of danger here."

Susanna sighed in resignation. "I suppose that would take precedence. Though, at some point you are going to have to tell me what this is all about."

"You know why I must see this concluded, Susanna," he replied.

"I do not, actually," she stated. "You haven't told me told me anything, Ian; I am completely in the dark about a seemingly large portion of your life."

"Are you upset with me that I am leaving town in the hopes to save a life?"

Susanna opened her mouth and closed it again, frowning. "No,

I am not saying that at all. I find it admirable you found this path for your life. You have my support, Ian, but it would be nice to have that trust reciprocated. I will soon need answers."

Ian nodded, staring in wonder at the woman before him. Her blind trust in him was jarring but he couldn't divulge everything just yet. For that tale, he needed more time.

"I promise you answers, but for now you will need to sit tight and stay vigilant. I must be off. Be careful and wary of Riverton. I will return for you."

He stood as she did, capturing her lips in a quick kiss before quitting the room, tugging his hat onto his head and escaping into the awaiting hackney.

That damnable woman and her attempts to save him would be for naught, he sighed as the hackney rolled him away from Susanna. She wanted answers, but he wasn't certain she would like the information she sought. This was who he was. It was all he would ever be. For his crimes he had to pay the price of happiness and life with Susanna.

Ian left town on a Friday. Susanna remembered specifically because Riverton escorted her to a soiree that evening. Saturday it was a drive around the park where she insisted Beverell attend her. The drive was thankfully cut short due to an afternoon storm that caught them off guard and sent them running for the safety of Bradstone House. Sunday was luckily free of Riverton, but a note came around Monday morning asking if she would join him at an opening of a new art exhibit at the Museum.

That was the invitation that prompted Susanna to tell her brother everything.

Riverton. Ian. Lady Day. Everything.

Sitting in his formal study, surrounded by dark, rich colors, mahogany and leather, Susanna was rethinking her decision to come clean. Andrew had not said a word to her while she told her story, simply sat in his chair behind his opulent mahogany desk, looking very ill-tempered and very imposing, every inch the duke. The carefree jovial brother she had grown up with was buried somewhere in him, but right now there was no trace. She was starting to wish she had included her sister-in-law in her confessional—Clara's presence would at least lend itself to softening Andrew's mood.

Rain pelted the window panes as though pebbles were being thrown down from the sky. The rattling noise set her nerves on edge.

"Why are you telling me this now?" Andrew asked. "What prompted your confession?"

Susanna took a deep breath, having wondered that herself. "The desire to no longer keep this a secret," she answered. "And Ian's absence has me on edge. I wanted someone else in my corner, I suppose."

"Susanna, I am always in your corner," her brother said, leaning forward on the desk, steepling his fingers against his chin. "I wish you would have told this to me sooner."

"Would you have stopped me?" she asked, braver than she felt.

He shook his head. "Not in the slightest."

"You are . . . you are comfortable with my establishment and running of Lady Day?" she asked.

"Had you come to me and told me what you wanted to do, I would have gone to look at properties with you," he replied.

Susanna sat back in her chair, rather stunned. "You never gave any indication you cared what I did."

He leaned back as well. "My inheriting the title was not easy," he replied.

"Yes, Andrew, I know it was difficult for you—" she began but he held up his hand to cut her off.

"My inheriting the title was not easy on anyone," he continued. "The circumstances that prompted it were life-changing for us all and we have all dealt in our own ways, ways that have not gone unnoticed by me. Had you approached me with this idea of starting a boy's school, I would have supported you wholeheartedly, just as I have in all your charitable efforts. In your own way, this is how you have dealt with Father and Sam's death, and this is how you honor them. Of course I would have given my support, as it seems you did not need my consent."

Susanna looked down at her hands, her fingers twisted around a handkerchief. It was curious how well her brother knew her, how well he could put into words what she had been feeling for years. There was so much pain and ugliness in the world, and having experienced a brief moment of such despair, she wanted to help others who might have to live with that misery. So she started a home for young orphans in the city, in a hope that if they were raised correctly, educated properly, taught right from wrong, they would not take to highways thieving and robbing another family of their loved ones. The cycle had to stop somewhere.

"Now tell me more about this business with Riverton," Andrew inquired.

"Ian believes him guilty of some crime, though he has not disclosed what exactly," Susanna explained.

"Ian works for the Home Secretary," Andrew stated, ignoring her use of Ian's Christian name. It seemed her brother had taken a liking to the earl.

Susanna nodded. "In some form, yes, and I believe he is technically still in the Army. He hasn't really said much about it, just that it is not espionage."

Andrew chuckled. "Yes, I suppose he is not the espionage type."

"Certainly not," she agreed.

"Do you trust him?" her brother asked.

Without hesitation, Susanna replied, "Unequivocally."

This seemed to surprise him. Eyebrows raised, he asked, "And you are certain of his character?"

Susanna took a moment to answer. "At first I wasn't," she

began. "But I've come to know him as having an excellent sense of humor, and a deep well of concern, capable of an immeasurable capacity to love. His mind is quite clever, and it is interesting to see how he sees the world, how everything is a jigsaw connecting the pieces. He is quite remarkable and quite absurd all at once."

Andrew nodded, a soft smile on his face, but he did not comment, just slowly and knowingly nodded his head.

"You think me a love-sick ninny," she said, huffing and crossing her arms across her chest.

He shook his head, chuckling. "In love, yes, but never a ninny."

"So what if I am in love with him?" she asked feeling defensive.

"I never said it was a bad thing, Susanna," he replied. "Does he return your affections?"

She felt the heat of her cheeks and prayed she wasn't as red as she felt. "I suspect so, but he has never said as much." It was incredibly embarrassing to speak of such things with her brother.

"Has he . . . erm . . . compromised you in any way?" he asked, shifting uncomfortably in his chair.

Susanna swallowed down her embarrassment. "Not in any way permanent," she replied.

"Good, good," he said quickly and looked as eager to be finished with this conversation as she was. "Now regarding Riverton, if Ian thinks him a threat and yet leaves you unprotected, what does that say about his character?"

"That he trusts me," Susanna mused. "Or that he trusts his ability to control the situation."

"Or possibly both," Andrew replied. "I agree that Riverton is no longer considered a suitable match, but from what you have told me it is imperative you not call the whole thing off."

"Ian says it will tip him off," Susanna added. "He merely gave me instruction to never be alone with the viscount."

"And you shall not," Andrew agreed. "I know it took courage to make this confession and I am grateful you have shared this with me. But you must heed Ian's warning with complete seriousness."

"I do," she replied nodding. "It is difficult to maintain the status quo without knowing what I am in danger of. He could suspect Riverton guilty of anything from manslaughter to kidnapping to grand larceny. I haven't a clue."

"If your relationship with Riverton should give indication of progressing whilst Ian is away, I am to play along?" Andrew asked.

She nodded. "Unfortunately, we all must act as if nothing has changed. I am to be smitten with a man who revolts me in order to free the man I love."

"Seems like an awfully dramatic way of putting it," Andrew grumbled. "But the explanation is just. We simply carry on as is."

Susanna nodded. "Should be simple enough."

Her brother nodded in agreement.

It was, in fact, not so simple. All week long, Riverton was there. Andrew did his very best to escort and chaperone her, rarely leaving her in his presence for more than a few moments. It was the most closely chaperoned she had been the entire year, much less the past month.

Riverton did not seem to notice, she hoped, though Andrew and Clara were careful about being too obvious. They simply expressed a desire to accompany them on all their evening outings, and Susanna insisted on having Annette or Beverell the burly footman with her during the day.

"There was a robbery in the park, not two weeks ago," she fibbed one afternoon late as they strolled through the park, trying to explain Beverell's constant presence. It had rained that morning and the previous two days, so walking along the footpaths of Hyde Park was a treat she could not pass up.

Riverton chided her timidity and she remembered how he had been the one to become visibly anxious at the appearance of Ian in Hyde Park scarcely a month ago. But she did not pay it too much attention, she had, in fact, rather gotten used to Riverton's ever-changing moods and demeanors. This past week he had been in a decent mood—fairly enjoyable almost. It was a shame Ian thought him a villain. Occasionally he was quite pleasant, albeit boring. He had a pleasant smile and a calm demeanor, but he never seemed fully comfortable with her, regardless of how much time they spent together.

After a night out with Riverton escorting her to a dinner party and a rout, Andrew and Clara in attendance as well, Susanna was eager for Ian to return and put the business of Riverton behind her. Sitting at her dressing table as Annette came in to help her prepare for bed, Susanna wondered what Ian's issue with the viscount was. He suspected him of something of great importance, and he said there was danger around Riverton, and yet his case out of town bore more significance? It just did not make any sense.

"My lady, this came for you while you were out," Annette said, handing over a cream, folded letter. She recognized the handwriting as Mrs. Jensen, her matron at Lady Day. Curious to what the letter could entail, as Mrs. Jensen had never written to her directly at Bradstone House, Susanna slipped her finger beneath the seal, breaking it into pieces and quickly unfolded the letter.

She scanned the words, her eyes growing to saucers as she read through the missive. The news from Lady Day was astounding, though Susanna could hardly believe what she was reading.

"Annette, this is of grave importance," Susanna said, refolding the letter. "Find me a footman to deliver a message." She pulled out a clean sheet of parchment and scribbled a note onto the paper as Annette fled the room with haste. She returned moments later as her mistress was folding the paper.

"Oh good, Clemmons," Susanna said, recognizing the footman. She smiled at him. "Please, a quid is in it for you to get this to Westcott House as quickly and quietly as possible. And discreetly," she added. "In fact, change your clothes before you go, best not to be seen about in your livery going between the two residences. Do not worry about your tasks just yet, I will give you leave from Howards. Please, this needs to get to Westcott."

"Yes, m'lady, right away," the footman replied, giving a quick bow and exiting the room.

Of course, Clemmons knew who she was talking about, there wasn't much business the staff weren't aware of, but Susanna did not mind.

"Lace me back up," Susanna said to Annette. "I must see to Howards and secure leave for the young man."

Annette quickly redid the buttons and ribbons along the back of Susanna's dress before she sought out the butler. She found him in the front hall, although it was quite late.

"I've given Clemmons a task, Howards," she said to him quickly. "There is no telling how long it could take. A couple hours at most, I hope."

"What is wrong?" Andrew asked, coming into the foyer.

"Something has come from Lady Day," she explained, pleased with how she spoke of Lady Day so freely. She handed her brother the letter and he quickly read through it.

"Ian must know of this," Andrew agreed.

"I've sent Clemmons," Susanna replied. "Ian sent a note yesterday; he was due back this afternoon."

A crack of lightening lit up the front foyer, reflecting off the well-polished floors, a clap of angry thunder just moments later. Susanna frowned at the storm rolling in.

"Let us hope this does not delay him," Andrew replied.

Susanna nodded in agreement. Deciding to wait it out for news of Ian's return, she returned to her room and changed into a cotton night dress before escaping to the kitchens, wrapping herself up in a thick knit wrap, her fingers laced around a heavy ceramic mug filled with chocolate. Cook had long gone to bed, giving her a tight squeeze on the hand. Andrew had joined her, having changed out of his dinner wear, retaining his breeches without stockings and a partially unbuttoned linen shirt. It was the most informal she had seen her brother in years, and while they were silent partners listening to the storm raging on, she was grateful for his presence. Near the warmth of the crackling fire, she could pretend the fury of the storm outside was in her imagination. The news in the letter was troubling and she wished she knew what it meant or what to do about it.

An hour later, the time approaching half past one in the morning, Clemmons came bursting through the servant's entrance just off the kitchen. Andrew and Susanna jumped to their feet. Susanna's heart sank as she realized he was alone.

"Your grace!" Clemmons exclaimed, shaking the water out of his hair. Howards came from his rooms having heard the commotion. With Howards and Andrew's aid, they were able to strip the layers of jacket and overcoat from the drenched footman.

"Here," Susanna said, handing him a cup of tea as Howards pushed him into a chair beside the fire. Clemmons hesitantly took the tea from her, his fingers cold and teeth chattering. "Had I known this storm was about to erupt I would never have sent you!"

"S'alright, m'lady," he said, downing the hot tea. Susanna quickly refilled it. "I made it to Westcott House, begged the person to admit me—I do not think he has a butler? I asked for his lordship but he had not arrived yet, so I was invited to wait for him. Then, just a bit ago, a rider arrived, it was an associate of his lordship, I suppose, riding ahead to tell the staff his lordship was delayed. It seems there was a carriage stuck in the muck of a riverbank and his lordship stopped to help. He sent his man along to warn his staff not to worry. I left the note with the butler and returned here. Westcott House is not too terribly far, I thought I would make it without any problems."

"But for the wind," Andrew finished for him, and Clemmons nodded. "You've done a great service and I applaud your bravery in facing this fearsome storm. Please warm yourself and rest and make certain you are well from your ordeal against the elements. We do not want you to catch a fever and send you to your death."

Clemmons let out a nervous laugh but nodded. "Yes, your grace. Thank you."

Andrew stood. "I, for one, am exhausted. Susanna, I suggest we retire as well. There is nothing more to be done, save pray for the safe return of your earl."

Susanna nodded, and tried to ignore the knot in her stomach. She hated the idea of Ian out in this storm, but she wasn't surprised he had stopped to help a fallen carriage, gallant prat that he was.

She followed her brother out of the kitchens, down the main corridor of the house and up the two flights of stairs to where the residents each had a suite of rooms.

"Thank you, Andrew, for staying up with me," she said, her hand on her door knob. "I appreciate the company."

"I am always here for you, Susanna," he replied. "And do not over worry about the earl. Ian is a resourceful chap. He will be fine."

She smiled gently at him and nodded. "I am sure you are right. Good night."

"Good night Susanna," her brother said and she disappeared into her room. Annette had tended to the fire while she had been in the kitchen, so the room was warm without being too hot. She nestled herself under her plush comforter, worrying about Ian as she watched the flames of the fire flicker and dance her into dreamland.

Chapter Eighteen

———— ✾ ————

It had been perhaps the worst week of Ian's life.

He stood, motionless in the darkness, watching Susanna as she slumbered, albeit restlessly. He felt raw, his emotions scraped down to their core and he needed her. He wanted her. He wanted to forget this entire week had happened. Again.

It was all Ian could do to stop from breaking down in tears or punching his hand through a wall.

He had ridden directly to her house, not even bothering to change from his wet clothes, soaked by the rain and the storm raging inside, mirroring the torment he faced on the inside. That poor girl . . . outside in the rain for days, and he couldn't save her. He couldn't save Beth; he couldn't save any of the other girls. What was he good for then?

He dropped his satchel near the window, peeling away the layers of wet clothing until he stood in nothing but his under britches. Scandalous.

He snuck under her covers, needing to be near her, to feel her warmth and her life. He wound his arms around her, pulling her close, her back to him, and nestled his face into her hair, breathing in her scent. She felt like home.

"Ian?" she said sleepily and turned towards him. He managed to smile at her in the darkness as her eyes peeked lazily open. "Hmmm, I missed you." She snuggled into him and he tightened his grip on her.

Something inside him was changing, whatever it was, this girl was the orchestrator. She made him hope there could be a life away from the darkness. He felt anchored to her, relief washing over him, and he held her tightly, knowing she was still here, not a figment of his tortured imagination.

"Ian, what's wrong?" she said, leaning away from him to look into his eyes. She blinked a few times, watching his face as his walls came tumbling down, brushing the hair away from his face. "Oh, Ian, darling," she whispered and leaned in to kiss him softly. "What has happened? What is wrong?"

He deepened the kiss, unable to explain the events of the past week and how she had irrevocably changed him. His need for her bloomed into full grown passion as she opened her mouth to his and he claimed her as his own.

Not breaking their contact, he rolled her onto her back, pressing his weight into her. "Tell me now, Susanna," he said huskily against her neck. "Tell me to leave and I will. Tell me to stay and . . . The choice is yours, love. But if I stay, I am not stopping."

"I do not want you to stop, Ian," she breathed, turning her head to kiss his cheek. "I want you to stay." It was all he needed to hear.

He traced along her collarbone, palming her through her cotton nightdress, buttons up to her neck. Her fingers were quickly releasing the buttons and he pushed the garment down past her waist, freeing her arms. He kissed her again, her tongue matching his thrust for thrust, neither one intending to end this game until the finish.

He cupped a breast in his left hand, rubbing his thumb over

her sensitive nipple. She gasped with each pass of his thumb. Her breast overfilled his palm as he massaged before leaning down to take her into his mouth and suck. Her nails raked through his hair, massaging his scalp, sending a tingling sensation down his spine as he savored her, teasing her other breast with his thumb, lightly twirling and twisting the nipple into a tight bud. Each twist of his fingers brought another tight gasp from her lips, brought him further and further to the edge.

He recaptured her mouth as he moved his hands down her torso, to the mound above her thighs, pulsing with need. He swallowed her groan of pleasure as he pressed his fingers into her, her folds slick with want.

"I need you, love," he said huskily against her neck as he stroked her inside.

"Please, Ian," she gasped, her blue eyes blazing with want and passion. She slipped her hands under his last remaining garment, freeing his shaft and stroking him long, as he did to her. The action nearly undid him and he leaned his forehead onto hers, closing his eyes with the pleasure of her hand. "Take me, darling. I am yours," she purred into his ear.

Pushing the rest of her nightgown away from her body, he removed the remainder of his clothing, covering her body with himself, pulling the down comforter over their shoulders. With his knees, he pushed her thighs further apart, revealing the most tantalizing view he'd ever had. Susanna, wide before him, ready with want and need, wet with desire. He kissed her lips, setting the tip of his arousal against her entrance, shaking from the exertion of holding himself back.

"Keep quiet, love," he whispered to her lips. "I hope to not cause you pain but . . ."

"Stop talking," Susanna said, pressing her hips up, pushing him into her with her slow thrust. Slowly he entered her.

He waited for a long moment, feeling her tightness around him begin to slowly give way as her muscles relaxed.

"S'not so bad, is it?" he asked, lightly, kissing the side of her neck.

"Ian, its heavenly," she replied in a hoarse whisper, with a silent gasp as he thrust through her maidenhood.

He chuckled against her soft skin. "Good." He withdrew completely before pushing forward and filling her again, her body taking him more easily this time. She moaned with satisfaction. The sound set him ablaze.

His slow tempo, gently stretching her and acclimating her to his intrusion, was soon forgotten as Susanna began to thrust her hips up, meeting his plunge and deepening the contact, quickening their movements until he was nearly pounding into her. She did her best to keep quiet, but her face showed the true depth of her ecstasy. Her blue eyes, afire in the moonlight, locked onto his and he found he could not look away. He watched as her eyes clouded with passion and pleasure, her delectable mouth awash with silent moans, the trust and need for him rushing through her eyes. With a feral groan, he leaned down to kiss her, recapturing what was his as he thoroughly claimed the rest of her. She was his, and he basked in that knowledge.

He could feel her tensing around him, and he pushed away from her lips so he could see her pleasure overtake her. Watching her come, the half-smile played across her lips, the dreamy look in her eyes as he could feel her orgasm pulse around him sent him spiraling into his own. He thrust twice more before finding his own release, panting into the pillow beside her head. She wrapped her arms and legs around him, holding him tightly as waves of emotion and pleasure and anxiety washed off him. Her touch was therapeutic, as she held him, he could feel himself breaking into two pieces. One, full of darkness and despair, wrought with guilt over past wrongs and failures. And another, light with happiness, loving the girl beneath him, soaking in her care for him, her attentions banishing the darkness and healing his wounds.

He pushed back to look at her, seeing the myriad of emotions and pleasures wash across her face, her eyes ablaze and sparkling with some sentiment he dared not name. He kissed her again, wanting to make sure she was real, wanting to remember this moment forever.

Her shock at what they had just done was less powerful than her need to comfort him.

She held him to her, his head buried in her neck as the waves of ecstasy rolled off him and it warmed her heart to know she could give that release to him. He held so much inside, never allowing anyone to know the true depths of his wounds.

When he looked at her—his eyes revealing something broken and shining with emotion—she loved him even more. But when he kissed her, it was as if she was his last lifeline to any sense of happiness, and he couldn't bear to let her go, her heart ached for him.

He rolled off her, breathing heavily, an arm draped across his eyes. She watched him in the darkness, the gentle moonlight casting shadows across his features, his nose and mouth appearing more angular.

"Ian," she said softly and he turned towards her, his eyes a stormy gale. "Please do not hide away from me. It does not help you heal from your wounds. Let me know what is bothering you."

"What would you know about wounds?" he asked, perhaps a bit harsher than he intended, but Susanna was unfazed by his tone. He turned his head away.

"I had both parents and a brother taken from me when I was young," she replied. Sitting, she pulled the sheet around her. "I understand how the darkness in life can feel as though it is consuming you."

"I understand your father and brother dying was quite difficult on you, Susanna," Ian began, but she cut him off.

"Do not for a moment think that I do not know the horrors this world possesses," Susanna softly cajoled him, her voice full of hurt and warning. "I may be a pampered and silly girl, but do not think that I have never experienced heartbreak. I was there, Ian. I was in the carriages as we went to Bradstone Park, when we were attacked by highway men. I sat inside, wrapped in the safety of my mother's arms until we heard the first shot ring out. Sam stood blocking the door to our carriage, shot before he could pull his pistol. I pulled my brother inside the carriage, as he was bleeding and dying. The horses were startled and took off down the road, leaving my father to die alone in the muddy road, like a common criminal. I was the one that pressed strips of my gown into my brother's wounds to stop the bleeding, but there was so much blood. I held him as he died, watched as his eyes, so full of fear, dimmed as the life left him, knowing there was nothing I could do. I know how ugly the world can be. I've had blood on my hands and it is the worst sort of memory to wipe away."

Ian sat up, wrapping his arms around her, holding her tightly.

"I had no idea," he whispered into her hair and she shook her head.

"No one did," she replied. "Mara and Mama were with Norah and I in the carriage. Sarah and Sam rode with the boys in the other, Father was outside on horseback. Andrew wasn't there and I've never told him any of this. Norah claims she cannot remember anything, just that there was so much blood, Mara was barely one-year-old. But I remember sitting with Sam as he died in my arms. I was ten years old, Ian."

He leaned down and kissed her softly on the lips. "I am sorry you had to endure something so awful," he said, smoothing the hair back from where a few errant locks had strayed to her face. "Things like that never leave you, they stay with you always."

"Please, Ian," she said softly, snuggling in closer to his warmth, the hairs of his chest ticking her face. "Tell me about her."

He held her for a long moment before leaning back on the pillows, pulling Susanna with him. She traced the outlines of the shadows across his chest, waiting for him to decide to let her in, hoping with every beat of her heart he would finally choose to trust her.

"Beth was lovely," Ian said eventually. His voice was soft and unhurried. "Eight years younger than I. She enjoyed horses and the pianoforte. She was fast, we would race up and down the expansive lawns at Ashford Hall, in Wiltshire. She was clever and cheerful, always had a smile on her face; she was rarely in a foul mood, never saw her have a bad day. Not one to want to read about things, or have someone explain the ways of the world to her. She wanted to experience and learn on her own; she was stubborn and determined to figure things out herself.

She was on the brink of womanhood when I left home and all I had from her in the intermediate years were letters. She was a beautiful writer, witty and funny. She told the best stories about our parents and their forgetfulness. I should have taken it as a sign something was wrong with their memory, it was blatantly obvious. But I pushed it off as their quirks.

"I left when I was nineteen. Bexley had just been through raving about the great time he was to have at Oxford with his cronies, your brother included. I was insanely jealous. I fought so hard against my father, but he did not budge. University was full of wanton distractions, he said. Studies that were worthless in running an estate. Never mind that school and society was where an heir would make friends and form alliances to help him in the House of Lords. Father never sat in the House, he spent all his time poring over his estate books, counting every penny, every piece of silver, making sure everything was accounted for. One afternoon, after a particularly intense row, I took my horse, D'artagnon, and we went out to ride off my frustrations with his censure. I decided I was going to enroll at University without my father's blessing, just forge the notes of mark and show up one day. But as I rode towards Oxford, I realized it wasn't far enough. He would come and drag me home. So I kept riding, until I reached London and found myself in front of the Home Office. I had heard about the war and knew France was too far away for my father to retrieve me. So I signed up and I was gone within a week."

"Tell me what happened with Beth three years ago."

"I arrived home on a brief leave. Beth had written to me of her courtship and I wanted to meet the man she was to marry and to be there for her wedding. I arrived home unexpectedly, greeted by my baby sister, who was no longer the freckled girl I'd left seven years earlier, and she told me she had become betrothed just two days prior. She was so very excited for a life away from from our parents, and it was then I realized the extent of my parents' mental illness. The staff had done their best, but the state of the house was deplorable. I felt guilty Beth had been living in such conditions, though she had tried her best to manage things in my parents' mental absence. The floors were a mess, the staff in constant rotation, the kitchens were unorganized. Furniture was missing paint and pieces, the gardens were beyond repair." Ian sighed and took a calming breath. "She went out that evening with my aunt as her chaperone, she was to meet her fiancé there and I was to meet him the following afternoon."

"Why did not you go with her?" Susanna wondered aloud.

He heaved a sigh. "She told me I wasn't properly attired. I had been traveling for the better part of seven years, France, Belgium, Spain and every corner of England, virtually a nomad, living out of my trunk; I had no proper evening attire. She asked me not to embarrass her and to wait. Waiting, it turned out, was a colossal mistake. She was abducted from the party she attended with Riverton. Had I met him before that night all of this could have been avoided."

"How so?"

"I am a fairly good judge of character," he replied. "One of the reasons I do not quiver in the presence of your brother, the Stone Duke. One of the reasons I immediately liked you."

"Flattery will not get you anywhere," she replied, but she could feel him smile. "Continue with your story."

Ian sighed again, but continued, pulling back the memory of a night he tried so hard to forget. "A messenger boy came with a ransom note, Riverton refused to pay, but I was willing except no one came to collect. Two days later, early in the morning, Beth's body was discovered in Hyde Park. She was nude and had been shot."

Susanna's quick intake of breath drew his attention but she urged him to continue.

"A note was pinned to her body with a knife, an apology note. Afterwards I searched high and low for the messenger boy, but he couldn't be found. There were no witnesses, no evidence, just two notes and a body. Riverton showed his true colors then and I have despised him ever since."

"You more than despise him," Susanna argued.

"Yes," Ian agreed. "I began to look for similar crimes in other areas of the country, wondering if perhaps it wasn't an isolated event, since it was very neat and tidy."

Susanna's brow furrowed. "What did you find?"

"Six more similar homicides," he replied. "And six more since then."

"Twelve similar murders?" she asked, a stunned expression on her pretty face.

"Each as gruesome as the next, as each with the same pattern. Engaged young woman, within two to three days of the proposal, the woman goes missing, usually at a large event, and held for ransom by persons unknown. In some cases, the family paid up, but in some cases, no one did. The fiancé never paid in any situation. He was always paid monies for a broken engagement contract when the woman turned up dead days later."

"What happened last week?" she asked.

Ian sighed. "We arrived in Little Horwood Friday night, the town where the Freeley family lived. Miss Jane Freeley had been missing since Thursday evening. Same set of circumstances, same timeline and same pattern. We inspected the Freeleys' house, the

Assembly she had disappeared from, and the house her fiancé had rented. Interviewed everyone—her parents, the people who had attended the Assembly, the townspeople who had not attended. We talked to her father's business partners, the magistrate, the inn owner, Miss Freeley's best friend—we interviewed everyone. People gave conflicting information regarding Miss Freeley, the Assembly, her fiancée, but there were pieces we verified as accurate and relevant. By Tuesday, we had some decent leads to look in to. But then the storm set in, forbidding us to leave the inn or we would have been drowned. It stormed for two whole days and we worked through the information, looking for connections and answers. And we found them."

"You found who took her?"

"We figured out what direction her abductors had gone and where she was most likely being held," Ian corrected. "When the rains let up on Thursday morning we raced to a forgotten plot of land in the middle of two estates, to the barn containing a wagon with a broken wheel that clicked like giant crickets as it raced down the lane."

"You found her?" Susanna asked. She could feel him tense, tightening his hold on her.

She looked up at him and he was looking at her, uncertain if he would continue. She smiled softly at him, hoping he would share this burden with her. He held so much inside, kept too much pain to himself. He needed to tell someone, needed to share the weight of his problems.

Ian took a deep steadying breath before continuing. "We found her, much as we found Beth. Stark naked, leaning against a tree, dead and soaked from days of rainfall. A note of apology pinned to her body with a dagger."

Susanna was careful not to let him feel her disgust, or her sadness for him. But her heart felt torn into a million pieces. The past week he had basically relived his sister's murder.

"We had a good indication who took her, but couldn't prove

anything, just like the others," he continued.

"You think it is the same man?" she asked and he nodded.

"It is too much of a coincidence for them all not to be connected."

"And you think Riverton involved?" she asked. "Why?"

He hesitated, but one pleading look from Susanna and he was resigned to his fate.

"Let me up and I will show you," he said and she moved off him. He stood, naked in the darkness, and crossed the room, and pulled a file of papers out of a traveling portfolio slouched on the floor by the window. He returned and settled onto the bed beside her, leaning over her to light the candelabra on the side table.

"I have a proficiency for sketching," Ian explained, showing her a few sketches of landscapes, one of a duck in the pond. "On a whim, I asked one of the victims's families to describe the missing fiancé to me in detail and I sketched as they talked." He handed her a few more sheets of parchment she was startled to see the face of Lord Riverton. Puzzled, she flipped through the papers, more sketches of Riverton's face. In some he had a beard, others darker hair, but it was his face in dozens of sketches. Each had a date etched into the bottom corner.

He continued as she looked through the different images. "We tried different noses, eyes, brows until it was as they said he looked. And the face that looked at me from the page was Riverton's. So I went back and did the same with the other families, with the same result. Sometimes he wore a beard, sometimes not, but in each situation it was the same face."

"Then why hasn't he been arrested?" she asked. "If they positively identified him . . ."

"I've never mentioned to any of the families that I might know the identity of the man in the sketch," he explained. "Riverton has an alibi for some of the times in question, yet has no alibi for others. He was still at home at the time of the first murder, and in the midst of finals at Oxford for another. Of all thirteen murders, there are only five he has no alibi for, and it does not make any sense for him to be there for five and not all thirteen."

"This is your evidence against him," she said softly, looking through the pages.

Riverton's face looked up at her from the parchments, little dates going back ten years. There was a last sketch, one not torn from the sketch pad and she reached across Ian to pull it closer.

"This one is from five days ago," she said, squinting to determine the date in the corner. "Yes," he replied.

She looked up at him in alarm. "But Riverton was here with me all week. I saw him almost every evening."

He nodded solemnly. "See why he has yet to be apprehended? All this evidence is completely circumstantial. I have no actual physical evidence against him, merely some drawings, and I am going to need much more if I am to accuse a peer of such a crime."

Susanna looked down again at the pad of paper in her hands, wondering how this could be possible. Finally, she understood his evidence against Riverton, his desperation for her to be away from him. But it did not make any sense. How could he be in two places at once?

She reached out and touched Ian's face with her palm, his eyes closing at the contact. She gently climbed onto his lap, straddling him as he had done to her earlier, pulling his face to hers. Brushing away an errant lock of sandy blond hair, she placed feather light kisses along the corners of his mouth, his nose, and his eyes. He took a deep breath and exhaled before opening his eyes, his eyes those of a man hurt and lost.

Susana leaned in closer, pressing a gentle kiss against his lips.

"What you said of me at the ball was true," he said, leaning back from her, brushing her hair back from her face. "It terrifies me that you are able to see me. I do everything I can to hide behind sarcasm, jokes, and flirting and for you to see past all that is unnerving. I have been running from myself, from my responsibilities, for so long I am not even sure of who I am or where I belong.

But there is a darkness inside me, Susanna, and I am terrified of it affecting you. You are goodness and grace and I cannot allow this to taint you."

"We all have a darkness inside us," she said softly. "You need not fear tainting me, Ian. There is no damage you could inflict that has not already been done." She leaned into him again, pressing her breasts to his chest, pushing him back into the bed as he pulled the sheet over their entwined bodies.

"We are doing this again, are we?" he asked as she kissed along the line of his throat, nipping at his pulse.

"It was such an enjoyable experience before," she said, sitting up to rest on his pelvis, knees on each side of his hips. "How much longer do we have until dawn?"

She watched Ian's eyes rake over her naked body, greed and passion pooling in his green eyes; he seemed to not hear her question.

"Susanna the Minx," he murmured, lacing his fingers behind his head. "Please, enjoy yourself."

She playfully swatted at his chest. "Very well, my lord, but we aren't quite there yet. I barely know what I am doing still. You'll have to show me."

"In that case," he said before he scooped her up off him, and flipped her on her back, pressing into her.

She laughed, but he cut off the noise with a deep kiss.

"Shhh, Susanna," he said against her lips. "Lest you wake the house and have the duke come tumbling in here, issuing our marriage license on the spot."

She smirked at him, one eyebrow raising in challenge. "Yes," she said breathlessly. "But not tonight."

"Exactly," he said, kissing her soundly.

Chapter Nineteen

The return trip to Lady Day was mostly spent in silence, as the two occupants of the carriage had gotten little sleep the night before they both took the opportunity to sneak a nap. Susanna sat beside Ian, her head on his shoulder, feet tucked up beneath her, with a warm blanket covering both of them. Ian had wrapped his arms around her, put his feet up on the opposite seat, and laid his cheek atop her head. They were rather comfortable for being in a moving carriage traversing the pitted roads, soaked from the storm the night before. Even Ian's well-sprung carriage—the luxurious one with the crest this time—did not adequately disguise the bumps in the road, but the couple slept on.

The driver rapped on the top of the carriage, alerting Ian to their proximity to the orphanage. He gently roused Susanna who was rather reluctant to give up her comfortable position tucked under Ian's arm. She sat up and arched her chest forward, stretching the muscles in her back, little moans escaping as she stretched.

"Careful, love," he chided. "With movement and sounds like that we might not make it out of this carriage."

"You are incorrigible," she said, shifting to the other seat to appear more proper when they arrived, though she was an unmarried woman arriving for the second time unchaperoned in a carriage with a man who was not her relation. He wasn't sure why she bothered any more.

"You quite enjoy my incorrigibleness," he rebutted.

She chuckled, shaking her head. "Please let us get through this with some respectability. We are here with a rather important purpose."

He nodded, her words sobering him a bit. He had been rather shocked to read through the letter sent to her by Mrs. Jensen. If what the matron claimed was true, then his lovely companion's boy's school might hold a key piece of evidence and a break in his three-year long case.

They descended from the carriage and quickly entered the house, which felt warm despite the damp and coldness of the morning. Susanna began pulling off her gloves, having just put them back on moments earlier and Ian did the same, yanking the gloves from his fingers, and annoyed they had to deal with such frivolities at all.

"He was quite beside himself after you left, my lady," Mrs. Jensen was telling them. Her face looked wearier than it had nearly a fortnight ago. "It took us nearly a week to get something sensible out of him. And when we heard his tale, we sent for you straight away."

"Yes, I apologize for my delay," Susanna replied, patting the matron on the arm, glancing at Ian as they began to climb the main staircase. "It seemed pertinent to wait for his lordship's return, which was delayed by the storm. But we are here now and eager to learn what the boy can tell us."

"We have him in one of the private rooms," Mrs. Jensen explained as they passed the doorway to the main dormitory rooms. "His hysterics were frightening to the other boys."

"Yes, of course," Susanna replied.

They were led to a doorway at the end of the hall and Mrs. Jensen cautiously turned the knob, though it wasn't locked.

Inside sat a young boy, probably around ten, huddled in a wicker chair. He was wrapped in a thick knit blanket, only his head peeking out from the top as he looked absently out the window and across the grounds.

"Miles," Mrs. Jensen said softly, but the boy did not respond.

Susanna knelt beside the boy's chair, brushing the hair from his face gently. "Miles, darling, how are you doing?"

The boy shrugged but did not look away from the window.

"We've come to see you," Susanna said, her fingertips lightly brushing back his hair in a continual motion. "We heard you've become quite the celebrity around the house."

The boy shrugged again. "I am nobody."

"Oh, that's not true," Susanna said. "You are somebody to me."

He turned to regard her, his face sad, his dark eyes hollow. Ian shifted his weight and the movement caught the boy's attention and he looked up at Ian. His eyes grew wide in recognition and horror.

And Ian recognized him too. It was the boy from before, the one who stared intensely at him, the one who had looked so familiar to him. Then, when the boy was well nourished, he had been unrecognizable, but something had told Ian he knew the boy. And looking at him now, his face thinner, his eyes more sunken, circles darkening under his eyes, he recognized him. It was the same messenger boy he had chased through the streets three years ago, the one who had been sent by the persons who abducted his sister.

Ian took a step back, realizing the implications of who this boy was and what he could reveal about that night. The boy scrambled out of his chair, practically tipping it over as he flattened himself against the wall, desperate to be away from Ian.

The boy was shaking his head, horrorstruck at the sight of Ian.

"Miles, sweeting, you are safe here," Susanna said, still kneeling. "Look at me, Miles, do not worry about him."

Miles tore his eyes away from Ian and stared at Susanna's face, his eyes wild with terror.

His breaths were coming in big gasping gulps, and he was visibly shaking. Susanna stretched out her hand to him and he hesitantly took it before collapsing in her arms, burying his head in her neck. His need for comfort was heart-breaking and for a moment Ian could see how incredible a place Susanna had built. He knew boys from the streets saw unthinkable horrors, and for them to have such a peaceful reprieve was a godsend. And at the heart of it was Lady Susanna, in her Macalister glory, sweetheart of the *ton*, wealth and riches abundant, her arms wrapped around a sobbing orphaned child.

Ian thought about the night he had seen this boy last, and could see it through the boy's eyes. Big angry men, a young girl just as frightened as he was; who knew what he had seen at their hands? His reaction indicated he had seen something horrific.

It took a few minutes for Miles's sobs to subside, and Ian slowly knelt beside Susanna, her hand rubbing along his back, murmuring soft comforting words in his ear. Ian couldn't make out what she was saying, but Miles was nodding, his face pressed against Susanna's shoulder.

Slowly he pulled back, his face red and tear soaked but he was no longer shaking. He glanced at Ian nervously before looking back at Susanna who nodded encouragingly.

"Miles, this is Ian," she said gently. The boy swallowed hard. "I believe you two have already met, though under less than ideal circumstances."

"It seems we might have," Ian replied, forcing gentleness into his voice as though he were talking to an easily spooked horse. "Miles, do you know me?"

Miles nodded and took a deep breath. "You were there at the house, the night . . . the night . . ."

"It is all right, Miles," Susanna cooed, her hand comfortingly on his back. "Please tell us as best you can what happened. Your tale can help Ian apprehend the bad man."

Miles swallowed again but did not take his eyes off Ian. "There was a girl and they . . . they . . . they hurt her."

Ian nodded. "That was my sister."

"They pulled me off the street and gave me a note and an address, told me I'd get a shilling if I delivered it and came back. I did and you were at the house." Miles took another breath and continued. "Then the next day, I went back, but he was there in the house with you so I ran."

Ian's mind was racing, fitting this new information into what he already knew. "Who was at the house with me?"

"The bad man," Miles whispered, his eyes darting around. "The man who hurt her."

The only man that had been in the house with him at the time had been Riverton, Ian thought.

"I think I might have a sketch, if you'll look at it for me?" Ian asked. "And tell me if you recognize anyone."

Ian stood and grabbed his satchel from beside the door, slipping it open and yanking out his notebook of sketches. He sat back down beside Susanna and Miles, flipping through some pages.

"This one, do you recognize this person?" Ian asked, holding out a sketch of Beth. Miles nodded. "That's the girl, the one they hurt."

"And this?" Ian asked, pulling out a sketch of one of the versions of Riverton who had scruff along his jaw. Miles eyes grew wide again and he nodded. "You recognize him? Who is he?"

"That's the man who hurt the lady," Miles replied in a whisper. "And the one who was in your house."

Ian was confused. "You saw him twice?"

"There were two men," Miles clarified. "That one—" he pointed at the sketch of Riverton with a scruffy jaw, "is the man who stayed by the docks with the lady. And that one—" he pointed at another parchment that had fallen from the stack, this one a sketch of a clean shaven Riverton, "was the man at the house."

"And you are certain they were two different men?" Ian asked, his mind racing.

Miles nodded. "After I ran from the house, when I went back to the docks later, they were both there, arguing."

"You saw both men standing beside each other?" Ian asked, holding up both sketches.

Miles glanced at them and at Susanna who nodded and he looked back at Ian and nodded firmly. "There were two different men that night. That one was with you, the other was with the lady."

"What else did you see?" Ian asked, placing the papers back into the leather notebook. "Were they working with anyone else?"

Miles shook his head slowly. "No, it was just the two. They argued about the lady, then about me. They did not see me, did not know I had come back."

"Why did you go back?" Susanna asked.

Miles looked down sadly. "When I saw the man in the house and I thought it was the same man at the docks, I thought I could sneak down there and the lady would be alone and I could untie her. But the man was at the docks too, and before I could leave, the man from the house came to the docks and I was trapped. I had to wait until they left, but they never did, and I couldn't untie the lady before they . . ." Miles looked down again, tears filling his eyes.

"You were a very brave lad, Miles," Ian said, placing his hand on Miles's shoulder. The boy flinched at the contact, but Ian did not remove his hand. "Not many would rush in to save the damsel. I truly appreciate you trying to do so."

"I couldn't save her," the boy said sadly, tears falling from his face. He leaned into Susanna again and she wrapped her arms comfortingly around him.

"Miles," Ian said gently. "It wasn't your job to save her. It was mine, and I failed. But with what you've told me tonight, I can catch the men who did this to her."

"I helped you?" he asked, wiping away his tears with the back of his hand.

"You've helped me more than you will ever know," Ian said reassuringly. "Thank you."

Miles nodded and sighed. He untangled himself from Susanna's arms and sat on the chair. Susanna stood, and kissed the top of his head, pulling the blanket around him.

"I think you should have the rest of the day to rest up in here," Susanna said, brushing the hair back from his face. "And tomorrow you shall have a haircut and rejoin the other boys."

Miles looked up at her, his brown eyes showing much more than simply gratitude towards his lady savior. It was loyalty and love and blinding admiration, much of what Ian felt towards Susanna.

"I will send up some chocolate for you," Susanna said.

"If you remember anything else, write it down and have Mrs. Jensen send it along," Ian said, pulling a blank sketchbook from his satchel. "Or, if it is easier for you, draw what you see. Sometimes it is just easier to draw instead of trying to find the words." He set the sketchbook and two unsharpened graphite pencils on the bed.

Miles's eyes widened at the generous gift. He carefully picked up the pencils and sketchbook, flipping through the blank pages and examined the unsharpened pencils.

"Have Mr. Jensen help you with shaving the end down to a fine point," Ian said, pulling a sharpened one from his bag. Miles examined it and nodded, hugging the sketch pad to his chest.

They left quickly, eager to return to London, but made promises to return to Lady Day soon. Mrs. Jensen promised to send along any new information Miles might remember and Ian gave her his London address directly.

They sat in the carriage in silence, Susanna watching him carefully as he digested this new revelation.

"There are two of them," Ian stated, his voice reverberating with shock. "Did you know? Could you tell?"

Susanna shook her head. "At the time, no, though I've always known him to be a peculiar sort, with strange moods. I suspect it was not moods, but different men entirely. So much of him makes sense now."

Ian agreed and nodded, his mind was racing through information and facts. How had he not seen this earlier? The different appearances, the shifting alibis, of course there were two of them.

"Though I have to wonder," Susanna mused, looking out the window.

"About what?" he asked. She turned to regard him, seeming to choose her words carefully.

"About which Riverton has been courting me and which Riverton courted your sister," she replied. "I am certain I have met both men during my relationship with him, but one of them must have had the initial idea sometime. And one of them chose Beth as well."

"I suspect it was a different Riverton who took you to the fair along the river," Ian mused.

"And probably the other when he escorts me about town," Susanna agreed. "It explains his seemingly strange choice in acquaintances, and the occasional flashes of rage he thinks I do not notice. Though, while this development might shed light on some of the more confusing aspects of this entire affair, you have to wonder, if one man is Lord Hanson Averly, Viscount Riverton, who on earth is the other man?"

Ian did not know, and that bothered him. But he intended to find out. "Scoot over, I am going to sit next to you."

He shifted to the left and she crossed the carriage in a smooth movement, settling beside him and laying her head on his shoulder. He pulled the blanket from the warmer and laid it across them both.

"How are you faring?" she asked.

"Perfectly well," he replied.

"We both know that's not true," she said softly, and he looked away from her, vexed that she could always see right through him.

"I saw your face when you recognized the boy, Ian, I know what those memories do to you. Just . . . just do not think you have to shut me out."

She did not say any more, simply wrapped her arms around his arm, snuggling into his side. He nodded, though he wasn't sure she could see his agreement. He sighed and rested his head atop hers, her fingers lacing through his, and he closed his eyes, and was content. For a few moments he could pretend the world outside the carriage did not exist, and all there was in the world was this woman and her unexplainable love for him. It had shaken him to see the boy again, but it was a bit easier to understand with a warm woman pressed up against the side of him, especially when he loved her as much as he suspected she loved him.

"Ian, I would like to meet your parents," Susanna announced.

Ian glanced sideways at her. "Why would you want to do that?"

She looked at him incredulously, which was the facial expression equivalent of rolling her eyes. "Because they are important to you."

Ian caught himself from making a snide rebuttal and held his tongue.

Realizing he had an inkling of interest in her meeting his parents, especially after her quick acceptance of his Warren relations, he asked, "Must we do it now?"

She laughed. "Heavens no, Ian, I doubt we have time. But soon."

She returned her head to its position against his shoulder and Ian watched her, wondering what she would make of the elderly and mad Marquess and Marchioness of Ashford. He wasn't embarrassed about his parents' condition, not exactly. He was more ashamed of his running out of their lives and not realizing there had been a problem. Had he noticed his parents' ailing minds, had he picked up on the clues in Beth's letters, he might have come home sooner. As it was, his parents had their good days and bad days, but they rarely recognized him. How would they react to meeting a complete stranger?

"Soon then," he agreed, hoping this meeting would not alter her perception of him. Their madness could be hereditary; she could blame him for their deteriorating state. Perhaps this would finally be the thing that repulsed her, or made her see why she should not place her faith in him. He had a tendency to let people down.

He gave himself a mental shake, hoping to delay the meeting as long as possible.

Chapter Twenty

❀

They visited Lady Day at the beginning of the week, but Susanna did not see Ian for the remainder, at least not during the day. Somehow, he managed to sneak in each night and she was content to sleep wrapped in his arms. She inquired lightly about what occupied him during the day, but he merely replied he was "working," which was just as well, because Riverton continued to pay her attention through the entire week.

Susanna was grateful for her brother's presence and protection, but it was Ian's teasing smiles she missed most. If Riverton noticed the continued change in her chaperonage, he did not comment. It was the Friday before the Newcastle All Hallow's Eve Ball when Riverton managed to get her alone.

They were attending a midday garden party, which was unfortunate because the weather clearly had not received the notice that garden parties traditionally took place outside. The sunny day was not warm and a blustery wind had begun to whip through the city. It was all Susanna could do to keep her bonnet upon her head, the ribbons tied tightly beneath her chin. It was such an accessory that sent Clara scurrying in another direction and Riverton seized his moment of opportunity. Clutching her arm almost forcefully, he guided her to a hedged walk, secluded from the remainder of the party.

She looked up at his handsome face, difficult to find him attractive any longer after what Ian had shared about him. Was it true? Had he murdered Lady Beth and all those other young women? Did he want the same for her?

"I beg your pardon if I am too forward," Riverton said, taking her hand. The contact had her startled; in the almost four months she had known him he rarely touched her.

"You do not need permission to be forward, I believe that is the point in being forward," she replied, blinking at him, silently chiding herself for using Ian's words now.

"Indeed," Riverton murmured, leaning in to place a light kiss against her lips.

Susanna's morbid curiously took over and she allowed her eyes to flutter closed, almost hoping she would have a reaction to his kiss, but determined to give the performance of besotted fiancée-to-be. As heated as the kisses between her and Ian were, she almost wondered if it was an exclusive situation; and she soon discovered it was.

Riverton did not deepen the kiss and pulled away a few moments later. Apparently her kisses with Ian were unique. She felt almost nothing when Riverton kissed her, except for longing for Ian. Clever that the one man who would not marry her had made it so she compared every man to him. Even if what he said about Riverton was true, she was forever ruined, and not just physically. She would forever compare everyone to Ian, and no one could equal him, the damned man.

Riverton, it seemed, from his flushed face and heavy breathing—*why was his breath so labored?*—was more moved by their exchange than Susanna was, and she quickly covered a laughing smile with her fan, hoping she appeared coy and smitten. Riverton looked as though he had just enjoyed a rather remarkable experience.

"If you would honor me, Lady Susanna, I ask for your hand in marriage," he said, holding her hands together.

And there it was, the words she'd been waiting to hear all her life, except now they came from the wrong suitor. She'd anticipated his proposal, though she was surprised all the same, as if she never fully believed they would happen. No declaration of love, or admiration or sonnets about the color of her hair, though she had not been expecting any. Riverton did not seem the sort to have any feelings, much less express them.

"Oh, my goodness," she said breathlessly, doing her bit of the act.

"I know this must seem sudden," Riverton explained quickly.

"Sudden" was not the word Susanna would have chosen. *Overdue*, she thought, *or perhaps unsolicited. Excruciating or unwanted; purposeless, unwarranted, or offended. But certainly not sudden.*

Riverton continued, unaware of Susanna's thesaurus musings or her lack of interest in the conversation. "But my admiration for you cannot come as a surprise. Over the time we have spent together, I had surmised we suit very nicely. I have a sizable income and will one day inherit from my grandfather. A lady of your years could not want for a better offer."

The veiled insult caught her off guard and she opened her mouth to snap a rebuttal at him, but she closed her mouth with a click of her teeth, plastering on a smile. The whole thing could be blown to shambles should Riverton not be convinced she was besotted.

"This is rather sudden, my lord," she said sweetly, nearly choking over the offending word. "Have you spoken to my brother about this?"

Riverton nodded. "Just this morning. He said he gave his consent if you were amiable to the pairing."

"Did he now?" Susanna murmured, thankful she had chosen to

disclose the ruse to her older brother. Andrew could have unknowingly tipped their hand.

"Interesting fellow, your brother," Riverton commented. "It was fascinating how he placed the decision solely in your hands, even though he had every intention of us marrying. He would not have allowed a courtship to go on for this long had he not known the eventual outcome. He must know your true feelings for me."

"My brother knows virtually all my secrets," she replied. "But this is such a large decision, my lord, I am at a loss. I must confess I had thought of us marrying, but now with the option before me, I must truly give this the thought it deserves. Please, would you allow me until the Newcastle Ball to give you an answer?"

"Of course!" he exclaimed. "I should wish you to enter into this contract with no reservations or hesitations. Very studious of you, Lady Susanna. Why, had you accepted my offer outright, I might have thought you too eager and wondered about your motives. Titles and fortunes are well and excellent, but if they were all you were concerned with you would have accepted without hesitation. Take the time until the ball to know in your heart we will suit for a lifetime."

Susanna felt a little like Elizabeth Bennett in *Pride and Prejudice*, having been insulted in every way possible during a marriage proposal. She tried to hide her disapproval and irritation with a flick of her fan and downturned eyes, hoping she appeared shy and uncertain. It was truly taking everything she had not to slap him across the face.

"Thank you, my lord," she said demurely. "I am sure I will come to see the wisdom of this match in my own time. Just give me a few days to come to the same conclusion that you have so wisely already arrived at. Shall we return to the party?"

She linked her hand into the crook of his offered arm and strolled along beside him, returning to the garden party and hoping with all hope Ian would come to sleep with her tonight. She needed a good dose of Ian to stamp out the Riverton in her life.

The same evening, Ian sat in the study of 4 Whitehall Place, having answered his third summons in the past month, more than he had received in the past ten years working for the Home Office. It was curious, however, as neither Mayne nor his counterparts received the same summons. The Duke of Leeds seemed to have the need to speak to him directly, and alone.

After a few moments of pleasantries, Leeds got down to the pertinence of the meeting. "Mayne has agreed to head to Ireland to work with Mr. Peel," Leeds announced in his gruff, no-nonsense tone. The news was surprising to Ian, though he was skilled enough to not let the duke on to his shock.

"Mayne will be a benefit to Mr. Peel," Ian replied, his tone measured.

The duke nodded. "Yes, I agree. You are to go into France and make your selections from this group of candidates." He patted the stack of files on his desk. Ian counted at least fifteen different files.

Ian swallowed, thinking of traveling to France, finding a replacement for Mayne, and most importantly, leaving Susanna. He did not think he could do it.

"Selections, your grace?" he asked, his mind honing in on the one abnormality of the duke's statement. Selections—plural.

"Yes, you will select four gentlemen to be trained," Leeds explained. "They will take the place of your team and add one additional to the task force." The duke took off his spectacles and rubbed the bridge of his nose. "Westcott, I intend for you to take my position."

Ian sat back in his chair, running his fingers along his chin. "I beg your pardon, your grace," Ian said, his mind racing. "I do not believe I understand."

"I am old, and the Home Secretary has granted me permission to appoint my successor," the duke explained. "You've been a part of this since the very onset. I think you will fare perfectly. You were the task force before I headed it up."

"If it is merely my time dedicated to the cause that is my only contributing factor in this appointment—"

"Allow me to finish," the duke cut him off and Ian clamped his mouth shut. "The past decade is not the single contributing factor in this decision, but merely one of the aspects. The past ten years you have performed admirably—you and Mayne have the highest closure rate among the group. However, you have the respect of the others, and you have their loyalty. They look up to you, Westcott, and you have become their leader, more so than I have ever been. They answered to me, but they have always followed you. It is time you took over a position you have been groomed to take on for a decade."

Ian stared at the duke, unable to come up with anything to say.

Leeds chuckled at Ian's silence. "Take some time to think this over. This comes with an appointment within the Home Secretary's cabinet—Inspector General of the Home Secretary. You will also be summoned to the House of Lords by a writ of acceleration under your barony title, Baron Carlisle. Your time out of the country and away from family would come to an end. You are welcome to retain your current position, should you choose, and someone else will be appointed to my position. However, the writ of acceleration is coming soon, nonetheless. The position under the Home Secretary is yours, should you desire."

Ian nodded numbly, mumbling he would need to think about it. Leeds gave him the weekend to make his decision, until after the Newcastle Ball as it would happen. After discussing a few things regarding the Riverton case, Ian made his bows and quickly left. There was one person he wanted to see, one person he needed to share this news with. He just hoped she was home.

Ian was admitted to Bradstone House with little effort, Howards was quite familiar with him by now. He waited in the lilac drawing room, glancing about the lovely, decorated room while Susanna was fetched from the depths of the house. He could hear noises and laughter and realized he must have come when the Macalister family were hosting a dinner party.

Deciding his news could wait, he scooped up his hat and gloves, and made for the exit. "Ian?" Susanna called his name, echoing softly in the front foyer.

He turned to face her, his expression sheepish. "I apologize, I was not aware you were entertaining."

She waved off his admission. "Do not worry about them. Howards said you had come to call?"

"I apologize for the lateness of the hour," he said. "I merely wanted to inform you that the information the young lad provided was beneficial. He has been a most helpful witness."

"I am glad for it," she said.

They stood in the front foyer, staring at each other. He wanted to scoop her into his arms and kiss her senseless but his trysting with Susanna must stop. He had already pushed it too far.

"I was offered a position," he said.

"Riverton proposed," she stated at the same time.

"Did he?" Ian replied, quirking an eyebrow up.

"I sent a note round to your house, but you must not have received it."

Ian shook his head. "I haven't been home today."

"Do not worry," she said with a glint of mischief in her eyes. "I will not marry him."

"I should hope not," Ian replied.

Susanna tilted her head to the side, her eyes narrowing a fraction. "What sort of position?"

He shook his head, thinking about the timing of Riverton's proposal. "Another time."

"Ian, you came here to tell me about it," she stated. "So tell me."

"I've been offered a position with the Home Office," Ian explained, sighing.

Susanna watched him carefully, her eyes narrowing in confusion. "I thought you already had a position with the Home Office?"

"This would be a higher position, actually. I would oversee the task force I have been working with for these past ten years. I would be the Inspector General of the Home Secretary. I will be summoned to the House of Lords by a writ of acceleration."

"Hmm." She did not seem to want to comment further. He stood a few paces away from her and watched as she studied his face. "Have you eaten?" she asked.

"I was on my way to sup at the club," he replied, though it was a lie. He had planned to pick at left overs at his father's house. Cook always left him a plate in the cold cabinet. "Do you have anything to say about what I've just told you?"

"Oh, I have plenty to say on the subject," she admitted. "Just none that I want to say at the moment. Come, your arrival pulled me from my meal and I wish to return to it."

"It would be most improper for me to crash your dinner party," he said.

She raised an eyebrow at him. "Improper?" she asked incredulously. "I did not realize you knew there was such a thing. Besides, it is not a dinner party. It is simply a family dinner with those of us who are on English soil."

"Oh, well—" Ian began but he wasn't allowed to finish as he was pulled deeper into the house.

"And later we will discuss this position of yours," she said. "Much later, when it is dark. And past our bedtimes."

He glanced sideways at her, understanding her meaning. She winked at him.

"Look who I found in the front hall!" Susanna announced to a room full of Macalisters as she paraded him into the dining room.

He was met with a rousing welcome, and was plopped into a chair beside a jovial young lord. A steaming plate of food was soon before him, the conversation budding around him as if he had been there the entire time.

He looked around at the occupants of the table and realized

what a large family Susanna truly came from. He had heard their names listed off in order, but to actually see them here, together, was a little surreal. It was striking to see almost all of them together, each resembling the next, yet each different. Though where his Warren relations had bright red hair, the Macalisters bore the same dark chocolate hair.

Lady Sarah Hartford—Lady Radcliff—was beside Susanna and engaged in a conversation with Susanna and the duchess, something regarding plans for Christmas. Lady Radcliff looked familiar to him, but he wasn't quite able to place where he knew her from. Lady Norah was detailing the events of a recent outing for the youngest Macalister, Lady Mara, who was eating up every word her sister spoke. Andrew was listening to a story told between two young lords, later introduced to him as Lord Nick and Lord Charlie Macalister. Andrew laughed at the end of the story, which apparently ended with Charlie in the lake and Nick sitting alone in a boat.

Andrew looked at Ian and asked, "Were you fortunate enough to grow up with a lake on your property?" Ian nodded, and was easily and effortlessly pulled into the conversation.

Clara and Norah began to discuss a current fashion of bonnets; Susanna and Sarah asked Mara about her studies, adding in tips as she described her instructors. Nick and Charlie listened aptly as Ian described an occasion where he had been forced into the lake to retrieve an errant umbrella.

Conversation swelled and flowed around him, wrapping him into their web of familiarity. He was both a participant and observer of this family, member and intruder congruently. He felt at ease as he did with his own family, which was interesting as he rarely felt comfortable anywhere. It was amazing how easily and smoothly they all welcomed him into their folds, as if he was truly a part of their clan and not a passerby.

Susanna glanced at him, her eyes sparkling at him before looking back at her older sister. He could see where she got her easy going, make-you-feel-at-home nature. Her gentleness with him made his heart swell. Perhaps he would make this work after all.

Clara leaned towards her husband and said something into his ear and he nodded. The duke cleared his throat once before tapping the side of his glass with his knife. The conversations quieted down and all eyes turned to him. He stood, holding his wine glass and cleared his throat again, more so out of nervousness than necessity.

"As my beautiful wife reminded me this evening, it is wonderful to have you all in residence," the duke said. "It is unfortunate we could not have Luke or Ben with us this evening, but their adventures abroad translate into their losses at home. It seems, however, this is an opportune time to share something with you all." He paused and smiled lovingly down at his wife, squeezing her hand. "Clara and I have happy news. Come late spring of next year, our numbers will increase yet again."

"You are with child?" Norah practically squealed and threw her arms around the duchess.

Clara nodded, laughing under her sister-in-law's embrace, tears in her eyes.

"Oh, a baby!" Mara said, clapping her hands together like a giddy toddler. "What wonderful news!"

Sarah leaned back in her chair, hand over her mouth, tears brimming in her eyes. Susanna leaned over and squeezed her older sister's hand. Sarah glanced at her, her dark blue eyes happy and sad at the same time, and nodded.

"You've no idea how difficult this has been to keep a secret," Clara said, dabbing at the corner of her eyes.

"Did you tell Mary-Claire?" Mara asked.

"We told her this morning," Andrew replied.

Clara added, "She is excited."

"Congratulations," Ian said, raising his glass in toast to the happy news.

He could feel Susanna's eyes on him, but was careful not to meet her gaze for fear she would see every emotion racing through them. He could not divulge the warmth in his heart, the longing he felt for a life like this. With the position he had just been offered, and with Susanna's love, it seemed possible. But with the mystery surrounding Beth's death and Riverton's connection not explained, he could not allow himself to want for too much just yet. He was terrified he would give in to the desire for a normal, happy existence and it would be snatched away from him. Dealing with Beth's murder had to come first, he had to see to the end of that episode before he could move on to anything else. If he did not, it would haunt him for the rest of his days. He wanted carefree and easy days with Susanna, not ones dogged by guilt and regret.

Dessert came and was consumed quickly, with playful jabs at the duchess for eating her own and half her husband's custard. Port and brandy were brought in; both young lords attempting to acquire a glass, but were quickly rebuked by the duke.

"All those tales about foods not agreeing with your constitution!" Norah exclaimed, laughing. "Goodness, what a wonderful actress you've become Clara!"

Ian needed to leave. It was all too much. The life he should have, the life he wanted was laid out directly before him, and well within his grasp, yet he was too stubborn to take it. The love shining in Susanna's eyes, the camaraderie and family radiating in the room, it was all a big tease, but he couldn't pry himself from it. It was akin to a drug, the laughter and playful banter between the siblings; the happiness over the news of the duchess's increasing, tossing names around for the new Macalister. He wanted this—he wanted this life.

And then something clicked in his head, a piece of the puzzle slammed into place. The noise around him faded away and he could see the importance of the timeline unreeling before him, like a well-drawn chart detailing the events of the scheme. Riverton had asked Susanna to marry him. If this followed the same timeline as the others, she had two or three days until she was kidnapped, two or three days' reprieve from the madness that awaited at the hands of her intended. The Newcastle Ball was in two days. The New-castle Ball is where Riverton would make his move. Innumerable things happened at a ball with no one to take notice and Susanna had said this was a masquerade ball—everyone in costume. No one would even notice she was missing for hours. And now Ian had forewarning, his saucy little bait had held up her end of the ruse. Riverton would make his move at the Newcastle Ball and Ian would be there to stop him. Two days from now, this would all come to an end. It was time for this to be over, it was time he reclaimed his life and place in it. He had put off his duties for a decade, he had paid his obligation to his country. It was his turn to want for something.

He refocused his attentions on the anecdote Susanna was engaging them with, hoping she would still have him, now that he could see the light at the end of a long, dreary tunnel, he had decided to ask.

It was hours past the end of the dinner, past when Susanna had sent Annette off to bed, past when the breeze from the window had extinguished the flames of the candles on her bedside table. There really wasn't a need for candlelight. The moon, near-ing its quarter stage, brightly lit up the cloudless night. Despite the rain the past few days, the evening was crisp and clear, warm enough to keep the window open, though not for long. Her menses had appeared the morning after their first sexual encounter, so even though he had snuck in to sleep with her each night after, they had done nothing more than sleep. Luckily she was blessed with four-day menses, and having ended the evening before, Susanna was eagerly awaiting Ian's nocturnal arrival.

Fortunately, Susanna did not need to wait as her sandy-haired suitor was as eager to see her as she was him. She wasn't quite sure how he did it, slipping into the shadows unseen and unheard. But when he stepped into the moonlight she was thrilled to see him, happy he had made it through the house undetected.

"Andrew would not be pleased to learn you are able to infiltrate his house so adeptly," Susanna said, swinging her legs over the side of the bed and standing up.

"I am adept at picking locks," Ian said softly. "And an expert at living in the shadows." She crossed the floor to him, wrapping her arms around his neck and leaning up for a soft kiss.

"Good evening," he said as she broke contact, smiling shyly at him.

"Why do I leave my window open if you come through the house?" she asked.

"Did you think I was going to scale the copper pipes along the house and sneak through your window?" he asked.

Susanna shrugged. "Something like that might have crossed my mind."

"I can walk lightly through a hallway better than I can scale the side of wall," Ian replied. "Besides, your window faces the front drive. Someone would see me trying to climb the drain pipe. And I do not want to fall to my death. The open window is simply a signal."

"Sneaking through the servants' quarters seems less like espionage and more like burglary," Susanna added.

"Well, my skills are more the burglar's than the spy's," he said kissing the tip of her nose. "So, shall we talk or shall we . . . ?" He wiggled his eyebrows at her and she chuckled. Ever the flirt, her earl.

"You are going to tell me why you hesitate against this new offer from the Home Office," she said, pulling him towards the bed. "After that, we will see."

Ian pulled her up against him, her back to his front as he wove his arms around her, holding her to him. Her neck dipped to the side, his lips finding the soft flesh along her jaw, teasing her breast with his palm as he nipped the delicate flesh.

"Talk to me, Ian," she pleaded breathlessly.

"Yes, what would you like to talk about?"

"Tell me about this position you were offered," she said in a harsh whisper. He stopped his torment and sighed, releasing her from his hold. She turned to look at him, seeing the wounded expression as he sat on the edge of her bed.

"What is wrong, Ian?" she asked gently.

Ian shook his head. "Nothing. Nothing is wrong, for probably the first time in a long time. This position, it will allow me to cease investigating cases, and I will stay in England. It will allow me to take over my father's responsibilities in everything except name."

"You sound as if these opportunities do not please you."

"Quite the opposite, love," he replied, pulling on her hand until she was sitting in his lap. "I find myself elated, excited even. It's the sort of stability I always feared would be thrust upon me and now that it is here, I do not find myself balking against it as I thought I would."

Susanna wiggled on his lap, loving his embrace around her, but hesitant at his words. "So," she began hesitantly, "this new position will keep you in England? And it will force you to sit in the House of Lords, and this stability does not frighten you?" He nodded after each question, kissing along the base of her neck.

"I never thought I'd see the day," she breathed. "Ian Carlisle, Master of Absurdity, brought back down to earth with the rest of us mere mortals, forced to live the life he was born to live." She paused as he nibbled on her earlobe.

Ian chuckled. "You make it sound like fate or something."

"Ha! And now he speaks of fate!" she laughed. "Goodness, whatever happened to the dashing rogue who almost trampled me to death?"

Ian quickly lifted her off his lap and onto the bed, holding her wrists in place beside her head. "I am still a rogue," he argued, kissing under her ear, and along her jaw.

"Yes, a rogue who attends Parliament," she whispered, smirking at him. "And holds a position within the government. Very rogue-ish."

With a growl he claimed her lips in a rough kiss and she drank from his ridiculousness, his kiss igniting the fire within she often tamped down to its embers.

"I am still dashing though, am I not?" he asked, slowly pulling at the tie wrapped around her. Parting her silk wrapper he stopped when he saw her nightgown underneath.

Nightgown wasn't quite the right word, Susanna acknowledged as she watched his possessive eyes trail over her form. She smirked at him, his appreciation of her eveningwear thrilling her. She could see the arousal blaze in his eyes and it pleased her she could create such a thing in him.

"What on earth are you wearing?" he breathed in a hoarse whisper.

"It is merely a nightgown, Ian," she said innocently and watched as his eyes grew hotter.

"Like hell it is," he replied. "Dare I ask where you acquired such a garment?"

Susanna shook her head. "Do you like it?"

The nightgown was made of a paper thin silk and it was deep red. Thin straps held it in place and the front dipped into a deep V, trailing down at the edge of her breasts.

"Darling . . ." Ian's voice trailed off as he looked down her again. "Seriously, where did you get this? Please tell me you did not order this?"

Susanna laughed. "I did order it, if you must know, but not recently. Last spring, we were helping Clara choose new clothing and a wedding wardrobe and I came across this in one of the catalogue books. So I added it to Clara's order, then I stealthily removed it from the packages when her new clothes were delivered."

"You ordered this . . . in May?" he asked slowly, his face clouding.

Susanna sat up and kissed him soundly. "I did not order it

with anyone in mind, Ian," she explained, reading the change in his mood.

"Then why did you order it?"

She shrugged, and traced her finger down his cheek, down along his jaw. "It was the fantasy of wearing it, I think, of being in a situation where someone would want me to wear it. It has been in the back of the wardrobe wrapped in its papers since then."

"And you decided to wear it now?" he asked hoarsely.

Susanna nodded, kissing the edge of his jaw. "I thought you might like it." She pulled back to look into his eyes. "Was I wrong?"

His look was hard and tormented and suddenly Susanna was doubting herself. Before she could question it more, he pulled her off the bed and set her before him.

"Susanna the Minx," he purred in her ear. "Let us see what we have then." And he leaned away and sat back on the bed.

Susanna was bewildered. "I do not understand."

"Well, love, nightgowns like that aren't exactly for sleeping in," he explained, smirking at her. "Those sort of garments aren't meant to be worn for long. The whole point is to remove them." He rolled his hand in front of him, indicating she should proceed.

"You want me to take it off myself?" she asked slowly, slightly enticed by the idea.

Ian's eyes glowed like a ravenous wolf as he nodded.

Susanna hesitated for a long moment, emboldened by the fire in his eyes, passion and anticipation flashing across his face. Slowly, her palms flat on her thighs, she slid her hands up her body, the soft fabric pulling up as her hands rose to her hips then falling back into place as she let go. Slowly she moved her left hand to her right shoulder, pushing the thin strap over her shoulder, pulling her arm free of the strap. With the opposite hand she did the same to the other shoulder, the strap falling from her arms and the entire garment flitted to the floor, leaving Susanna standing perfect and bare naked in the moonlight.

She never took her eyes off Ian's and despite the cool in the air, she felt on fire. He reached for her hand and pulled her to the edge of the bed, trailing his fingertips down her bare arms. She shivered in pleasure.

Not breaking eye contact, he bent and dipped his head, taking her taut nipple into his mouth and sucked, hard. Susanna breathed a low growl from deep within her and her eyelids drooped. He continued to suck, tortuously palming her other breast, while she stood naked before him. Sensing the torture he was creating, he released her breast and stood beside her, guiding her hands to his cravat, wordlessly indicating she should remove it.

Susanna continued. It was all too arousing to be standing naked in her room with him looking at her as if he wanted to devour her; she wanted to see as much of him as he was of her. Carefully, and rather skillfully she wanted to point out, but refrained from doing so, she removed his cravat, slowly pulling it free from his neck and tossing it aside to lie with her discarded nightgown. Next she worked off his jacket and his dinner vest, pulling the edges of his shirt free from his pantaloons. He helped her lift the shirt over his head, as he was a good six inches taller than her, and soon his shirt joined his other clothing on the floor.

With a shirtless Ian before her, Susanna could fully appreciate how beautiful he was. He wasn't overly bulky with muscles, but he looked strong, his toned abdomen and chest scattered with light curls, a thin line leading down below his pant line.

Glancing down, Susanna said, "You are going to have to do your boots yourself."

"Funny, I thought maybe you were appreciating something else that direction," Ian lamented, sitting and yanking his boot from his foot, the lines of muscle and sinew pulsing under the strain of pulling on his boot. Susanna watched appreciatively as his muscles flexed when he removed his boots. He stood back up as he set his boots aside and Susanna resumed her removal of his clothing, wanting to see how far down the trail of curls went.

His garments removed completely, Ian stood as naked as she,

and she admired him as openly as he did her. His shoulders were broad and muscular, his hips narrower with a nicely rounded bum and finely shaped legs. His erection stood strong and upright and she wanted to touch it, but wasn't sure if that was something that was done.

"How long are we going to stand here naked, Ian?" she whispered to him. He had been staring quite unashamed at her and she longed for him to touch her, to tease her, stroke her, and ride her into oblivion.

"Until I come up with something sarcastic to say," he whispered honestly. "You've quite stolen my words, Susanna. God, you are beautiful."

She stepped closer to him, trailing her hand down his chest, along the line of curls leading to his cock, standing erect before him. Before she could overthink it, she took him in her hand and stroked. Ian closed his eyes and groaned.

"Susanna, you minx," he said, capturing her mouth with his, pushing her to the bed and then back into the thick down. "You will undo me rather quickly if you continue and I have no intention of rushing this time. I intend to take my time."

And take his time he did. He loved every inch of her. Pulling her nipples into tight peaks with his teeth, lavishing them with his tongue, blowing soft air across with his hot breath, sending shivers of pleasure down her spine. Desire pooled deep within her and she came into his mouth as he ravished her warm feminine folds with his tongue.

Eyes burning with pleasure and emotion, he settled the top of his cock onto her opening, kissing her deeply, Susanna relishing in the taste of him and herself on his tongue.

"You wanted to know what happened to the rogue in the park?" Ian asked, huskily against her mouth before pulling back to look at her face. "You happened. You make me want things I've scarcely thought about, have been too afraid to ask for. You maddening woman who somehow became mine."

Susanna leaned up on her elbows and kissed him softly, pressing her breasts against his chest. "And you, my darling, are mine."

"Damn right I am," he said darkly, pushing himself into her, her folds soft and willing for his intrusion. Susanna sighed with fulfillment.

He took her slowly, rocking into her deeply and steadily, the embers of her orgasm slowly building again, threatening to engulf her as their tempo increased. She met him thrust for thrust, pushing into him as he was to her, the deepness and fullness stroking something deep inside her. Whether it be the side she hid from the world, or the part of her she longed to be, Ian pulled her out of her head and into the moment and made her feel as though she was the most important, most beautiful woman on the planet.

She came again, pulsing and tensing around him, waves of passion rolling over her, and she buried her face into a pillow to muffle the high pitched moan that ripped from her throat. Ian found his own pleasure a few moments later, tensing as he thrust deeply into her. She could feel his cock pulsing inside her, spilling his seed deep within her womb.

After catching his breath, Ian rolled off her, pulling her to him and she snuggled against him.

"I cannot believe you wore a red, silk nightdress," Ian whispered after a few minutes. "When will you ever cease to amaze me?"

Susanna turned her face to kiss his chest, running her hands through the soft curls. "Hopefully never," she whispered.

"That is undoubtedly true," he agreed, wrapping his arm around her and soon they were both fast asleep.

Chapter Twenty-One

———— ❁ ————

*D*ue to her tiring nocturnal activities and a bed partner who departed in the very early hours of the morning, Susanna felt she was entitled to a lie-in the next morning or, at the very least, a leisurely morning in bed. Her sisters, unfortunately, felt otherwise.

Norah wanted to have a rather serious conversation about the duchess's increasing status, and rattled on in an overly dramatic fashion about how she was to be the only one left at home when the love-birds welcomed their little darling. Norah seemed under the impression that Susanna was on her way out, and quick, though Susanna could not bring herself to agree.

"I do not know why you are overly worried about this," Susanna told her sister, flipping through the gossip magazine. It was rather devoid of anything interesting, mostly commenting on who danced with whom at the ball two nights prior and was thankfully devoid of any marriage announcements between herself and Riverton. At least he had agreed to her terms and had not forced her hand by tipping off the gossipmongers. Susanna glanced guiltily at her sister, who was flopped on her back, her arm thrown over her face in mock despair. She did not like keeping such a thing from her sister. They had used to be quite close, but lately . . . Norah's choice in friends made it difficult to take her seriously.

"You are going to marry an earl and run off happily ever after," Norah moaned in anguish.

Susanna did not want to ask which earl she meant, though one was still technically a viscount. "For now I am here with you, my dear," Susanna said. "Do not count your eggs before they hatch."

Norah sat up and gave her an unconvinced look. "They're technically your eggs I am counting," she replied. "And you have two gorgeous lords falling at your feet. Surly one will eventually come up to snuff."

"The key word there is 'eventually,'" Susanna reminded her. "I am at present unattached and could remain that way for some time."

Susanna did not want to think about how much time that could be. She had promised Ian patience, and she truly did love him. She just wanted him to choose her over his work, over his obsession with Riverton and Beth's murder. She did not understand his refusal to put down the case and walk away.

Norah left with as many dramatic airs she had when she entered and Susanna attempted to settle down in her comforter and pillows in peace.

Clara was in moments later. They chatted about her pregnancy, how she was feeling, et cetera, but really Susanna wasn't all that interested. She was happy for the couple and excited to be an aunt, but really it wasn't the first pregnancy she had experienced. Her mother had spent most of their lives pregnant and Susanna had been present at her sister Mara's birth, even though she had been merely nine years old. Susanna just wasn't in the mood to fantasize about baby bonnets and booties and baby names with their beloved duchess. The conversation came around to Ian and Riverton eventually and, having been briefed by her husband, Clara was eager for any new information or developments. Susanna filled her in as best she could, but aside from Miles the former messenger boy, there really wasn't much else to report that she was aware of.

Sarah was in moments after Clara left, wanting to talk about Riverton and Ian. With all her meddlesome sisters, Susanna thought she might just have one big conference to hash it all out at once instead of repeating the conversation multiple times. Sarah was so motherly and so sweet, she merely encouraged Susanna to be as agreeable as possible and allow the men to come to their own realizations about how incredible she truly was.

Susanna wanted to roll her eyes. Her sister meant well, but it was something her mother would have said to her. "Be brave, Suzie-Bee, you can be as daring as the men if you choose to."

"You are beautiful and smart, Suzie-Bee, do not let those boys tell you what to do." Mother had been a bit of a forward thinker, always encouraging her daughters in ways most mothers of their time did not. Susanna appreciated her sister's sentiments but it felt odd coming from her. Sarah was such a motherly person, stepping into the role of Mother upon the death of theirs so soon after their father and Sam's.

Susanna knew the announcement of Clara's pregnancy must hurt Sarah, though her dear sister would never admit it. Sarah and her husband had been unable to conceive during their marriage and, as a result, Lord Radcliff died without issue. Family and children of her own was something she knew her sister desired more than anything. Susanna could see it in the way Sarah's smile did not quite reach her eyes when talking about the future Lord Hadleigh, the Bradstone courtesy title. But then, with a reassuring squeeze to her hand and a promise that everything would work out, Sarah was off and Susanna was alone in her room again.

At this point she decided she may as well get up and dressed for the day. She donned a pretty, yellow and grey pinstriped dress and Annette wove her hair into a loose plait and pinned up atop her head. There was decent light outside, even if the air was crisp, as the end of October was upon them. Deciding some painting in the side garden would stave off her boredom, she scooped up her paints, brushes, and two fresh canvases from her stack in the corner and made for the garden.

She did not get very far. As she was descending the last set of stairs into the front foyer, Ian was walking through the door, tipping his hat to Howards, who did not even bother to ask for his card or offer him a sitting room.

Ian's face lit up when he saw her and he bounded up the stairs towards her, meeting her half way. "Just the woman I wanted to see. How are you, love?" he asked, kissing her cheek.

"Tired," she replied, swatting at his upper arm. "But my sisters seemed intent on discussing the current events so I am attempting to escape to the garden to paint. Will you join me?"

"It does sound rather tempting," he admitted. "But alas, I am here on other business. I am requesting the pleasure of your company."

Susanna blushed and but did not break his gaze. She knew just how pleasurable his company could be. "When?"

"Right now," he replied. "I would like to drive you somewhere."

Susanna frowned. It was much too early for the fashionable hour in the park.

Ian understood her confusion. "We are driving to a specific location, not just round in circles through the park. We are driving somewhere, not taking a drive. Big difference, you know."

"Yes, I conceive there is a difference," she replied. "It's the destination that has me curious."

"All in good time," he replied. "Now pop up to your room, deposit your supplies and return with a hooded cloak as quickly as you can. It's a bit chilly out."

She quickly went up the stairs and did as he requested. She was back in the foyer, pulling her heavy wool cloak around her shoulders as she descended the last stairs.

"Howards, if there are any inquiries, I have stepped out for a drive with his lordship," Susanna said to the butler as he opened the door. Howards eyed Ian warily but nodded.

"Yes, m'lady," he replied with a curt nod.

Susanna smiled thankfully at him, knowing he would only mention her absence if someone should notice.

"We should not be gone more than an hour or two," Ian replied, tipping his hat to the butler.

"Very good, sir," Howards replied and closed the door behind them as they exited the house.

"Good chap, your butler," Ian commented, handing Susanna into the covered carriage, the Ashford crest on the side.

"Howards is the best," Susanna replied. "He would never let me out of the house alone if he did not trust my company."

"It seems your entire house is conspiring to get us together," he said, winking at her.

She nodded. "Probably."

It was a quick trip to their destination and Susanna did not recognize the large house they pulled up to.

"Welcome to Westcott House," he said, opening the carriage door. Her eyes grew wide as she realized the reason for their visit. As she descended from the covered carriage, she took in the brick structure rising three stories above the street. It was decisively smaller than Bradstone House, but that wasn't really a fair comparison. Bradstone House was a massive Park Lane mansion; Westcott House looked awfully plain in comparison.

Ian chuckled. "It is not much, I give you. But when the Marquess acquired it, it was merely for use while in town for the season. His usual residence was Ashford Hall in Wiltshire. The Marquess was rarely in London and had little need for a mammoth of a house." He ushered her inside, taking her cloak from her. His butler seemed to be absent.

"It looks . . . charming," Susanna offered hesitantly. She really did not want to be insulting to Ian's house, but the interior wasn't much better than the exterior.

"Susanna, love, I do not expect you to like it," he said, taking her hand. "I do not like it. I merely stay here when I am in town because I own it. Or rather the Marquess does."

"Ah," she replied, not really knowing what else to say.

"You can turn back now," he suggested, his eyes hoping she would agree and they could flee.

Susanna shook her head. "You've brought me this far. I would like to meet your parents."

Ian scoffed, but led her up the stairs and into a sitting room that was very pink. Pink upon pink. "I cannot imagine why you'd want to meet them," he mused. "They will not know who you are. They do not even recognize me."

Susanna smiled sadly at him, laying her hand on his arm and kissing his cheek. "They're a part of you, Ian," she said softly. "I want to meet them."

He sighed and nodded, laying her cloak and his overcoat over the back of a pink upholstered chair.

The room was a strange room for a study, as that is what it appeared Ian used it for. In addition to the rose print wallpaper—which was fading—the furniture was covered in pink upholstery fabric—which was yellowing—and every flat surface was covered in small porcelain figurines of animals holding bouquets of roses. A portrait of a young woman hung above the mantle, directly across from the desk on the opposite wall.

"She is beautiful," Susanna murmured, looking up into the face of the long dead sister who haunted Ian's every step. She had bright green eyes and a strawberry tint to her blond hair, her soft smile almost forced, like she had been strictly instructed to hold still and maintain her composure, and the stillness had been enough to drive her mad.

There was another frame hanging to its left, a family portrait featuring both the Marquess and Marchioness with Ian and Beth. Ian strongly resembled his father, even as an adolescent, and Beth strongly resembled their mother both in appearance and coloring, but Ian and Beth looked nothing alike. Coming from a family in which each branch was decisively a Macalister, it was interesting to her that Ian and his sister bore no resemblance to each other, save for the same base color in their eyes. Where Ian's were light green and stormy, Beth's were a bright evergreen.

"Mother and the Marquess were actually older during this painting than they appear here," Ian said coming up behind her. "Mother instructed the artist to paint them younger. I think on some level her childless years bothered her. She was in her forties when she had both Beth and I."

Susanna nodded. "My mother was the opposite. She was pregnant most of her married life, it seemed. She lost as many babes as she bore to full term."

"So there could have been more of you?" he asked in a mock horror.

Susanna nodded. "Ten was enough, I think. It made for interesting dinners to say the least."

"I bet your family never threw potatoes at each other," he replied.

Susanna chuckled. "Peas, once," she replied. "Nick would always dangle the bones of his chicken legs in front of Norah and tell her the bones of all the dead chickens were going to haunt her. Andrew tossed a roll at Sarah once and part of it broke off in her eye."

"I cannot imagine your stoic, ducal brother throwing a roll," Ian said, chuckling.

"You did not know us back then," she told him. "We were a little less refined, a little more rowdy."

"What happened?" he asked.

She turned to regard him seriously. "We all had to grow up. Now let us get on with the reason for our visit. We can reminisce about our drastically different childhoods later."

Ian sighed and nodded, clasping her hand in his, and led her out of the pink study. A nurse was coming down the stairs just as they started to ascend and Ian stopped to speak with her briefly about the state of the Marquess. Apparently his breathing was labored after his last fit, but he had finally fallen asleep. The nurse advised them not to wake his lordship.

"But Mother is awake?" he asked her and she nodded. "How is she today?"

The nurse shrugged sadly. "It's not a good day for visits, I am afraid."

"We will make do," Ian replied. The nurse bobbed a light curtsy before continuing down the stairs. Ian glanced at Susanna with a look that seemed to say, "You asked for this."

She gave him a reassuring smile, encouraging him to continue. The room directly above the rose sitting room was the Marchioness's room. It was bare, save for a large bed, a side table with a few framed miniatures, and an arm chair near the window where an elderly woman silently watched the drizzle of rain as it fell on the Mayfair streets below. Her face was wrought with wrinkles, her hair turned from its burnt strawberry blond to a wispy white.

"Mother?" Ian said softly, kneeling beside her chair. "How are you today?"

The Marchioness turned her head towards him, her eyes cloudy, confused. "Who are you? What are you doing in my house?" Her voice was light and raspy but her tone was firm. She was a woman who was accustomed to her orders being met.

"I am your son, Ian," he said to her. "I brought someone for you to meet."

"My son's not here, so you cannot possibly be him," she said accusingly. "Have you come to rob me?"

"No, Mum," Ian replied. "I've brought someone for you to meet."

The marchioness turned to look at Susanna and frowned, confused. "That's not my daughter."

"No, this is Lady Susanna," Ian said.

"It is nice to meet you, your ladyship," Susanna said, giving a small curtsy. "I want my daughter," the marchioness demanded. "Where has she gone?"

Ian swallowed and glanced at Susanna. "Beth isn't here, mum. She is passed on."

The marchioness's eyes unfocused as she thought over Ian's words. Her eyes narrowed at him.

"Ah, that silly girl must be out riding again," the marchioness replied, waving off Ian's attentions. "My Ashford does not approve of course, but I will not tell him if you will not."

"Yes, of course," Ian mumbled in reply.

"She gets it from her brother," Ian's mother continued. "That boy would be on his horse for all hours of the day if Ashford let him. But Ashford was always hard on my boy. Wants to raise him right, you see. But my boy had better be careful, or he will ruin us all." She turned to regard Ian shrewdly. "You mark my words. If that boy of mine does not come home this time, we will all be doomed. Losing him will break us all."

"You did not lose me, Mum," Ian said gently. "I am right here. I've come home."

The marchioness looked at him annoyed and glanced at Susanna again before crossing her arms in annoyance.

"Where is my daughter?" she asked again. "I want my daughter to attend me."

"Beth's not here, Mum,' Ian repeated gently. "She is no longer with us, remember?"

The marchioness narrowed her eyes at him. "I remember you," she said. "You were here when she died, when they found her body in the park. You killed her, did not you?" She rose from her seat onto shaky legs and Ian stood to help her. She swatted him away.

"You killed my daughter, you fiend!" the marchioness rasped at him.

Ian shook his head. "I did not kill Beth. I am your son, Ian."

"No, no, no, you are not Ian!" she cried. "My Ian was a good boy, until he ran off and joined the war. You killed my baby! You killed her! You killed us all!"

Ian took a few steps away from her shaking his head as his mother screeched at him. "You killed her!" the marchioness cried, her eyes blazing and wild. "You killed her!"

Susanna watched his face crumble as tears welled in her eyes. She looked away; she did not want him to see her weep for him.

She understood. Finally, she understood why he needed to find his sister's killer, why he needed to close this chapter before he could move away from all of this.

Susanna tilted her head up, taking a deep breath and blinking away her tears. Ian had not moved towards her and she prayed he did not see how this affected her. It was heartbreaking to watch him endure this. His mother might be in a state of repetition, reliving a horrible past, but Ian did not have to endure that over and over again. It was purgatory.

The nurse returned just then and coaxed the woman back into her chair. The marchioness fought against her, raving at Ian about how he killed her daughter, how he killed her baby.

Ian took Susanna's hand and pulled her from the room, down the stairs and into the sitting room covered in rose print wallpaper. He poured himself a double brandy from the decanter on the desk and tossed it back. He poured another and offered it to her but she declined. He downed it as well before collapsing into the chair behind the desk.

Susanna looked around the room, her mind reeling from the madness of the marchioness—the old woman's cries could still be heard in the room above. What a place to live, even when one was briefly in town. She understood why he avoided London, and yet why he felt compelled to be here when he was. He felt he owed it to them to be here after so many years apart. He needed to find Beth's killer because he felt like it was his duty to put it right, as if it was all his fault in the first place.

Susanna shook her head. This place was toxic. "Is this house entailed?" she inquired.

Ian shook his head. "No, the Marquess purchased it when they came to town for Beth's debut. He meant to give it to her as a wedding gift."

"Why is it named Westcott House?" she wondered.

"No idea," he replied. "Best I can gather is the Marquess forgot his current title when he purchased the house. Because I doubt he bought it for me."

"Ian, you need to sell this house," she said softly. He sat with his head leaning back against the back of the chair, his eyes closed.

He sighed. "I do not know if I could."

She knelt beside him, taking his hands in hers. "Ian, this house is draining you of every ounce of life you have. Your parents would be better off at a distant country estate, away from constant reminders of what transpired here, of the loss they endured while living here. They need happier surroundings. And you do, too."

He opened his eyes and looked down into hers, torment and emotion racing through them. It tore at her heart to see this side of him, to see what damage he had endured. The loss of a loved one was difficult enough and will change a person in profound ways, but to have a constant reminder, to live those moments on repeat, was inconceivable.

"Ian, you need to let this house go," she insisted. "You cannot right all the wrongs of your past, but you can give your future a fighting chance. This house will drive you mad."

"Seems to have worked out well for my parents," he said sardonically, his mouth twitching to the side, his normal response to anything remotely serious.

She wasn't going to allow him to charm his way out of this discussion. "Ian, you need to move on."

"Susanna, you do not seem to understand—there is no moving on from this, this is my life." His posture was stiff, jerky, and he was clearly agitated. He gulped down the remainder of his brandy and set the glass on the table beside him, his thumb and pinky finger tapping a quick beat against the snifter.

"Explain it to me, then."

He stood up abruptly, crossing the room to the window. She did not follow. "This house is part of me, a part of my father and of the estate," he replied. "I cannot escape it any more than I can escape becoming the Marquess one day."

"Is this not a welcome concept?" she asked.

"I am not sure," he replied slowly. "I never really thought about becoming the Marquess, other than as something that's bound to happen, and I dread it all the same. I never daydreamed about running the estates and sitting in Parliament. I never wanted any of it, I never wanted to become my father."

"You will not become your father; you'll simply inherit stewardship over his title."

He turned his head sharply at her, quizzing her with his gaze. "What do you mean?"

"Well, your title does not really belong to you," Susanna explained. "You will be the Marquess, yes, but it is not entirely yours. Each person who inherits the title adds a little bit of himself to the lineage, changes the course of the Marquessate to fit his own needs. It does not belong to you alone; it belongs to all of you. All those who came before you and those who will come after. You only get to take care of it for a little while. It is a part of you and a part of them. You are not required to be the same Marquess as the previous ones have been. If your not wanting the estate stems from reservations about turning into your father, then you are looking at it all wrong."

He watched her as she spoke and she realized he had never considered any of this. "How should I view it?"

She rose slowly, stepping lightly on the polished wooden floors, her slippers quiet as whispers as she crossed the few steps to him. Gently, she reached a hand up to his face, cupping her hand lightly against his skin. "As an opportunity to be different," she replied softly.

He covered her hand with his, leaning into her soft embrace

and sighed. "But what if I do it wrong?" he whispered, staring heavily into her eyes, his green eyes stormy with torment.

"You couldn't," she replied. "I will not let you."

He closed his eyes for a moment before pulling away.

"I know I cannot escape being the Marquess," he said, not looking at her. His head was hunched down, his shoulders slumped. His posture was broken, as if something inside him was deeply wounded. "But I cannot drag you into this with me, Susanna. My life . . ." He sighed heavily and looked up towards the ceiling, his arms hanging as dead weight at his sides. "My life is not fit for a lady."

Susanna's eyes narrowed and she glared at his back. "Bollocks," she snapped at him. He whipped around and stared wide-eyed at her, surprise radiating off his face.

"I beg your pardon?" he asked with a half laugh.

"You heard exactly what I said," she retorted. "You have created this entire reality in your mind in which you are not fit for someone to love you. Well, I hate to break it to you, but I love you and you cannot do a thing about it. You are stubborn and arrogant, but Ian, you have such goodness in you, why can you not see it?

He clamped his mouth shut, swallowing his retort, his brows pulling together. "You love me?"

Susanna let out an exasperated sigh. "Of course I love you, Ian."

Her admission seemed to take all the steam from his sails. "I had hoped you did," he replied quietly, watching her carefully as if she was making a joke.

"I love you quite ardently, I am afraid," she stated. "Nothing you could do would change that."

"How could you love me when I have all of this?" he waved his hand around the room, but it wasn't the room he was indicating. It was all the baggage that came with him. His parents. His sister. His hunt for justice. His audacity, his wit, his charm. His loyalty, his courage, his intelligence.

"Ian, it is because of all of this that I love you," she replied. Rising on her tip-toes, she met his lips with hers and attempted to express her affection this way, in a way he might possibly understand.

"I am not good for you, Susanna," he stated, pulling away from her. "I have tried and tried to get you to see this, but you refuse to grasp that I am trying to protect you from the darkness that lurks beneath the surface. I am barely a shell of a man who cannot offer you the full and loving life you so deserve."

"Yes, you can," she replied earnestly. "Why have you so low an opinion of yourself that you cannot accept you are capable of such a life, that you deserve such a life?"

"Oh, I do not know, perhaps because everything until now has told me that I am not capable of such things?" he replied with a dark laugh. "I am not someone who can be relied upon, Susanna; I am not your savior. You have built me into this fantastically good man and I am not him."

"Then tell me who you are," she demanded. "Tell me what is so wrong with you that you will not allow yourself to be happy."

"I do not deserve happiness," Ian answered. "The things I have done . . . it is not in the cards for me."

"You are making no sense," she replied. "You do not even hear yourself and the nonsense you are spouting." *How can he be so clever and so dense at the same time?*

Ian shook his head. "I ruin everything I touch. Beside me you will only find darkness, Susanna. I have let every person down in my life, just as he said I would." Ian was breathing heavily, his arm outstretched, pointing at the corner of the far wall. "I had one job and I couldn't even properly handle that. And I must live with the consequences of my selfishness."

"Oh, stop being so dramatic," she chided. "And who told you that would let everyone down?"

His silence answered her question.

"Your father?" she asked and he nodded. She sighed. "You are allowing the musings of a cranky old man and the ghost of a dead sister run your life. Grow up, Ian, and take some responsibility."

"I broke him, Susanna," he said forcefully, the pain in his eyes nearly stealing her breath away.

"My father was a solid and proud man and my abdication broke him." Ian shook his head. "If I had not left, none of this would have happened."

"Oh, Ian, darling," Susanna said softly but did not reach for him or touch him in any way. "What you did was for the best. He sounds like an abusive man who preyed upon his son, one who was so eager to please. Had you stayed, their minds would have faltered and you would be left unprepared to handle it. When you left your father, you proved to him you had the strength and the courage to do what was necessary. You escaped a destructive situation and you made yourself better than you would have been if you stayed."

"But my sister . . ." Ian began and sighed a deep breath. "Had I not left, Beth would still be alive."

"Maybe," Susanna replied. "Maybe not. There is no way of knowing what your life would have been like had you chosen a different path, and it is pointless to dwell on it further. What would have happened if my father and brother had not been killed in a highway robbery? Andrew would not have been the duke and chances are he would not be married to Clara. I would not have wanted to start Lady Day. Our choices in life do not define us, Ian. It is what we learn from our choices, the good and the bad, and how we choose to live that define who we are. You are not at fault for the tragedy that befell your family, any more than you are at fault for sunshine outside."

"You have such blind faith in me," he said softly, cupping her face. "I do not deserve you, Susanna."

She laughed. "Yes, you do. You deserve happiness, Ian, not to live imbedded in the sadness of the past."

"How am I to get past all this?" he asked.

"First, you accept your writ of acceleration until your father passes and you become Marquess," she instructed. "After that we will figure it out."

"How will *we* figure it out?" he repeated.

She nodded, leaning up to him, pulling the points of his jacket collar down to meet her mouth with a kiss. "One kiss at a time," she replied.

He leaned into her kiss, seeking comfort and release, and Susanna was happy to oblige.

Chapter Twenty-Two

───────── ❀ ─────────

T he night of the Newcastle All Hallow's Eve Ball had finally arrived.

Sarah and Norah had already left for the ball with their respective friends, leaving Susanna alone in the sitting room with their graces, all listening as Ian described the details of the evening and what to expect.

In truth, Susanna only was half listening. She knew what to expect and it terrified her, though she was not going to let Ian know the depth of her fear. Who would want to knowingly be taken hostage? What sort of person would choose to put the person they loved in harm's way?

True, Ian had never said he loved her, but Susanna was fairly sure he did. And she knew why he was doing this, why he was willing to put her in danger and while she knew he wasn't being reckless, she worried that his desire to catch his sister's killer might overpower his more rational side.

As if he had a rational side, Susanna mused. But if endangering herself this way, agreeing to go along with this was the only way to free him for the shackles of his past, then it was worth it, right? She was making the correct choice, she told herself, and truthfully, she had made this decision weeks ago when Ian had first warned her about Riverton and asked her to act as bait.

She knew then she wanted this man as her own, and she wanted him freed from the guilt and regret of his past decisions. She was risking herself, risking their happiness and their future together, all in an attempt to heal the parts of himself he had left open for so long. It was a calculated risk, one with a certain degree of uncertainty and peril, but the greater the jeopardy the greater the compensation. And Ian was the most treasured prize conceivable.

They all stood to leave, their graces exiting the sitting room first, heading downstairs and to the awaiting carriage. Ian stopped Susanna at the door.

"He will attempt his abduction tonight," Ian stated firmly. "During the ball. It is always during a busy event where no one will notice a disappearance until hours later."

"Yes, you've already said as much," Susanna replied.

"I do not want you to worry, love," he insisted. "I will not let him harm you."

Susanna was worried nonetheless. "Are you certain this is wise? What if he slips me out without your seeing?"

"You will not be in any danger, love," Ian reassured, smoothing the hair away from her face. "I have three associates in attendance tonight. We will not take our eyes off you."

Susanna nodded and took a steadying breath.

"You look lovely, darling," he said, moving an errant brown lock from her cheek.

Susanna glanced down at her attire. "I haven't worn white in a while," she acknowledged. She had chosen to go with a white, Roman style gown, loosely fitted and billowy in the layers of fabric, a golden cord wrapped around her waist giving the impression that with one tug the entire garment would dissolve. Her hair was pulled back in curls, a halo of greenery resting upon her head with a delicate, daisy-encrusted hairpin tucked into her curls.

Ian glanced at her hair with a smirk. "I see you've worn your new hair pin again. Excellent."

"It seemed wise," she replied.

"It was," he agreed, pushing something into her hands. "As is this." Susanna looked down at the small pistol he had placed in her hands. "Slip this into your reticle, just in case."

"In case of what?" she asked, looking back up at him. His eyes exposed the pain in his soul and he kissed her roughly, desperation and worry radiating off him.

"In case I cannot be there to save you too," he said softly, leaning his forehead against hers.

"Oh, Ian," she sighed and wrapped her arms around him, his arms holding her tightly against him. They stood together, motionless, each taking steadying breaths for different reasons, but needing the comfort of each other's arms all the same. After a long moment he set her away from him, flashed her a devious grin before disappearing out the door and into the darkness.

Susanna took a deep breath, slipping the small silver pistol into her reticule as instructed.

Giving herself a mental shake, she followed him out the door into the awaiting carriage.

No one spoke in the carriage as they rolled towards New-castle's Mayfair mansion on the other end of Park Lane. Ian rode along outside the carriage, a silent champion in the darkness.

The jostling of the carriage made her uneasy and she couldn't shake the pit of worry deep in her stomach.

They arrived at the ball, descending from the carriage and going into the mansion before Susanna could change her mind. They were announced, a glass of champagne was in her hand, music was filling her ears, and Riverton was at her side, smiling shyly at her, all before she could manage another reassuring glance from

Ian.

When the invitation had come, written in red and gold ink, Susanna had thought the Duke of Newcastle had discovered an unknown flair in his penmanship. Now, looking around the ballroom, she realized it was more he had discovered an unknown flair for the dramatic.

She marveled at the extravagance of the room, as did everyone else in attendance.

Extravagant was the only word she could think of to describe it. Gaudy, perhaps, but certainly he had taken his masked circus theme over the top. Bright-colored tent tops hung from the ceilings, draping down to the floor, creating the illusion of being inside a circus tent. Jugglers and jesters and even a magician on stilts, made their way through the guests, entertaining everyone. Susanna thought she saw a fire breather along the opposite corner. Along the far wall were tents set up with palm readers and fortune tellers.

Of all the places one would want to kidnap someone, this ball provided immeasurable possibilities. Susanna cringed.

She looked at Riverton's handsome face, wishing this whole ordeal would be over tonight. Whatever Riverton's involvement, she wanted Ian free of this darkness.

"Good evening, my lady," Riverton said and bowed over her hand.

"Good evening, Lord Riverton," Susanna said pleasantly. "How are you this evening?"

"Quite well, thank you," he responded pleasantly. "And yourself? Do we have reason to celebrate tonight?"

Susanna smiled shyly. "I believe we might," she admitted, lying through her teeth. She gave herself credit, she was a much better actress than she thought. "But we should wait until the dinner, I think. I'd rather not have everyone's attention just yet."

"Understandable," he agreed and clinked champagne glasses with her. "To our little secret, then?"

Susanna gave another shy smile before drinking from her glass, careful not to down the contents for courage.

They danced a quadrille set before Riverton fetched her a second glass of champagne.

Susanna chatted and laughed with Gemma and Monica, having brought them into her confidence just after Riverton's proposal, and they helped keep her in their attentions. Thus far Riverton had not found an opening to remove her from their group.

As she stood nursing her third glass of champagne, she wondered where Ian lurked. She knew he was here, she could feel his gaze on her, but the masks and costumes hid him from her. It was probably a good thing she did not know his costume or she would not have been able to keep her eyes from him.

Someone pushed by, jostling the glass of champagne in Susanna's hand and the liquid sloshed clumsily onto Susanna's gown.

"Oh, goodness," Susanna said, her hand dripping with alcohol. She set her near empty class on the tray of a passing footman and regarded her soaked garment.

Fantastic, she thought. Right when she was supposed to be on her guard, something as simple as a spilled drink could make her lose her focus. She should probably retire to the refreshing rooms and attempt to dry her dress.

She looked up at Riverton and stilled. His eyes were hard, his jaw clenched tight, his expression guarded as his eyes bore into hers. It wasn't what she was expecting from him. This was it, she realized. He had been looking for his opportunity all night, and this was it. She teetered on the edge of what she was about to do, what was about to happen.

"Lord Riverton, might I request your assistance?" she asked, silently determined to see this through. "It seems I am in need of freshening up."

Susanna felt Clara tense beside her, saw Gemma and Monica look pointedly the other way; she could feel the fury radiating from her ducal brother and Riverton nodded, accepting her bait, seizing her misfortune to get her away from the protective eyes of the ballroom.

"Yes, of course, Lady Susanna," he replied, offering his arm. "I will do what I can to assist you."

"Thank you," she said, and accepted his arm. She gave her family and friends a reassuring smile as they departed their company. She would be fine; Ian would make sure of it. Nothing would happen. It wasn't as if she was about to be abducted, held for ransom and found dead in the park. She was just *pretending* that was about to happen. No one need worry.

But Susanna was worried and she was doing her damnedest to hide it from her escort.

Praying Ian was following them, she moved through the crowded ballroom with Riverton hoping this all wasn't some colossal mistake.

In the hall, Riverton removed his arm from her gasp and took a couple steps away from her, turning to look at her, pain flashing across his face. His lip tightened, his jaw clenched; he looked as though he were about to explode.

"Riverton, what is wrong?" Susanna asked, his change in demeanor alarming her.

"Come with me," he said gruffly, gasping her hand tightly and pulling her down the hall.

Susanna tried not to panic, though she was more in shock he was actually going to go through with his plan. Ian had been right all along.

"My lord," she managed to say, and tried to pull her hand from his vice-like grip but to no avail. "Riverton, you are hurting me." She looked around wildly, hoping to see Ian swoop in to her rescue, but the hallway was completely void of anyone.

Riverton pulled her down the corridor and into the first room he could find with an unlocked door.

It was a sitting room of sorts, though it was mostly full of dead animals, stuffed and hung for display. The stuffed bear and lion might have proved a distraction, or even the zebra skin on the floor or the moose head on the wall, but she ignored the troubling taxidermy.

"Riverton, please, you do not have to do this," she said, attempting to reason with him.

"I am not going to hurt you, Lady Susanna. I am trying to save you," he stated and it stopped her in her tracks.

She blinked dumbly at him, in shock. "You are . . . trying to save me? From what?"

He shook his head. "It is much too complicated to explain. I had hoped my engagement to you could be overlooked, that he would not notice. Then I brought Mother to town, made a big show about our impending engagement, but it did not work. You are too much of a prize."

"Lord Riverton, what are you talking about?" Susanna asked. "Who are you talking about?"

"The other Riverton," he said dismissively, as though this should be obvious. "My brother."

Susanna's head was spinning. The best she could do was to play dumb. "Your brother? There are two of you?"

"Well, not exactly," he explained, trying another window. "Why did I choose the only room with bolted windows?"

"Hanson, explain!" she demanded. Her use of his Christian name neglected to pull his focus. "Riverton!"

"There is a man, an imposter who looks exactly like me," he explained quickly as he tried another window. "He is a cousin from my mother's side, no connection to the Riverton title. But it is remarkable how similar we are. He has placed my family under threat for nearly a decade and we are forced to do his bidding."

Susanna sat down. Was this the truth? Was this the real Riverton telling her the truth or the other Riverton spinning lies? She did not know what to believe.

"This is madness," Susanna said to herself. She looked at Riverton, wondering what to do. "We have to find Ian," she decided. She did not want to figure this out alone.

"What?" he asked whipping around, looking distressed.

She was shaking her head in anticipation of any argument he would have. "We have to find Westcott, he must know of this."

"What does Westcott have to do with any of this?"

"You have your secrets, I have mine," she replied. "Come now, we must find him."

"Lady Susanna, we cannot return to the ball. Gideon is out there—it is not safe."

"Yes, but Ian is out there," she replied, yanking the door open. "We are much safer out there with him than in here without."

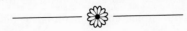

One moment his tempting Roman goddess was in his line of sight, the next some clumsy matron was tripping all over him and once she was righted, Susanna was gone.

Mayne's spilling of Susanna's drink had been inspired, but the untimely matron had drawn his eyes away from Susanna for the briefest moment and when he looked back, she was gone.

Ian cursed under his breath, trying to tramp down the cold dread that stole down his spine. He moved through the crowd as best he could, ignoring the terror clawing at his heart, the rush of fear roaring in his ears. Drowning out the music and voices of the ball, he could only think of Susanna and finding her again. It was madness to put her in harm's way like this. After tonight, no matter what happened with Riverton, he was done. He couldn't take this any longer.

He tried his best not to panic, making his way towards the edge of the ballroom, steps from the door nearest where he had last seen Susanna with Riverton.

He would kill Riverton if he harmed a hair on her head.

It would destroy him if she was lost. A choking, painful, gut-wrenching dread almost stopped him in his tracks. His sister's lifeless body flashed before his eyes, mangled and bloody in the park, and he fought to shake the image away. Susanna would not suffer the same fate as Beth.

He searched every masked face for Susanna's, none of the eyes were as bright a blue as her eyes were. Her smile was not on anyone's face—what if he never saw her smile again?

He fought to breathe, knowing his panic would not help anyone. He stepped away from the stiflingly hot ballroom, into the cooler hallway. Deep breaths and oxygen filled his lungs and his head cleared after a moment. The corridor ran towards the middle of the house and turned left towards the back garden. His earlier surveillance of the house informed him it was the most direct route out of the house aside from the front door. Riverton would have to be a fool to attempt to march her out through the front door. And a fool this criminal was not.

Ian tried each of the doors along the corridor, finding each one bolted tight. Voices coming from around the corner caught his attention and he straightened just as a mass of white silk ran directly into him.

"Ooh!" came the noise, and he would recognize her voice anywhere.

"Gads, Susanna," he said, righting her. She looked up at him with relief and he wrapped his arms around her, thankful she was safe.

"Ian, you must hear what he has to say," she was saying and Ian realized they were not alone.

Riverton was standing a few paces behind Susanna, a frown on his face. Ian pushed Susanna behind him and pulled out his pistol.

"Do not move," he instructed the viscount, lifting his arm to turn the gun on his suspect. "Ian, listen to him first," Susanna said, pushing his arm away and stepping in front of him, putting herself between him and Riverton.

"Susanna, move," he said forcefully, but she stood her ground.

"Ian, I think you were wrong about him," she said quickly. "Please, trust me." He paused and watched her, knowing he trusted her with his life and the life she could be carrying. The thudding in his ears came pounding back and he swallowed, attempting to dampen the panic.

Susanna stepped towards him, placing a soft gloved hand onto the arm at his side. The contact had an instant soothing effect, and his boiling blood calmed in this veins.

"Riverton, tell him what you told me," Susanna said, her voice soft but commanding.

Riverton launched into an elaborate tale about an identical cousin who had been terrorizing their family for years. It was outrageous, and it was insulting that Riverton even attempted to create such a fiction.

Except that a small part of Ian was inclined to believe the man. His preposterous tales did explain a lot of the blind spots in the past three years.

Susanna cocked an eyebrow at Ian, as if to ask, "Well?" Ian wasn't sure what to believe.

"Did you know what he would do to her?" Ian asked calmly. "To my sister."

Riverton shook his head and looked down at his hands. "Beth was to be my escape from him. I truly loved your sister, Lord Westcott. Instead, I enraged him. I did not think he'd have the gall to attack a lady of quality, but I underestimated him. I had hoped to escape this nightmare by marrying her. Instead it made him worse."

"Then what is your business with Lady Susanna?" Ian asked.

Riverton glanced at Susanna. "I learned from the ordeal with Lady Beth. I made sure not to make the same mistakes this time. I chose a lady with high ranking family, someone well known in society. I had hoped this would dissuade my cousin from coming to collect."

"You have let a distant relation run your life for over a decade," Ian stated. "Why not toss him out, call his bluff?"

"That is what Lord Riverton attempted," Riverton replied. "My . . . father. And Gideon killed him."

Ian noticed the subtle change in Susanna's posture but he

ignored her discomfort. He had him talking now.

"He would leave us be for months on end before popping up with some outlandish demands. At first it was money, then he needed an alibi, and before long he had pulled me into his schemes, determined to ruin our family. I have three younger sisters, Westcott, what would you have done?"

Ian did not want to feel sympathy for this idiot and certainly did not want to believe his insane tale, but there was something that rang in his words. Old Riverton had died rather suddenly, drowned in a creek from what he could remember.

"He has not allowed Mother to leave Lincoln—he has her terrorized. He has bullied my sisters. When he sends for me, I am expected to appear. I had hoped Lady Susanna's family and position would be enough to dissuade him, but it only seemed to provoke him further. Bringing Mother and the girls into town was the last effort. If I married in a very public fashion, he would have no choice but to accept it."

"Why did not you mention any of this after Beth's disappearance?" he asked. "Why did not you come to me?"

Riverton looked pained and confused. "How would you have been able to help?"

Ian's surprise overtook him for a moment and he lowered his weapon. "Beth never explained to you why I was away?" he asked cautiously.

Riverton still looked confused. "She said you did investitures in someone's home office?"

"Oh, good lord," Ian said, shaking his head. "I investigate crimes for the Home Office." Due to his own idiocy, Riverton would have no reason to assume Ian could be of assistance in her safe return.

"Had I known . . ." Riverton began but trailed off, realizing his effort was futile. "You made up your mind about me from the beginning. You decided you knew what sort of gentleman I was and even now I see I am not dissuading you."

Ian seethed. "I saw you for the spineless simpleton that you are, Riverton," he snapped at him. "Forgive me if this tale has not changed that opinion of you. I know the sort of gentleman you are, when you did nothing to help save my sister and then had the audacity to ask for her dowry in exchange for a broken contract."

"That was Gideon," Riverton explained quickly, shaking his head, irritated. "He forced me to ask it from you. Never in my life would I have done so out of my own desires."

"Then you would not have taken my dowry either?" Susanna asked.

Riverton blanched. "I told you that to appease you," he explained, embarrassedly. "But in truth the estate needs the funds. Gideon has bled us dry."

Susanna's shoulders tensed and Ian wished he could see the fury on her face. She was so lovely when she was angry.

"I wish it were not so, but Westcott was correct in his assessment of you," Susanna said. "I am satisfied to have aided him in his investigation."

"Investigation?" Riverton asked, swinging his eyes back to Ian.

Ian nodded. "I have been investigating you for the crimes against my family and the murder of my sister. Along with this inquiry, I found the crimes you committed, the murders you carried out for him, and the ones he did in your place. You are both going to hang."

Riverton was shaking his head again. "No, it was all him. He forced me into all of it. I was an innocent in all of this, you must see that!"

"Perhaps years ago you were an innocent in all of this," Ian said almost remorsefully. "But you stood by and watched as a man terrorized your family. How are you innocent of that?"

"Oh, he is not as innocent as he seems, I can assure you," came another voice from behind them, followed by the click of a round sliding into the chamber of a pistol.

Chapter Twenty-Three

Ian spun around to the left, his outstretched arm swiveling to point at the other Riverton—Gideon?—leaving Susanna standing between Riverton and Ian.

At least she wasn't weaponless, Susanna mused. It was a slightly consoling thought. Her arms had been tucked across her middle section throughout Ian's interrogation of Riverton, her hand gripped tightly around the small pistol Ian had instructed her to store inside her purse. The reticule did a decent job of concealing the weapon and Susanna was grateful for Ian's forethought.

"Oh, my goodness," she said upon looking into the face of the other Riverton. He truly could have been the viscount's twin.

"Mr. Lydon will do, or simply Gideon," the man sneered. "It seems my dear cousin has finally let the cat out of the bag. Took you ten years, old chap. Solid constitution, this one."

"Continue in this way and you will not survive this evening," Ian stated.

"Most gentlemanly of you to forewarn me of my impending demise," Gideon replied. "But I assure you it will be the opposite.

In fact, none of you will survive. Well, Riverton will, as in I will, but the other Riverton will not."

"You will not get away with this," Riverton snapped, taking a step towards his cousin. Susanna snapped her head to her former suitor and stopped him with her glare.

"Oh, I will, in fact," Gideon replied. "No one is going to question me when I finally step into your shoes, brother, the one and only Riverton, once and for all."

"Hang on," Ian said suddenly, "I am confused. You said cousin before, but now you are saying brother?"

"Brother, cousin, same thing," Gideon said with a shrug. "I am him. Or I should have been. We are not just relations who look similar, we are in fact identical. When we were born, there was no distinction made between the two of us, there is no knowing which of us came first. So our dear grandfather, the earl, made the decision to have one of us sent away. I was sent to the wilds of Wales and raised as a lowly relation of the Riverton name. Then, to my luck, we ended up back in Lincoln. From then on, Hanson was gone. I chose to be Riverton."

Something clicked in Susanna's head, something Riverton's mother had mentioned.

Susanna frowned. "Evil twin seems like such a cliché ending." Ian glanced back at her, his eyes wide in surprise.

"I beg your pardon?" Gideon asked.

She shrugged. "I am simply saying that if your claims are true, then you are just as daft as Riverton. It is an awfully unoriginal ending. Plausible, yes, but it is simply awfully done."

Ian was watching her curiously. "What would you like the ending to be?" he asked.

"Oh, the hero would win, of course," she replied. "That's you, darling, you are the hero. But it's the heroine that no one expected. She is the one wild card who the villains suspected was a simple society miss with marriage on the mind and a bonnet on her head." She turned towards Riverton, shaking her head. "You really should not underestimate the heroine."

"What is she blabbering about?" Gideon asked his brother.

Though his question sounded like a rhetorical one, Riverton responded, "I have no idea."

Riverton lunged for Susanna, knocking her hands free of her reticule, dropping the pistol on the floor. She ducked away from him but he got his arms around her, holding her tightly to his chest. Susanna stomped down hard on his foot with her heel and, as he released her, she pulled the daisy hairpin from her hair, holding it before her. He lunged at her again and her hairpin blade connected with his hand, slashing his palm. Riverton released her, shouting in pain.

In the same time, Ian had disarmed Gideon and held him with one arm twisted behind the man's back, one weapon on the ground, Ian's pointed at the man's head.

"Well done, sweetheart," Ian said with an approving nod. "Though you'll have to explain because for once I am lost."

"Not surprising, really," Susanna replied. "The rub of the riddle is that they are both imposters. Ten years ago, the tale this Riverton spun earlier was partial truth. These two came into the house of the Viscount Riverton and threatened the family. The Old Riverton and his son, Hanson, attempted to protect their family and the Old Riverton was killed. I suspect Hanson was wounded and they pumped him for information, planning on slipping into his life once they killed him as well. One twin went off to Oxford the following fall, becoming the Viscount Riverton, the other remained to look after the family. They held the Averly family in terror for a decade, threatening their lives for their compliance. The crimes through the past decade are both their doings, as they like to take turns with everything. Oxford finals, carousing about town, courting young women—together they became Viscount Riverton, each taking a piece of his life.

"The best part is that I doubt they are actual brothers of the original Hanson," Susanna explained with a laugh. "Hanson had not attended Eton or Harrow, people would have only known him starting at Oxford, where one of these two showed up as him. They quite effectively slipped into his life. No one knew what he looked like before, so they became him. These two are undoubtedly twins, just of no relation to the real Hanson Averly."

"Which one of you courted my sister?" Ian asked.

Susanna nodded towards the man holding his bleeding hand. "I suspect this one. His emotions when talking about Beth were genuine, and he called her 'Beth,' instead of 'Lady Beth.' It's the hint of familiarity that gives him away. I suspect it is the same one who courted me."

"How can you tell?" Ian asked.

"When he realized we knew each other as more than just casual acquaintances, he looked mad, as if someone had taken away his favorite toy. He looked possessive of me," she explained, and looked at Ian. "It is how you look at me. Though I quite like it when you are looking at me. It is rather revolting when he does it."

Ian was beaming at her. "You are rather incredible."

She nodded. "You have barely even scratched the surface of how incredible I can be."

"That is not true! Any of it!" Gideon claimed wildly.

"Give it up, Gideon, we are caught," Riverton said, head slumped down.

"Jarrod, shut up!"

"Oh, Jarrod is it?" Ian asked, his eyebrow quirked up. "Shall we leave you alone to get your stories straight?"

Gideon glared at him. Riverton—Jarrod—looked pained. "How did you know?" he asked her.

"Lady Riverton said something peculiar during the dinner party," Susanna revealed. "She was terrified of you, they all were. She spoke of her son with such affection and reverence, and yet looked at you with horror and fear. She said two men died the day her husband died, and from then *her* Hanson was gone. It seemed grief-stricken ramblings at the time, but it just did not sit well.

And then you two appear, and I realized as you rambled on with your nonsense story that no one ever knew who Riverton was until he appeared at Oxford. Quite clever, finding someone who had not been introduced to society, only known by his family. Even the senile earl would not have seen through your lies."

"I wanted to end it all," Jarrod said, pleading with her. "I tried to save you. I wanted to marry you and live an actual life, not half of a stolen one."

"It would have still been a stolen life," she replied, frowning. "And I haven't intended on marrying you for over a month. I was simply carrying on to aid Lord Westcott in apprehending you."

"You cared for me, I know you did!" he exclaimed, fighting against Ian's restraints.

Susanna smiled sadly at him. "I am just that good at acting like a marriage obsessed society miss." She raised one eyebrow and said very flatly, "If only you weren't such a prat and a bounder, and a murderer, then I would not have to watch you hang. For I will be there when they hang you."

Ian grinned at her, love shining through his eyes.

"You would not let them!" Jarrod exclaimed.

"Oh, no, I would," she answered, nodding determinedly. "You lied to me, intended on using me for my dowry, and planned to kill me. Not to mention you killed his lordship's sister and what sounds like twelve other girls, including one just last week. Death is too merciful a punishment."

"He killed them," Jarrod was saying, pointing at his brother.

"Aye, that's true," Gideon replied. "Once I had my taste of the first one, ahhh, there were so many more to enjoy."

"He may have killed them, but you penned the apology note and stabbed it into each girl's heart," Susanna snapped at Jarrod, knowing she was correct. "You could have stopped him, but instead you went along with the game, happy to play Riverton when it suited you, happy to go along with his murderous intentions when it suited him. You wanted to live different sides of the same life, and this makes you both equally guilty."

Ian was nodding. "She is right, you know," he stated and looked at her. "We should get married."

"Are you actually asking me this time, or just implying that is the end result?" she asked impertinently.

Two other men arrived at that moment, preventing Ian from answering, Ian nodding to them in recognition. "Mayne, Haslett, look who we found."

"Double the trouble," Mayne muttered, hauling the bleeding Riverton to his feet. "Lady Susanna, pleasure to see you again."

"Likewise, I suppose, Mr. Mayne," Susanna responded.

"I was hoping for one early evening this week," Haslett said, winking at Susanna. "Guess we will have to clean up his lordship's mess."

"Whatever," Ian said shaking his head. Turning towards her, he said, "Susanna love, I do have to take care of this, but I am leaving you in the very capable hands of Lord Haslett here; he will get you safely home."

"Ian, I am quite capable of finding my own way home," Susanna said. "I can just return to the ball as if nothing has happened. I am becoming quite good at that, you know."

He shook his head. "Fine, Lord Haslett will return you to your brother and you will inform him that you need to return home." He laced his fingers through hers and leaned his head closer to hers. "And I am serious about marriage. This is me formally asking you, Lady Susanna Judith Charlotte Macalister, to become my countess and eventually my marchioness and all that, but my feelings will not be repressed. You must allow me to tell you how ardently I admire and love—"

"Ian, that's from *Pride and Prejudice*," she said, squeezing his hands in hers.

"Lead me not from temptation, but—"

"Oh, all right, stop making a mockery of yourself," Susanna said, cutting him off. "Yes, of course I will marry you. How could I resist such a romantic declaration?"

He grinned at her. "Forgive me for my inability to form an original declaration of my affection, love. All the good ones have been taken, I am afraid." He might have said it with an edge of silliness, but his stormy grey-green eyes, bright with love, completely gave him away. "But I can honestly say, darling, I love you so very much I can scarcely breathe. You are my very best friend and I want to give you a world of happiness. Please do me the honor of becoming my wife? I promise to only make you regret it once or twice, but the rest will be filled with laughter and love, and maybe a little adventure. What say you?"

She nodded, tears brimming in her eyes at Ian's sentimental declaration, knowing her life with Ian would not be without its challenges, and it certainly would not be boring.

He took her into his arms and kissed her soundly in front of both Rivertons and his colleagues, but she did not care.

He pulled away from her, grinning from ear-to-ear, and she laughed. It was a rather absurd way to get engaged, but her love was a rather absurd man. There was no point in taming him when she loved him just as he was.

About the Author

*E*rica Taylor is a mother of two and military wife married to her high school sweetheart. Raised in the mountains of Colorado, she holds a BA in History from the University of Colorado. Erica has been writing stories since she can remember. She picked up her first romance novel while on a beach vacation as a teenager, and fell in love with falling in love, sexy heroes, and the feisty women who challenge their lives.

A self-confessed geek, Erica loves anything *Harry Potter*, *Doctor Who*, or *Star Wars*, can spend hours in Target with a Starbucks, and truly believes a cat makes a home. Currently living in South Africa, Erica can often be found writing during soccer practice or piano lessons and is not afraid to let dinner burn if it means getting the story out of her head.